In Search of the Fuller Brush Man

A Novel

Douglas B. Carlyle

This book is a work of fiction. Names, characters, places, and incidents are products of the author's imagination or are used fictitiously. Any resemblance to actual events or locales or persons, living or dead, is entirely coincidental.

ISBN: 978-1453694206

Acknowledgements

I would like to give special thanks to my sister, Sandy, for taking on the awful task of overall editing. In addition, she supported me by providing continual pointers and motivation. I'm not sure what this says about our relationship, but doing so brought us closer together.

I must also thank my beta readers, Patti, Shannon, Ruby, and Mrs. VP, who prior to my publishing this novel, gave me invaluable critical input.

I would like to recognize the Writers' League of Texas for offering workshops enabling me to create a piece of work worth publishing.

Last but not least, I must recognize my wife, Peggy, and my daughters for providing their support and lending their ears as I read this novel to them…over…and over…and over.

In Memory of Mom and Hilary

In Honor of Dad

In Celebration of the Institution of Marriage

Dedicated to the Urbana High School Class of 1973, Urbana, Illinois. Go Tigers!

Chapter 1

DIXIE WOKE UP FROM her restless sleep and was immediately troubled by the sensation she was once more alone. Rolling over in her California king-size bed, she reached for the empty side of the bed that should have been occupied by Sean. Putting her hand under the comforter covering the Egyptian cotton sheets, she quickly felt the cold and knew Sean had not come to bed. Such had been the case more and more frequently ever since her husband of thirty-plus years discovered he could purchase a video copy of *The Fuller Brush Man* on the internet. Starting the day he received it almost seven years ago, that movie had initiated the slow transformation of what had been nothing more than a latent curiosity over his mother's final words, into a manic fascination that was slowly sucking him into its darkness.

Dixie hated—no, feared—anything having to do with the Fuller Brush Company. She'd read how people sometimes could become obsessed with finding answers to their most out-of-the-ordinary questions. Likewise, she was all too aware that while such fixations could push deranged people over the edge, they could also send otherwise normal people down a path of self-destruction. In Sean's case, all it took was a silly black and white movie, and four words—the last four words his mother had written in her journal twenty years ago. Those, for whatever reason, were the same as the movie's title.

Dixie's devotion to Sean and their marriage was unwavering. The moment she stole his heart back in college, she vowed never to let anyone, or anything, get between them. But his obsession was clearly getting the better of him now, and he was completely blind to its danger. If it were a bus, Sean would be dead, flattened, and sun-baked in the middle of the road. He'd kept his wits about himself thus far. Just how long she could protect him was anyone's guess. Her concern was that any additional disturbance might just be enough to bring Sean crashing down.

PREPARED TO OFFER HERSELF as a distraction, she crawled out of bed wearing her new nightie, complete with matching printed knickers she had imported from London. It wasn't so much that she wanted to entice Sean with sexy lingerie. Rather, she wanted to show off her more slender frame she had trimmed down with a new exercise and diet plan. She was proud of her new figure. Sean had yet to make a comment about it.

She approached the dimly illuminated room that was Sean's office in their Lake Forest home. It had increasingly become a storage facility for anything remotely connected to the Fuller Brush Company. She found her husband staring at his computer monitor. He never noticed as she walked up next to him. It was as she feared. If only he had been staring at internet pornography, it would have been a peculiar blessing. Instead, he was perusing the website for the Fuller Brush Company…again.

"What are you doing?" Dixie asked, trying not to sound too perturbed.

After removing his bronze Giorgio Armani glasses and rubbing his eyes, Sean replied, "Just retracing some old steps." Pointing at the screen, the knowing automobile dealership executive continued, "Look at this credo from Fuller Brush—'Make It Work; Make It Last; Guarantee It No Matter What.' Sounds like something General Motors, Ford and Chrysler overlooked."

With as much empathy as she could muster at 0-dark thirty, Dixie said, "Honey, it's going to be dawn soon. You have got to get some sleep. It's Group Meeting Day and you know how grumpy Daddy is at those meetings. If you show up exhausted, he'll eat you alive." Her words brought no reaction. She was talking to a man mired in the quicksand of his own making.

"Think about it, Dix, the Fuller Brush Company was started in 1906. There were plants in Philmont, New York, and East Hartford, Connecticut. The company moved in 1976 to its present location in Great Bend, Kansas. I've been to Philmont and East Hartford twice in the past year, both times looking through antique stores for any hint of a connection to Mom's words."

"Sean, I'm well aware of your comings and goings. I also know you buy anything with even the slightest association with the company."

"I need to go back to Kansas again."

"Honey, you've been to the plant in Kansas four times now."

Leaning back in his chair, ignoring everything Dixie had been saying, Sean asked, "Did you know Billy Graham was a Fuller Brush Man?"

"No, and I don't care," Dixie replied, shaking her head.

"Did you know Janet Blair played Ann Elliot in *The Fuller Brush Man* and that Lucille Ball played Sally Elliot in *The Fuller Brush Girl* and that I grew up on Eliot Drive? The street was spelled with only one 'l,' but maybe that's insignificant."

Dixie couldn't find a kind response.

"Then again it might have something to do with 1948. That was the year *The Fuller Brush Man* was released. Maybe it's that year in Roman Numerals…MCMXLVIII. Could those letters be a cryptogram? Perhaps an acronym? Maybe even an anagram? I was born in 1955, but sis was born in 1948. That's got to be more than just a coincidence."

"Sean!!" Dixie ran her fingers through her soft, shoulder-length brunette hair, pulling it back from her face as she tried to regain her composure after yelling at him. "Honey, you have got to stop obsessing over this. It's really progressed over the years to the point where it's beyond unhealthy. You hardly exercise anymore, you drink coffee non-stop, and you don't get enough sleep. When you take off your glasses, I can see bags under your eyes that didn't used to be there. Frankly, the family thinks you're losing it."

Sean didn't bother to cast a glance at Dixie, and his insensitivity was palpable. "Your family."

"They're your family, too, remember? We both stood in front of the same judge."

"Yep, that was Frank's big day, wasn't it? Nothing like having your only daughter elope. I'd kill any punk who did that to Callie. No wonder he hates my guts."

Dixie crossed her arms. "Hey, if Daddy hated you as much as you say he does, you never would have gotten as far as you have in the Group."

That got his attention. Sean stared irritably at his wife. "Meaning, I'm the man I am because of your father?"

"Well, he certainly helped. Wouldn't you agree?"

"I guess if being a pain in Frank's ass all these years has made me a success, then I'd have to say you were spot on."

She began to pace back and forth. "Good. That's really good. You're obstinate, inconsiderate, and now on top of everything else, he thinks you have some sort of OCD thing over your mother's last words."

"OCD, huh? Then you figure it out. I simply can't accept the answers people give me. I mean, they try and try to convince me that twenty years ago when Mom was lying on her death bed, her mind had simply quit working. That doesn't add up. Sure, the cancer had taken a toll on her body, but her mind had remained keen. All those years of working various types of puzzles and brain teasers had kept her sharp as a tack. No, she wrote those words for a reason. I'm absolutely convinced the words were directed at me!"

Suddenly, Dixie realized the entirety of her remark had finally sunk in as he said, "Well, if he thinks that, it's only because you've discussed the subject with him. I certainly haven't talked to him about my research."

"Research?! Does he think that? Sean, I think that! Look at all of these piles. This room looks like a Fuller Brush rummage sale. Could you obsess over computers or cars or golf or women in lingerie or something half-way normal? No! You obsess over a company everybody over the age of 50 has forgotten, and nobody under 50 has ever frickin' heard of!"

Sean's tone was as bland as the subject matter. "It's actually a thriving business. Anyway, these are collectables."

"Right! What's in this box?" Dixie proceeded to dump the contents on to the floor. "Brushes. What's in this box?" She picked up another box and dumped it out on his desk. "More frickin' brushes. Wait! Here's a mop head!" She reached into another box and pulled out a bottle. "General purpose house cleaner?" Continuing to pull items from various boxes, she added, "Look, a squeegee! Look, window cleaner! Oh, wow! A duster—just what I always wanted! Whoo-whoo! Air freshener! These aren't collectables, Sean. It's a bunch of crap we don't need!"

Dixie watched with curiosity as her husband maintained the most serious expression while he defended the ridiculous.

"You don't understand the connections, do you?"

"Connections?! Connections to what? What's the connection between this 1948 Life Magazine with an article about the Fuller Brush Man and your son's new French girlfriend? What's the connection between this Fuller Brush letter opener and your daughter's imminent first week at college? Just what every man needs—a Fuller Brush rose-beige, pressed-powder compact. What's the connection between that and me? Here's a poster signed by Freddy the Freeloader. Yeah, that's got something to do with this month's auto sales, right?"

"It was Skelton playing Red Jones, not Freddy the Freeloader. Red couldn't hold a job until he became a salesman. Yet, Dad and I have always been gainfully employed." Pointing intently at Dixie, Sean continued, "And what about the murder plot in the movie? There was also a murder in the sequel, *The Fuller Brush Girl,* made in 1950. Was this a clue to some unsolved murder? When I was growing up in Urbana during the 50s and 60s, the local Fuller Brush Man was Floyd Drake. Could she have been alluding to him? There were all those rumors about his alternate lifestyle and, after all, he did die rather mysteriously. He's buried in the same cemetery where Mom's buried. His headstone's simple enough—just a name, birth date, and date of death. No clues there."

Grabbing an old, yellowed newspaper, Sean went on to explain, "The newspapers never mentioned anything earth-shattering about the guy; just that he died of natural causes at home. Yeah, right. He seemed to have lived a modest life in his home up by the fairgrounds until a neighbor found him dead. There was no indication in the records that his death was considered foul play. Could the police have missed something?"

Sean threw the newspaper back onto the thick, disorganized stack from which he'd pulled it. "And Red, he took on the nickname Philo Jones in the movie. That's a take-off of the name Philo Vance from S.S. Vine's detective novels of the 20s and 30s. You see? There's the mystery angle again. There almost had to be some type of foul play going on."

Pulling out and unfolding an old, coffee-stained Rand McNally roadmap of Illinois, Sean drew an arrow pointing at a particular landmark. "As for Philo, that's the name of the little town south of Urbana. I've turned that town upside-down chasing that red herring."

Dixie stopped ranting. Her eyes moistened with the beginnings of tears as she truly worried about the possibility her husband was on the verge of losing his mind. She pulled up a chair and sat next to him.

"Honey, I had lunch with Momma and Katie yesterday. It wasn't ten minutes before they started talking about your behavior. I tried to make up excuses, but I can't cover for you anymore, Sean." With a hint of ill-timed sarcasm, Dixie added, "I mean, your *research* has been going on ever since you got this wild hair seven years ago when you came across your mother's journal in the attic."

"Excuses? Cover for me? Wild hair? Tell them the truth," Sean said, getting face to face with Dixie. "Tell them that my mother was trying to send me a message twenty years ago, and I've been trying without success to figure out what that message is! They can either help or stay the hell out of the way!"

Struck by the intensity of Sean's rebuttal, Dixie took a moment to study him before asking, "Does that include me? Do you want me to stay out of the way, too?"

"You can either be a part of the problem or a part of the solution. Pick one," Sean said, sitting back in his chair once again.

Dixie stared at her fatigued husband. Her emotions at that moment ran the gamut from anger, to fear, to empathy, to devotion. Finally, she said, "Honey, I think you need to see someone about this."

"Someone as in…?" Sean asked, making no eye contact with his wife.

"…A therapist of some kind. I think you need some distance from me while you sort this out. I don't think I can be of any help to you."

Still refusing to look at her, Sean asked, "Who needs distance from whom in this separation you're talking about?"

"Sean, I'm not talking about getting a separation," Dixie said calmly as she put her hand compassionately on his shoulder. "I just want you to be able to speak with someone who is objective. Quite frankly, I'm not that person any longer."

With a facial expression that almost answered his own question, Sean asked, "You think I'm nuts, don't you?"

"Sean!" Stepping back as she pointed her finger at him, she said, "Don't back me into a corner. If you want me to call you nuts in order for you to seek help, then I'll do it. Just, please, get some help."

Her persistence finally secured Sean's consent. Holding out his hand for Dixie, he said, "Alright. I'll see someone. Maybe they can see what it is I'm overlooking."

Reaching out again and putting her hand in Sean's, Dixie replied, "Or maybe they can just help you move forward…help you get past these thoughts you're having." After a short, but symbolic embrace, Dixie added, "Will you come to bed now?"

"I'll be right there," he replied with half a smile. "Let me make a few more notes about my thoughts tonight and I'll join you."

"I love you, Sean," Dixie said as she made her way to the door.

"Ditto, babe."

Pausing before she passed through the doorway, Dixie turned and added, "I think it's best for now that we not tell Daddy anything about therapy, alright?"

Weakness of any kind, whether it was perceived or real, would never be tolerated by the old man. Frank always said in meetings, 'The weak are there to be dominated by the strong.' His credo sounded nothing like 'Make It Work, Make It Last, Guarantee It No Matter What.'

"I agree. This talk of a shrink is between us."

Before she left the room, Sean closed the conversation with, "Hey. You look good in that outfit. Have you lost some weight?"

Dixie knew Sean always had a way of ending a confrontation with an olive branch. Reaching out to take it, while realizing all might not be hopeless in their marriage, she seductively replied, "Come to bed, honey."

AFTER DIXIE WAS GONE, Sean poured himself another cup of coffee. Restarting the movie, he set out to check the spelling of the names he had written down for the minor cast members in the movie and those of the Director, Producer and others in the opening credits. Without an accurate spelling, his internet searches the next evening for each of those people would be a complete waste of time.

But as the names began to scroll across the television screen, Sean became distracted by his earlier thought and began to jot down the Roman Numeral letters representing 1948 in various combinations, altering the sequence of the letters, looking for any type of pattern.

Chapter 2

"HONEY!!" DIXIE YELLED FROM the office doorway.

Sean nearly fell out of his chair, startled by her voice.

"I can't believe you slept in that chair all night. You said you were coming to bed. What am I going to do with you?"

After slowly getting out of his office chair, Sean ignored the sad reality that he had once again fallen asleep at his desk. He went about saving the open files on his computer and putting the papers scattered about on his desk into neat piles or manila folders. Once done with his countermeasures, he pulled a comb out of his pocket and twice ran it through his graying, red hair.

"There. How do I look for Daddy?"

Sounding not the least bit amused, Dixie told him, "You look like shit. I'll make you some coffee and something you can take with you to eat in the car. Go get showered, shaved, and dressed."

Dripping with sarcasm, Sean answered back, "Ah, those sweet, motivational words that a man hears come out of his wife's mouth the first thing in the morning. They do so set the tone for the day."

Maintaining her serious tone, Dixie said very bluntly, "You have fifteen minutes. I'll call Daddy and make up a reason for why you're late."

Sean closed his eyes and puckered his lips with great exaggeration as if to woo a kiss from his wife. His intentions were for naught. She turned and left. Sighing, he realized he was off to a bad start for a Tuesday morning.

FIVE MINUTES LATER, THE shower was doing little to invigorate him. As soapy water ran from his head down over his eyes, Dixie surprisingly joined him. Sean turned and rubbed the water from his eyes in time to see Dixie holding his insulated coffee travel mug in the cleavage between her all-natural breasts. Not many women could do that, but then not many women would choose to do it even if they could. She had this wild streak that would inexplicably come to life from time to time, and this was one of those moments.

"I brought you your coffee. Want some?" Dixie asked with a wink.

Understating his enthusiasm over the spectacle, Sean replied, "This would be a great commercial for Starbucks. Let me get the video camera."

"No. There's no time for that. Besides, the cup is starting to get hot. Drink up while I test you."

Sadly, Sean knew she was right. After removing the cup from its firm, fleshy holders, he drank from it while Dixie lathered up his chest with soap.

"How many units have you sold this month?" Dixie asked in a business-like manner that was completely out of context with what was taking place.

"On target for one hundred Toyotas and fifty Lexi."

"Year-over-year sales?"

"For the month, up seventeen percent. For the year, up twenty-two percent."

"Why aren't the monthly year-over-year sales up more than the total year-over-year? Is your business declining?"

Sean scanned his wife from head to toe more than once. His facial expression and body language poorly concealed his lusting desires. "If it weren't for those slippery, wet knockers of yours, I'd swear you were Frank asking the questions."

Shaking her head, Dixie said, "Don't even joke about being in a shower with soap and Daddy. Now stay on task. Answer my questions."

"Our allotment of our two hottest selling Toyotas decreased in the last two months."

"Why? Did allotments drop at Smith's Midwest Motors? Did they drop at Grand Lake Motors? What about the rest of the northern region?"

"No. Only ours decreased."

"How do you know?"

"Inside research."

"So, were you on the phone twice a day trying to increase your allotment?"

"Yes. Religiously."

"Then why weren't you on the phone three times a day?"

After that cross-examination, Sean couldn't have spelled erection, let alone achieved one.

"Tell you what, Dixie, there's no question you're a Darling."

His wet, voluptuous, naked wife cocked her head to one side. "Thank you, I love you, too."

The worn out joke was that Dixie really was a Darling—daughter of successful North Shore businessman, W. Frank Darling and his wife, Suzanne. It was only because she married Sean against her father's wishes that she dropped the family name and became a Marcum. There wasn't even a hyphen. But without question, Darling blood was thick…really thick. And Dixie had plenty of it pumping through her veins.

"So, how did I do?" Sean asked.

She playfully flicked water from her fingers into his face. "He's going to kill you." She shook her head before continuing. "You know he depends upon your growth. That's about all the Group can count on these days. You could be up thirty percent and he'd still treat you like a step-child."

"Or a son-in-law."

"Right, or a son-in-law."

Dixie quickly finished washing both sides of Sean's body. It appeared by way of her lingering hands that she was taking note of his physical attributes. In spite of his increasingly sedentary lifestyle, he was still in quite good shape for his age. There was even a bit of a 6-pack still visible under the hair covering his abdomen, and his bum was still firm.

After glancing seductively downward, then back into Sean's eyes, she asked, "So, how's your growth doing right now?"

Anticipating a turnaround at any moment, Sean answered, "Uh, you'll notice that it's pointing straight down."

"I see that," she replied, pressing her body affectionately against his. "That's a bad thing, don't you think?"

"I'm going to be late as it is, and…" His argument went weak when she grabbed on to something that definitely got his attention.

Following a coquettish grin, Dixie said, "No, you're not. I called Liz and asked her to tell Frank Junior that the meeting was delayed until 9:15. He's going to be late." After kissing Sean slowly on the lips, she ended with, "We only need twenty minutes."

Sean's day began to take a well-deserved turn for the better.

TRAFFIC HAD BEEN FORGIVING, and thankfully Sean arrived at the Group's main office just shortly before the meeting was scheduled to start. The Group Meetings, as they came to be known, were less of a business review and strategy session, than they were a fight for survival. Frank had a way of pitting the principals of the dealerships against one another in a sort of ritualistic battle to the death. Sean always came out with his shirt on his back, largely because his dealerships were the only ones consistently showing increases in revenue, profit, market share, and repeat customers. The gamble he had made years earlier to take on the dogs of the auto industry, as Frank called them at the time, had made him a huge success. Frank's sons got the cash cow businesses of an earlier era. Frank Junior was General Manager of Cadillac and later the waning Hummer dealership. John was General Manager of Buick and GMC and at one time had Oldsmobile until that brand became obsolete. Stephen was General Manager of Chevrolet, the commercial truck businesses, and Pontiac until that brand joined the Dodo, too.

Sean's anti-American brands were Toyota and Lexus—and he was kicking butt. Frank always cast the American brands in a positive light regardless of how poorly those businesses were performing. Sean, on the other hand, always had to prove himself worthy of his General Manager title to the rest in the Group. Surviving Frank's monthly assault had become a predictable rite, one that he was familiar with, and one he had mastered. That he could absorb all of the stones Frank and his sons threw at him on a regular basis and walk away unscathed and unaffected, truly grated on their collective nerves. Of course, it didn't hurt that Sean was married to the oldest sibling, Dixie, or that she had Daddy in the palm of her hand and could crush her younger brothers at will as she had her entire life.

Recently, tensions were worsening between the Darling boys and Sean. Sean was generating so much cash from his business that he wanted to expand into BMW and Volvo. Such an expansion, though financially justifiable, required the unanimous approval from the other principals—an approval that, thus far, the other Group executives had denied him.

Frank Senior had fulfilled his obligation to his country as a Marine during the Korean Conflict. He once led a platoon to the heroic completion of their critical mission after his senior officers were killed early in battle. For his bravery, he received a meritorious combat field promotion to the rank of Sergeant. He conducted his affairs to this day as if he never left the Corps. He remained vocal, opinionated, domineering, aggressive, and right one-hundred percent of the time. Few dared challenge him. Though in his late seventies, Frank still carried his six-foot three-inch, two-hundred-twenty-pound frame proudly upright. His sons never mastered his brutality in business or at home, though Frank Junior and Stephen often tried. John, the middle son, was actually halfway decent in Sean's eyes, due in large part because he married a gem of a woman, Katie, who was also Dixie's best friend and closest sister-in-law. Their relationship was so extraordinary, Sean and Dixie chose John and Katie to be Godparents to their children, Callie and Will.

On the flip side of family harmony, Frank Junior never forgave Dixie for naming her son, William Frank, after their father, eliminating the unique possibility of there being a third generation Frank, as in 'the III.' Then, when Dixie began calling him Will instead of Frank, she simply added insult to injury. Frank Junior was convinced Dixie privately influenced their father in ways that worked against him as part of their perpetual sibling rivalry—and he was probably right.

FRANK ALWAYS MADE A grand entry, and generally made a point of expressing his displeasure about something right off the bat.

"Stephen! Where's your idiot brother?"

"He should be here," Stephen said. "I saw his car in the driveway when I drove past this morning."

"Bunch of damn bankers, that's what I have in this Group." Glancing momentarily at Sean, Frank asked, "Sean, how's my daughter?"

Frank never asked how Sean was doing, but his daughter had better be happy and healthy or the consequences would be anything but pleasant.

"Great, Frank. We enjoyed coffee, then something to eat, before I left the house."

Sean noticed as John turned to look out the window in order that Frank wouldn't see him snickering at the innuendo. Frank quickly reined John back into the discussion.

"John, I need Katie to call Mom later. There may be a conflict at the Club over the use of the pool for JJ's birthday party. Mom's going to deal with it this afternoon. Tell Katie that if there is any problem getting that pool, to get in touch with me. I'll make one phone call and fix it."

It became clear to Sean long ago that it was dogma that Frank could fix anything, command anything, or arrange anything, with one phone call. Recipients of those phone calls invariably promised themselves never to be in the position to get another one.

Frank looked at his watch before yelling out the door for his secretary. “Francis!”

One of the other assistants, Phoebe, entered the conference room with her phone and notepad in hand.

“Where the hell is Francis?” Frank asked.

“She said she had to take her son to the doctor. She’ll be in around eleven o’clock.”

“Does anyone around here realize this is a business?”

Phoebe’s wise reply showed Sean that she wasn’t stupid. “Yes, sir, Mr. Darling.”

“What about the rest of you candy-asses?” Frank continued, scanning the others in the room.

Sean, Stephen, and John just sat there in silence, soaking up the abuse.

“And why are you in slacks?” Frank asked, pointing at Phoebe. “You know I don’t approve of women wearing slacks to the office. When Francis gets in, go home and change. If you want to wear slacks, go work someplace else.”

“Yes, sir, Mr. Darling. I apologize.”

“Call Frank Junior on his mobile and find out where the hell he’s at. Tell him he’s late.”

“Yes, sir, Mr. Darling.”

Phoebe had no sooner walked out the door when Frank Junior appeared with a puzzled look on his face. By his reaction, the others could tell he knew he was late. It only took seconds for Frank to wield the hatchet.

"Glad you could make it, Frank. Meet the punctual members of the Group—John, Stephen, and Sean. They're here for our regular monthly Group Meeting that happens at nine o'clock every goddamn first Tuesday of every goddamn month for the last eleven goddamn years."

"Dixie called Liz and told her the meeting was postponed until 9:15," Frank Junior stated in his defense.

"Are you really that stupid?" Frank asked his eldest son unsympathetically.

Continuing to defend his tardiness, Frank Junior foolishly replied, "Sean probably had Dixie in bed and needed a smokescreen so that…"

"Stop!" Frank shouted. "Don't ever say the word 'bed' and your sister's name in context with Sean, do you hear me?"

Knowing how to really start the fireworks, Sean came to Frank Junior's rescue.

"He's right, Frank. Dixie got in the shower with me this morning and I simply couldn't resist the…"

Frank threw his hands into the air. "Jesus Christ!! Make me throw up!" He whispered futilely in his gruff voice as he continued, "It sickens me to even think she had sex with you even twice to make those two wonderful grandkids of mine. I'd hoped it stopped at that."

"No, Frank. Dixie's a regular minx. I found that out before we were married."

Frank pointed the finger-of-death at Sean. It was like having a referee hold up the red card in your face at a soccer match, only you were never lucky enough to be sent to the locker room. You had to endure the ongoing punishment from the bench.

Reminding Sean that some wounds never heal, Frank muttered his perception of his daughter's matrimonial status. "You eloped with my daughter. You didn't get married."

THE PRINCIPALS TOOK THEIR seats, then proceeded to sit in silence for what seemed like an eternity as Frank shuffled through reports, all the while making a myriad of grimacing facial expressions. The silence ended with Frank's usual analysis of the combined Group's performance.

"Pathetic," Frank said.

Sean wasn't going down without a fight.

"You're right, Frank. I'm only up twenty-two percent this year. I was hoping for twenty-five."

The other principals squirmed in their chairs, clearly wishing they had Sean's numbers and probably wishing he had simply let the matter drop. But Sean always liked playing slap the bull with Frank.

"That's your problem, Sean," Frank said. "You always set your goals too low."

"Did you notice margins are holding up nicely?" Sean countered. "Not to mention the fact that we'll start the next model year with less than thirty units from the last model year."

"Why so many?" Frank asked.

"Because, you cut my television advertising budget last month to zero."

"You're a bright young man," Frank said, his voice dripping with sarcasm. "Why do you need television for a crutch?"

"Oh, it's not a crutch. It's just my opportunity to get Callie in front of the camera. People notice when she's in the commercial…just like they remember the commercial when Dixie's on screen."

And that's how it worked. Sean would set it up so that Frank could be right, be the hero, and take that hill one more time, and Sean would usually get the desired outcome.

Frank reflected on Sean's comment. "I was thinking only yesterday that I hadn't seen Dixie or Callie on television lately. A couple of weeks ago, I was golfing with one of the coaches at Northwestern, and he asked about Callie. He said he'd see what he could do to get her a volleyball scholarship there."

"She's going to the U of I in Urbana, Frank. That's already been settled."

"What a waste," Frank said. "Send a beautiful girl like that away from her home in Lake Forest, when she could be close by her family and still get exposure in advertising. You still have time to reconsider."

"Classes begin in less than two weeks, Frank."

"Not a problem, Sean. One phone call from me, and she'd be in any program you want at Northwestern."

Sean needed to get the conversation back on track. "So, do I get ad time?"

Probably knowing Sean wasn't going to back away from his demand, Frank ended the matter on his terms. "Fine. You get one prime spot each day for the next three weeks."

Wasting no time, Sean quickly took advantage of the offer. "I'll start shooting tomorrow."

"Bullshit!" Frank Junior interrupted. "I'm due for a shoot tomorrow, Sean. You'll have to wait until we're done."

Playing his trump card, Sean tantalized Frank. "I thought I'd do a back to school pitch with Callie and Dixie. What do you think, Frank?"

Sean knew there was no way Frank would turn down his proposal—not with both of Frank's girls in the spotlight.

"Frank!" The senior said. "Film later in the week!"

Sean winced as Frank Junior argued.

"Fine, then. I'll shoot with Blue Lake Advertising."

The old man pointed his finger-of-death at Frank Junior. "You'll use Lakeshore Media, no ifs, ands, or buts. Remember this, the weak are there to be dominated by the strong. Sean just made a damn good argument. If you weren't such a candy-ass, you'd have had the filming done last week and be running ads now. God knows your business is in the shitter."

That shut Frank Junior down…for now. Sean could tell that a volcano stirred in his brother-in-law's gut. Frank looked for new victims and it didn't take long.

"Stephen, John, your numbers are atrocious." Frank slammed the palm of his right hand on the table. "I want a plan on my desk by this time tomorrow morning."

Frank Junior grinned, having escaped that assignment. His moment of glory was short-lived.

"Frank, your performance is by far the worst of all. Stay after the meeting. We need to talk." Looking around the room, Frank continued, "Honestly, gentlemen, this is the worst performance I've seen out of this Group since…I don't know when. We can't continue like this. We need a solution before the end of next quarter. Jameson at the bank is getting erectile dysfunction over the size of our note. I need to give him something more than a promise. Also, our temporary lot out on the Tri-State is going to cost us twice as much starting in October. Gibson says he can get more than double what we are paying if he leases it to the State for snow removal equipment and surface treatment storage. He owes me a favor so he's giving me a break on the price, but nonetheless, what he's charging us is still piracy. We need to drop our combined inventory by four-hundred sixty-two vehicles, which is, at last count, what we have collecting bird shit on that lot."

Frank closed his notebook which meant the meeting was over. Sean knew his timing was poor, but he had to ask the group once again for a pledge to expand his operation.

"Frank, can we at least discuss BMW and Volvo?"

Frank's response wasn't entirely what Sean had hoped for.

"I've decided to consider the investment further, but this meeting's adjourned. I have something to discuss with Frank Junior, then I have an appointment. Sean, I'll drop by your office later…say fifteen-hundred. I'll let you know my plans then."

Frank Junior's face took on an expression indicating he knew something, but wasn't about to share it with the others. This usually meant Sean would reap some of the benefit of Frank's decision, but one or more of the other principals would garner the lion's share.

Sean decided to take Frank's offer at face value. "See you at three." He wasted no time packing up his folio and leaving ahead of the others.

Chapter 3

SEAN BRISKLY PULLED HIS small black Toyota sedan into the parking space reserved for him and shut down the purring motor. Both of his dealerships were always immaculate in appearance, and he prided himself on hiring and retaining only the most passionate and respectful employees. He couldn't help but notice a dozen prospective buyers on the lot looking at vehicles and several more in the showroom. On top of that, there was more than the usual number of guests in a nicely appointed VIP lounge that had been the brainchild of Sean's Director of Customer Satisfaction, April Knudsen.

As much as the brands in Sean's businesses sold themselves, April's personal attention to customers' desires at both of his dealerships, before, during, and after sales, had easily increased his business by fifteen percent. The people-friendly layouts of the lots, the abundant, tasteful landscaping, the supervised playscapes for children of clientele, and the ever-changing selection of drinks and foods, had all been her ideas. Everyone who purchased a vehicle left with her mobile phone number, and she frequently made personal calls to customers weeks and months after their purchase to ensure they were satisfied, would strongly consider

Sean's dealerships in the future, and hopefully recommend them to others in the market for a vehicle.

Sean's dealerships were next to one another, giving him easy access to both. His expansion plans included razing a waning, circa-1960 strip mall next door, where he would build his Volvo and BMW businesses. The demographics in this northern Chicago region were perfect for a line of upscale family vehicles made by Volvo, and the more expensive, fashionable, and high-performance brand, BMW. But start-up costs were going to be substantial and, though he had the means to establish the dealerships himself, he preferred to tap the deeper pockets of the Group in order to bring his plans to fruition. The owner of the mall recently mentioned to Sean that there was another unidentified party taking serious interest in the property, and that he needed to make a decision soon or risk losing the opportunity.

April was waiting for Sean in his office so she could review some recent customer feedback data. She was quite a few years younger than Sean and a looker to boot, a quality that hadn't gone unnoticed by him. Regardless of what she wore to work—a suit, sweater and slacks, blue jeans and vest, or even a Chicago Blackhawks jersey—her sleek, five-foot eight-inch tall, and shapely figure made the ensemble look better than it otherwise would. He had always kept their relationship completely professional, which probably added to her feeling of freedom to push the limits of what she could do. She had a magic touch for getting anything done, faster than expected, and usually at lower cost than budget. Her list of resources filled her Blackberry, and her relationships with local civic organizations, politicos, contractors, and suppliers were impeccable.

As successful as she was in business, behind the scenes, her personal life was in tatters. Her ex-husband, Scott, was a naval officer who was forever on long deployments. She suspected at one time that he had a girl in every port and confronted him about it. He denied the specific allegation, telling her defiantly that he had only *two* girlfriends—one in Europe and one in Asia. How convenient it was that his assignments year after year had taken him to one of those destinations. Needless to say, as a Command Officer, he needed a wife if only for image, and she needed a husband for, well, no particular reason, actually. She ultimately divorced him, but kept her wedding ring on her finger. That, and regular conversation about a nameless, faceless significant other in her life, kept away the many casual suitors.

APRIL GREETED HER BOSS with her usual, cheerful smile. "Good morning, Sean. How'd it go with Frank?"

Setting his folio on his desk, Sean replied, "Not good enough, too late, try harder, the weak are there to be dominated by the strong."

"So, it went as always," she said.

"Actually, the dichotomy of the weak and strong got us some air time. We got daily prime spots over the course of the next three weeks, but we need to shoot tomorrow, and it *has to* include Dixie and Callie."

April radiated confidence. "No problem. I'll call them and set it up with the agency. Do you care what time?"

Taking a seat at his desk, Sean replied, "No. Just work around Dixie's schedule. Callie shouldn't be doing anything she can't break away from. All she's doing is packing for school. I have her keys because she stayed out too late Saturday night. She should be at home or with Dixie. Be sure to give the spot a back to school flavor."

After sitting down in a plush chair in front of Sean's desk, April gracefully crossed her legs. "Callie's really done well in front of the camera. I think she's a natural. Has she picked a major yet? She'd be terrific in marketing or advertising; even theater or acting for that matter."

"That she has. It's called wallet depreciation."

April laughed so hard at Sean's response, she almost spilled her coffee.

"I'm serious, that girl has no self-control. She wants something, she buys it. She sees something, she buys it. If I say no, her response is always, 'Grandpa will get it for me.' She doesn't even bother dropping 'mom' into the argument. I swear, Frank and Suzanne have masterfully spoiled her."

Still chuckling over Sean's dilemma, April suggested, "She got some of that from her momma, didn't she?"

"I don't know. What Dixie has given up in quantity, she has made up for in quality. Just last week she bought these Pratesi Egyptian cotton sheets made in Italy. Cost as much as a monthly lease payment on a Ferrari! I pray every night that Callie doesn't get the taste for high-end items that Dixie has. However, I may be facing my first test on that subject tonight. Callie wants to talk new car with me."

"Don't you think that's natural? After all, she's the next generation of an automotive family."

"She has a car. I got her a nice Solara. Hell, it's more of a car than I drive. I think she's going to drop the Lexus Coupe bombshell on me tonight."

"Hey, every upscale freshman, prospective volleyball star, and sorority pledge needs a 'Coupe.'"

"Remind me to keep you far away from her during the shoot tomorrow."

April giggled some more before offering, "Can I get you a cup of coffee?"

Getting up from his chair, Sean replied, "Let's walk together. I need to talk to George about our discounts. We need to move some vehicles for the Group. I think this new ad might bring in some incremental business from parents sending their kids away to college, and I want to make the most of it."

THE TWO MEANDERED THROUGH the Lexus showroom floor, schmoozing with the staff and customers as they went. After about ten minutes, they made their way to the lounge.

"What's Will going to do after this year?" April asked. "Has he decided on grad school?"

"That's another huge debate. He's set to graduate with a degree in Finance at U of I after this year. We've toyed with the idea of him going for his MBA right after he graduates, but Frank wants him in 'the biz' the day after graduation. He says he'll send him through the Kellogg School at Northwestern."

"Sounds like a sweet deal."

"Right," Sean said with reservation. "Well, here's the catch." Making sure they were alone, Sean whispered, "I don't think Will wants to be in *the Biz*."

"You're kidding?" April replied, looking astonished.

"No, I'm dead serious. He met this French girl from Marseille at school this summer, and she's really got his head spinning. She's getting a Finance degree, too, but her family is in the hospitality businesses—lodging, wine making, and restaurant management. She wants to open a bed-and-breakfast or castle lodge in some glamorous old home someplace, and run a chic eatery alongside it."

"What's Will say about it?"

"Oh, he's too busy drooling over this girl to think straight, but I think he's going to follow her dream."

"Are there wedding bells?"

"He says they're going to live together this year and see how it goes."

"Ummm. That sounds serious. Does Frank know?"

"Hell, no. Frank will shit an Osterizer when he finds out. Right now, with Callie starting her freshman year there, Will is worried that Callie will figure out the arrangements and spill the beans."

"She's going to be too busy with her game schedule and pledging to spot those details, don't you think?"

"No. She's always messing in his life somehow. She's been watching Dixie screw with Frank Junior for as long as she can remember."

April's phone chimed indicating she'd received a text message. After a pause to read it, she ended the conversation abruptly with, "I'd better get moving on that ad shoot. I'll let you know if I need any help. We'll talk later about the customer feedback."

"Great. I'll be tied up with Frank this afternoon after three o'clock, so try to catch me before that."

"What's the subject, if I may ask?"

"BMW, Volvo...and something to do with Frank Junior."

"Oh. Well, good luck."

"If I don't show up for work tomorrow, start looking in the trees for a middle-aged man with a noose around his neck. That'll be me."

Putting her hand on his shoulder supportively, she said, "You'll do fine. You always do."

AN AFTERNOON RAIN SHOWER had just ended when, exactly two minutes before fifteen-hundred hours, Frank pulled his full-size Cadillac next to Sean's much smaller sedan. The contrast was clear and purposeful. It was anything but accidental that Frank parked so close to Sean's driver's side. There was no way a person could open the door. Symbolically, Sean wasn't going anywhere. Frank climbed out of his vehicle, briefcase in hand, and began his calculated two-minute march to Sean's office, taking a moment to glare disapprovingly at Sean's car as he passed by.

One after another, Sean's employees greeted Frank with smiles and salutations, only to be scrutinize as if they were soldiers standing in formation as the senior officer strutted past. Needless to say, Frank wasn't a Howdy Doody sort of guy.

Sean was on the telephone with one of his suppliers when Frank opened the office door and let himself in. He was just wrapping up a conversation, during which he was negotiating an increase in his allocation of some of the more lucrative and hard to come by models. It hadn't gone well.

"So you'll call me back by Friday? Monday? OK. I'm counting on you, Terry. You, too. Bye, now."

Sean hung up his phone, then sat back in his chair, anticipating Frank's unsolicited remarks.

Frank didn't disappoint. After taking a seat, and without any attempt at concealing his criticism, he said, "Let me ask you, Sean, how does a guy like you survive? From listening to this end of the conversation, you just put your balls on a platter and handed that guy a knife."

"You weren't here for the entire discussion, Frank. It went quite well."

It actually hadn't, but Sean wasn't about to admit that.

Mocking his son-in-law, Frank said, "Do you think I told troops during battle, 'Let's take that bunker Friday. No? What about Monday, then? I'm counting on you, boys. Go, fight, win…'"

"We each have our own way of conducting business, Frank. How I work with my suppliers has served me well. But thank you for reminding me, once again, of our differences."

"You know, Sean, it's not about *you*. It's about *us*…the Group. It's about Dixie and Callie and Will. You're not fighting hard enough for an upside in allocation. Was that Terry Nakamura?"

"Yes, it was. Why?"

"You need to call Kitajima. Start at the top. Nakamura's a bozo. I'll give Kitajima a call first thing in the morning."

"Frank, I'll let you know when I need your help. Please stay out of it."

"That's your problem, Sean," Frank responded, leaning closer so he could pound his fist on Sean's desk as he spoke. "You wait too long to call in reinforcements. You need help and you don't even know it. Meanwhile, the rest of the Group is circling the toilet."

Deciding he had heard enough, Sean changed the subject to what he wanted to discuss, and hopefully bring Frank's visit to an expedient end.

"Frank, what about the new dealerships. You know it's the right thing to do. Why are you so reticent?"

"It's the same issue with you, Sean. I don't think you have the guts to tough out a new market. I mean, Toyota? Lexus?

Anybody can sell those. Hell, they practically sell themselves. Of course, you have to rely on a woman to be the face on your business—several women, mind you. You have Dixie, bless her heart, out there marketing your products for you. Callie's coming up right behind her. And April, she does nine-tenths of the work around here. Hell, you ought to fire half your sales people. They're all standing around outside, waving at me like a bunch of idiots."

Sean could feel his muscles tightening as Frank's diatribe went on and on.

"Volvo and BMW? That's a new ball of wax. The product is European, not Japanese, and the customers are go-getters, not a bunch of tree-huggers. Why, people who buy BMWs eat people like you for breakfast. That's why they can afford to buy BMWs."

"Frank, I know all about the products, and I know my market. So, are you behind the investment or not?"

"That's just like you. You think all you need is money, and the business will take off on its own. Let me tell you something, young man. It takes a real driver to launch a business like the one you're talking about."

The conversation was beginning to take on ominous undertones.

"Frank, answer my question."

Frank's expression took on an appearance Sean imagined the old man had many times in past conflicts when he would drive a bayonet into the squirming body of an enemy soldier—a mixture of delight, fanciful pleasure, and accomplishment as he watched the life in that person drifting away.

"I like the idea, Sean. The Volvo and BMW lines will be a good addition to our Group. And here's the part you've been waiting for…"

Sean suddenly felt as if his life was flashing before his eyes.

"…I'm going to give the Cadillac business to Will—kind of a graduation present from his granddad."

It was a reflex action, much like pulling one's hand away from a flame as Sean blurted out, "He doesn't want anything to do with the business, Frank." After the words were spoken, Sean regretted opening his mouth.

Frank vehemently disagreed. "What do you mean? He's a Darling. He *will* be in the auto business. It's in his blood."

Going for broke, Sean explained, "I'm pretty sure he wants to get into the hospitality business."

The finger came out as Frank reacted. "That's faggot crap! You need to put a stop to it, now!" Frank stopped for a moment to study Sean, then continued, "Or is this some idiotic idea of yours? It sounds more like something you'd dream up, instead of something my grandson would think of."

"And he's probably getting married."

"Bullshit! If that was the case, Vaughn would have told me."

"He isn't marrying Kristy Vaughn. He has a new girlfriend, and I think he is considering tying the knot with her."

"Like hell he is! You need to put an end to that right now! He's been dating Vaughn's daughter for three goddamn years. I'll make a phone call right now and get this fixed."

"Frank! Keep out of it!"

The glass windows that make up the walls in Sean's office were no longer sufficient to keep the argument out of the ears of passersby.

Sean could tell Frank was chewing on his tongue. He did that instead of shouting 'Oorah' when victory was imminent.

"When he finds out he's getting the Cadillac business, he'll come around. I'll see to that."

It was a foregone conclusion, but Sean had to know. "So, what's Frank Junior going to do if, as you propose, you turn over his business to Will?"

The grin that unfolded across Frank's face was most sinister. "Volvo and BMW, of course."

Sean smirked, though not with disbelief. "Frank, that has to be the lowest thing you've ever done to me."

"What? Giving Will a job that most young men would kill for?"

"You know what I mean. You're using the excess cash generated by *my* business, and taking *my* idea to benefit Frank Junior. It's just wrong."

"Boo-fuckin'-hoo. What are you going to do about it? Are you going to deny your son the greatest opportunity ever thrown at him?"

Sean stood up before Frank knowing that was something he disliked. Frank often said he never wanted to look up at anyone.

"No, Frank. I won't deny him the opportunity of a lifetime. I'm going to make damn sure he marries the love of his life and goes into business for himself like he wants."

Standing up opposite Sean, Frank coldly replied, "We'll see."

The two stared at each other for what seemed like an eternity. Frank ended the face-off. "You have a great day, Sean. Oh, by the way, Senator Bogenkamp is swinging through town Tuesday next week. I want to have a reception for him…right here, followed by dinner at the Club. I want him to see the property I'm buying next door. The owner's his son-in-law. Did you know that?"

Sean wasn't aware of that fact. Nor was he aware that Frank was the other unidentified party interested in buying the old strip mall. He detested Bogenkamp even more than he did Frank, and never had reason to look into any of his ties or holdings.

"There will be a fundraiser at the Club at nineteen-hundred that evening. You know—cocktails at six, dinner at seven. Five-hundred a plate; twenty tables for eight. I want you to set it up for me, and that means a set of butt cheeks in every chair. Call me tomorrow with your plans. You see, Sean, that's how families work together. They get things done. I suggest you get your shit together real fast."

Chapter 4

IT HADN'T BEEN THE worst day in Sean's life, but it was certainly close to the top. He had no sooner arrived home, dropped his folio on a chair in the kitchen, and opened a bottle of beer when Callie walked up to him. It was clear she was operating with mission parameters. That didn't matter. Sean was unhappy with her, and it was time they had yet another serious discussion about her priorities.

With the passing of each day, his eighteen year old daughter looked more and more like Dixie at the age of twenty-two. Callie was all too aware of this, and she could sense her father's resolve quickly weaken whenever she wanted something from him. If beauty was the only ticket to success, Callie had it made. She was a siren with Dixie's long, wavy, brunette hair, exquisite facial features, pouting lips, hazel eyes, and a figure that belonged on the cover of a gentleman's magazine. But along with her looks, April had been correct with her observation that Callie had no trouble commanding attention, getting straight to her point, or standing her ground.

Sean leaned against the refrigerator and tried to glare at his daughter. "April tried calling you all day today, and you never returned her call. She has an advertising gig for you and your mother, and the two of you need to get it done tomorrow."

"I was busy. Didn't you get my text message? Oh, wait. You don't have text messaging, do you! That's right—I remember reading somewhere that there are three Neanderthals on this planet, and you, who still don't have text messaging."

Dealing with Callie's smart mouth would have to wait. He needed to address the business first.

"Just a phone call, Callie. It would have taken you all of five minutes. What were you doing that you couldn't return her call?"

"I was test driving cars. I was at Uncle Stephen's driving a Vette, and Uncle Frank let me drive an XLR Roadster."

"I have both sets of your keys in my coat pocket. Who took you?"

"Grandpa."

Her sly grin that followed indicated to Sean it had been a conspiracy. *So that was the appointment he had before three o'clock.*

"Put those cars out of your head. You're not getting either of them."

"That's okay, Daddy. I really want one of your Coupes."

"Sweetie, we've had this conversation. You have the Solara. That's your car."

"Daddy, you don't get it, do you? I mean, are you really that stupid?"

Sean was watching his daughter turn into a creation of Frank and Suzanne's before his very eyes.

"I mean, it's like you're trying to keep me from being the best. You own a car company, right? I mean, why can't you just get me another car? Like, I do all of this advertising for you, right? And, like, you never paid me crap for doing it, right? So, this is, like, your chance to settle up with me."

After calmly taking a gulp of his beer, Sean answered his spoiled, belligerent daughter. "Let's see, Callie. There's tuition, room and board at Kappa Kappa Gamma if they accept you, gas money, your allowance, all of your expenses for volleyball that won't be covered…"

"Grandpa thinks I should go to Northwestern. He says he can get me onto the team there and into any sorority I want. He just has to make a phone call. Then, like, if you want me to do advertising for you, I'm close by."

Sean was surprised Callie played the Frank card so quickly.

Doing well to stand his ground, Sean said, "Is that so? Well, I'm your father and you're going to Illinois. Period."

Right on cue, Dixie pulled up. Sean wondered whose side she would take. But before the three of them engaged in what was certain to be a house-divided argument, the kitchen phone rang. Callie quickly answered it.

Making certain her father could hear the conversation, Callie greeted the caller. "Grandpa! How are you doing?"

After angrily grabbing the phone from Callie's hand, Sean yelled into it, "I told you to mind your own damn business!!"

A calm voice replied, "Golly, Son, I missed you too."

Realizing the caller was *his* father, Raymond, Sean apologized. "Dad…I'm sorry. I thought you were…"

"Frank?"

"Yeah, Frank."

"So, are things a little tense up there?" Raymond was a master of understatement.

"No. Everything's under control. I'm just having a little disagreement with Frank. That plus Callie's being a pain in the ass."

Callie stuck her tongue out at her father.

"Did you just call your daughter a pain in the ass?" Dixie asked as she walked in with a bag full of groceries.

"Yes I did. Did April get in touch with you today?"

"April?" Raymond asked.

"No, Dad. I was talking to Dixie."

"Do you want me to call back later, Son, say in about four years?"

"Dad, hold on."

"Yes," Dixie replied. "April called me, and we're all set for nine o'clock tomorrow."

"Great, can you explain what's going on to your daughter?"

"Mom, Grandpa wants me to go to Northwestern."

"Why does Raymond want Callie to go to Northwestern, Sean? I thought he was looking forward to her going to school in Urbana."

"No. *My* father does want her to go to Illinois. It's *your* father who wants her to go to Northwestern."

"Really, well maybe we should consider that."

"Dixie!"

"Son, do you want me to call you back?"

"Mom, Dad won't buy me a new car.

"I'll talk to your father, Callie."

"Dixie!"

"Maybe this isn't a good time, Sean."

"Dad, it's good. It's good."

Having completely lost control of his heart-to-heart with Callie, Sean gave up, taking the phone into his office where he took a seat at his desk.

"What's up, Dad?"

"Well, I called to give you some news…actually, some bad news, I'm afraid."

Sean snickered before saying, "Hit me with it, Dad. Nothing can make my day any worse than it is at this moment."

"Alright. Brace yourself. Kimmie died this afternoon."

Sean couldn't speak—his heart was in his throat.

"Did you hear me, Sean?"

Trying to breathe without gasping, Sean struggled to answer. "Yeah, I heard."

Sean's hands began to shake and his eyes filled with tears. Raymond's words were ones Sean hoped he would never hear.

"Are you alright, Son?"

After considerable delay, Sean answered, "No, Dad. I think I'm going to be sick."

"Well, just take a deep breath. I called Ben and gave him our condolences. He sounded the worse for wear, but he's pretty stoic. I told him I'd let you know, and he said for me to tell you it was a long time coming and that he's doing fine. He said if you wanted to call him to wait until tomorrow some time."

Poorly concealing the devastation he felt, Sean asked, "When's the funeral?"

It was clear to Sean that his father had dealt with a lot more death in his time. Raymond seemed to not have any outward problem having a rational conversation about such a highly emotional topic—the death of Sean's first true girlfriend, whom Raymond had loved like a daughter.

"He wasn't sure, but he said sometime the first part of next week. I assume you're coming home to attend the services?"

Dixie poked her head in the room and asked, "Honey, did you say funeral? Is everything okay?"

Choking on his words, Sean replied, "No, Dixie. Kim died this afternoon."

"Oh, Honey, I'm so sorry," Dixie said. She walked up behind her husband, leaned over and gave him a hug.

Back to Raymond's question, Sean answered, "Sure, Dad. You know I'll be there."

Dixie released her compassionate hold, then quickly scribbled the name *Bogenkamp* on a piece of paper, holding it up in front of Sean. He unkindly grabbed it from her hand, crumpled it, and threw it across the room. Dixie left in a huff.

"You won't have any trouble getting away, will you?" Raymond asked.

"Dad, I'm the General Manager. It's no problem."

"Sure, Son, if you say so."

Sensing there was beginning to be a subtext within the conversation, Sean asked, "What's that supposed to mean?"

"Well, I kind of get the feeling from all the chatter up there that things are a bit, how should I say, in a tizzy right now."

"No, Dad. Everything's fine," Sean said. His answer was so unbelievable, even he knew he was in denial.

"Did I hear Callie say something about Northwestern?"

Sean let out a sigh. "Yes, you did. Frank's stirring the pot as usual. Now, Callie thinks she wants to go to school at Northwestern."

"What a waste," Raymond said without a moment's hesitation. "It's simply unjust to keep a beautiful girl like that at home in Lake Forest, when she could be spreading her wings at a good college here."

Sean sat quietly for a moment, letting what had been nearly the same words as Frank had said earlier, only with different grandparental perspective, whiz around in his head.

"Sean, are you there?"

"Yeah, sorry. I was just thinking about what you said."

"That would be a first," Raymond said.

Sean sensed his father was moving the subtext closer to the main topic in their conversation. "No it's not, Dad. I listen to you all the time…well, some of the time. But honestly, do you really think it's a good idea for Callie to go away to school? There's a lot to be said for staying close to home."

"Are we speaking about Callie or Sean, right now?"

"Jesus, am I that transparent?"

"Well, I am your father."

After reflecting on a fork in the road of his distant past, Sean said, "In truth, Dad, I still have regrets about moving away from home and establishing roots in the Chicago suburbs."

"It isn't like you're a thousand miles away, son."

"I know, but I feel as though I missed so much when I wasn't across town from you. I mean, I should have done more for the grandparents, mom…even Kim."

"You did enough. Don't beat yourself up for being what you are. Besides, you turned out pretty good. But since you brought it up, let me ask you this. If you come up with a believable answer to this question, maybe that will help you with Callie's situation. Have you ever understood why you left home?"

Sean had actually come to grips with this very question many years ago. "I had to find myself, Dad."

The delay in Raymond's retort was calculated. After letting the gears in Sean's head churn for a few more moments, he replied, "You will be sure to drop me a postcard when you have that epiphany, won't you, Sean?"

Sean laughed at his father's observation. After all, he left home nearly thirty years ago, and he was still searching for that something which would give him peace of mind.

"You want a piece of advice, Sean?"

"Sure, Dad, what is it?"

"It's only money, Sean. You've sold your soul for money."

"No I haven't. I'm nothing like Frank."

"I didn't say you were like Frank. If you were, we wouldn't be having this conversation right now. I just think you confuse money with success. I'm here to tell you, they aren't the same thing."

"Dad, I hate to break this to you, but Frank Capra died a few years ago."

"Alright, smart ass, put this in your pipe and smoke it. Let me tell you a story about a young boy I once knew. Occasionally, I'd put him on the train to go see his grandparents. That boy loved trains. He told me once that he got to see the countryside from a different perspective. At the end of the ride, his reward was the open arms of his grandmother or grandfather. The reward at the end of the ride was love. Some years later, I stood on a railway platform outside of Chicago with that same fellow, only he was an adult now. We watched as two or three trains flew by, never stopping at the station. That young man asked me, 'Why didn't the train stop?' I told him, 'It was an express train.' Then he asked, 'Where was it going?' to which I replied, 'It was probably taking most of its passengers to work.' You know what he said next? He told me, 'I hope I never get stuck in that rat race. I like the stops along the way, and the arms of someone at the end of the ride.'"

The young boy and young man to whom Raymond referred was of course Sean, and he knew it.

"So, as I said a few moments ago, Sean, it's only money. Maybe when you come down for the funeral, you can take a few days off. You could probably use a vacation. Sounds like you need to get your shit together."

It amazed Sean just how dissimilar his father was from Frank, and yet they sounded alike in so many ways.

Changing subjects all together, Raymond went on to say, "Hey, Will brought Giselle over the night before last. The two of them made Barbara and me a fabulous supper, and then stayed to visit a while. That son of yours sure knows how to cook. He must have got that talent from Dixie's side of the family because you could never even make a grilled cheese sandwich."

"Well, I can almost guarantee that talent, if it does come from the Darling side, is a very, very recessive trait."

"And Giselle, she's something. Made me wish I was twenty-two years old again. Damn—pretty, smart, sexy, outgoing, the whole nine yards. She's got that accent thing going for her, too. Have you gotten to know her very well?"

"Some. Will brought her up here on their way to an art exhibit in Chicago. They only stayed for a little while before they headed out. And while I'm thinking about it, Frank doesn't know any details about her, so kindly keep it hush-hush for now."

"Got news for you, Sean, they're shacked up in a real nice place just east of campus. I think it's her condo. Girl's family has a lot of francs in the banks, if you know what I mean. Won't be long before Frank's radar picks up on it, or worse yet, Callie gets wind of it. You need to have Will get Frank in the loop. Once he gets to know Giselle, he'll like her. Tell him to set something up on Dad's Day, and me, Will, and you will corner Frank and straighten him out."

"Straighten him out?"

Raymond chuckled. "Well, it sounded good anyway. Hey, listen, I have to run. Barbara and I are going over to see some friends, play some cards, and drink some bourbon. I'll let you know when I hear some details about Kim's funeral. And like I said, take some time off and stay with us for a while. Bring Dixie. She's always welcome."

"I'll probably do that. She can hang with Callie…assuming she's still going to school there. I'll talk to you later."

"Bye, Son."

"Bye, Dad."

After disconnecting from the call, Sean reached deeply into one of his desk drawers, pulling out an old photograph in a simple silver frame of Kim at Allerton Park. It was the only one he still had of her. She was sitting on the hood of Sean's car with the statue of the Sun Singer behind her. As she gazed meditatively toward a spectacular central Illinois sunset, her face was illuminated by the peach and orange hues of the clouds. It was as though she was looking for guidance, much as one might imagine was the case with the bronze statue of the Greek God Apollo—his arms raised to the setting sun. One thing was for certain, Sean didn't have to reach as far into his mind, as he had for the 5 by 7, photograph for memories of their time together. Kim was frequently in his thoughts.

In Search of the Fuller Brush Man

KIM TABER AND SEAN went steady for five years beginning in the autumn of 1970. He often told her she was *The One*, and to even the casual observer, it appeared they were destined to be a pair for eternity. Kim plucked Sean out of a group at Carle Park during a Sadie Hawkins Day celebration. In the years that followed, the two were inseparable. Beginning that blustery mid-November day, their chemistry made for a long union. She was feisty and had just the right amount of zeal in her behavior to keep the relationship moving forward, but not so much that she would drive away a much more timid Sean. Her enthusiasm for life was second only to her perpetually happy nature. Sean's senior yearbook was full of personalized phrases from schoolmates that underscored everyone's belief that they were going to become Mr. and Mrs. one day.

Kim's parents died when she was barely a young teenager. After the death of her parents, she came to live with relatives in Sean's home town. Once Kim embarked on her relationship with Sean, she took an immediate liking to Sean's mother, Nadine. Their loving adoration was mutual. Sean would frequently come home from his part-time job to find Kim and his mother laboring over puzzles, cooking, or watching game shows on television. Nadine and Raymond did everything they could to nurture the love and friendship between Sean and Kim. She even had a job at the Marcum Pharmacy. Needless to say, it came as a devastating blow when, out of the blue, Sean developed a wild streak, and ended up in the grip of Dixie Darling.

Sean often wondered—to himself of course—what would have become of his life if he hadn't walked away from Kim? They certainly would have had children. They would have made a good home together in Urbana. They would have made a mark in the community. And most importantly, they would have been there for all of life's trials and tribulations as grandparents, parents, extended family members, and close friends grew older. They would have been there for all of life's celebrations and for all of its tragedies. However, as Sean sat there in his office, one thing he couldn't get off his mind at that moment was that if the two had been husband and wife, he would now be faced with a funeral. And the thought of having to bury a spouse, much as his father had, sent chills down Sean's spine.

FINDING HER HUSBAND STILL sitting in his office staring at a wall after two hours, Dixie tried to jolt him back to reality. "Sean, are you going to sit in here and mope all night?"

"I appreciate your understanding, Dixie."

"What do you want me to say, Sean? You lost a dear friend. Your life goes on and you have a lot to do."

"I'm not so sure about that anymore, Dix. Your father jerked the proverbial rug out from underneath me today on the BMW and Volvo expansion. It seems that he sees it fine and dandy to take all the cash I have created for the Group, and use it to go ahead with the expansion, but then give it to Frank Junior."

"If you want it badly enough, fight for it, Sean,"

"Do I look stupid? That's what Frank says…oh, and yes, Callie. No, last time I did the math, four against one was a bit too lopsided."

"You know Daddy's just doing this for your own good. If you fight for it, he'll give it to you. If you don't, you probably would have buckled under the stress."

"Now that's a perspective I hadn't thought of. Do you think Frank's still awake? Maybe I'll call him and thank him for looking out for me."

"You just don't know how Daddy works."

"Like hell I don't! He's a carnivore right out of a science fiction movie. The only difference is most carnivores go for the throat to bring a swift death to their prey. Frank goes for the belly. He likes to watch his victims scream in pain as they bleed out. Do you know what he wants to do with Cadillac? He wants to put Will in charge."

"I told him that sounded like a good opportunity for him," Dixie replied without hesitation.

The shock of Dixie's remark was profound. It hadn't occurred to Sean that Dixie had any inkling about Frank's plans, let alone given input to it.

"Will's twenty-two years old, Dix. He'll graduate at the ripe old age of twenty-three. The Cadillac business is a mess right now. Talk about stress."

"Daddy said he'd be there to work with him."

"I guaran-damn-tee Frank will be there. He probably has paperwork prepared to legally change Will's last name to Darling. And where the hell am I in all of this, Dix? How could you be discussing all of this with Frank behind my back?"

"Discussion? With you? How, Sean? You have your nose stuck in your computer night after night buying up the Fuller Brush Company one bristle at a time. You watch that frickin' movie over and over, night after night. I can't talk to you. You aren't here. Your mind is in Kansas. You want to talk? Then get your shit together and let's have a conversation."

"If one more person tells me today to get my shit together, I'll..."

"You'll what?"

Sean didn't know how to finish the statement. Tapping his fingers on his desk, he finally said, "You know, you're right. So are Frank and Dad. After the funeral, I'm taking a week or so off. I need some time to regroup."

"So, how are you going to pull off the fundraiser for Senator Bogenkamp if you're not here? Not only can you not afford to take time off for vacation, you can't afford to take off for any funeral...unless you want it to be your own."

Holding his hands out as if they were a balance, Sean said, "Gee, Kim...asshole Senator...Kim...asshole Senator. I guess Kim wins."

"She's dead, Sean! So is your mother!" Dixie pointed her menacing Darling finger in Sean's face. "Are you going to be as obsessed about her as you are Nadine? Because if that's the case, you're on your own. I'm not having anything to do with it."

They stared at each other for a few seconds, before Sean replied with a single word. "Good."

Dixie stormed out of the room. Sean took a few gulps of his warm beer before turning on his television. Soon, *The Fuller Brush Man* was playing.

Chapter 5

EVEN THOUGH BEN BARNETT grew up on a different side of Urbana than Sean, he, along with the other grade school children in the surrounding area, were thrown together in the town's only middle school. After all the moving and shaking was over, cliques formed and friendships bloomed. As soon as the two met in seventh grade math, they quickly became the best of friends. Sean's father was the local pharmacist, and Ben's father owned the hardware store. The patriarchs were masters of their own destiny in a modest way. Sean often coveted the promise of owning a small business. He realized later in life that the challenges faced by men like his father and Ben's dad were essentially the same as he faced himself, only on a different scale. And whereas there was no Frank in their midst, there was always adversity of some type. Sean's just had a face to it.

Teenage years in the late sixties and early seventies proved to be quite a challenge—the counterculture rebellion, Vietnam, drugs, political unrest. Ben became class president and often reflected during class reunions that, as a whole, and in spite of great adversity, the class of nearly four-hundred actually turned out to be pretty successful. Sean was moved by one particular vestige of his high school years. By the mid to late 60s, teens were broadly classified, willingly or otherwise, as greasers, hicks, hippies, jocks, or nerds. Sadly, there were strong racial divisions as well. But, by the time graduation had rolled around, one could safely say that all outward manifestations of such profiling were gone, and there truly was a unity among the young men and women in Sean's graduating class. That in and of itself was something the class prided itself on. In the years after graduation, the class still held in common the belief that they remained 'one'—no one was better than the other, and most certainly, nobody was weaker or stronger. These fundamental tenets that guided Sean in his life ran against the grain of the Darlings. His life was forever to become a delicate balancing act.

DIXIE WASN'T ON SPEAKING terms with Sean the next morning, so he felt uncomfortable calling Ben from home. She didn't have the relationship with Ben. It was all Sean's. To say that Ben disliked Dixie wasn't entirely true. The events that led to Kim falling in love with Ben began when Dixie lured Sean away from her...against Ben's advice. To that end, Ben was a very lucky man. The friendship between the two comrades waned after college due to distance and commitments to jobs and family. By the time Kim was first diagnosed with breast cancer ten years ago, Ben and Sean were once again almost as close as brothers, Kim and Sean were amicable, and even Kim and Dixie found some common ground. Now, it had come to this moment. The most difficult phone call of Sean's life was about to take place from the driver's seat of a two-year old Avalon. He managed to raise Ben on his house phone.

"Hello?"

Ben's voice sounded tired and scratchy.

"Ben, it's Sean."

"Hey, man. Good to hear from you."

Suddenly, Sean couldn't find anything to say.

"It sucks, Sean. This really sucks. I've had this day in the back of my mind for ten years. It ain't like we didn't think it could happen. But, shit, man, this really hurts."

Sean had to pull off the road before he could continue with the conversation.

"I'm sorry I didn't know she was doing so badly, Ben. The last time we spoke, she was hanging in there."

"That was a month ago, Sean. Here's a news flash for you. People who are this sick can crash quickly."

"I wish you'd called me, Ben."

"I wish you'd called, too, Sean. She really wanted to say goodbye to you."

That was all it took, and Sean lost it. It wasn't long before Sean could hear Ben crying, too, on the other end.

"I would have liked that, Ben. I don't have to tell you that I feel like I've lost a huge part of my heart and soul."

"We both have."

"How are Tim and Michael doing?"

"They're alright, considering. Nobody is ever truly ready for this. Tell you what. They had one hell of a mother. She was always there for them…always."

"Yeah…yeah. Hey, is there anything I can do, man? Anything. You name it and I'll take care of it."

"Well, please don't have Frank make any phone calls," Ben replied with a little levity mixed in.

Sean had often vented his frustrations over Frank to his friend. Of course, Ben always reminded Sean that he brought it all upon himself. However, he never belabored the point too much because, again, the outcome left Ben, in his own mind, the luckier man with Kim as his wife.

"No way, dude. This is personal. You call me, you get me. Got it?"

"Well, obviously, I want you here for the funeral."

"When is it?" There was some hesitation in Sean's voice.

"It's likely going to be Monday, but perhaps Tuesday next week. Obviously we're waiting on her brothers and sisters. Also, do you remember Nancy?"

"McAllister?"

"Yeah, now Caswell. She's flying in from Austria for the funeral, if you can believe that. So, we're holding off a bit for her to get here."

"Jesus, that's really a special friendship."

"So, you should have no problem being here, right?" Ben asked once again, looking for a commitment from Sean.

"Did you say Tuesday?" Sean asked as if the date mattered at such a time as this.

"Don't tell me you're going to fuckin' miss Kim's funeral, man! Do not do that to her!"

"No way, Ben. I'll be there. In fact, I'm planning on coming down later this week after I take care of a few things."

"It's Dixie, isn't it?!" Ben asked. His angry tone indicated he didn't believe the words coming out of Sean's mouth.

"What do you mean?"

"She owns your balls, Sean. Ever since she spent the night with you at the hospital when you broke your goddamn ankle, she's owned your balls. When she doesn't have them, ol' Frank's got 'em in a vice. Let me tell you something, friend, Kim talked about you almost to her dying breath. But you didn't have the decency to pick up your phone and say shit to her."

"Ben, you're..."

The litany continued, "If she hadn't asked me to make sure you came to her funeral, I'd have hung up on you the moment you called. And to think that she would even have to make that request, Sean? What does that say about you, huh?"

"Ben, I..."

"It says your friendship is worthless, Sean. It tells me that all those years she loved you as a girlfriend didn't mean squat. It tells me that all the years I've known you as a friend—hell, practically a brother—don't mean a damn thing to you."

"Ben, please..."

"So what are you going to do at our next class reunion, Sean, when you walk past the easel that has the photos of dead classmates? Are you going to walk past it like you always have? Are you going to just breeze past with only a few moments of reflection about the person whose picture is staring back at you? It'll be Kim looking back this time, Sean. Will you stop and stare, Sean? Will you shed a tear? Or will you let Dixie pull you away so she can flash her perfect smile at all of her adoring fans while she drags you along for show?"

There was a long period of silence during which Sean rationalized that Ben's rant was an outburst fed by loss and sorrow. Sean looked at his phone to see if he and Ben were still connected.

Eventually Ben spoke up. "I'm sorry, Sean. I didn't mean the things I said. I miss her so much already."

"I miss her, too, Ben. Hey, I'll give you another call tomorrow, alright?"

"Thanks, buddy. I'm sure I'll need to hear your voice by then."

"And I will be there later this week—I promise."

"I know…I know. Hey, I almost forgot."

"What's that?"

"Kim wanted me to send you something. I need to wrap it up and mail it. Where do you want it to go?"

"What is it?"

"At the risk of sounding like I'm conspiring with the dead, she asked me not to tell you. She just wants me to send it to you.

There's also a letter she wrote that's addressed to you. I haven't read it. She said for you to read the letter, then you'd know what to do with the item that's in the box."

"Ben, go ahead and read the letter, man. There's nothing involving Kim I won't share with you."

"I know. Besides, it's not exactly like you're a threat to my marriage anymore. No, I'll respect her wish and just do as she asked. If you want to tell me later about the letter, we'll cross that bridge when we get to that point."

"Well, mail it to my office. That way, I know there will be somebody who can receive it. Do you have my address?"

"Yeah. Kim kept your card by our phone."

"Alright, then. As soon as I get the package, I'll let you know I have it."

"Hey, I just thought of something else…my mind's not working very crisply, so bear with me."

"No sweat. What is it?"

"We're putting together some pictures for the service. It's going to be a slide show of her life. Anyway, Kim was looking for a picture from a long time ago. She said you took it of her when the two of you were together. You're at Allerton and she's sitting on the hood of that hideous Toyota you owned with the Sun Singer behind her. She said she liked the composition and the lighting in the picture. She was unable to find it, and this picture in particular she wanted framed and on an easel. Do you know the picture I'm talking about?"

A chill went down Sean's spine as he answered, "I sure do. I have to be honest, Ben, that's the one picture I still have of her."

"Can you let me borrow it?"

"I can do better than that. I should have the negative stashed in my closet. I'll find a way to make a high quality digital image for you. I can bring the JPEG down with me on a memory stick."

"That would mean a lot to me. That would mean a lot to Kim. Thanks."

"Think nothing of it."

"Well, I do." After a short hesitation, Ben asked, "Tell me something, Sean. Why did you keep that one picture of her?"

Sean had to think for a moment before responding.

"Sean?"

"Yeah, I'm here. I was trying to think of the answer to your question. I had to blow off a lot of cobwebs. I think it had to do with Allerton Park and Monticello. We used to go there all the time, but mostly whenever Kim was in a funk. She used to tell me how she imagined there was a small town in heaven, and it looked just like Monticello. She wanted to live there someday. We'd go see the Fu Dogs, the tower, the ornamental gardens, the Sunken Garden, then always end with the Sun Singer. There was something about that landmark…sort of like it was the conclusion of something. Anyway, it always brought her great joy. We'd frequently sit there for an hour or more just talking. The light of the day would fade away, and the color in her face would change. It was as if all the pain and anguish that was tormenting her were leaving. I can understand why she wanted that picture. Just sitting here telling you about it, I recall many times feeling the same way myself."

Chapter 6

DIXIE WAS ON HER way to the commercial shoot with Callie in tow, when she noticed Sean parked off the side of the road in a restaurant parking lot talking on the phone. After letting traffic clear, she made a U-turn in her luxury Lexus SUV and went back to see if something was wrong. By the time she pulled up next to him, he had put his phone away. As she approached his car, she could tell he was upset about something.

"Mom, what's the matter with Dad?"

"I don't know, Callie. Wait here."

Sensing it would be best to speak with him while inside his car, she went around to the passenger side and climbed in.

"Honey? Is something the matter?" She had never seen Sean this distraught since his mother passed away.

"Yes. I'm half sick to my stomach. I just finished talking to Ben a little while ago."

"Oh, I just saw you on the phone. Was that Ben?"

"No. I was just speaking with April."

Sean's remark made her skin crawl. "So, you're practically in tears over Ben and Kim, and you don't feel the need to call your wife? No. Instead, you call April. What's going on here?"

"What are you talking about?"

Waving her hands about, Dixie replied, "You…April? Duh?"

"Dixie, I called April so she could get to work on that asinine fundraiser for Bogenkamp."

"April? Daddy asked you to personally take care of it."

"Well, that's not going to happen. I'm heading off to Urbana toward the end of the week for Kim's funeral."

"No you're not!" Dixie said. She was dead serious. "You have commitments here, Sean!"

"Dixie, I have a lot of commitments a lot of the time. They have to be prioritized. I *am* going to Kim's funeral."

"I mean it, Sean. You have to pull off this fundraiser or Daddy will really be pissed."

"Why? What's he going to do, Dixie, that he won't do anyway? I can't stand Bogenkamp, not to mention the fact that Frank has his nose up Mr. Senator's ass in order to get a deal on the land next to *my* dealership."

"You're right, Sean. That should be you kissing ass, not Daddy."

"Nope. I'm more than happy to let your father have the deal. I'm sick and tired of butting heads with him. The fact is, Dixie, I found a financier who will allow me to break away from the Darling Group. After the funeral, that's the direction I'm heading."

"That's ridiculous, Sean. You'd leave the group over some petty differences? I won't let you do it, Sean. You can't make that kind of business decision without me, and I won't support you."

"As if you ever have, Dixie!" Sean said, pounding the steering wheel with his fists.

It was so unlike Sean to lose his temper like this. During the course of their marriage, Dixie could count his outbursts on the fingers of one hand. The effect of getting riled up so seldom was that doing so typically had a powerful effect on the person at the receiving end. He apparently forgot that Dixie had been trained by a professional—Frank. And she was more than capable of standing her ground.

"Let me tell you what you will be doing today, Sean, since you appear to have lost focus. First, you will call your father-in-law and inform him of your progress, not April's, in making arrangements for Senator Bogenkamp's reception and dinner. Next, I expect you to take Callie and me to lunch at the Club as compensation for shooting a commercial for you. Immediately following lunch is your nephew's birthday party for which you are gleefully staying. Your brothers-in-law will be there, and I expect you to be cordial at a minimum. Daddy will probably stop by as well, so you had better be on your best behavior. When that's over, you need to take you daughter car shopping. I don't want her leaving for college in an under-powered, unsafe, unfashionable car. If she wants a SC09 Coupe, then buy her one. You're a General Manager of the Darling Group, for Christ's sake. Act like it. Finally, after today, you need to find someplace else for April to work. She's beginning to get on my last nerve."

Sean didn't reply to any of Dixie's diatribe. All he did was toggle the door lock button and say, "It's unlocked."

BY THE END OF the afternoon, Sean had accomplished everything he had set out to do that day and then some, but deliberately none of the tasks Dixie had asked of him. He knew he was going to be on the hot seat tonight, and he had no desire to hurry home. The thought of straying had never crossed Sean's mind, but inside he was seething over his bout with Dixie earlier in the day and was still upset over his conversation with Ben and the death of Kim. If there was ever a weak moment, it was about to confront him.

"Hey, Sean. I see you're finally off the phone," April said.

"It's been a crazy day."

"Tell me what's been going on."

After a moment, Sean replied, "No…there's just too much to discuss. I don't want to bother you."

April kept the conversation going. "I thought you'd like to know that I have all the seats filled at the fundraiser. In fact, I could use three more tables. Maybe you could call Frank and ask him for more?"

Sean shook his head. "Naw. You did all the work. You call him."

"Very well. I'll give him a ring tonight. You're sure you don't want to do it?"

Clenching his fists, Sean replied, "April, I am ever so certain I want nothing to do with Frank tonight."

The conversation might have ended at that point. Then, April sat down and said, "We got the commercial done today. Callie was fantastic."

Sean agreed, in part. "She certainly has the talent. She just needs to fix her attitude."

"Oh, come on, Sean. Don't be such a dad. She really did a fabulous job."

There were a few more awkward moments of silence until April spoke up.

"Can I ask you something, Sean?"

Casually leaning back in his chair with his hands behind his head, Sean replied, "Sure, go for it."

Nervously fiddling with her scarf, April said, "I've done a lot of work with Dixie before. Today, she was an entirely different person. If I had to describe it, she was very distant; aloof; angry; preoccupied. I don't know exactly what was going on."

Sean didn't say anything.

Staring at her lap as she spoke, April continued, "And now, I'm speaking with you, and you're not exactly what I would describe as engaged in this conversation. All day long, you've done nothing but make phone calls behind closed doors and come and go, come and go, come and go."

Again, Sean didn't say anything.

Turning her gaze toward her boss, she asked, “So, my question, Sean, is this…is everything okay between the two of you? I mean, it’s really not my place to ask, but then, maybe it is…as a friend, of course.”

After a few moments, Sean said, “Close the door.”

April did as he asked, then returned to where she had been sitting.

“First, let me thank you for taking care of the commercial shoot and the fundraiser. That took a huge load off of me.”

“No problem. Anytime. Now, get to the point. What’s bothering you?”

Grinning at her directness, Sean opened up. “I’ve just about had it with the Darling Group, April. I’m seriously considering going independent.”

“How serious are you?”

“I’m serious enough that I have financing and an attorney lined up.”

Nodding her head, April said, “I’ve sensed for a long time you needed a change…that you were ready for a fresh experience. You deserve better than the way Frank treats you.”

“Yeah…maybe…I don’t know. My head’s spinning right now. As if the job wasn’t enough, next week is the twentieth anniversary of my mother’s death, and I guess I have a lot of baggage about that.”

“I’m sorry. That must be really hard for you. Do you want to talk about it?”

Suddenly feeling more comfortable with the conversation, Sean resumed, "Wait, there's more. A dear friend died yesterday. I need to go to her funeral, and that's causing a lot of stress at home."

"What's causing the stress? Is it the funeral or the fact that the deceased is a *her*?"

Unsure why he felt so liberated discussing Kim and Dixie with April in such a manner, Sean replied, "Ah, you are very perceptive. It could be an aunt, for all you know." It appeared April was thoroughly enjoying the candor of the conversation.

"No, judging from Dixie's body language today, this isn't just any woman in your life who died. Am I correct?"

"That you are. She was my high school sweetheart and steady girlfriend up until the time I met Dixie."

"So, what was her name?"

"Kim Taber. Later, she married my best friend, Ben Barnett."

"So, did you still have feelings for her?"

"Well, I'd have to say there was still an attachment. I love Dixie. But at the same time, I can't ignore what took place between Kim and me. That and I was always a bit jealous that it was my best friend who married her. Even more so, I envied the quality of marriage they had. It was textbook perfect in every way…all the way until Kim died."

"Sounds like a very tangled web you have woven, Mr. Marcum."

"Don't be so critical, Ms. Knudsen. My life's not that screwed up…well, maybe it is."

April giggled, confirming for Sean that she was comfortable with the degree of freedom with which they spoke.

"So, does Dixie feel threatened?"

"Not directly of course. The rub is that Kim's funeral will probably be the same day as the Bogenkamp fundraiser, and I plan to be at her funeral. Dixie thinks my priorities are out of sync with the best interests of the Group."

"Don't worry about the fundraiser, Sean. I have it under control. I have the list of attendees, and the menu is set. We even have a short program by a Catholic school choir—the same school from which Bogenkamp graduated."

April had scored big. It suddenly occurred to Sean that she not only solved this particular problem for him, she went way beyond the call of duty…and he wasn't sure why. Yet, being the thoughtful person he was, Sean complimented his partner.

"Thanks, April. It does sound like you have everything under control. I'm amazed, though I shouldn't be. You always come through for me. You always go the extra mile. There's nothing I can do for you that could equal what you do for me. Seriously, I'm in awe of your thoroughness, support, and kindness." He choked on his words toward the end.

"Sean, I'll always be here for you. Always."

Those words tore at Sean's heartstrings. Kim had said those same words many times during their relationship. And they were true. She *was* always there for him. In the end, he couldn't make the same claim. To avoid showing his emotions to April, he turned away from her.

IT HURT APRIL THAT she couldn't do more for the man in pain sitting across from her. She felt a certain degree of pity for him. That a woman could mean so much to a man as Kim obviously did to Sean was simply exhilarating. Certainly, April thought to herself, no one had ever felt that way about her. At that moment, she wanted so much to take him in her arms and hold him close. She yearned to reach out to Sean without crossing the invisible line that kept them at arm's length all these years.

Alas, she was wise enough to know that doing so most certainly would alter their relationship and possibly end her career, not to mention his marriage. Though unafraid of any of these prospects, such changes necessitated planning in order to achieve as yet clearly defined objectives. Nonetheless, she felt a desire for him she had long ago lost for her first husband, and was most certainly absent from the relationship with the current man in her life.

"So what's bothering you the most? Your job, your home, your mother, or Kim?"

After giving April's question some thought, Sean answered, "I think it's the confluence of all of these things at once."

"So, you need some help sorting things out, right?"

"Please don't tell me I need to get my shit together," Sean said.

"No. I would never do that. However, have you ever thought of talking with a therapist?"

"So he can tell me I need to get my shit together?"

"I don't think that's exactly what they do, Sean. I would highly recommend the psychologist that I see."

Turning around, Sean asked, "You see a shrink?"

Comfortable with her choice for dealing with problems in her private life, she replied, "No. I see a therapist, who happens to have a Ph.D. in psychology. He's really helped me through a lot of rough times."

"You? Excuse me for being so blind. I didn't know you had any problems."

For a moment, April was taken aback by Sean's seeming lack of familiarity with her personal life. In a way, it hurt that he was so unobservant of her, yet was so strongly connected to a dead girlfriend.

"Uh, yeah," she answered, bristling. "I had a husband who was gone all the time, not to mention unfaithful. I would like to have led a normal life, but I was, for all practical purposes, neither married nor single, leaving me with the worst of both worlds."

It appeared it was Sean who was now startled by the degree of candor in their conversation. "Golly, April. I had no idea."

All traces of her once-friendly smile were now gone. "Well, I guess the ups and downs of our personal lives aren't the kind of thing you and I would discuss."

"That's not true. Based upon your earlier remarks about Dixie's behavior today, you have a fairly good idea of how things are going between the two of us. And, you talk about Scott from time to time. I just assumed you were the typical wife of a typical naval officer."

His remarks further stirred her ire. "So, Sean. What's typical? Was it typical for a naval officer to have one girlfriend in Naples, and another in Guam? Was it typical for a naval officer to be gone for years at a time at his own request? Was it typical for a woman like me, in the prime of her life, to remain faithful, waiting for the philandering pig to come home eventually? How do you think that made me feel, Sean?"

In a tone now as terse as hers, Sean replied, "Put in those terms, I would have to think he made you feel like shit. What about this other man you speak of occasionally?"

"What about him?!" April asked.

It took a while, but Sean finally said, "I'm…speechless."

In all the years they had worked together, April had never confided so much detail about her personal life, let alone in such an embittered manner. This was a secret side of her that likely changed his once immaculate perception of her. She sensed his growing interest.

Reaching across Sean's desk, April grabbed a notepad and proceeded to write.

"Call this man. His name is Sterling Berkowitz. He's good. Talk to him. Be honest. Be candid. Do it while you still have control. Do it before you make a mistake you will regret."

"What kind of mistake are you talking about?"

Was he daring her to answer? Was he blind to the response she might give? Was he hoping she was the *mistake*, wishing for her to make the first move? She couldn't take that chance—at least not now. She had to at a minimum throw some water on the fire, but leave the coals smoldering.

Leaning provocatively over his desk, she replied, "Sean, are you really that stupid?" She then departed.

April had presented a door to him. It was up to him to walk through it or remain safely on the other side.

APRIL NEVER HAD A chance to phone Frank with an update on the fundraising preparations. He practically ran over her as he made his way to Sean's office, and it was apparent he wasn't going to stop and give her the time she needed to tell him herself. He walked right over to Sean's desk and took a seat squarely in front of him that only moments ago had been graced by April's svelte physique. April was kind enough to close the door.

"Do you mind telling me what the hell's going on in that vacuum that sits on top of your shoulders?"

In no mood for Frank's impending confrontation, Sean replied, "I've had a stressful day, Frank. Excuse me, but piss off."

The finger-of-death was quickly drawn. "You can be a disrespectful pecker-head to me all day and all night for all I fuckin' care, Sean. But don't you ever disrespect my daughter, my granddaughter, or the rest of my family ever again. You got that?"

"Let's talk about respect for just a minute, Frank! That appears to be something you have no clue about!"

"I respect real men who earn my esteem! It's a goddamn short list! I promise you this much, your name will never grace it!"

"Thank you, Frank. That's the most gracious offer you have ever made."

Pointing his thumb over his shoulder in the direction of April, Frank continued, "So, once again, you have a woman doing all of your work. I suppose she was giving you the up-to-the-minute details? Let me guess, you told her to call me with the sob-story that she can't find enough people to seat at all the tables. You're so chicken-shit you make me puke. She didn't even have the nerve to tell me the sorry news to my face, did she?"

"April's fulfilled your request and then some, just as she always does for me. In fact, Frank, she needs three more tables. Do you think you can stop with the rampage long enough to make one of your phone calls and secure her some more space? If not, I'll have her contact those twenty-four individuals to let them know they didn't make your cut."

Frank chewed on his tongue for a moment before answering, "I'll get her five more tables—the three she asked for, plus one more for my four General Managers and their wives, and one more for my grandchildren."

Standing his ground, Sean said, "There's going to be at least one empty seat, Frank. I'm not showing up."

"So, you'd embarrass your family? Is what you're telling me?"

"No, Frank, I'm going to a dear friend's funeral. Sadly, I'll find more pleasure doing so than listening to Bogenkamp's bullshit."

"Right—Dixie told me all about her. She tells me a lot about you, Sean, and frankly, I find it all very disturbing. Tell me, Sean, why didn't this girl you loved so much marry you? That way Dixie could have had a real wedding to a decent man."

"I won't disgrace Kim's memory by discussing her with you, so let me end your visit with these words, Frank. I love Dixie. The fact that she's your daughter is something you know as collateral damage. She's worth everything to me that you're not. Now if you don't mind, I'm calling it a day. Phone me first thing in the morning and let me know if you were able to come up with three more tables. If you're unable, or unwilling to do so, I'll ask April to handle it. I'm sure she can get it done."

Sean got up before Frank once more, knowing full well he hated it, and opened the door for him.

Frank stood up and eased toward the door. Before leaving, he said, "By the way, I've got word out to the banking community that it would be a huge mistake to finance your little fantasy. Don't think for a second you can pull it off without the Group's support. The project belongs to me. Don't fuck with the big dogs, Sean."

With a confident smile, Sean pulled out his phone, scrolled through a list of recently called numbers until he found the one he was looking for, and pressed the connect button. It took only a few rings until his call was answered.

"Good evening. This is Sean. I'm doing fine. Are we still a go? No, nothing's wrong here, though I thought I felt a small rumble in The Force. I'll be in touch. You have a good night."

Sean flipped his phone closed and put it back in his shirt pocket. "Good advice, Frank," he said, pointing at his father-in-law, "You shouldn't fuck with the big dogs."

Needing to get in the last word, Frank closed with, "You're going down."

SEAN ARRIVED HOME, LOOKING forward unrealistically to both a little quiet and a chance to make up with Dixie for what she most likely saw as mean-spirited, unforgivable lapses in judgment earlier in the day. The conversation he just finished with Frank all but sealed the deal in Sean's mind—he was going to have to break away from the Group if he was going to maintain any self-respect, not to mention any financial security. There would not be any support from the others in the Group. The other principals, even John, would never take a position opposed to Frank's. Sean's biggest concern now was how to preserve his marriage in the face of such a secession.

Trouble met him at the door with a small duffle bag over her shoulder. She was eighteen years old, going on twenty-five, and all Darling.

"I cannot believe you! You diss'ed me today! Mom's been crying! Grandpa's pissed!"

Sean uncharacteristically slammed his folio onto the kitchen table with a bang. "Young lady, I am the adult in this conversation, you are the child. If you expect to gain anything from this tête-à-tête, fix your attitude and your mouth right now."

Callie yelled at the top of her lungs. "I am not a child!"

Holding his hands out to her, palms up, to make his lo-and-behold point very clear, Sean countered, "Hey, you act like a brat, you get treated like one."

"So, like, are you and Mom getting a divorce? I mean, I asked her and she wouldn't say 'no.' She wouldn't even look at me! I'm starting college in two weeks, Dad. Like, I'm trying to pledge the same sorority that Mom and Grandma belonged to. I have try-outs for the volleyball team. Do you know what having your parents go through a divorce in the middle of all of this will do to me? You are totally so self-centered! All you think about is you! And another thing, if that bitch you're crying over had been my mother, I'd probably have killed myself. So you need to go to Mom and beg for her forgiveness, and then go kiss Grandpa's butt or whatever."

Callie headed for the door.

"Where do you think you're going, young lady?!"

"I'm spending the night with Uncle John and Aunt Katie."

"No, you're not!"

"What are you going to do? Tackle me!"

With total disregard of her father's objection, Callie opened the door to leave.

In a fit of rage, Sean forcefully shoved the door closed. Unfortunately, Callie was carrying her duffle in her left hand, and it got caught between the door and the frame. There was a sickening thud, followed by a loud scream, and the bag dropped to the floor. Realizing what he had just done, Sean jerked the door open to the sight of Callie writhing in pain on the stoop, holding her arm.

Sean knelt over her. "Honey, I'm so sorry. Let me look at your arm."

By now, Callie was crying in pain. "Leave me alone!"

Like a mother bear running to the aid of her cub, Dixie appeared in what seemed like a split-second. She pushed Sean aside. "What's wrong baby?"

"Daddy broke my arm! He frickin' broke my arm, Mom!"

Dixie delicately pulled Callie's right arm to the side to look at the injured arm it cradled. It was obvious to all three by the deformity in her normally straight forearm, that Callie's arm truly was broken.

"Start the car, Sean!" She was furious.

"Dix, it was an accident."

"Accidents don't result in breaking your daughter's arm! Go start the car!"

Chapter 7

FOR SEAN, THE LOW point of the previous evening had to have been watching Frank escort the police down the hallway of the hospital's emergency department to interrogate him. The senior Darling wanted to press assault charges against his son-in-law. But loyalty outweighed anger over what had taken place, and Callie told the doctors and her mother that it really had been an accident. In the final analysis, she really felt considerable devotion for her father, contrary to her outward manifestations. Such was not the case with Frank.

The Darling network quickly activated. When Callie didn't show up at John and Katie's at a reasonable hour as planned, they called to check on her, only to find she was at the hospital. Within fifteen minutes the wagons were circled, and all three of the Darling aunts and uncles, plus Suzanne and Frank had an almost military occupation of the lobby and treatment room. As expected, Frank made one of his phone calls and within an hour, one of the best orthopedic surgeons in the region, who happened to be a Darling Cadillac customer, was at Callie's bedside.

Despite Callie's assertion that her father didn't deliberately cause her injury, Frank persisted with his own version of the story, painting Sean as both verbally and physically abusive, and insisting on a protective order that would keep Sean away from Callie pending an investigation and hearing. Sean couldn't deny having yelled at Callie, and he didn't deny closing the door on her arm during an argument. With a great deal of hesitation, Dixie went along with her father's wishes. After contacting a judge, coincidentally a Darling GMC customer, by phone the next morning, Frank had his way.

SEAN'S LATE MORNING ARRIVAL at the office wasn't enough in and of itself to generate the unusual behavior of his staff as he entered the building. Noticeably, their eye contact was short-lived if they looked at him at all, conversations tapered off to nothing as he approached, and the typical salutations were replaced by truncated greetings. Word of what had taken place the night before was definitely out among the ranks. Fortunately, one person stood by him...April. She followed him into his office.

"Good morning." She was her usual, perky self.

Sean noticed that her attire today was a little more edgy than usual. She had on a low-cut, beige, polka-dot wrap dress that was *very* low cut. Over that she wore a conservative, red, corduroy vest. When he first noticed her on the showroom floor, it had been buttoned up all the way. When she entered his office, it was gaping open.

"Are you certain you want to be seen in the company of a criminal?" Sean asked.

"You're not a criminal...are you?"

Unsure if he enjoyed April's attempt at humor, he quickly asserted his innocence in light of his first question. "It was the ultimate Frank Darling circus, April. There are no charges. My attorney will get matters straightened out before the end of the week. As for Callie and me, we'll be alright. It was an accident, nothing more."

She must have sensed Sean was desperately in need of a friend, and she made certain he knew where she stood regarding the matter. "Sean, I know you. I know it was an accident."

Sean found the diametrically opposed reaction of Dixie and April to the incident involving Callie's broken arm to be particularly striking.

"Can I do anything for you?" She asked in what Sean could only describe as a truly compassionate voice.

"Hey, there's work to be done. Let's get on with business."

"What about Dixie and Callie? Do they need anything?"

Humbled once more by her thoughtfulness, Sean replied, "Thanks for asking, but for now I think it's best to leave them alone. I'll check on them later after some of the emotions have calmed down."

"So where is Dixie in all of this?"

All Sean would say was, "She's a Darling."

Sean had regrets about his answer. What he said indicated that he and Dixie weren't on the same page. It also planted a seed that he might be searching for solace at some point. He had to quickly figure out how he would respond if and when that moment arrived. It scared him to death that he was even having such thoughts.

"What's that you have?" Sean asked, pointing to a package April carried under her arm.

Pulling the package out and reading the label, she said, "Oh, it came for you overnight delivery. It's from Urbana...Ben Barnett. Isn't that your friend back home?"

"I'll be damned, it's here," Sean said. The hair stood up on his arms.

"Do you know what it is?"

"It's something Kim wanted me to have. Ben was instructed to send it to me."

Offering the package to him, she asked, "Are you excited to get it?"

"I don't know if excited is the correct word," he replied. He took the box. "To be honest with you, I'm terrified of what might be in here."

"Why?"

"I don't know. I guess it's because Kim had...how should I describe it...an interesting way of communicating messages. She used to tell me that life was an endless series of lessons, and she frequently came up with a symbolic way to get her point across. It could have been something she said, an action, a gift, any number of things. But the intent was to deliver a message subliminally."

"And you think she's done it again with this package?"

"I'm almost certain of it. Don't get me wrong. It's not a bomb or anything like that. But I can guarantee that along with the contents of the box, there is a hidden message. I'm going to have to figure it out, and to be honest with you, I'm not sure I'm up for that kind of stress right now."

"It might do you some good to get your mind off of last night if you at least opened the box."

Sean was afraid doing so would put him in a vulnerable position. He quickly dismissed her suggestion. "No, I'll do it later." He pulled out an old negative from his shirt pocket. "Hey, can you take care of something for me?"

"Absolutely."

"Would you make an 11" x 14" print of the picture on this negative, and also get it converted to a JPEG and put it on a memory stick? It's a picture of Kim that I told Ben I'd get for him to display at Kim's funeral."

"I'll get it this afternoon," April said.

Sean sensed a brazen eagerness to please him, but he didn't take issue with it.

"I'm taking the final list of attendees and the menu for Senator Bogenkamp's fundraiser to the Country Club. I'll take care of it while I'm out."

"Did Frank get you your tables?"

"That he did. He got me five more. He also asked me to remove your name from the list. Are you sure about that?"

"Completely."

Tossing out the next test question, April continued, "Did you know Dixie's name is still on it?"

"That's up to her. She has to make a choice."

Out of the corner of his eye, Sean noticed April's nostrils flared ever so slightly.

AS APRIL APPROACHED SEAN'S office around six o'clock, she found the mood was palpably different. Through the glass, she could see Sean shooting baskets with his toy Nerf balls and basketball hoop he used usually when he was in a particularly good frame of mind. Something must have happened to brighten his day.

"Look at you shooting hoops. What's up with that?" April asked.

"Terry Nakamura called back. We got our upside. The delivery trucks will begin arriving here starting Monday."

"What did you get?"

"Sixty-four units—all good stuff, too. Supposed to be forty-eight Toyotas and sixteen Lexi. "

"Great! They ought to be here just in time for the back-to-school upside we're expecting. Where are they coming from?"

"Not sure, don't care, didn't ask. Another thing, since I'll be gone, I need you to take care of one vehicle in particular—a red Coupe with my name on it."

"You didn't…"

"I did. I figured a broken arm justified a new Coupe. What do you think?"

It was with a sour expression and a particularly catty tone in her voice that she indicated she didn't agree with Sean's decision. "Callie will be happy, that's for sure."

"So, you think a Coupe is a bad idea? Earlier, I thought you said to get her…"

It was time for some tough love, and April proceeded to dole it out. "Sean, I fancifully suggested the other day getting her a Coupe because it appeared that you in no way were going to get her that car. So, what's the deal? You break your daughter's arm and that entitles you to make her into a little rich-bitch? It's the last thing she needs, and it's especially the last thing she needs from you." April held her hands up to her mouth, regretting that she blurted out exactly what was on her mind.

It was obvious Sean was perturbed by her remark. "I've made a decision, April. Deliver the car to Callie. If you don't want to, I'll get someone else to handle it."

Point goes to daughter, she thought to herself. *Regroup, and make it fast.*

Seeing that April had a thin cardboard folder with her, he asked, "Is that the picture?"

She couldn't wait to show him. She desperately needed to get back on Sean's good side. After taking a seat at his desk, she set the folder down in front of him. He took a deep breath, then slowly flipped it open. The print was breathtaking. She watched as Sean was overcome with emotion. She owned the moment.

"She's beautiful Sean. Did you take this picture?"

"Yes I did," Sean replied. He began reflecting on that time in his life. "Both of us dabbled in photography. She did nothing but black and white. I shot color. She was eighteen or nineteen at the time. We'd been together several years by then. Who did this print for you?"

"Scarborough's."

"I'll have to thank Deanne personally." Sean's voice began to break as he continued, "This picture captures everything about Kim."

Seeing that her boss was really struggling with all the present and past events in his life, April suggested, "Why don't you take the rest of the week off, Sean? This whole thing's really been hard on you, and you should probably spend some time at home before you leave for the funeral."

"Well, that's not exactly a practical idea since I can't be at home when Callie is there until this protective order crap gets resolved."

For several minutes, Sean sat and stared at Kim's picture, and April sat and stared at Sean. It was obvious to April he had a lot of feelings pent up inside. She offered her heart-felt support to him once more.

"Sean…talk to me. Tell me what's going through your mind right now."

Rocking nervously in his chair, Sean asked, "Would it be too much to ask for you to open Kim's package for me?"

April half expected, even hoped, that Sean might casually offer to take her for an after-work drink. Depending upon the weakness in his heart at that moment, he might even invite her out for *more*. But this, this was so much better. This was a man in pain putting his heart and soul on display for her to examine, decipher…and manipulate. She began to feel a growing power over him.

“I can think of nothing I’d rather do for you, Sean, than to get you through this awful time. Where’s the package?”

Sean reached under his desk and pulled it out, handing it to her.

As if it were a priceless heirloom, April took the item with both hands before proceeding to delicately slice off the wrapping paper with a letter opener that was lying on Sean’s desk. The paper removed, Sean and April were left staring at a nondescript box intended for a ream of print paper, much as one would find at a commercial copy and print store. After setting the box on his desk, April gingerly slipped the lid off, revealing a sealed letter-sized envelope sitting atop what appeared to be a printed document wrapped in thin, light-blue tissue paper. The words, “Dear Sean” were scrolled across the front of the envelope in India ink.

April held the envelope up to Sean, at which point he spoke as if he was identifying state’s evidence at a trial. “She was very much into calligraphy.” He studied it for a few moments. “The lines and strokes are shaky—probably an indication of her condition when the words were written, and that likely wasn’t too long ago.”

"Do you want me to read this?" April asked. She knew full well there was no way she was not going to do so.

Sean tried to say yes, but his voice only made a squeak. His simultaneous nod told her to press on. Making eye contact with April one final time, he motioned with his hand to get on with it.

Dear Sean,

It has come to this—my last words to you. I had hoped to deliver them in person, but as so often was the case, that moment together with you was not to be. You have before you what took much of my life to put into words. Your life—yes yours. As strangely possessive as it may sound, Dixie took you from me, but I never completely let go of you. That subtle distinction produced this memoir.

You may remember how I started writing a novel my freshman year of college. Think for a moment. What was the name of that book?

April looked up at Sean. His eyes got wide as he obviously struggled with Kim's first test of their past devotion. Finally, he managed to say, "I believe it was called, *The Road to Monticello*."

After letting his thoughts settle, April continued reading.

That was to be a celebration of our life together. Well, we know how that ended up, don't we? Let me say for the record, that although your completely selfish act tore my heart out and threw it in front of the snowplow, I led an extraordinary life with Ben. Had it not been for you and your actions, I never would have experienced the unqualified happiness I've had with Ben and our two sons.

Looking up at Sean once more, April asked, "Are you doing okay with this?"

"Uh…yeah. I'm still trying to think of the name of her book. Does she say anywhere what it is?"

After looking at both sides of the letter, April replied, "Nope. Sorry." She watched as Sean rubbed his obviously sweaty palms on the legs of his pants. "She has quite a way with words, doesn't she?"

Sean wiped away the tears from his eyes. "You've just begun to get a taste."

"I mean, 'you threw my heart in front of a snowplow'? Kind of melodramatic, maybe?"

Sean waved his finger at April as he explained, "Ah, you see, this is where the nuances of her message begin. She had this sad, bizarre infatuation with snowplows. To her, the snow was trillions of tiny, harmless, beautiful snowflakes. Then, just as Dr. Seuss created Whoville, they became populated, tiny, harmless, beautiful snowflakes. So here is this universe of life, as she called it, trickling out of the sky and piling up on the ground in God's own artistic way. Along comes this horrible, metallic, bone-crunching machine that brutally swooshes all of these tiny worlds into oblivion."

Nodding her head in pseudo-agreement, April said, "It sounds horrific. Gosh, you really broke her heart, didn't you?"

"Major league heartbreak. Major league. This plow thing had legs, too. About fifteen years ago or so, I was back on speaking terms with Kim. Of course Ben and I were still close, and Dixie tolerated the situation. Dix and I visited home that winter, and Kim got us both Christmas gifts. Well, mine was this implausible sweatshirt with the picture of a snowplow on the back, and on the front were the words, 'My Other Car is a Snowplow.'"

April smiled and chuckled, clearly showing that she enjoyed the anecdote.

"Ben just thought it was clever, and Dixie thought it had something to do with the auto business so she just blew it off. Let me tell you, for about half an hour, there was so much non-verbal communication between Kim and me. I still have the damn thing. I'll have to wear it to the funeral."

"Jesus! This chick was good! What did she get Dixie?"

"Oh, that's the best part," Sean said. A huge grin spread across his face. "Kim got her a sweatshirt with a bunch of tiny snowflakes on it. Dixie actually liked it. Do you get the message? I mean, do you get the message?"

Applauding, April replied, "I would have really liked this woman."

"You would have, April. She was really extraordinary in so many ways, just like you."

Sean was lost in thought—probably analyzing Kim's words up to that point. April was picking her jaw off of the floor after Sean's last remark. He had just likened her to his first love…a woman who still held tremendous power over him.

Apparently not realizing the impact of what he had said to her, Sean said, "Read on. I'm ready."

After clearing her throat and shaking off his shocking comparison, she carried on.

Which brings me to the point of this gift. I find it incumbent upon myself to bring peace to your otherwise mediocre and miserable life, Sean.

"What did she just say?" Sean interrupted.

"She seems to feel you are leading a, quote, 'mediocre and miserable life.'"

"Why would she say that?" Sean asked with a bitter tone in his voice.

"Let's read on. Maybe she will clear that up."

You see, Sean, I know you. I know all about you. We beat of one heart for too many years. Where you are in life today is not where you had hoped to be. The big business, the huge home in the suburbs, the trophy wife, the perfectly matched Y and X children, and all the money a person could want and then some, just doesn't become you.

"How does she come off saying this?" Sean asked. He stood up from his chair. "We haven't been that close since we broke up in college. She has no idea what I want in life. How can she possibly know if I'm happy or not?"

But all is not lost, Sean. Buried deep inside of you is a soul that I once touched. It was a soul with dreams so vivid and a passion for life that was palpable. I know. I felt it. We nurtured it together. Remember?

"This is really starting to piss me off, April. Is she really saying this? You're not making this up, are you?"

"Sean, why would I make this up?"

"I don't know. I just can't believe she's saying these things. Don't you find it offensive?"

"Maybe she really cared about you, Sean. Let's finish reading the whole letter before we jump to conclusions. Okay?"

My final request of you is simple. You must read my book. It is your only hope for salvation. I know that right now, you are most certainly in denial that there is anything wrong with your life. I wouldn't be asking you from the bottom of my heart to read it if I didn't think your situation was truly critical. There is time for change, Sean. You deserve a better life. You have to find it. My book will help get you there.

You must promise me one more thing. You must not read the last page of the book until you have reached the end. I have sealed it in yet another envelope to help you fight the temptation to jump to the answer. It won't work that way, Sean. Your life is a labor of love...my love.

So here's to you, Sean. May you find yourself so that I may rest in peace. With greatest love...Kim.

Sean sat quietly for a moment, absorbing Kim's challenge to him from beyond the grave. April knew he had questions, and she was the only one around to ask. She needed answers. Without asking permission to do so, she sliced open the tissue paper covering the manuscript of Kim's book. There on the first page, the title confirmed one thing—that Sean had remembered the name of the book correctly. It was, indeed, *The Road to Monticello.* April turned the box around so that the manuscript faced Sean, unsure if it was a pot of gold or Pandora's box.

"She wanted to be a writer," Sean said.

"I beg your pardon?"

"Her father was a professor of journalism. Her mother was a fiction writer with a few books to her name. They both passed away when she was young. Kim wanted badly to follow in their footsteps.

She began this book as a tribute to our love. I can't imagine it ends along those same lines."

"There are ways to convey love without saying, 'I love you.' I think she is reaching out to you, Sean, in a way no other woman can."

"She's dead, April. That's impossible."

"No it's not, Sean. Look at all the great works we've read in our lifetime from authors who have long since passed away. Their works still touch us in fantastic ways. I'm sure hers will, too."

"All this crap about my mediocre life—I think there's something vengeful about this."

Going for broke, April asked, "Sean, tell me, are you truly happy?"

"My life's not mediocre!"

"Well maybe not, but what gets you focused? Who lights your fire? Is it Frank and his acidic, verbal carnage, or plain-spoken John? Maybe she chose harsh words because she knew that would get you engaged in her book."

Sean simply sat, listening to April's analysis.

"Sean, this was the most impassioned letter I think I have ever read. When she says she never let you go, she means it. When she says you have vivid dreams and a passion for life, I, too, see that from time to time. But in recent months they've become suppressed. When she says she is asking from the bottom of her heart, that's no exaggeration. When she says you deserve a better life, you do. When she called it a labor of love, it was. Don't throw her heart in front of the snowplow again, Sean. Do as she asks. Read this book."

Further engaging Sean in conversation, April asked, "If you don't mind me asking, how did you end up parting ways with Kim? Obviously it had a significant impact on both of you."

"It shows?"

"Oh, yeah. It shows."

"Do you promise you won't think any less of me if I tell you my darkest secrets?"

"Sean, come on. I'm your friend. Consider this a warm up for when you speak with Berkowitz."

"Do I have to pay you?"

"In kind," she replied. She was only half-joking.

"Here's the short version. Ben and I have been close friends since seventh grade. Kim was one year behind us, and when I went to college, I began to see things I hadn't noticed before."

"Other women?"

"Well, yes, among other things. I couldn't flirt with anyone in high school and I was hands-off to all females. It was a small school and people would have noticed immediately."

"Did you want to flirt?"

"Probably. I think all guys do. It's a reflection of their insecurity."

"So, you think it's fair to be unfaithful because other guys do it?"

"We're getting off the subject here, doctor."

"Sorry. You're right. I'm doing too much active listening. I'm not passing judgment, Sean. I simply want you to know I am connecting with you on this subject. I guess in some way I'm trying to figure out what went through Scott's mind." As she spoke, she made sure her body language indicated she was completely at ease with the conversation.

"So, I began to develop a more independent and wild side. Ben and I started playing rugby our freshman year, and along with that came all the rabble rousing, drinking and so forth."

"How did you get away with drinking?"

"It was funny. The town dropped the legal drinking age to nineteen during the time I was in college. They raised it back to twenty-one after I graduated. They must have used me as a poster child as to why combining beer and nineteen-year-olds was a problem."

"Did Kim like you drinking?"

"No. I never took her along. She didn't much care for the whole rugby environment, and I could see the strain in our relationship."

"What about sex?"

Sean looked startled by her frank question. "What about it?"

"Well, did you?"

"That's kind of personal."

"This entire conversation is personal, Sean. Did the two of you have sex?"

"Actually, no. Almost, but in truth, no."

April waited anxiously for Sean to elaborate, but it was clear that topic, for now, possibly out of respect for Kim, was off the table. She wasn't going to press the issue.

"So, when did Dixie come into the picture?"

"Well, the beginning of my junior year, I was pretty much an Animal House kind of guy."

"You?"

"Yep. Yours truly. And Ben and I hated anything Greek."

"You mean fraternities and sororities?"

"Right. We used to say we were pledges of Slamma Cramma Jamma."

"Sounds like a fine institution."

"Well, it was rush week in Greek town, and Ben and I were drunk as shit. We decided to streak the sororities. We'd made it through three of them when we decided to go for the one with the reputation of having the bitchiest girls—Kappa Kappa Gamma."

"I'm with you there. And did you succeed?"

"This is embarrassing. We were on the third floor of the place chasing girls out of the shower. All of them were screaming bloody murder, and Ben and I were in absolute heaven. Well, I slipped and fell, breaking my frickin' ankle. Between being shit-faced and in pain, I couldn't move. Then we heard sirens. I told Ben to leave and I'd deal with the fallout. He managed to escape, and I figured I was toast when this gorgeous brunette stepped out of a shower stall with nothing on—I mean nary a stitch of clothing."

"Dixie?"

"The one and only. I'll be damned if she didn't get me a blanket and help me across the hall to her room. She managed to get me into the top bunk where she slept, and hid me under a bunch of pillows. When the cops came searching door to door, she flashed them and screamed like they were intruding, and they immediately left the building with their tails between their legs."

"Lucky you."

"You got that right. So, the next thing I know, she's helping me dry off and she wrapped my ankle up in a pillow. Her roommate showed up and they found some of her boyfriend's clothes, got me dressed, and drove me off to the school infirmary."

"Why did she do all this for you?"

"She said I was cute."

"I guess I can see that, but it sounds sort of lame as a real motive from what I know of Dixie."

"Well, the reality was, she was a rebellious college girl, and I was perfect material to piss off her father."

"Frank?"

"Yep, good ol' Frankie boy."

"Where was Kim?"

Sean squirmed uncomfortably as he spoke. "This is where it gets sad. She showed up at the hospital the next day and caught me and Dixie in an awkward moment."

"You were having sex?"

"You got it. I mean, down and dirty, right then and there, riding like a cowgirl on top, shaking the light fixtures sex."

"Dixie?"

"Hey, she's got a wild streak. It doesn't come out to play as often as it used to, but she can put a smile on my face, if you're with me."

This was too much information, and April had to get off that subject. She asked, "So, I guess Kim freaked out?"

"No, Kim just retreated. Ben, of all people, freaked out. He couldn't believe what I'd done. I might as well have banged his mother."

April felt a personal affront to his past behavior. "You asshole."

"I thought you weren't going to be judgmental?"

"I'm not. I'm just saying what Berkowitz will be thinking when you tell him this. He's a trained professional and won't be so blunt. I, on the other hand, can call you an asshole. No wonder she was so hurt."

"Thank you for your understanding, April. Note to self, don't confide in April ever again."

In actuality, April found the conversation between her and Sean absolutely exhilarating.

Sean looked at his watch, then started to ask, "What are you doing…?"

But before he could finish his question, April interrupted him. "Have you called Berkowitz yet?"

He was about to ask her out. She had heard the line many times, and seen the same expression in the faces of countless men as they proposed a tryst. A man in need didn't even need to complete the question. But if she were to jump in now, not only would she bring down Sean's life about him, he would never learn what Kim was trying to teach him.

"No," Sean answered.

"Call him. You can't do this alone, Sean. Get a professional on your side."

Her message to him was clear. She couldn't—or at least wouldn't—be his first line of support in this matter. If she crossed that line, they would be in bed. He needed to be sitting across from a therapist…at least for now.

"You're right, April," Sean said. He looked somewhat embarrassed.

"Do you still have the number I gave you?"

He reached into his wallet and produced the note with Berkowitz' phone number. But, he didn't let what had almost transpired go without remark.

"Hey, what you did just now was very special to me. You kept me from changing our relationship. I truly, truly thank you, April."

She just smiled as she thought to herself, *my time will come.*

Chapter 8

SEAN DIDN'T BOTHER CALLING before showing up at the house. He expected nobody to be there, and depending upon Callie's plans for the evening, she might end up spending the night elsewhere. He never knew anymore where she would be. She was having a hard time with the imminent long-distance relationship she was destined to have with her boyfriend, Rick, when the two would go off to different colleges. As such, they were spending as much time together as possible, likely doing things Sean didn't want to think about. If she showed, he'd make alternative plans for the night.

Thursday nights had been a traditional night out at the Lakeside Dinner Club for the Darlings as long as Sean could remember. It was a spectacular, circa-1902, lakefront home that had been converted into a swank dinner club for those who could afford it. As they did in so many ways, the Darlings made certain their noses were into any social activity that took place on the North Shore. Thursday night was popular among the social elite because pictures taken that evening would end up in the society section of Saturday newspapers. Frank would often say, "We're either giving or we're getting so we're going." Nobody argued. Sean did have to acknowledge that in spite of Frank's dictatorial, heavy-handed business acumen and brusque personality, he did a lot for the community. If there was a need, he would see to it. If he couldn't handle it alone, he'd make phone calls. His reputation as a 'heavy hitter' served the public time and time again.

Sean actually looked forward to an evening alone with his new read while Dixie fulfilled her obligation, and feeling scorn for the social circuit as he did simply made his private evening that much more rewarding. After pouring himself a goblet of cabernet, he retreated with wine and book to the peace of his screened-in porch that overlooked the nicely-manicured backyard and woods that bordered it.

Perhaps it was the object of the book—Monticello—that caused Sean to reflect on this view for a moment. During the years he and Dixie had occupied their home at 10 Tarleton Gardens, he had taken great pains to personally maintain lush flower gardens, fine statuary, and ponds throughout his five acres. What's more, despite Dixie's arguments to the contrary, he insisted upon leaving the woods in their natural state. The outcome was a strong likeness to the gardens and woods at Allerton Park. Until now, he had never understood the importance of his choice in landscaping, nor its relevance. But at this very moment, it was clear to him that he had made subconscious choices along the way to retain something that had been very dear to both he and Kim.

As for Monticello, it was as Mayberry as a town could get. A river ran through it, as did a railroad line. It was the county seat and, accordingly, was home to a magnificent courthouse and requisite town square. The population was enough, but at the same time, not too much. The town was surrounded by rich, rolling Illinois farmland. Architecture was for the most part modest and utilitarian, but always well-kept. Then, there were the estates adorning several tree-lined blocks known to locals as Millionaire's Row. Architects and historians recognize them as some of the early twentieth century's most splendid residences. In fact, one was so large, a philanthropic soul had turned it into a local hospital. Yet despite its wide demographic spread, there was no overt poverty or in-your-face opulence among the population. People blended together as a community, and, as much as anything, that's what drew Kim and Sean to visit the town time and time again during their years together. In the fictional future that young lovers paint for themselves, the two hoped Monticello would be a place they called home one day, where they would raise a family, and where they would live out their lives together.

Having never read a single page of the book before, Sean had no idea what to expect. All he knew was this—he had to read it. If ever there was a vow not to be broken, it would have to be his final promise to Kim that he would read and cherish every word of her book.

It began:

There is only one first love. No matter the outcome of that relationship, nothing takes the place of that first love. It is the benchmark against which all others will be judged. Many relationships will be worse, and with luck, at least one will be better.

For me, that first love was Mark.

"Mark, huh?" Sean said to himself. "Guess I'll have to think out-of-body for this project." He took a sip of his wine before continuing.

His was an appropriate name, for it was I who had my sights on him that autumn afternoon. It was Sadie Hawkins Day, and I wanted a man. And it couldn't be just any man. No, this choice required particular vigilance because I wasn't going to do this again. Even at age sixteen, I vowed that I was playing for keeps. The trick was not to let my prey know this.

Sean sat for a while, thinking about all the details he could remember of that day. A cold front had blown through that morning and the temperature was a cool, wind-backed fifty degrees when the high school let out at three forty-five. Anyone who had to take a bus home was gone, and a high percentage of the foot soldiers and those with their own cars thought the entire Sadie Hawkins Day activity was a bit over the top. And then there were those who felt it was amusing enough to stick around and watch from the sidelines. That's where Kim found him. In truth, he was trying to lay low until Judy Nixon looked his way. She was Sean's fantasy girl—in his dreams, but probably way out of his reach. They were friends, but he always wanted to take it a notch, or two, higher. Then, just as Judy looked his way, he stood up, only to be grabbed from behind by Kim.

He knew Kim, but not particularly well. As circles of friends go, theirs overlapped. But they each were just outside the other's circle. At first he was amused by her tenacity. She simply wouldn't let go. After dragging him across the finish line—the prerequisite for marriage—he remembered sitting with her until after sunset, by designation the defining moment, and getting to know her as she discovered more about him. Sean all but forgot about Judy Nixon that evening, and his relationship with Kim was underway.

A few pages later, Sean was struck by another passage in the *Road.*

DeeDee asked me what I saw in Mark. "After all, Collette," she said, "he's the most pathetic dancer I've ever seen."

I told her it was his car. What seventeen-year-old man can drive a 1969 Toyota Corona and retain any dignity unless his character is exceptional enough to lift him above that impediment?

She's Collette, he thought. *She always liked French names. But she wanted me for my car?* Now, more than three decades later, Sean found himself still driving a Toyota. *Was this all about character?* He recalled one of his greatest forays into manhood as a teenager. He was going car shopping with his father and grandfather. When they parked at the auto dealership, they stopped in front of a yellow 1968 Mustang Fastback. He remembered his heart racing like he knew the cylinders would in that muscle car. He felt Steve McQueen's blood running through his veins. But as they walked toward it, Raymond redirected Sean to the right—to a white Toyota 4-door. As defining moments go, this was about as clear as they got. As a father himself, Sean knew Raymond's choice had been the best one. Had he bought Sean the Mustang, it would have completely altered his personality. Now, as he was facing a similar decision about a purchase for Callie, Sean was certain, for reasons he didn't understand at the time, that getting her the Solara last year was the right thing to do. He'd have to call April tomorrow and have her release the Coupe for public sale.

It was maybe an hour, three glasses of wine, and forty-five pages into the book before the topic of sex was introduced. Without a doubt, the delay in text reflected reality.

There was this race once. The first to cross the finish line, as we all know, was the tortoise, followed by the careless hare. Long afterward, Mark's lips crossed the finish line. I finally gave up waiting for him. While our friends would be either making out or making love, I couldn't get Mark to kiss. I had survived the summer of '69 a virgin, but I never thought I'd be waiting on my first kiss.

Within ten feet of where I first landed Mark, I held him in my arms, and slowly pressed my lips against his. They were met with incredible passion. Surprisingly, that was all it took. Oh my. I never knew one kiss could transform a boy into a man, but I know he grew a beard that very moment. Something else grew as well, but that's a subject for another chapter.

It had been a spectacular kiss, Sean recalled. He had kissed a few girls by that time, and, probably because a great kiss is for the most part an acquired talent, they had all been terrible. But Kim's was a delight. Kissing came naturally for her. Her lips were pouting and soft. As all of his senses raced to full alert, he remembered the smell of her hair, the faint taste of the cola they had just shared, the roundness of her butt cheeks as he held them in his hands, and the firmness of her breasts as she pulled her body intimately close to his. And to think that, at the time, Sean felt he was experiencing all the sexual attention he would ever want from Kim—just a kiss. That didn't last long. But, as with the kiss, Kim would always be the one to make the next move—the one to drag him to the next base on the field, so to speak. Yet, though she would invariably initiate the next move, she always let him finish the act.

And so the story went, but not for too long. It might have been the long night or the difficult day or the superb wine on an empty stomach, but about eighty pages into the *Road*, Sean's eyes closed and he was soon asleep.

THE TOYOTA, AS IT turned out, had many exceptional features, not the least of which were the fully-reclining, front bucket seats enabling Sean to sneak Kim into the house via the garage and close the door without the nosy neighbors taking notice. The black light was on in Sean's bedroom, Santana was playing, the incense was burning, and the parents were gone for the weekend. It was all set to be that perfect evening for two. The unusual illumination made the setting surreal. It made skin look incredibly tan, then highlighted any light-colored clothing to the point one would think it could cast a shadow. Smiles revealed iridescent teeth. The down side was that it made every spec of dirt and flake of skin stand out like stars in the moonless sky. But those were the least of Sean's worries tonight. Foremost on his mind was to somehow remove Kim's clothing, without throwing up from the worst case of nerves he'd ever experienced. It wasn't as if he could bluff his way through it either. He shivered like a new Boy Scout on his first overnight winter camping trip where there was a real threat from wildlife.

Even with his vulnerability completely exposed, Kim took it upon herself to find a way to calm him down. Following a most adoring kiss, Kim encouraged Sean by saying, "It's okay. Just relax. It's only me and there's nothing to prove."

Her words only made him shiver more. She knew she had to distract him, and hoped moving matters along would bring relief to his anxiety. As her lips left his again, she whispered, "Take off my clothes."

His hands remained firmly planted on her waist.

It was obvious to her that this endeavor was going to require a little more nurturing. She let her hands fall from where they had been cradling the back of his head, to the bottom of his sweater.

There, she grabbed the garment from both sides and in one quick upward movement, had the sweater over his head.

Sean removed it the rest of the way so he could get his hands free once again to place on Kim's body...anywhere on her body. Now, it was his turn to remove an article of her clothing. For some reason, that night she wore a button-down cardigan.

The challenge of the buttons proved to be almost too much for Sean's trembling hands, so while he slowly fumbled with the top three buttons, she quickly unfastened the bottom three. Soon, her sweater joined his on the floor, and Sean's hands moved quickly to Kim's shirt-covered breasts. Her nipples began to get hard, and even she was surprised he was able to get a rise out of her. Perhaps there was hope for him after all.

Though Sean's shivering soon stopped as his attention focused in on Kim's intentions, the pace was agonizingly slow—too slow for her. After encouraging Sean to sit on the bed, she removed his shoes and socks, then unbuckled his belt and loosened his blue jeans. There's a point at which autopilot turns on in most young men, and Kim had finally reached it. As she stood before him, he loosened her brown corduroy pants, and with a few lithe wiggles of the hips that only a woman can do, her pants were on the floor. Realizing they were piled around her shoes that he had neglected to remove, she quickly and without much ado slipped them off.

He stood up once again and his jeans joined the growing piles on the floor. They were now down to shirts and undergarments. Without making a fuss, they simultaneously removed each other's shirts. Fitting with the times, Kim wore no bra. Sean now stood looking at the bare breasts he had caressed so many times, but until now had never set eyes upon. He ever so slowly placed first one hand, then his other on both of her breasts. As Kim let out a reflexive sigh, Sean's confidence jumped an order of magnitude.

It was now time for the Hail Mary. Not only were Sean's white Jockeys blinding in the black light, they were doing a poor job restraining what was concealed within them. Kim got down on her knees and slipped them off. She had only heard from some of her girlfriends about the one-eyed jack that was now staring at back at her. This was the real deal—a fully-erect penis that was both loaded and ready for action. As she had been coached to do by her best friend Zoe, she kissed the head of his penis one time, not lingering long, but showing she was ready to play, before getting back to her feet.

The last vestige of clothing was Kim's panties. Sean made quick work of them, and the two embraced flesh to flesh for the first time. The unique sensations defied description. Now feeling a genuine chill herself, Kim pulled back the bedspread and sheets on the bed, and the two huddled beneath the covers, holding each other passionately. For the next hour, they completely explored each other's bodies for the first time.

After a while, the problem wasn't lack of warmth. It was too much warmth in the form of heightened sexual desires. Sean seemed to know what he was doing as he fondled Kim's genitals. Once he initiated his touching and stroking in earnest, it took a remarkably short period of time for Kim to experience her first orgasm at the hands of a man. Sean pressed his lips against hers as she moaned and gasped. When her breathing slowed and the rhythmic pulses ceased, she opened her eyes and gave him an endearing smile.

"You did it," she said, relaying to him her verbal approval of what had taken place.

"Did you have an orgasm?" He asked, still doubting the reality of what had transpired.

"Yes. It was fabulous."

"How do you know? I mean, have you had one before?"

The black light concealed Kim's blush as she replied, "Yes. Does that surprise you?"

"No, I guess not. After all, guys…well, you know."

Kim reached down for Sean's penis which was still rock hard, and had been since she had removed his underwear. As he raised himself up to give Kim better access, she quickly positioned herself under his body with her legs apart.

After kissing him and marveling at how hard he was, she posed the challenge every young man longs for, yet dreads at the same time. "Let's make love."

He had no response to her offer. As he relaxed onto her warm, welcoming torso, she guided him into position. All he needed to do was push and he'd have his home run. Instead, he kissed her repeatedly and brushed the hair from her eyes. Maybe the fact that she was willing to accept him into her body, sacrificing her virginity to him, was all it took to satisfy his immediate desire. In any event, he couldn't go through with it.

His flameout deeply troubled Kim. "Is it something I did?" She asked.

"No, babe. I just think we should wait. I love you, Kim, and I don't want to do anything you will regret."

"Uh, I think I know what I'm asking for, and believe me, I have no plans to regret it."

"What about getting pregnant? Aren't you worried?"

"Nope. I've cleared you for landing with Catholic Air Traffic Control."

Uncomfortable that Kim was able to remove all of his barriers, he asked, "Why do you want to make love?"

Kim rolled her eyes as she replied, "We have a very serious role reversal going on here, Sean. You're supposed to be relentlessly pounding me into the mattress while I scream, 'No, Stop!'"

"No. Not tonight, Kim," Sean said firmly.

As Kim looked over Sean's shoulder, she asked, "Ben, what's with this guy?"

Sean turned around, and there stood Ben in his bedroom with no clothes on.

"What are you doing here?!" Sean asked, startled by the spectacle.

"I'm taking over where you left off, you moron," Ben answered.

"What do you mean?"

"Get off of her," Ben demanded.

"What?"

"I said get off of her!" Ben repeated.

Without further objection, Sean crawled out of bed. Where his body once lay on top of Kim, Ben now took that position. As Sean watched helplessly, Ben and Kim began making love. He was unable to speak and was frozen in position. He looked on as his love was stolen by another man—his best friend. He closed his eyes so not to watch what was taking place. When he opened them, he found himself staring at an approaching snow plow. His feet were frozen to the roadway. There was no escape. He felt the thud as the huge metal blade struck his body, sending it hurdling through the air. As he was about to land, two arms reached out to catch him, breaking his fall.

"Sean! Wake up!"

Sitting in his chair, soaked with perspiration while his arms flailed wildly about, Sean opened his eyes to see who was holding him. It was Dixie. Frank and the rest of the Darlings were standing right behind her.

Chapter 9

"PATHETIC!"

"Daddy, shut up!" Dixie wanted desperately to understand what was going on.

"What's he doing here anyway? There's a protective order keeping him away from..."

"Frank!" Dixie never addressed her father by his first name unless he was one step from being verbally thrashed. It had happened on a few occasions before, and shocked the Darling sons as much as it had stunned Frank. But, they each knew Dixie had given them fair warning. One more remark against Sean, and they'd be hoisted by their own petards.

Before matters escalated, Suzanne intervened. "Frank, dear, let's leave them alone. I'm certain Dixie can take care of matters. Boys, come along."

Seldom did the matriarch of the Darling family give such explicit instructions. So seldom in fact, they invariably trumped anything Frank would say, let alone his sons. As Frank, his sons, and their wives filed out of the house, Frank made a parting gesture—he was chewing on his tongue for Sean to see. He was clearly savoring Sean's moment of anguish and embarrassment. Dixie and her mother exchanged hugs, followed by John and Katie. After the door closed, Dixie pulled up a chair next to Sean. He looked like he'd been through ten rounds of a prize fight.

"What's going on?" She asked.

"I was reading Kim's book and I fell asleep."

"What book are you talking about?"

Sean found himself facing the harsh reality that he'd yet to inform Dixie about *the book*. This was unlikely to go over well.

"Uh...Kim wrote a book about me...I mean us...I mean, all of us."

Dixie just glared at Sean while tensing her jaws.

"Actually, it's a fictional story based on people like us, doing things that she and I...I mean, all of us...oh, fuck it! I'll tell you later."

"When did this book appear? I mean, she really *is* dead, isn't she?"

"Yes she's dead! What a horrible thing to say. She'd been writing it for a long time. Ben mailed it to me at the office. I just started reading it."

"Why did he mail it to the office? Were you trying to hide it from me?"

"No, Dix. I just wanted to make sure someone would be around to sign for it."

"So, why all this emotion? You're soaked in your own sweat. There's snot running out your nose. There are tears in your eyes. You've obviously been drinking. You were freaking out about something in your sleep. Were you dreaming? Is there something in this book you need to tell me about…like right now?!"

Sean glared back at her. "Did it bother you when Kim caught us making love at the hospital?"

If Dixie had been up to that point approaching Sean from the perspective of a caring wife, that tact just vanished.

"What the hell are you talking about?"

"When I broke my ankle back in college…do you remember making love to me in the school infirmary?"

"Of course I do. That was our first time to…"

"Did it bother you when Kim caught us?"

"No, Sean. Not in the least," Dixie replied. Adding insult to injury, she revealed a secret she had kept to herself. "Kim called the room that morning while you were asleep. I answered the phone. I told her I was your nurse and she asked me to tell you she would be by after her eleven o'clock class to see you. I knew she was coming. I think my actions speak for themselves, don't you?"

"You mean to tell me, you wanted her to catch us?"

"It attained the desired result. Here we are over thirty years later, still husband and wife."

Sean got up from his chair and began pacing angrily about the room. "I can't believe you set her up to catch us like that!"

"Sean, there are winners and losers in life. That just happened to be her day to lose."

Turning to face her, Sean shouted, "Jesus! I'm hearing Frank come out of your mouth word for word!"

Standing up to confront him, Dixie fired back, "My father is driven to achieve objectives. So am I Sean. A long time ago, that objective was you, and I've never regretted what I did to get you. Are you telling me our end didn't justify my means?"

"You crushed her, Dixie!"

"No! We crushed her, Sean! Making love takes two, and you were just as much a part of that moment as I was!"

Sean must have realized she was right. Although he hadn't understood the pretenses until just now, he was as guilty as Dixie in breaking Kim's heart. Angry with this revelation, he let out a loud growl and pounded his fists on the porch table.

The situation was probably going to escalate further except that there came a knock on the kitchen door—the same door through which everyone had just left a short while ago, and Callie had her accident the prior evening. Dixie went to see who it was. It was John and Katie.

Pulling the door open vigorously, Dixie asked, "What?"

The friendship Katie had with Dixie was crucial at this moment, and the sister-in-law used it to her advantage. "I forgot my purse. We heard shouting. John and I thought we'd see if you guys needed some…referees."

Dixie tried to restrain herself, but she broke down crying on Katie's shoulder.

"I'll go see about Sean," John said, leaving the ladies to sort things out in their own way.

SEEING HIS BROTHER-IN-LAW APPROACHING, Sean greeted him with, "John, this doesn't involve you."

"Bullshit, Sean."

"Hey, I'm fuckin' serious. Stay out of it."

"Nope. Not a chance. You're destroying your entire life, Sean, and I'm not going to stand by and let it happen."

"You mean my 'mediocre and miserable' life, don't you?"

"What the fuck are you talking about?"

"Oh, never mind," Sean replied. He didn't want to bring undue negative criticism to Kim's book.

John went to a small refrigerator and pulled out two cold bottles of beer. Handing one to Sean, he said, "In case you haven't taken notice lately, you have a gorgeous, loving wife. You have two great kids. You live in a fabulous home at a prime location. And you have a terrific career. True, your father-in-law is a Nazi. But excluding that small detail, I'd say your life is far from mediocre and miserable."

Sean stood with his beer unopened long enough that John opened it for him. John then twisted the top off of his and held it up to Sean for a toast. After a few moments, their bottles clicked.

"So, what's going on, Sean?"

If there was a friend in Sean's life, it was John. And besides, Sean didn't care about repercussions at this point.

"I've got to get away from Frank, John. I want out of the Group."

"So, leave," John said.

"Just leave?"

"That's right. It's obvious to all the principals that you want out as badly as Frank wants you gone. The only reason he hasn't had some thug blow up your car with you in it is that you're Dixie's husband. And in case you didn't know it, Dixie is commander-in-chief of the Darling Group. Seems to me there should be no reason the two of you—actually, the three of you—can't come to some agreement."

"You mean me, Frank, and Dixie?"

"Well, you can't do anything affecting the partnership without her approval. She is your co-signatory. If the two of you get on the same page, I don't see why you shouldn't be able to split off. In fact, I think with Dixie on your side, you both could walk away with a really sweet deal. After all, your dealerships are the big money-makers these days."

Sitting down at a picnic table, Sean responded with a less than enthusiastic, "Hum."

There was a pause while John took note of Sean's less than robust response to his suggestion.

"Okay, let's try this again. What's going on, Sean?"

He still refused to open up.

"I have to tell you up front that if this is where you tell me you've fallen out of love with my sister, or worse yet you're having an affair, I'll have to hurt you."

Sean sipped his beer and chucked at the meek threat. He eventually said, "I'm just wading through some baggage, John—

some left over from my mother's death, and now some left over from the death the other day of an old girlfriend."

"Dixie told us about that at dinner tonight."

"Us? At dinner?"

"Well, it's hard not to talk about you, Sean, especially when you're not around. You're such an easy target."

"Gee, thanks, buddy."

"Think nothing of it, pal."

"I won't."

"So what was going on when we walked in on you tonight?"

Going for maximum shock value, Sean replied, "I was dreaming about screwing my old girlfriend."

"Ooh. That's pretty hot stuff," John said. He was unsure if Sean was telling the truth, so he prodded him further. "Was she good?"

"You're sick."

"No, really," John said while making thrusting motions with his arm.

Reluctantly, Sean told more of the story. "Actually, I was dreaming that I was watching my best friend make love to her."

"Ooh. Voyeur stuff. Now that's really hot."

"No, it was disgusting."

"Oh. Okay, if you say so." After a pensive pause, John asked, "So, I guess this is where a therapist would ask, 'So, Sean, what do you suppose that dream meant?'"

"And I would answer, 'Mind your own damn business.'"

"That's not very constructive, Sean. Seriously, why do you think your best friend nailed your girlfriend?"

The truth in Sean's answer hurt him deeply as he replied, "Because I nailed your sister."

Not being naïve, John realized he had hit upon something in the past of his sister and brother-in-law that he had previously only suspected.

"Are you telling me my sister stole you from this woman?"

"Stole is probably not the right verb. Let's cut to the chase scene. Kim caught Dixie and me in bed."

"In college? Before you were married?"

"Don't tell me you thought your sister was a…"

"Virgin? Damn right I did. I figured Frank would have killed any dude who he thought took his little Dixie to bed before her wedding night."

"Well I hate to piss on Frank's parade, but your sister could write volumes about pre-marital sex."

"Uh, okay. This is where I stop talking about sex and my sister."

It was a good thing that the two men reached that juncture in the conversation because at that point, Dixie and Katie joined the two on the porch. Dixie sat on the bench next to Sean. Whatever Katie had said it had calmed Dixie down.

"Katie had a good idea," Dixie started. "She thinks we should go away for a few weeks as soon as Callie goes off to college. The time away would be a good thing for us. What do you think?"

Sean's response showed he wasn't ready to commit. "What do you have in mind?"

It appeared Katie and Dixie had rehearsed how to respond if, but more certainly when, Sean gave a vague answer to her question. "There are all kinds of places to go. We could go to Canada, the Caribbean, Germany, Switzerland, Australia, or London. You pick—anyplace, including any destination I didn't mention. We'll simply pack up and go."

Picking the wrong time to give a gut response, Sean said, "Let's go to Monticello."

Katie and John could tell from Dixie's expression that he'd hit a nerve.

"What did I say, Katie?" Dixie said. She quickly stood up. "What did I say? I told you he'd give me some flip answer. I'm tired of this shit. I'm simply tired of it."

Before anyone could say another word, Dixie's cell phone rang. It was Callie.

"Hi, sweetie." Dixie's expression became maternal. "He what? I'm so sorry, honey. Where are you? Are you okay? Are you sick to your stomach?"

"What's wrong?" Katie asked, trying to get Dixie's attention.

With her hand over the mic of the phone, Dixie replied quietly, "Ricky broke up with Callie. She's hysterical."

"Yeah. I can come get you. Where are you? McDonald's? Which one? Okay. I'll be there in ten minutes."

"Dixie, let me and John go get her. She can stay with us tonight," Katie said.

"Hey, sweetie? Would you like to spend the night with Aunt Katie and Uncle John? Okay. They're leaving here now to pick you up. I'll send some clothes and overnight stuff with them. Call me before you go to sleep. I want to talk to you some more, okay? Hey, Rick's a jerk, what can I say? Alright, he's not a jerk. Northwestern? We'll talk about that tomorrow. Sorry. I'll talk to you later. Love you, Cal." Dixie disconnected the call.

"Jesus Christ. Goddamn Rick Paternek dumped Callie. She had a conniption, and then threw up in his car so he dropped her off at the McDonald's over on Sheridan Road and bailed. Callie says he's hooked up with Tammy Hrabski because they're both going to Northwestern. Now, she's certain she wants to go there. What a mess."

"Tammy Hrabski? She's the senior class slut," Katie said.

"Tell me about it," Dixie acknowledged.

"Is she sick?" Katie asked.

"I think her pain medication is getting to her. That doctor put her on a pretty high dose of Vicodin. She's never had that before, and I think it's making her nauseated."

"John, go get her and swing back by here to pick me up," Katie said. "I'll get her things ready."

"Right. I'll see you guys after a bit." Before leaving, John added, "Sean, remember what we talked about. And for what it's worth, I think a vacation would be a great idea for you two."

Before Sean could respond, Dixie did in kind. "Bite me, John. Just bite me."

John saw the door and went directly for it.

Walking up to face Sean, Dixie asked, "So, mister I-don't-give-a-shit father, why aren't you the least bit upset about your daughter being dumped at a fast food restaurant?"

Sean was all too casual with his reply. "You know, I think it was the best thing. I didn't trust that guy. I think he was getting too serious with Callie."

"Too serious?" Dixie was incredulous. "You mean, sex? I have news for you Sean. I put Callie on the pill over a year ago and from what she's told me, they've put it to good use."

"You what? Why didn't talk you to me about that first?" Sean asked. He was unable to fathom Dixie's past action.

Getting in Sean's face, she replied, "Because the Fuller Brush Company doesn't sell birth control pills! I figured you wouldn't care!"

"Alright! Both of you! Cut it out!" Katie said. "I can't stand listening to you two! You're husband and wife! Act like you love each other! Now!"

Not about to rest the argument, Sean continued, "You talk about Fred Hrabski's daughter being the school slut! Then, in the next breath, you tell me you put our daughter on birth control! What kind of hypocrite are you?!"

"I'm a concerned parent protecting our daughter from unwanted pregnancy! You break arms! Got anything else you'd like to say?!"

"I'm surprised you didn't invite Rick to hop on top when Callie was post-op this morning! I figured having sex in a hospital bed was a dominant trait passed on from mother to daughter!"

"La-la-la-la-la-la…hearing way too much," Katie said with her hands cupping her ears.

"You know what, Sean? As I recall, you had to take muscle relaxers for a week in order to wipe off the smile I put on your face, not to mention the fact that when you blew your wad, it all but came out my ears! Don't for one second act like you weren't having the time of your life!"

"Way too much information…way too much," Katie said to the uncaring couple between whom she was standing. She had heard enough, and left the room to go pack Callie's things, leaving the two warriors alone.

Dixie and Sean stood practically nose to nose. Their breathing was fast. Their nostrils were flared. Neither of them wanted to back down. But in time, Sean couldn't take it anymore, and said half-heartedly, "It came out your ears?"

Dixie suddenly felt herself suffer Kim's pain. "While she watched us…right at your moment of glory. Gosh that was a shitty thing to do to her."

Sean let his forehead touch Dixie's. Moments later their arms wrapped around one another's waist.

"We've never fought like this before, Sean. I don't like it. I don't like it one bit."

"Me either, Dix. What do you want me to do?"

"I just want my husband back, Sean. I love you and want things to be the way they used to be."

"I have an idea."

"What?"

"Instead of going off to on some bizarre vacation, we can book a room at the hospital and relive our first time. What do you think?"

After a short giggle, Dixie replied, "Anything you want, honey. Anywhere, any place, any time."

Katie happened to be listening as the two were reconciling their differences.

"So the two of you really did do it in a hospital bed?"

Dixie put her head on Sean's chest as she looked toward Katie and nodded. A genuine smile graced Dixie's face.

"Right…," Katie said. Getting back to the business at hand, she continued, "Now then, Dix, I have Callie's sweatpants and top, some clean panties and a bra, socks, tennies, make-up, hairbrush, toothbrush, and this lightweight coat. Anything else?"

"Yeah, I need to get her pillow and her medicine. And the doctor said her arm might start throbbing tonight. She needs to keep it the same level as her body and that should minimize her discomfort. And she's going to be upset about Rick, so whatever you do…"

"Dixie," Katie interrupted, "I can handle it. Cal and I are like sisters. Go get her pillow and medicine so I can get out of here."

Dixie left the room just as John pulled up in his Suburban. Sean expected John to honk or come through the door. He was surprised when Callie came in. She hesitated for only a moment before she ran into Sean's arms crying.

"Daddy, Rick broke up with me."

"I know, baby. I'm sorry," Sean replied. He kissed his daughter on her head and held her closely. "I'm sorry about your arm, too, Cal. I never meant to hurt you."

"I know Daddy." Sensing his vulnerability, she asked, "Can we at least talk about me going to Northwestern?"

Sean cradled her tightly as he answered, "We'll talk tomorrow. Okay?"

Callie buried her face in her father's chest and bawled her heart out. Dixie came back with the pillow and a bottle of pills to witness a reunion she had only hoped for.

Katie whispered to Dixie, "I think everything's going to work out, Dix. I think it's going to be good." After walking up to her niece, Katie put her arm around her and said, "Come on, Callie. Let's go make us a root beer float."

After giving her father a crushing hug, Callie said, "Goodnight, Daddy." She then ran to Dixie's open arms and exchanged a hug with her. As she parted, she said, "Rick really was an asshole."

It would be days if not weeks before Callie came to grips with her true feelings about her ex-boyfriend. But for now, she seemed to be dealing with the situation as any eighteen year old would—denial.

SEAN AND DIXIE WATCHED as the Suburban pulled out of the driveway and turned left for the half-mile drive to John and Katie's home. They walked back into the house hand-in-hand. After closing the door, Dixie systematically went about the house turning off lights. She caught up with Sean at the door to their bedroom. He stood holding a bottle of wine.

"What's that?" Dixie asked, pointing at the bottle.

"It's the 1984 Sattui. Remember when we bought it?"

"I don't think I've ever had such a good time at a winery. Jesus, we were drunk."

"Me either. So, we said we'd save it for a special occasion. I think tonight makes the grade."

Dixie obviously agreed. "I'll draw the bath and light the candles. See you in a few minutes?"

"Be right there. I have to go get the Lalique goblets."

"Going all out, eh? Sounds good. Hey, I'm feeling a bit like a cowgirl tonight," Dixie said with a wink.

"I'm certain we can work something out," Sean replied, unable to conceal his smile.

Sean went to the dining room and retrieved the slender, crystal goblets from the china cabinet. As he walked past the porch, he saw the box with Kim's book lying open. He carefully packed it away and took it to his office where he left it lying squarely in the center of his desk. He put his hand on the box as he said, "Goodnight, Kim. I'll get back to you later."

A STRONG BREEZE MUST have broken off a limb that crashed loudly onto the roof over the master bedroom awakening Dixie. She reached over for Sean, only to find him gone and his side of the bed cold. The clock read just after three-thirty in the morning.

Dixie had performed this scene in her life's tragic play too many times. She slipped her pajamas and robe onto her naked body before going to Sean's office. Once again, there he was—asleep on the sofa. This time, it was Kim's book he had scattered about in several piles on the floor instead of documents related to the Fuller Brush Company. Quietly, she picked up Kim's book, and took it back to the bedroom.

Being careful not to confuse the stacks, Dixie quickly scanned through the pages reading snippets of the book, and looking for anything she might consider inflammatory or harmful to her or to Sean. Spending only about one-half hour reading the excerpts, nothing stood out to her until she came to a sealed envelope at the bottom of the box. Written across its face were the words, "My Dear Sean, Promise Me You Will Not Open This Envelope Before You Are Finished Reading My Book." Dixie couldn't resist the temptation, and certainly lacked Sean's allegiance to Kim. She sliced open the envelope with a nail file and read from the single page it contained.

"Oh, my God," Dixie said quietly to herself. "Sean will go crazy when he reads this."

It only took a moment for Dixie to decide what needed to be done. She found a blank sheet of paper, folded it, and placed it in a new envelope. She then sealed it, tucking the original envelope with the last page of Kim's book in the bottom of a box in her closet. Afterward, she returned Kim's book, in its various piles, to where she found it earlier. She looked at her husband as she thought, *I can't let her do this to you, Sean.*

Before leaving, she remembered a request from her father. He wanted to know the number Sean had called earlier that day when the two met at Sean's office. Dixie found Sean's phone, scrolled through the list of dialed-numbers, and jotted down the number in question on a scrap of paper.

Chapter 10

"SEAN, LEAVE THOSE FILTHY boots at the door," his mother shouted from the kitchen.

"What makes you think I haven't already taken them off," he replied. He began retracing his steps so he could take his snow-filled boots off and set them on the designated rug by the front door.

She peeked around the corner, catching him in his all too ineffective act of deception, and pulled her eyeglasses down disapprovingly on her nose.

"You're in trouble now," Kim said.

Sean wasn't aware Kim was at the house.

"How did you get here so early?"

"Things at the store were quiet because of the storm so your dad let me off work at three. I came right over to help Nadine with dinner."

"Chili?" Sean asked.

"Is this game night?" his mother answered.

Kim, Sean, and his parents went to every home hockey game. Tonight, Illinois was playing Loyola—always a good match-up. The precursor to all hockey games was Nadine's chili followed by hot apple cobbler. She and Kim had been perfecting the chili recipe since Sean and Kim began dating. The recipe had morphed to a quality deserving of the title *cuisine*. The smell permeating the household was wonderful, reinforcing what would become an indelible memory.

At eighteen, Kim acted like a daughter-in-law in almost every respect, and Nadine treated her every bit as one. It was one thing to be so special to Sean, but the bonus points came in that she revered Nadine like a mother and a friend. The two spent countless hours together in the company of Sean, but countless more in the company of each other. Sean's older sister, Kelly, was quite a bit his senior and had graduated college, married, and moved out of the house the summer before that fateful Sadie Hawkins Day. Kim filled a void left in Nadine's heart as much as Nadine filled a maternal void for Kim.

Skidding down the wood-floor hallway to greet Sean, Kim unabashedly wrapped her arms around him, kissing him on the lips. She was proud of her love for Sean and public displays of affection were commonplace. Putting her warm hands on Sean's cheeks for only a moment, he let out an approving sigh. In the winter months, Kim almost always wore any number of sweaters with the sleeves pulled down over her hands. She could extend her hands to perform tasks in an instant, then quickly retract them back into her sleeves. Cold hands were one thing she could not tolerate.

After making his way to the stove, Sean helped himself to several samples of the chili using the same wooden spoon his mother had cooked with for years. When he was younger, she had used it to paddle his butt on those frequent occasions a whipping was well-deserved. Few objects in the house had as much disparate sentimental value as that spoon.

"What do you think?" Kim asked.

"Okay, you changed it again, didn't you?" Sean replied.

Kim nodded and donned a coy smile as she asked, "What's different?"

"It's a lot spicier, I'll tell you that much," Sean replied. He took another taste.

Kim egged him on some more.

"A bit sweeter, too," he said, taking yet another.

She continued to push for more.

"The meat tastes different as well. So, maybe some more cayenne pepper, some brown sugar, and something about the meat I can't put my hands on."

Jubilantly, Kim said, "Almost got it. Yes, we spiced it up a notch or two, and, yes, we did throw in some brown sugar, but also molasses. As for the meat, Ben's dad gave us some venison sausage yesterday that was simply screaming to go into the chili. And last, but not least…" Kim reached behind the percolator for a brown paper bag, and pulled out an empty red wine bottle.

"Crap! How much did you put in this chili?" Sean asked.

Starting to laugh somewhat uncontrollably, Nadine replied, "Well we started with one cup of wine for the chili, then added a second, and then we had to drink the rest."

Kim put her arm around Nadine, and they both began singing an Engelbert Humperdinck tune into the bottle. By the time they got to the third verse, they were both laughing too hard to continue. It was then that Raymond arrived home from work to the sight of the mayhem in the kitchen.

"Uh oh. Sounds like Mom's been in the sauce again," he said.

"Dad, Mom got Kim blasted. Look at her."

"I see her. She'll be a cheap date if you keep bringing her here first."

Raymond gave Kim a kiss on the forehead, something he couldn't do at work where the relationship had to be purely professional. He then gave Nadine a warm hug and a swat on her rear end.

"I gotta wash my hands, then let's chow down. Game's in an hour," Raymond said, enthusiastically keeping everyone on task.

"I'll be right back, too," Nadine said as she, too, headed off to her upstairs bathroom. In her case, it was to put on lipstick. She always had to wear lipstick to dinner. Nobody ever understood why.

Putting her arms around Sean's waist, Kim said, "I want us to be like them in twenty-five years."

"I want to be like them now. Why wait?" Sean posed the question as he swatted her on the rear.

Spontaneously, Kim pulled up her sweater and blouse, flashing her breasts at Sean right there in the kitchen. Sean quickly kissed both of Kim's nipples while he had the chance. She soon regretted her indiscretion.

Fanning her sweater, Kim cried out quietly, "You must have had chili on your lips. My tits are burning off." Realizing both bathrooms were occupied, Kim grabbed a kitchen dish towel, ran it through cool water several times, then patted her breasts with it. All the while, Sean was laughing uncontrollably.

With a desperate look on her face, Kim said, "It's not funny, Sean." It was all she could do to not laugh at herself.

Before she was able to cool herself down completely, she heard both Nadine's and Raymond's footsteps approaching the kitchen. She quickly folded the towel and placed it back by the sink.

Raymond took his place at the table, and Nadine began serving. She grabbed Raymond's bowl, but before scooping any of her chili into it, noticed some unacceptable water stains. As it would happen, she grabbed the same towel Kim had just been rubbing across her nipples to wipe the spots off the bowl. At that point, Kim lost all control.

As she buried her face inside of her sweater while she laughed, Sean covered for her hysteria by saying, "Mom, don't give Kim any more wine. See what you did?"

Quick to acknowledge, Nadine replied, "I see what you mean. No more for her, that's for certain."

"Okay, everyone. Cut the crap. Game's in fifty-five minutes," Raymond reminded the revelers.

Once dinner was set, and all were at the table, Raymond asked, “Kimmie, would you say Grace, please. Maybe that’ll settle you down.”

And it did. Kim never took the Lord’s name in vain, and laughing during Grace would have been tantamount to blasphemy. After a lovely prayer, the four indulged themselves.

As usual, few words were exchanged as they devoured this week’s chili masterpiece. That is until Raymond had to say, “Damn good chili, girls. I don’t know what’s in it, but this is gold medal stuff.”

“If you’d excuse me…” Kim said. She bolted upstairs to the bathroom.

“Is she alright?” Nadine asked Sean.

The three could hear muffled laughter coming from the direction of where Kim was.

“I think something got her funny bone, and on top of that, you got her drunk. She’s probably embarrassed.”

“Tell her to get back down here,” Raymond said. “Laughter’s good and needs to be shared. Besides, the game’s in fifty minutes, and we need to get the show on the road.”

SEAN WENT UPSTAIRS TO fetch Kim. After knocking on the door, he let himself in. She was crying as she sat on a stool in front of the mirror.

“What’s wrong?” he asked.

"I just can't believe she's gone. I used to sit in this chair while Nadine would curl my hair for me. It's one of the many memories of her I'll never forget."

"Is everything alright?" The voice came from the doorway. It was Ben.

Suddenly, Sean realized the circumstances had changed. He looked at the reflection of himself and Kim in the mirror. They were much older now. Confused and having a difficult time understanding what was taking place, Sean excused himself and walked back downstairs to the living room. It was full of his family's friends and relatives…and Raymond. One person was noticeably missing—his mother. A woman with a young boy and girl in tow came up next to Sean. It was Dixie with Callie and Will.

"Does anyone know what's going on?" Sean asked the group.

The room fell silent.

"Seriously, what happened to my mother? I can't remember."

"She's okay. Find the Fuller Brush Man. He knows."

Sean turned around. It was Kim who had answered his question.

"What do you mean?"

"Sean, it's all about the Fuller Brush Man," she said, trying ever so hard to make him understand.

"Kim, I hear what you're saying, but I just don't get it."

"She's nuts, Sean," Dixie said, adding to the confusion.

"No, I'm not, Dixie!" Kim said. "When Sean finds the Fuller Brush Man, it will be good for you, too."

"Why do you care what's good for me?" Dixie asked Kim.

"To be honest with you Dixie, I don't care what's good for you…only Sean. But the reality is, what's good for him, will be good for you. Help him find the Fuller Brush Man, Dixie. It's your only hope."

"You know what I hope, Kim?" Dixie asked with a frightening look on her face. "I hope you die."

Defiantly, Kim replied, "Fine. Sean will find the Fuller Brush Man without you. Then you'll be sorry."

"I may be sorry, but you'll be dead…you'll be dead…you'll be dead…"

SEAN WOKE UP ONCE MORE. Sweat covered his body. His head pounded. Looking around the room to get his bearings, he saw the light of dawn out the window, and smelled coffee brewing. Creeping into the kitchen, he found Dixie sitting at the table. She was clearly upset.

"What am I supposed to think, Sean, when you go to bed with me, and wake up with your ex-girlfriend?"

"Dixie, she's dead. I fell asleep reading her book. She's not a threat."

"That's bullshit, Sean!" Dixie shouted as she slapped the table with the palm of her hand. "She was never a factor in our life until three days ago. Now, you might as well be having an affair with her. You're fixated. If there's anything good about this whole thing, she's created a diversion so that you're not thinking about that other matter I'm afraid to mention."

"You mean, Fuller Brush?"

Dixie gave Sean a disapproving look.

Taking a seat at the table with Dixie, Sean explained, "I've got news for you. I think there's a connection between, Kim, my mother, and the Fuller Brush Man."

Shaking her head, Dixie asked sarcastically, "You know this because?"

"I was having a dream. Mom had just died, and we were having a wake at the house. Kim was there, and she was trying so hard to tell me to find the Fuller Brush Man. She said he would help me…she said he would help us."

"Sean!!" Dixie shouted, so loudly it startled him. "Do you have any recall of the two of us together last night? Do you remember how nice it was to soak together in the bath; the wine; the candles; making love?" Dixie started to cry. "That was my husband. Can Kim help me find him? Because if she can't, I don't ever want to hear her name again, is that understood?"

Sean wouldn't respond.

Cautiously, Dixie said, "Honey, I know you're reading her book. But, I have to tell you I have this inexplicable feeling that she's out to hurt you."

"She wouldn't do that, Dix," Sean said, completely discounting her assertion. "You need to read the cover letter she sent.

It comes across fairly negative at first. But when April talked to me about it…"

"April?!"

There was no question that Dixie was lit up by the fact that Sean had covered intimate territory in Kim's book with April first, before discussing it with her. He knew matters were about to go from bad to worse.

Dixie stood up, tried to speak, but was only able to put her hands up in front of her. With great effort, she finally managed to say, "Not only am I subordinate to your dead, ex-girlfriend. It appears I'm subordinate to your current, live one, too."

"Dixie, April's just a…"

"A what, Sean? It doesn't matter what you call her. She's replaced me as your friend and confidant. I assume you've taken her to bed, too."

"Dixie, stop this…"

"That would explain so much, you know? Is all this Fuller Brush crap just a smoke screen so you can communicate with her via computer all night long? You're doing everything possible to drive me away from you so that when she finally makes her move, you'll be more than happy to run to her and away from me. For that matter, I'll be happy to see you go. Is that the plan?"

"Dixie, you need to let me talk…"

"No, Sean. You've had plenty of chances to talk. I'll make this real simple for you. I'm moving back to Mom and Dad's for a while. That'll give you time to sort out where you are in your relationships with Kim, April, and the fucking Fuller Brush Man. Callie can stay with me. You have free reign of the house."

Dixie grabbed her purse and car keys.

"Where are you going?"

"I'm going to John and Katie's for a while until I can figure out how to tell Daddy what's going on. I'll be back for my clothes at nine. Don't be here. If you are, I'll call the police."

Dressed only in her pajamas and robe, Dixie bolted out the door, slamming it on the way out. If Sean had an ounce of gallantry in his body at that moment, he would have done whatever it took to stop her from leaving. As it was, he sat in the chair wondering how the Fuller Brush Man could possibly help him out of this mess.

Chapter 11

AS SEAN WAS DRIVING to work, his phone rang a familiar tone that was uniquely identified with April. Finding a safe place to pull over, he answered the call.

"Good morning. What has you calling so early?"

"I need to let you know something," April replied with a cautious tone in her voice.

"What's that?"

"I just got a call from Shirley over at the main office. Frank's called a meeting at an undisclosed location that includes Frank Junior, John, and Stephen."

"And it was an oversight that I'm not requested to attend?"

"She said you were deliberately left out. Get this—Rabinowitz is going to be there."

Marvin Rabinowitz was the attorney for the Group. He was, for all practical purposes, owned by Frank. This wasn't good.

"Well April, it looks like the coup de grâce is underway. I'm sure Frank's looking for a way to tie my hands behind my back and put a noose around my neck."

"That's not all," April continued.

"I'm sitting in a parked car. Hit me with it."

"Frank offered me a job this morning. He called me about thirty minutes ago and said he'd give me a twenty-five percent raise to come work directly for him in some poorly-defined corporate promotions capacity."

"What did you tell him?"

"I told him 'no,' of course. I worked for him once. I'm not about to do it again. Why would he offer me a job, Sean?"

Looking back at the morning's discourse with Dixie, Sean hypothesized, "I'm pretty sure it has to do with Dixie. Are you alone?"

"Yeah, what's wrong with Dixie?"

"She and I had an argument this morning. She's moving out of the house and in with Frank and Suzanne temporarily."

"Sean, I'm so sorry. You mean you're separated?"

The lightness in April's voice didn't match the words of concern coming out of her mouth. Sean thought perhaps it was the phone connection.

"I guess you could say we're separated, though I really don't like using that term."

"What's going on, if I may ask?"

Sean knew he had to level with her as it was now affecting her life, too.

"Dixie is having a lot of issues with my behavior. She doesn't like my obsession with the Fuller Brush Man…"

"What obsession with the Fuller Brush Man?" April asked.

It occurred to Sean at that moment that he'd never divulged to her any of his torment concerning the Fuller Brush Man. He'd always disguised his fascination as issues with his mother's death.

"It's a very long story, April…a very troublesome story."

Without hesitation, April said, "I'd love to talk with you about it sometime."

Sean stood before the door to April's heart once more. This time he pushed it open slightly.

"I suppose we could do that. But therein lays yet another problem I'm having with Dixie."

"And that is…?"

After balking for a moment, Sean answered, "She thinks there's something going on between you and me."

Without so much as a pause, April asked, "Is there?"

Having not immediately denied the plausibility, April decisively cast herself as a suitor. Sean found himself shaking nervously, just as he had so many times when Kim had pushed him into uncharted territory.

"Maybe there is, April. I've never thought about you that way before." After giving April his answer, Sean realized it was a lie.

"I'd love to talk with you about us some time as well."

Moving onto the next topic as quickly as he could, Sean continued, "Then there's the matter of Kim's book. I'm glued to it, and Dixie can't accept my emotions about the book or my past relationship with Kim. When she found out you had read part of the book to me, that was the final straw and she told me she was leaving."

"Would you like me to go with you to the funeral? I feel I can relate to Kim very well. We have something in common—your well-being. I love the way she writes, and I'd love to help you along as you read it."

Sean was so glad at that moment he'd had sense enough to be having this conversation while sitting in a parked car. Had that not been the case, he most certainly would have driven into something.

"You'd do that for me?"

A firm 'no, thank you' from Sean was the appropriate response if there truly was nothing for Dixie to be worried about. April was as close now as ever to crossing the very threshold that had concerned Dixie.

Like a gazelle running from a cheetah, Sean said, "I'm going to give Berkowitz a call today. I think I need to speak with him before I use you in that manner."

"Good idea," April replied. "He should have an opening. In light of what's taking place between you and Dixie, I already cancelled my appointment for this afternoon so I could be available to you."

Sean found April's remark all too peculiar. He had just told her of their falling-out. *Why would she have already changed her appointment?* He wondered.

"Did you bring the book with you?" April asked.

"Uh...yeah. Why?"

"Maybe we can read some at lunch. Did you read any yesterday after work?"

"A lot of things happened yesterday after work," Sean replied, thinking of all that had truly transpired. "Did you say you changed your appointment because of the fight Dixie and I had this morning?"

There was a short pause before April answered, "No, silly. You just told me about that. What I meant to say was I knew you would be bothered by what Frank was up to." Not waiting to hear if Sean had a response, April wrapped up the conversation with, "Hey, I have to see a customer. I'll catch you after a bit."

"Okay. I'll be at the office in twenty minutes or so."

"Great. And Sean, we'll get through this. It's just a bump in the road. And one last thing, don't ever think that you're using me. I don't see us that way."

SHE DISCONNECTED BEFORE SEAN could muster a response, which was just as well because he was completely out of words for April at that point. In fact, he was so flustered that April was so forthcoming about her feelings, and that he did absolutely nothing to ward her off, he decided to give Berkowitz a call before he did anything else. In doing so, at least he could say to himself he was trying to work out his problems, and, more importantly, remain faithful to Dixie.

After fishing the note with Berkowitz' number from his wallet, Sean reluctantly dialed it. Expecting to get voice mail so that he could leave a message, he was completely caught off guard when a human voice answered.

"This is Doctor Berkowitz."

Sean didn't reply.

"This is Doctor Berkowitz. Is anyone there?"

Sean disconnected. He sat in his car, debating if he should try calling again. Finally, deciding he didn't have the guts to call a therapist after all, he put his car in drive and started to leave when his phone rang. Reflexively, he answered the call without first looking to see who it was.

"Hello?"

"Yes, this is Sterling Berkowitz. Did you just try to call me?"

Sean braked to a stop and put the vehicle in park before replying, "Uh, yes. I did."

"Fine, then. Did you want to speak with me?"

"Well, until about sixty seconds ago, yes, I did."

"With whom am I speaking?" the doctor asked.

"My name is Sean…Sean Marcum."

"Oh, yes. April's friend. She told me to expect a call from you. How can I help?"

Sean was uncomfortable with the thought that a therapist was anticipating his call.

"I've been having some issues, and we thought I should speak with a Specialist such as you."

"That's always good. Tell me, Sean. Do *you* think you should speak with a Specialist? You said *we*, and I'm not certain that is inclusive of *you*."

"To be honest with you, I've never spoken with a therapist before, and I'm quite uncertain about the whole thing."

"That's understandable. One must develop a trusting relationship with his or her therapist, and that requires effort on the part of both. I'm willing to give you a shot. Are you willing to give me the same benefit?"

"I guess I could," Sean replied without commitment.

"Well, Sean, here's how I reach out to my clients. The first visit is free. I feel it's important to break the ice and maybe hit on some high-level subjects, but not necessarily dig real deep. I find that too presumptive if I push hard on a first-time client. That said, whereas my follow up visits are typically one hour, my first visit is two. I find the first hour is sort of like a first date—we talk about the weather, one's taste in food, and household pets, instead of all the things we are truly interested in discussing."

"I can see how that might be the case," Sean answered.

"What are you doing at two-thirty this afternoon?"

"Uh…I guess I'm sitting down with you?"

"Excellent. I look forward to it. Do you know where I'm located?"

Sean didn't know, but he was familiar with the office building Berkowitz described on the access road of the highway near the dealership. There was some degree of comfort for Sean knowing

Berkowitz' office was away from his normal route of travel home so there might be less of a chance anyone might see him there.

"Alright, Sean. You have a great day, and I'll see you this afternoon."

SEAN'S EMPLOYEES RECEIVED HIM just as cautiously as they had the prior morning. It was clear his role today would be to make little more than an appearance, then tuck himself away in his office. He owed Ben a quick call to confirm he had received Kim's book, but the conversation, as he would soon find out, took longer than he expected.

Ben answered his phone after four or five rings, "Hello?"

"Ben, it's Sean."

"Did you get the box I sent you?"

"As a matter of fact, it arrived yesterday. I intended to call you, but I got sidetracked. Did you know it was her book?"

"Of course I did. I watched her wrap it in tissue paper and place it in the box."

Wondering why Ben had been so secretive about it in the first place, Sean asked, "Have you read it?"

"Sean, Kim labored over the damn thing for almost three decades. I could probably recite it chapter and verse—except for the end. She kept that part to herself. You know she never got over how you and Dixie betrayed her."

"I see that now. I thought she'd moved on. I mean, we were able to talk and be civil all these years."

"There was a lot of hidden pain, Sean. You'll never know how much."

Still in denial, Sean asked, "Why didn't you tell me?"

"Sean, I'm not in the mood to make your memory of Kim fit your wish. It is what it is."

"Then tell me, Ben, what's your memory like of me? What do you think of my life? She used words like mediocre and miserable."

"I think she was being generous."

"Really?" Sean replied, upset by Ben's answer. "How long have you felt this way?"

"Since that day you screwed Dixie at the hospital."

"That's a fairly narrow event to judge a person by, don't you think?"

"Sean, you sucked, man. I happened to be driving home from class that day when I saw Kim leaning up against a tree on Pennsylvania Avenue, crying and barfing her guts out. I stopped to see if she was sick, and she told me what had happened. Don't tell me how to judge you. You weren't there to see what you did to her. I was."

If Sean was looking for support in his conversation with Ben, it hadn't happened yet.

"Ben, her book seems to be some fictional tale about a guy that sounds a little like me who is making all the wrong choices in life. I'm struggling to see the connection between me and what she's saying."

"Jesus, Sean. You're so frickin' blind. The guy in that book is one hundred percent you."

"So what's the point of the story?"

"Read it, Sean! That was Kim's request. I thought she was very clear."

"So reading her book is going to solve all of my problems? Don't you think that's perhaps giving her a little too much power?"

There was a long pause during which Sean wondered if Ben had disconnected.

"Sean, Kim told me you might react this way. She said if it became necessary, I was to tell you the following. Are you listening? Because, I'm only going to tell you this one time."

"Hey, I'm all ears."

"She said you came to her six or seven years ago and asked her about something your mother wrote in her journal. You couldn't figure out what it meant, and you hoped she could shed some light on the matter. Do you recall that discussion?"

"Yes, as if it was yesterday."

"And what did she say?"

"She told me my mother intended to send me a message at some point during her final days. She said it wouldn't necessarily be straight forward, but it was up to me to solve the riddle. In doing so, I'd find true happiness."

"And have you solved the mystery?"

"No."

"Have you found happiness?"

"I'm not unhappy, Ben."

"Answer my question as it was asked, Sean."

"No, alright? I'm not happy. I'm upset as hell that I can't figure this thing out. It's tearing me up."

"Exactly, and it bothered the hell out of Kim that you perpetually missed every opportunity to come to grips with what your mother was telling you."

"Did Kim know what she was trying to tell me?"

"Yes."

"Are you going to tell me?"

"No, Sean. In any case, she never completely disclosed to me what the message was. She did say there was a common thread between her book and your mother's journal, and that at some point it would become immediately obvious to you."

"Does it have something to do with the Fuller Brush Man? Can you at least tell me that much?"

"Read her book, Sean."

Sean was more frustrated now than before his call, but he knew he'd pushed Ben hard enough.

"When will you be here, Sean? You're still coming, right?"

"Yes. I'm leaving tomorrow."

"Are you bringing Dixie?" Ben asked. The tone of his voice telegraphed his desired answer.

"No. To tell you the truth, Ben, Dixie and I are separated."

There was a pause in the conversation as Ben struggled for a proper response. He finally offered an unbelievable, "Sorry to hear that. When did this happen?"

"Just this morning. I don't think it's permanent. I'm going to seek some professional help, and, hopefully, that will resolve some of my issues."

"For what it's worth, Sean, Kim really wanted you and Dixie to be happy. She hoped you would be as content someday as we were. I'd like to see that, too."

"Thanks, Ben. Hey, I got the picture you wanted. It turned out to be spectacular."

"Great. I can't wait to see it. Call me when you get into town. Do you want to get together for dinner or something?"

"Let's play it by ear. I need to hook up with Will and his new girlfriend. I think there may be a wedding in their future, so I want to get to know her as soon as I can."

"Shit. That's hard to believe, man. To think at one time you and I were making forts in snow drifts together. Now our kids are going to college and getting married."

"I know. It's all happening so fast. See you tomorrow."

"Bye."

Chapter 12

FOLLOWING HIS PHONE CALL with Ben, Sean spent virtually all of his time at the office reading more of *The Road to Monticello*. Try as he might, the hidden meaning of Kim's book and any connection to his mother's journal remained elusive. He probably would have given up had it not been for April's patient analysis of the book.

Initially, Sean hesitated to bring April in on any more of the book. The content had become highly revealing and deeply personal, and Sean felt that level of exposure would deepen the intimacy April was beginning to feel for him and vice-versa. But she was persistent, and, in truth, he found a great deal of comfort in her presence. When it finally came time for Sean's appointment, he thanked April for her insight, then set out for Berkowitz' office.

DR. BERKOWITZ WAS A very unassuming individual. He stood a little shorter than Sean—less than six feet tall—and had a full beard he'd obviously been grooming for many years. His lips looked almost plastic as they pushed through the salt-and-pepper brown whiskers. He had either lost weight or didn't know how to choose the correct pant size, for his Dockers were probably two sizes too large.

On his feet were a pair of loafers, the style of which Sean hadn't seen in probably twenty years. He wore a flannel shirt several months before that degree of covering was needed, and, over that, had on a tan, tweed coat. His shirt collar was held together with a bowtie fashioned after two fish heads joined at the knot. All in all, the bespectacled psychologist wouldn't win any award for best-dressed, but then, that wasn't what he was being paid for.

His office was utilitarian—a chair for him, two additional matching chairs of another style presumably for a client or the occasional couple, a coffee table, and bookshelves with a clutter of book titles Sean had never heard of which looked entirely too academic to be enjoyable reads. One entire side of the office was glass, but a privacy fence prevented a clear view of what would have been a parking lot and the passing highway. The removal of what would have been a distraction was undoubtedly a good thing.

"Sean, it's good to meet you," Berkowitz said as he met his new client at the door of his bare-bones waiting room.

"The pleasure's mine…I hope," Sean replied.

Pointing a finger at Sean and with raised eyebrows as bushy as spring caterpillars, Berkowitz said, "Ah! Humor! I like that in a person, especially when I am about to extract their brain."

Not exactly a reassuring response, but it was quickly apparent Berkowitz wasn't going to be an *I ask—you answer* kind of therapist.

"Come right in and have a seat over here," he said, pointing at the matching deep blue, cloth-covered, plush chairs. Sean took a seat in what seemed to be a chair of Scandinavian design.

Berkowitz sat down, and fell into what appeared to be a comfortable position with his legs crossed. Sean was unable to get comfortable in spite of the posh upholstering that obviously went into making his chair.

Trying to deflect his nervousness, Sean asked, "Aren't you going to need a note pad to write on?"

Turning his palms up to display his empty hands, Berkowitz replied, "If you are concerned about my ability to retain data, I noticed as I glanced out the door, you arrived in a black 2007 Toyota with what I assume is an Illinois vanity license plate, DAMSAM1 and a Lake County tax sticker in the window. You have hazel colored eyes that are tinted blue with contact lenses, a shirt most likely from JC Penney's, a thirty-six inch belt wrapped around a one hundred eighty-five pound, six-foot, one-inch frame, and a tailor-made suit—probably from Siegfried's in Mundelein. I have one just like it. A note pad? I don't need a note pad."

"Point made," Sean said, clearly unable to challenge the man's acute ability for details.

"Also, your tax sticker expires at the end of this month," Berkowitz added with a sly grin.

"Yes, thank you for pointing that out."

"DAMSAM? That can be interpreted in several ways, I presume. Are they initials?"

"Right, DAM is Dixie A. Marcum, and SAM is Sean A. Marcum."

"Clever. That would mean Dixie's initials before she took your name were DAD—which I suspect is a reflection of her father's indelible handprint upon her."

"Do you know Frank?" Sean asked.

"But of course. The Darlings are a well known family—'Darling Deals from Darling Motors.' Wasn't that the jingle in the late eighties?"

"Can you recite the preamble to the Constitution?"

"No, who reads that nonsense. I stick to important details. You had a new advertisement on television last night. *Back to school* was the theme."

"Well, I'm glad it made an impression on you. Are you in the market to buy a car?"

"No. Not for another six or eight years anyway. That's Dixie in the commercial and, I suspect, given the uncanny resemblance, your daughter Callie. Am I correct?"

"Right again."

"They're very natural in front of the camera. I study such things—the content of the commercial is secondary or tertiary in significance to me. But the performance is of utmost importance."

"You make me wonder if I'm wasting money on commercials."

"If you're trying to sell me a car, you most certainly are. On the other hand, my wife likes a new car now and then. But she wants a Volvo, and Darling doesn't sell that brand."

Sean perked up as he said, "Give me nine months, and I'll be selling Volvos and BMWs."

"Expanding, are you? Business must be good."

"My business is good."

"You said that with a certain degree of pride, and a bit of arrogance."

"When you're good, you're entitled to a little arrogance."

"Does your success create a little, how should I say it, tension between you and your brothers-in-law?"

"Damn right it does."

"And how does that make you feel?"

The smile on Sean's face gave Berkowitz his answer.

"You're my hero, Sean," Berkowitz said, raising his clenched fists into the air. "So far, we've determined you're in the fortieth percentile for weight and waist size, the eightieth percentile for height, you're expanding your very successful business as you rub your nemesis' noses in it, you have good taste in men's clothing, a lovely daughter and wife, and you have a Volvo customer waiting in the wings. Your only problem is your Lake County tax sticker is about to expire. What the hell are you doing here?"

By now, Sean was comfortable enough with the setting, and Berkowitz' demeanor, that he wanted to air all of his problems.

"Try this on for size," he began. "I'm haunted by the Fuller Brush Man, the twentieth anniversary of my mother's death is right around the corner, my old college girlfriend and wife of my best friend passed away this week, and her funeral is Tuesday as is a fundraiser my overbearing father-in-law has arranged for our dear Senator Bogenkamp. On top of that, Frank is trying to run me out of business, my wife left me this morning, I accidentally broke my daughter's arm the night before last, and that same college-bound coed is trying to empty my pockets of my last dollar. Finally, my son may have a chance to be his own man and become a businessman in his own right, and might get married to a lovely French girl, providing he doesn't get ambushed by his grandfather."

"Fantastic!" Berkowitz said. "It's the perfect storm, isn't it? We could spend months, maybe years dealing with all of these issues. Oh, by the way, you failed to mention the *other woman* in your life."

"I didn't mention there was another woman," Sean said suspiciously.

"I see," Berkowitz replied. "You've discussed none of these matters with anyone other than your wife? That's quite impressive, Sean. Most men would have found at least one soul—usually a lonely and beautiful woman—with whom to speak. After all, yours is quite a considerable burden, don't you agree?"

It was evident to Sean that the good doctor could see straight through him and his tailor-made suit from Siegfried's.

"I'm quite fond of April," Sean admitted. It was the first time he'd said anything along those lines, and he found a certain relief in expressing these words. "But that doesn't mean we're having an affair."

Berkowitz sat motionless, looking at Sean and expecting him to give up a little more information about that relationship.

"She's a great listener," Sean continued. "When I speak with her, she hears what I am saying. I can tell by the way she interacts and the look in her eyes. We have this…connection."

"I see. And when you discuss these matters with Dixie, do you get the same connection?"

"I think she wants to connect her right fist to my jaw. I really don't go into a lot of detail with her about these subjects anymore."

"Well, that certainly paints an interesting landscape—a storm on one edge of the painting, sunshine on the other, and a man in the middle. Which way do you suppose that man wants to run?"

Looking down somewhat embarrassed, Sean replied, "Toward April…I mean the sunshine."

"What do you think will happen to the storm if he does that?" Berkowitz asked.

"Oh, it would probably get so big, it would consume the entire painting," Sean surmised.

"Tell me, Sean, under what circumstances would that man turn toward the storm?"

"I guess if he's convinced he has to confront all of his demons, he might do that."

"Is there any way he might find happiness if he turns and runs toward the sunshine?"

"You mean, if he takes the easy way out? No, the demons will eventually catch him."

"You use the word 'demons.' That's very interesting. Why did you choose that word?"

"Because these things are tearing me up inside. They're destroying my life and the relationships I have with the people I love. They're ever-present and beginning to join together into one giant, fucking problem…excuse my language."

"No, that's okay. I would have used the adjective 'giant,' too," Berkowitz said, putting Sean at ease with a dose of humor. "You mentioned many things that trouble you Sean. Is there any relevance to the order in which you mentioned them?"

"I know this sounds crazy, but I think my problems are tied to my obsession with the Fuller Brush Man."

"Is this a person? Are you speaking of those men who used to sell products door-to-door years ago?"

"You remember them?"

"But of course. I'm older than you. I was born in '52, and you were born in '55."

"I didn't tell you when I was born. How do you know that?"

"I'm sure it showed up at one point or another in the society section of the Trib. Your birthday is July 5th."

"I hope you don't mind me saying this, but you're penchant for personal details is a bit creepy."

"Really? I have certain attributes of a savant, and I love to absorb trivia for playback at later times. I'm also a forensic psychologist, so I make a living memorizing personal attributes and categorizing people. I find doing so keeps me mentally sharp."

"So, you profile people. I thought that was frowned upon."

"Oh, Sean, surely you don't think profiling is a vulgar pastime of wayward law enforcement personnel? It's quite a tool. I'm not a stalker, mind you. Frank's birthday is June 6, 1932. Dixie's is May 29, 1956. Senator Bogenkamp was born in Louisville, Kentucky on December 19th, 1940. Oh, and I neglected to mention earlier, your left-rear tire looks low—probably about twenty-six pounds. Toyota recommends thirty-two for that tire on that vehicle, as does Bridgestone."

"What cologne am I wearing?" Sean asked, testing Berkowitz ability for observation.

"I'm not quite sure if you're wearing any at all. It's masked by the faint scent of Ungaro perfume—the same perfume often worn by our mutual acquaintance, April."

April had given Sean a long, cheek-to-cheek hug as he left for his appointment. Some of her perfume must have transferred to him during that moment of intimate contact. If it was noticeable to Berkowitz, it would certainly be noticeable to Dixie. Both the doctor and Sean had this same epiphany. Fortunately, Berkowitz didn't belabor the point but for one comment.

"It appears you turned toward sunshine today. Let's think before doing that again, shall we?" He paused, then followed with, "Now, back to the Fuller Brush Man. Tell me about this."

FOR THE NEXT HOUR, Sean proceeded to enlighten Berkowitz about Nadine's journal and her final words, his obsession with those words and his determination to discover their meaning, and his recent dream in which Kim had told him to find the Fuller Brush Man. Sean gave him detail ad nauseam, thinking perhaps Berkowitz' proclivity for connecting the dots might enable him to shed some light on the matter. He also gave Berkowitz his summation thus far of *The Road to Monticello.* As Sean spoke, the psychologist offered little insight, providing only occasional words that encouraged Sean to elaborate on something he had just said. When Sean seemed to finally come to an end for the time being, Berkowitz offered his thoughts.

"You've told me a lot, Sean. Let me make this observation, if I may. I sense that you found the separation from your mother, after you and Dixie got married and moved to the suburbs, quite troublesome."

"I've always regretted moving away from Urbana. I never realized how much I would miss it until I no longer lived there."

"What do you call home? Urbana or Lake Forest?"

"Urbana, of course."

"Even after all these years? Certainly you realize you have lived *away* from Urbana longer than you lived *in* Urbana."

"I still would call Urbana home."

"Which do you miss more—your mother or the town?"

"I'd have to give that some thought. I miss them both."

"That's fine. Now, let me ask you this. I sense you found the separation from Kim also quite troublesome."

"I really screwed her over, Doc."

"That's not an answer to my question. How did you feel about that separation?"

"She was a huge part of my life. I left that behind, and Dixie didn't fill the void."

"Dixie didn't fill it, or you wouldn't let her?"

"She didn't fill it. I gave her plenty of opportunity."

"Why is it *her* responsibility to bring *you* happiness?"

Sean thought about Berkowitz' question for a long time. He knew this was the point at which he needed to take ownership of his problems and not pass them on to someone else. With great reluctance, Sean answered the question. "I suppose it's not up to her."

Not thrilled by Sean's answer, Berkowitz suggested, "I suppose you loved your mother a great deal."

Somewhat bitter, Sean said, "No, I loved her a lot. There was nothing to 'suppose' about it."

"And I suppose you miss Kim a great deal, too."

Sean realized what Berkowitz was getting at, and said, "Alright, it is not up to Dixie to bring me happiness."

Berkowitz grinned, having made his point.

"Certain words, Sean, are like lightning rods to me. 'Suppose' is just one. You'll encounter more as we continue to meet. Suppose lacks commitment…focus. You need to take a stand, grow some balls, I don't know, pick your favorite euphemism, but please steer clear of this namby-pamby stuff."

Without encouragement from Berkowitz, Sean said, "I think April wants to bring happiness into my life."

"Let me suggest to you, Sean, that April is quickly becoming a victim in this situation. You have a need, she has a need, and what either of you has to offer to the other at this time will surely result in a great deal of trouble. All I can do is implore upon you to keep her at arm's length for now, and that doesn't mean having your hands on the cheeks of her ass. Use the following litmus test—if Dixie saw April and me doing X-Y-Z, she would…? If you can honestly say she wouldn't care, then have at it. I suspect right now that's a very short list. You definitely don't want to invite her out for a drink, and you absolutely don't want to use her as a sounding board, as much as that might bring you comfort."

Disagreeing with Berkowitz, Sean said, "She's offered to accompany me to Kim's funeral."

Shaking his head, the doctor countered, "No, Sean. She's invited you to divorce your wife and marry her. Attending Kim's funeral is step two. Step one was lending you a compassionate ear as the two of you read Kim's book."

"No, she's not that way, Dr. Berkowitz. She really is a friend."

"Oh, pul-ease, Sean, don't insult me that way. Okay, consider this. What would Kim say if you were to show up at her funeral with April instead of Dixie?"

"She's dead, Doc. She won't care."

"Nonsense!" Berkowitz insisted. "She's more alive in your heart today than she was a week ago. You know damn well Kim would disapprove of April at this point. That's not to say April can't be a part of your life to some degree today, and who knows, the two of you may become man and wife someday. But, now is not the time to replace the love once extended to you by Kim and your mother, with that of April. That's not fair to her, and you'll never understand what you have been searching for all these years."

Sean ran his hands over his face and through his hair as the intensity of the discussion began to hit home. The doctor picked up on this.

"I think we've discussed enough for one day," Berkowitz said. "What do you think?"

Reflecting on the previous hour and a half, Sean agreed. "I'm exhausted. I'll be going over this in my mind all night."

"Let me end by suggesting a couple of things. I think you blame Dixie for taking you away from Kim and your mother. The fact that your old sweetheart and your mother were so close only makes the torment that much worse. Not only did they lose you, to a large degree they lost each other. That weighs heavily on you, doesn't it? For in the final analysis, it's not Dixie who was ultimately responsible for your actions. It was you."

After deliberating whether or not to admit it, Sean said, "You're absolutely correct, Doc. I shouldn't have made Dixie the culprit all these years."

"A second point I wish to make. I used the word 'blame' a moment ago for impact. From now on, it joins 'suppose' in the collection of words to be stricken from our vocabulary. You're sorting matters out and learning about yourself. The goal is for you to walk away with a new view of your life and your place in the lives of others. If we accomplish that, we can call our time together a success."

"Fair enough."

"Finally, I have an assignment—I always end with homework, if you will."

"What's that?"

"Two things. First, at our next session, I want you to tell me what you feel about Mark in Kim's book. Think hard about the answer, as I won't accept some trite response. Second, if you could say one thing to Kim today, what would it be?"

"You don't want to talk about the Fuller Brush Man?" Sean asked, disappointed that subject might not be on the agenda the next time they spoke.

"Think of this as a math problem, Sean. I see the Fuller Brush Man as the product in this equation. We're searching for the multiplier and the multiplicand. If we find those, we'll quickly have the answer you've been looking for."

SEAN LEFT BERKOWITZ' OFFICE exhausted, but hopeful. He wanted nothing more than to get home so he could read more of the *Road.* Quickly leaving, he pulled onto the freeway just as he heard the beeping of his cell phone indicating he had missed phone calls. Instead of leaving well enough alone, he decided uncharacteristically to listen to four voice-messages as he drove.

His phone announced the first message: "Dad, it's Will. Hey, I know you're coming down for Kim's funeral. Giselle and I want to talk to you about something over dinner. We're cooking at our place. Let me know what days you'll be here so we can set something up. Take care. Oh, and sorry about Kim."

His phone announced the second message: "Sean," it was April, "I just wanted to tell you that if you want to talk about your session with Berkowitz, I'm available. I'll be leaving the office early today, so give me a call if you want. The first meeting can leave your head spinning. Also, let me know if you want to take me up on my offer to go with you to the funeral. The offer still stands. Call me. Bye."

The third message was from Frank: "Sean, the Executive Committee met this morning to discuss your recent behavior. Jameson and Rabinowitz were both present as was Dixie. It's been decided that I will take over day-to-day management of your dealerships until our next E-C at the end of September. No need for you to make an announcement. I'll do that first thing tomorrow morning. Get your shit together."

Sean expected Frank's actions. Nonetheless, he was livid. He pressed and held the button to delete the message for several seconds longer than was necessary. Finally Sean came to the last voice message. This one, too, was from Frank: "By the way, Sean, I spoke with your friend Sam Ricci today. I told him about your drinking problem, your emotional instability, the court order keeping you from your daughter whose arm you broke, and lastly your separation from Dixie. He said he's no longer interested in providing you with the capital you need to start up Volvo and BMW. He did say, however, he was very interested in working with me. I'll give you a private tour of my new dealerships a week before our grand opening. You have a terribly nice day, Sean."

Pressing the accelerator, Sean raced past eighty miles-per-hour as he threw his phone against the windshield of his car. He was beside himself with anger. Just then, his phone, which had landed on the floor of the front passenger seat, rang with April's tone. He had to speak with her. After reaching down to pick it up, he sat upright just in time to see a wall of brake lights—four lanes of stopped traffic not more than a hundred feet ahead. In a last, desperate attempt to avoid slamming into the rear of the stopped vehicles, Sean pulled his car sharply to the right. He felt the wheels on the right side leaving the ground, and soon his car was rolling...once...then twice...then over and over down an embankment. Sean recalled landing hard in some bushes, then blacking out.

THE SOUND OF SIRENS rings peculiar to a person when they come about as result of what you have just done. Sean slowly opened his eyes to see several strangers hovering over him and holding his body in such a way that he couldn't move.

"Looks like he's coming around," one of the paramedics said. "Sir, try not to move. You've been in an accident, and we need to take you to a hospital."

Sean had seen enough hospitals for one week, and he wasn't about to go this time. As he tried to sit up, he was met by equal resistance from several rescuers who insisted that he remain stationary.

"Let me up!" As he struggled, he felt intense pain in his back and his right chest wall. He also felt the blood that was running from his forehead into his left eye and down the side of his head. It was quickly apparent to him that struggling was not in his best interest. When he opened his eyes again, he saw a familiar face—that of April's.

"Are you alright?"

"April? What happened?"

"You rolled your car down the side of the highway. People who saw the wreck and stopped to help say you got thrown out through the sunroof and just missed getting run over by your own car. You landed over here, and you've been unconscious for ten or fifteen minutes."

"Sir, were you wearing your seatbelt?" asked one of the medics.

"I always wear a seatbelt," Sean answered.

"Sir, we don't see any marks from a seatbelt. It doesn't appear that you were wearing one. Do you know where you are?"

Sadly, Sean was disoriented by his unusual route during this journey, and he gave the medic the name of his normal route home instead of his present location.

"Do you know your name?"

Again, Sean was confused by his previous discussion with Berkowitz that was still fresh on his mind and told the medic his name was Mark.

"This guy's out of it. He's going," one of the medics called out to several firefighters who proceeded to get a stretcher out of a waiting ambulance.

"I'm not going anywhere!"

"Sean!" April called out. "You have to go the hospital, okay? Listen to these guys. They're only trying to help you. You could be seriously hurt. Now go with them, please. Do it for me."

Sean could see the anguish in April's face, and he wasn't able to think straight enough to fend off the rescuers any longer.

"Alright," he finally said.

"Ma'am, do you know this person?" a highway patrol officer asked.

"Yes, I work for him," April answered.

"Is he Sean Marcum from Lake Forest?" the trooper asked, looking at Sean's driver's license.

"Yes, sir," April replied.

"Do you know his family?"

"Of course, I know all of them."

"Would you do me a favor and make contact with them? I'd like you to inform them of the accident and that he'll be taken to the hospital."

"Sure. I'll call his wife right now." April looked at Sean. He appeared to be losing consciousness again. "Sean, if you can hear me, I'm going to call Dixie. Okay?"

SEAN SQUEEZED APRIL'S HAND. She wasn't sure what that meant, but under the circumstances, she had no alternative but to phone Dixie. After several rings, April's call went to Dixie's voice mail. She left a short message, then proceeded to phone John. Before long, John answered the call.

"Hello?"

"John, this is April Knudsen."

"What's up?"

"Hey, I'm out here on the Tri-State. Sean's been involved in a bad rollover accident, and they're taking him to the hospital right now."

"Jesus! How bad is he?"

"It looks bad, John. I don't know. He's in and out of consciousness, and when he's awake he's not making any sense. He got thrown out of the car through its sunroof."

"Holy shit! Does Dixie know?"

"No, I tried calling, but all I got was her voice mail."

"Okay, I'll get in touch with her. She's at Frank's. We'll be there as soon as we can."

"Thanks, John. I'll see you at the hospital."

No sooner had April finished her call than rescuers finished immobilizing Sean on a board with a stiff collar around his neck and an oxygen mask over his bloody face. She tried to get one last word with him, but she was held back by several firefighters who advised her that the medics needed to leave right away. As she stood watching the ambulance leave, she felt something blow up against her leg. It was a sheet of paper. It only took a second for April to realize the box containing Kim's book had been thrown out the sunroof along with Sean, and its contents were blowing about along the edge of the road. Quickly engaging a group of bystanders and emergency workers, April and the others set out collecting all the pages they could find. After twenty minutes or so, April was able to account for every page of the book, though some were tattered and torn or stained by blood, mud or footprints. She even found the envelope that contained the last page. She felt a sense of relief knowing she had spared Sean from the loss of some, or possibly all, of Kim's book.

Sean's folio, containing Kim's photograph, hadn't been as fortunate. It was crushed between the driver's seat and the center console of the vehicle, and there it remained for all intents and purposes, permanently wedged inside the carnage that used to be Sean's car. Such as it was, Sean was very lucky to have survived the accident. With the box tucked safely under her arm, April set out for the hospital, hoping she could see Sean before the rest of the Darlings arrived.

Chapter 13

JOHN WAS UNABLE TO contact Dixie, who was holed up in a guest bedroom at her parent's house with her phone off, until he went over and physically knocked on the locked door. Frank and Suzanne had taken Callie and several other grandchildren out to eat dinner when John notified them about the accident. Frank headed directly to the hospital. Suzanne drove home by way of Katie's house to be with Dixie. John's plan was to pick up Dixie and drive her and their mother to the emergency room. For a few anxious moments, John wasn't sure that Dixie would go to the hospital at all. It all boiled down to his delivery of the news and Dixie's reaction to it.

"Dixie! Open the door. It's John," he said as he knocked repeatedly.

Suzanne arrived shortly after her son and quickly joined him.

"Has she answered yet?" Suzanne asked.

"No. When did you last see her?"

"About two hours ago. She had a migraine and said she was going to take some pills and go to sleep."

Suzanne and her son exchanged concerned looks. Given Dixie's emotional state, pills, a locked door, and the fact that she wasn't responding to their calls, it didn't bode well for her.

"Can you get the door open?" Suzanne asked desperately.

"It's locked, but I can open it with a nail file. Do you have one?"

"Yes. I'll be right back," Suzanne said. She scurried down the hallway to the master bathroom.

"Dixie, open the door!" John called once more to no avail.

Suzanne returned without delay, and John quickly had the door open. Dixie was under the covers and, from what they could tell, completely motionless—to the extent that both John and his mother feared for the worst.

"DIXIE, SUZANNE SAID, STROKING her daughter's face. "Dixie!" She called out a second time, this time arousing her from her deep sleep.

Looking around to gain her bearings, Dixie asked, "What's going on?"

"Are you alright?" her mother asked.

"Mom, I told you I was going to take some medication for my migraine. I also took a sleeping pill. I'm so tired," she said, dosing off again.

"Dixie," her mother said once more, awakening her again. Once she felt she had her daughter's attention, she informed her, "Sean's been in an auto accident. He's been taken to the hospital."

The whole situation seemed dreamlike, and Dixie at first didn't believe what she'd been told. "Is this some kind of joke?" She asked.

"No," John stated very clearly. "It sounds pretty bad so we need to get going."

Seeing the concern in John's face made Dixie move more quickly. "What happened?"

"All I know is he rolled his car out on the Tri-State, and he got thrown out of the vehicle. He's in and out of consciousness. Now, come on, let's go. I can tell you more while we're driving."

Looking at her mother for comfort, Dixie frantically called out, "Mom?!" An instant later, Dixie was crying in her mother's arms, and anticipating the worst possible circumstances. "I knew something like this would happen. It always does. You have a fight, then someone dies, and you can't take back what you said."

She stood clutching her mother, dressed only in her underwear and bra, while John looked on anxiously.

"Hey, Dix, don't think like that. We don't know the extent of his injuries. Get some clothes on. We have to get going," John said.

"Where's Callie?" Dixie asked tearfully. "Does she know?"

"I dropped her off with Katie," Suzanne replied. "She knows about the accident. I told Katie we'd call as soon as we knew something. Now, let's get going."

"Where's Daddy?"

"He's on his way to the hospital," Suzanne answered as she went to a closet and picked out some clothes for Dixie to wear. "John, step outside, please, and call your father. See if he has any news. And be sure your brothers know."

"Right, Mom."

Dixie was so wobbly from the medications she had taken, she had to sit on the edge of the bed while she got dressed.

"How many of those pills did you take?" Suzanne asked disapprovingly.

"Probably more than I should have," Dixie answered, rubbing her hands over her face. "I didn't want to see anyone else today. I just wanted to wake up sometime tomorrow."

"Well, don't do that again," her mother scolded. "I don't want another trip to the hospital."

"Mom, I'm alright…really."

"You act and sound like your drunk. You didn't drink anything with those pills, did you?"

"No, Mom. I just took them with water."

While Suzanne helped Dixie get dressed, the two said little to one another for fear anything one said might be misconstrued and set the other off. After a few minutes, John reappeared.

"Is everyone ready to go?" he asked.

"Yes," Dixie answered. "Did you get in touch with Daddy?"

"He's at the hospital. The doctors are examining Sean as we speak."

"Is anyone else there?" Dixie asked. She was expecting Frank Junior and Stephen to be there.

"Just April," John replied.

Dixie froze where she stood next to the bed. Her expression changed instantly from explicit concern to unconcealed disbelief.

"Why is she there?" Dixie asked.

John must not have known he had just opened a can of worms

"She called me, Dix, to tell me about the accident. She was there when it happened, I guess."

"Why was she at the accident? Was she in the car with Sean?"

"Dixie, I don't know. All I can say is she called to let me know about the accident, and she said she'd meet us at the hospital. Now let's go. We're wasting time."

"No! Forget it! I'm not going!"

"Dixie!" John shouted.

"Nope. He made his bed, and he can sleep in it with his girlfriend for all I care," Dixie said. She removed her sweater and threw it on a chair in the corner of the room.

John was shocked by Dixie's remark and asked, "Do you think Sean and April...?"

"They're having an affair, John!" Dixie yelled. "Is that clear enough for you?"

As calmly as anyone could be under the circumstances, Suzanne interrupted, "John, go on without us. We'll be along in a few minutes. I need to speak with Dixie alone."

Defending Sean, which was without a doubt a huge mistake at that moment, John said, "Dixie, I know Sean and April, and I just don't see them having an affair. I think you owe it to Sean to..."

"I don't owe Sean shit!" Dixie shouted back at her brother.

Suzanne nodded for John to leave, and he didn't need to be encouraged a second time. Once they were alone, Suzanne went to work on her daughter.

"Dixie, John's right. I think you're jumping to conclusions."

"Mom, did I ask for your opinion?"

Dixie's words hurt, but Suzanne wasn't about to back down.

"Fine then. Let's for the sake of argument agree that Sean's screwing around. What are you going to do about it? Are you going to let her take him away from you? If you want something, you have to fight for it like Darlings always have. Darlings never give away something that's important to them. There's never been a divorce in this family, and as long as I'm breathing there's never going to be one."

Dixie wasn't buying what her mother was saying. "Mom, that's easy for you to say. You've never been in my shoes."

"Oh yes, I have."

Dixie couldn't believe what she'd just heard.

"Mom, are you telling me Daddy's..." She couldn't finish her remark.

"Your father isn't the saint you think he is. You don't need to know any more than that, and don't you ever repeat this to your brothers. This is woman-to-woman. But I'm here to tell you this. No hussy was going to take him from me. A certain redhead and I had a confrontation she'll never forget. She told me she'd have me thrown in jail, and I told her to hurry up because I'd kill her if she ever got near him again. That was the end of that. Now, when I think Frank's got too much twinkle in his eye, I yank him up short. But nobody's ever going to take my husband; not until they pry my cold, dead hands from his throat."

Dixie was speechless.

"So, your role in life now, Dixie, is to be by your man's side. If she's in the way, push her out. If he doesn't respond to you, then you get on your knees. From there you can either beg him to be faithful or bite his nuts off. Either way, he'll learn to stay by you. Am I making myself clear?"

Dixie nodded.

"Now get in the car, and let's go see your husband."

IF SUZANNE HAD DONE everything possible to shore up Dixie's commitment to Sean, Frank was busily doing everything he could at the hospital to make sure April got to him first. The emergency room physician quickly examined Sean for obvious injuries. He soon thereafter requested a CT scan of his head to determine if there was any internal bleeding or concussion, and a full series of x-rays to look for chest, pelvic, neck and spinal injuries. As the technicians wheeled Sean back from his scan, Frank insisted that April be allowed to see him. Their reunion was touching to say the least.

"How are you feeling?" April asked, resting her hand on his sheet-covered chest.

"Are you sure that car didn't run over me?" Sean asked trying to ease April's fretfulness with humor.

It worked. His comeback put a smile on her face.

"I really need to get off this frickin' board they have me strapped to. It's killing me."

"The doctor said as soon as he sees your test results, he'll try to get you off that board. Do you need something for pain?" I suspect they have all the latest street drugs here, not to mention the legal stuff."

"Actually, I could use something. My back is killing me."

"I'll go ask the doctor."

"No. Stay here with me," Sean said, reaching behind April's waist and pulling her closer. He met no resistance. "I'm surprised they let you back here with me. How'd you pull that off?"

"Frank insisted that I be allowed back here."

"Frank?" Sean said. The lack of trust was loud and clear. "April, I don't need to tell you that he's up to something. Does Dixie know about the accident?"

"Uh-huh. I tried calling Dixie, but could only leave her a message. I then got in touch with John, and he contacted everyone.

Frank says John is bringing Dixie in later on. She had to take care of some things."

"Had to take care of some things?" Sean asked. He was surprised and somewhat hurt by Dixie's apparent lack of urgency considering the potentially grave circumstances. The depth of their falling-out was becoming apparent.

Making sure they were alone, April got close to Sean's ear and said, "I have some bad news for you."

"Does it have to do with Frank stealing away my Volvo and BMW dealerships?"

"How did you know?"

"The asshole left a shitty voice message informing me. That's when I threw my phone against the windshield like some idiot. Then you called, and I was trying to pick up the phone from the floor of my car to answer it when I wrecked the car."

"I'm so sorry, Sean. I had just heard the news from Francis, and I was trying to tell you. That's why I was calling. When you didn't answer, I thought I could catch up with you at Berkowitz' office. You weren't there, so I was heading home when I drove up on your accident."

"Well, I wish I'd heard it from you and not Frank. I probably wouldn't be laid up like this. I suppose you heard he's taking over day-to-day control of my dealerships?"

Wishing she didn't have to tell him the dirty details, she said, "Frank's telling everyone you had a nervous breakdown."

"You're kidding me?"

"No. Sorry to say I'm not."

Everything was playing to Frank's favor: Sean's obsessions, his lack of sleep, being caught asleep after drinking, the incident with Callie, Dixie leaving him, and now this traffic accident. There was one thing Sean had to keep from Frank.

"April, please don't tell anyone I'm seeing Berkowitz. The last thing I need is for Frank to get a hold of that tidbit. He'll use that put the final nail in my coffin."

"How will you explain being where you were? You seldom travel that part of the Tri-State," April pointed out.

"I don't know. I'll come up with something. But under no circumstances can you tell Frank or Dixie anything about therapy...please."

Taking Sean's hands in hers, April said, "Whatever you say, Sean. I'll do anything you say." After they spent a while staring into each other's eyes, April asked, "So how did it go this afternoon with Dr. Berkowitz?"

"Intense is about the only word that comes to mind. That and I feel violated. The man can practically see through you."

"He's something, that's for sure. Did he give you homework?"

"Yes he did. I'm supposed to tell him how I feel about Mark in Kim's book. Part two is more difficult. He wants to know what I would say to Kim if I could speak with her one more time."

Twisting her mouth in acknowledgment, April said, "Those are good subjects. Would you like some help with them?"

Recalling what Berkowitz had said to him earlier, Sean asked with some reluctance, "Do you feel like a victim by way of our friendship?"

April smirked as she replied, "A victim? Get real. Did Berkowitz suggest that?"

"He says I'm not being fair with you—that I'm replacing a love I once felt from Kim and my mother with...your feelings for me."

April was without a doubt now on the verge of taking Sean's heart.

"Are you? Because if that's the case that would make me...very, very happy." Tears began to well up in April's eyes as she spoke.

Before Sean or April could say another word, Dixie spoke up from the doorway. "Tell me, Sean, are you replacing my feelings for you with hers as well?"

Dixie moved up next to Sean so that he could see her standing next to April. The expression on April's face at that moment reflected her extraordinary discomfort.

As Dixie removed April's hands from Sean's, she turned to her saying, "You're finished here, April. Please leave."

Trying to cover her tracks to the extent possible, April said, "Dixie, I'm just so glad Sean's not too badly hurt. You have to understand that I..."

"April...leave!" Dixie firmly reiterated. "I'm not going to ask you again."

NOT WISHING TO BE humiliated any further, April quickly walked out the door. Standing just outside were Suzanne, Frank Junior, John, and Stephen. They said nothing to her. It mattered not in the least what was truly going on. Clearly, the Darling family had made up its mind about her and Sean. As she reached the door to the parking lot, April encountered Frank leaning against a brick column. He was chewing on his tongue, obviously satisfied with what had taken place.

"You set me up, didn't you?" April asked, confronting Frank.

"That's harsh coming from a sweet thing like you," Frank replied, not denying he was behind the confrontation. "I'd prefer to say you performed very admirably, my dear."

"Why can't you leave Sean alone? He's the best of all the principals in the Group. All he's ever done is make money for you. In spite of all the obstacles you put in his way, he still presses on year after year. Are you so frightened by him you can't let him be a success?"

"Frightened by him? Sean's a putz. Anyway, I couldn't care less about him. I do, however, care about you. You're not getting soft on him are you? You need to remember who you're talking to."

April's caution light flashed brightly as Frank spoke. Standing close enough to feel his breath, she said, "No, it's *you* who needs to remember who *you* are talking to."

Not the least bit intimidated by her, Frank said, "I have a proposition for you April, and you can only say yes to my offer, so the decision should be quite easy. You are coming to work for me at the main office beginning Monday, no ifs, ands, or buts."

"And if I say no?"

"Then it's been real nice knowing you," Frank said with a twisted grin.

"You can't just fire me, Frank. There's too much at risk with a move like that."

"The hell I can't. My name's on every payroll check you get. I am human resources, as it were. I've just offered you a promotional opportunity making more money in lieu of your old job that I just eliminated. You have no basis for a fight. Take it, or leave. I'll see you Monday morning at nine o'clock, or not at all."

With that, Frank turned and went back into the hospital. April broke down in tears and ran to her car.

Chapter 14

IT WAS TERRIBLY DIFFICULT for Dixie to start a conversation on good terms with Sean given what she had just witnessed between him and April. While she exchanged looks with her husband—looks that ran the spectrum between commitment, trepidation, love, and denial—the words of her mother played back in her mind over and over. Whether or not there was a relationship between Sean and April, she had to see past that for now, and salvage anything there was left between them.

Standing precisely where April earlier stood and holding the same hand, Dixie asked, "So, how do you feel?"

"Why are you here?"

She had to swallow her pride in order not to tell Sean what she was truly feeling at that moment and leave, but she managed to say with some degree of sincerity, "You're my husband, Sean. In spite of what's happened in the past week, I still love you. Right now, I'm afraid. I just found out my husband was in a terrible accident, and I'm trying to find out if he's alright. It's not that complicated."

"Why did you chase away April? Are you still operating under this delusion that she and I are having an affair?"

"Sean, I'm trying very hard to make this a conversation about you, interjecting maybe a little of me into it. I don't want to talk about April now. As far as I'm concerned, she has nothing to do with your accident. What's more, she's not a part of our marriage, and I intend to keep matters that way."

"Why is it you think you even need to mention that? She's a co-worker for Christ's sake," Sean insisted. He should have let Dixie have the last word.

Remaining as calm as possible, Dixie clarified for Sean, "An attractive co-worker who is divorced; a co-worker who has taken a keen interest in my husband's private life; a co-worker who has replaced me as his soul mate; a co-worker whose name continues to come up at the most provocative times; a co-worker who appears out of nowhere to be at my husband's side after an accident on a road that is off the normal routes either of them travel; and a co-worker, mind you, whom he just suggested was replacing the feelings he once felt from his mother and Kim, and whom welcomed that opportunity as she held his hands most fondly. So, Sean, that is why I mentioned it. Now getting back to you, how do you feel?"

Apparently deciding it was best to get off of the subject of April, Sean replied, "I really want to get off this board."

His was not an answer to her question, but at least he had moved away from the topic of April.

"Do you remember what happened?" Dixie asked.

"I sure as hell do," Sean answered. "I was pissed that the Executive Committee, along with you, met and decided to put me on hiatus."

"How did you find out about the meeting?" Dixie wondered given that the meeting was supposed to be a well-kept secret.

"Well, obviously you didn't inform me of the meeting…or the outcome for that matter. The news came by way of a vindictive voice message from Frank. What I'd like to know is how the hell Frank found out about Ricci."

Dixie concealed her guilt like a pro. It had been Ricci's number she retrieved from Sean's phone before passing it along to her father. Nonetheless, it hurt her deeply that it was her dispensation of Sean's private information that resulted in Frank knowing with whom Sean was dealing in his new endeavor.

Quickly changing subjects, Dixie said, "Sean, you're not yourself these days. We felt a month away was in your best interest."

"You arrived at this without getting my input into the decision?! You assumed it was in my best interest?! What kind of shit is this, Dixie?"

"Why weren't you able to answer the phone when Daddy called?"

Sean evaded answering her question.

"Can you go see if the doctor can get me off of this board?" he asked.

Reluctantly, Dixie replied, "Sure. I'll be right back."

She bent down to kiss Sean on his right cheek—the one that was not covered in dried blood. That was, as it turned out, the same cheek that earlier had been pressed against April's. As Dixie's lips left his skin, she got an unquestionable whiff of perfume—the same perfume she had smelled on April when they had worked together earlier in the week. The moment only served to confirm her fears.

Without saying anything further, Dixie left the room. She left his room and kept walking...right on through the exit of the hospital. Suzanne followed along with Frank and Dixie's brothers. She continued to a bench in a landscaped area at the side of the emergency department entrance. There, she took a seat, closed her eyes, and proceeded to take slow, deep breaths. Her mother was the only one brave enough to approach her. She sat next to Dixie, waiting for the right moment to ask a question.

"I gather you're not sitting out here because of Sean's condition?" her mother asked as delicately as possible.

As Dixie shook her head, a tear rolled out the corner of her eye.

"Remember what I said tonight, Dixie. The fate of your marriage rests in your hands."

Eventually, Dixie replied, "Sean's going to be alright. All of you can go home. Tell Callie I'll call her after a while. Also, give Will a call for me and let him know Sean was in an accident, but that he will be fine. Ask him to call his grandfather, but not to bother with his Aunt Kelly since she's out of the country right now." Finally looking at Suzanne, Dixie asked, "Mom, can you leave your car with me and go home with someone else?"

"As you wish. You're sure you don't want me to stay with you?"

"I'll be fine. But, I want to have a word with Daddy before you leave. Would you ask him to come over here, please?"

After giving her daughter a hug, Suzanne went over to Frank and gave him Dixie's message. She then informed the others they could leave which one-by-one they did. Frank cautiously took a seat by his daughter, not knowing what to expect.

Dixie chose her words carefully. "I'm going to ask you this one time, Daddy, and I want an honest answer. Did you arrange for me to run into April with Sean tonight?" The circumstances were right out of the Darling playbook. It was the same set-up she had used on Kim.

"Dixie, of course not. Why would I do such a thing? She was here when I arrived."

Mostly satisfied with that answer, she went on to ask, "Do you have any idea why she was at the accident?"

"Honey, I don't want to cast dispersions against April or Sean. All I know is they both left work early today in separate vehicles, and ended up in a location full of restaurants, bars, and hotels on the Tri-State. I'll let you be the judge of what transpired."

She took a deep breath before asking her father, "Daddy, I want that woman away from Sean. Can you take care of that for me?"

Frank grinned as he said, “It’s already been taken care of, honey. She’ll be over at the main office where I can keep a close watch on her, and out of Sean’s hip pocket, starting Monday.”

Dixie wrapped her arms around her father, rewarding him for his gallantry.

“Are you going to stay here?” Frank asked.

“I’m not sure. I’ll stay at least until they release Sean or get him settled into a room. We’ll see what happens from that point.”

“Call me if you need anything, Dixie, and I mean anything.”

“Alright, Daddy.”

She watched as her parents drove off. Her mind was going a million miles an hour. Mostly, she just wondered how her marriage had gotten into the condition it was in at that moment. It was difficult to blame the dead, the Fuller Brush Man, or even herself. She simply felt the victim of a wide range of dire circumstances that all came together at the same time. Then, she spotted someone to whom she could assign responsibility. April was walking across the parking lot back toward the emergency room. Dixie met her before she could get to the curb.

“Now what are you doing?” Dixie asked, looking for a fight.

“I left without giving this to Sean. It’s Kim’s book.”

“I know what it is. What are you doing with it?”

“It flew out of his car at the accident. I collected all the pages and put them back in order. They’re all accounted for.”

"Now that's special," Dixie said in a catty tone. "Tell me, what were you doing at the accident in the first place?"

"Not that it's any business of yours, mind you," April replied, sounding equally annoyed with Dixie. "I was running an errand when I came upon the accident. I recognized Sean's car and stopped to help. Don't bother thanking me."

"And was Sean helping you with this errand? Because where the accident took place is not between work and home."

April lashed out. "Your husband is a kind, generous man and a wonderful boss. He has a need for a degree of compassion right now that you're apparently unable or unwilling to deliver. I have decided to be there for him when he needs a friend. It's not progressed beyond that point, Dixie. If it does, you have only yourself to blame."

"He's not going to change the woman in his life like you change underwear. Despite our differences at this moment, we are entirely devoted to each other. Don't go looking for the love that's absent from your sorry life in Sean. Somebody will get hurt."

"Is that a threat?"

"You can interpret it any way you want, April. I'm putting you on notice. Don't go near him ever again."

"Or you'll what?"

The words no sooner left her mouth than Dixie slapped April with such force and so surprisingly that she dropped the box containing Kim's book. After staggering for a moment as she regained her balance, and her self-control, April responded only verbally to Dixie's assault. The quiver in her voice was the only outward affect April allowed Dixie to see. The redness on the side of her face was masked by the dim lighting.

"If it weren't for my feelings for Sean, I'd have you arrested on assault charges. But he doesn't need that crisis in his life right now on top of everything else. You've made your point, though with the complete lack of grace I've come to expect from the Darlings. I'll leave you to your husband, Dixie. But mind you, he knows where and how to find me. And if he seeks me out, all bets are off."

The two faced-off with stares only a woman who was in emotional pain could muster. Eventually, April said, "I'll let you deliver the book. He knows I retrieved it for him. I was there, you weren't."

"He'll never see Kim's book again," Dixie replied.

"That would be a huge mistake, Dixie. Nothing means more to Sean right now than that book. He thinks it holds the secret to his happiness, and he's hell-bent on deciphering that mystery. If you destroy that book, I promise you he'll hear about it, and God help the person responsible for denying him that deliverance."

Dixie was about to repeat her earlier act of violence, but the situation was defused when a security guard approached the two.

"Ladies, what seems to be the problem? We've been watching the two of you on our closed-circuit camera so we know what's going on."

With her king held in check, Dixie said, "We're just ironing out a small difference of opinion."

The guard came up next to April and asked, "Ma'am, we have everything on tape. Do you want us to contact the police for you so you can press charges against your assailant?"

"My assailant?" April asked, basking in Dixie's moment of discomfort. After letting her squirm for a few moments, April replied, "No, I don't think that will be necessary."

"Do either of you have business here at the hospital?"

"Yes," Dixie replied. "My husband is here in the emergency room."

"And you, ma'am?"

Knowing she wasn't welcome, April answered charmingly, "No. I was just leaving."

"Then, let's wrap this up," the guard said, as if that would put an end to the feud.

April turned and tossed her handbag over her shoulder as she strutted away from the altercation. It was all Dixie could do to find the strength not to tackle April from behind. Instead, she reached down and picked up the box before proceeding back to Sean's bedside.

SEAN WAS SITTING UPRIGHT in his bed when Dixie returned, looking not the worse for wear aside from the blood on his face that a nurse was preparing to clean up. The blood from his head laceration had clotted without medical intervention, and the doctor had determined no stitches were necessary. All of his tests came back negative. However, due to the spectacular nature of the accident, the doctor wanted to keep Sean overnight for observation and to repeat several tests again in the morning as a precaution. Sean wasn't thrilled about the hospitalization, regardless of how short it was, due to his pending departure for Urbana the next day.

When he first saw Dixie, his attention was drawn to the box. "Where did you get that?" he asked.

Being surprisingly honest, she said, "April salvaged it from the accident."

Taking it from her, Sean quickly opened the lid and took inventory of the contents.

"Sean, it's all there. She made sure she found everything, and she put it in order."

Careful not to upset the relative harmony of the situation, Sean remarked, "Thank you for bringing this to me. I would have been devastated if I'd lost it."

A nurse entered the room with a hand full of supplies. After getting her attention, Dixie asked, "Are those for cleaning Sean's injury? If so, I'll be happy to do it. I'm his wife."

"Have you ever done this before?" the nurse asked.

"No, but I think I can figure it out. I'll come get you if I need help."

The nurse was more than happy to let someone else do that chore so she could tend to other patients.

"Great. Here is the cleanser, some sterile water, and gauze. Just don't rub too hard on the cut or it might open up again. When you're done, I'll put on a steri-strip to hold it closed."

"No problem. Thanks for letting me help." As she began cleaning the wound, Dixie continued, "So, I see the doctor got you off the board. Did he have anything to say about your injuries?"

"Overall, I'm in good shape, but I can expect to be sore," handing the box back to Dixie. "Hell, I could have figured that out myself."

"Are you being discharged tonight?" She asked while setting the box on a chair in the room.

"No. He wants to keep an eye on me tonight to see if I drop dead or something."

"Seriously, Sean, what did he say?" Dixie asked as she returned to caring for Sean's wound.

"He said I have bruised ribs and muscle spasms in my back that are playing havoc with my mid-spine. I can tell you right now he's correct with that diagnosis. I might have a small bleed in my spleen that he wants to check tomorrow morning. I have a slight concussion, and there's always a concern about something called a subdural hemorrhage. The cut on my head is fine. It just needs to be cleaned up. All that and my pride is shot to hell. He's giving me some oral muscle relaxers and pain medication which I plan to down as soon as I get them. He said they would probably knock me out. Then, they're sending me to a room for the night."

Dixie said as she began to clean the blood from Sean's face, "You did say you wanted us to check into the hospital for a night of R & R. Of course, I thought the circumstances might be a little different, but what the heck."

Recalling the same conversation, Sean said, "I don't expect you to stay with me, Dixie."

"I wouldn't have it any other way. For better and for worse, in sickness and in health, remember?"

"There's probably only a chair for you to sleep in."

"Fine. I've slept in chairs before. Besides, who said I was sleeping in a chair?"

Not prepared to repeat the misdeed of an earlier era, Sean hesitantly said in response to Dixie's suggestion, "I'm probably going to be asleep before…"

"Sean, I'm not leaving you tonight, and that's final," she stated firmly. She then continued removing the last trace of blood from his face. After drying off the left side of his face, she kissed him, following with a tight hug.

Noticing she was crying, Sean asked, "What's wrong, Dix?"

Stepping back just enough so that he could see the tears were genuine, she replied, "When John came to the house and told me about the accident, I was so afraid I'd never be able to speak with you again. He said the accident was bad, but couldn't give me a lot of details. You have to realize that for about thirty minutes, I thought this was my worst nightmare come true—that maybe you were dead." Having said those painful words, Dixie buried her face against Sean's chest.

He held his wife closely, comforting her. Without a doubt, Sean was comforting himself as well. It was at that moment he realized what she was saying was true. His accident had almost been a deadly event. It occurred to him that when he left Berkowitz' office, he was so absorbed by what they had spoken about that he did in fact forget to put on his seatbelt. That tiny oversight nearly cost him his life.

IT TOOK NEARLY AN hour and a half, even with Dixie's constant hounding of the hospital staff, to get Sean into a private room for the night. Once settled in, Dixie made it perfectly clear to the nurses that she would be Sean's caretaker during his stay. If he became symptomatic with his injuries in any way, she would quickly notify them. Otherwise, they were to give the couple total privacy. The hospital staff wasn't about to do otherwise as the Darlings practically held celebrity status. Frank and Suzanne had personally contributed a seven figure sum of money toward a recent hospital expansion, and the Darling Group had matched that figure—those funds going to a neonatal unit.

Certainly not the quality of a spa, or home for that matter, the accommodations still were comfortable to say the least. Sean was without a doubt in considerable pain as evidence by his slow walk and bent posture when he tried to stand upright. Dixie tried coaxing her husband into a hot shower with her, perhaps hoping some heat would help loosen him up

"Dixie, like I said earlier, I'm really not up for a lot of physical activity," Sean said.

She knew that the suggestion of a romp with his wife in a semi-public setting brought with it a considerable degree of excitement.

"Honey, you don't need sex right now. You just need me." She made certain that her offer sounded confident and comprehensive. It worked. As she enticed him into the shower and closed the door, she began to warm up the water.

"What does *me* bring with it?" he asked.

Turning the hot stream of water onto Sean's chest, she began to lather it up with the contents from a bottle of liquid soap. The antiseptic smell was inescapable. The humor of that moment brought smiles to their faces.

"What does *me* bring?" she answered. "It brings a hot shower, a whole lot of touch, a warm heart, and someone who wants to listen…not to mention soap that smells like cheap dog shampoo."

Taking a hand full of soap, Dixie spread it over her chest. She took Sean's hands and placed them on her breasts. She assumed he knew what to do from that point forward.

Dixie went on to say, "I have a confession to make. I read parts of Kim's book this morning while you were sleeping."

Her tactic worked—Sean had nothing to say about her admission. The diversion of lathering her body absorbed most of the shock. In fact, it may have brought with it an added benefit.

"I have a confession to make as well," Sean said. "I mean, it's only fair that we have some degree of mutual tit for tat…so to speak. I saw a shrink today. I had just left his office when I had my accident."

Dixie instantly ceased what she was doing and stared at Sean. It occurred to her that she might have been terribly unfair in her earlier judgment about her husband's afternoon activities, not to mention the right-cross she gave April a few hours earlier.

"Why didn't you say something?"

"And give your father the ammunition he needs to completely throw me out of the business? You know he doesn't tolerate weakness, and going to a therapist is probably the one thing that would in his mind underscore that characteristic."

"Honey, he wouldn't do that," she replied, rinsing the soap off of him. "Besides, I told him I wanted you to see a therapist. I cleared the way for you."

"I thought the other morning we decided not to discuss any of this with your father?"

"He was asking lots of questions, Sean. I owed him an honest answer. Anyway, John also spoke up for you today at the Executive Committee meeting. He told the members it would be a good idea for you to see a therapist."

"You discussed this at the EC? Dixie, I've never felt so exposed in my entire life, and I'm not speaking of being naked here with you in the shower. Babe, here's a news flash for you. Frank wants me gone. He's wanted me out for years. He plans to push me out and give my business to Frank Junior. He's using the guise of putting Will over Cadillac as cover. He's torpedoed my financial backing to expand into Volvo and BMW, and now plans to expand into those markets himself. I'm all but out on the street and for that matter, so are you…unless you have something going on that I'm unaware of."

She was all too aware of all Frank's motives, so couldn't feign surprise. Moving the conversation back to her own terms, Dixie posed the question, "What would Mark do?"

"Who the hell is Mark?"

"That's the name of the character Kim has portraying you in her book, right?"

It must have occurred to Sean the degree to which Dixie had consumed Kim's book.

"How much did you read?"

Dixie turned him around so his back was under the hot water. Massaging his back, she replied, "Bits and pieces. She really didn't like me, did she?"

"Why do you say that?"

"Well, correct me if I'm wrong, but my name in the book is Esmeralda. That's not particularly flattering. Mark—nice name; Collette—beautiful name; Esmeralda—sounds evil to me."

"Did you read the ending?"

She had blatantly lied to Sean so few times, she couldn't think of the last time she had done so. This reply was added to that short list.

"No. She said in her cover letter not to read it. I wouldn't want to spoil the ending for you." Sensing his disappointment in her answer, she continued, “So, what would Mark do? It appears he is destined for a great change in life. He just doesn’t know what it is or when it will take place. I get the impression from the quickening crescendo with which events are shifting in his life, something’s about to happen. What do you think it is?”

“I can’t live my life vicariously through a book, Dix.”

“Well, whether or not you want to, that’s the card Kim’s played for you. So what are you going to do?”

Sean didn’t answer.

She turned him around and looked deeply into his eyes before again asking, “What are you going to do, Sean? I need to know, because whatever it is and wherever you go, I’m going to be there with you.”

She pulled him closer until their lips met. This, too, would be a night at the hospital to remember.

Chapter 15

MARK HADN'T BEEN GONE more than a few years before I could detect noticeable changes in virtually all aspects of his behavior. This came as no surprise. When people haven't been together for some time, otherwise subtle changes stand out like a carbuncle on one's nose. Typically, the changes are physical—look at the weight he's gained, or he shaved his beard off. But with Mark, the changes came from within. And, despite the many I could discern, one thing never varied—he needed a woman in his life to take the lead.

Whereas I used to be that woman, Esmeralda now carried that torch. I suppose that was a good situation for Mark given the fact that his in-laws all had it in for him. He figured that after he and Emmy—he called her that because she had such a hideous name—tied the knot, they'd accept him into their clan. NOT! His good fortune in marrying a wench with such a repugnant name was her ability to keep her kind off his back, at least to the extent that it served her purpose.

A quick inventory of the parts of Mark that now adorned a marble monument at some park for missing-in-action included, but was not limited to, his lust for life itself, his quick wit, his compassion for others, his smile, and, of all things to lose, his dedication to home and family. Poof! All gone.

The first time I noticed conspicuous changes was during a visit by him to his hometown of nearly a quarter of a century in the winter of 1979. It had been a fierce winter that year, and snow was abundant. I encountered him at an old haunt—the one where I had brought him into my life many happy years earlier—Carle Park. I was returning from DeeDee's house to my apartment via a shortcut through the park when I found him standing alone at the pavilion, staring off into the marvelously snowy landscape. The winds had whipped up the many inches of snow on the ground into huge piles as tall as he. Gone was the green grass of spring. Gone were the children of summer. Gone were the leaves of autumn. All that remained were the countless winter villages of the Who. At one time, he would have seen all the life before him. But I could tell by his nervous sway, as he stood fighting against the cold, winter gale, he no longer could see the Who. All he could see was a barren landscape.

"Mark?" I called out to him. I knew it was him, but a swat on his derriere or a hug around his waist was no longer appropriate.

Without turning around, he replied, "Collette?" At least he hadn't forgotten my name.

I found this part most peculiar: the only vehicles in sight were locked-in by snowdrifts. Either he had walked to the park, in the cold, through the snow, against the wind, to accomplish his mission, or he had been beamed to his current locale by the crew of the Enterprise. Judging from the footprints in the mounds of the Who, it was the former—drat!

"What are you doing?" I asked.

He turned and proceeded to give me a look that told me he had been stripped of his soul. This was confirmed when he replied most uncharacteristically, "I have no idea."

Mark always had an idea. I expected him to tell me something awe-inspiring such as that he was counting snowflakes. He could always give me a number, and who was I to challenge it? Without fail, he would tell me the temperature and approximate wind chill. He loved and respected winter so dearly, and he understood all aspects of it. But instead of showing me something that would confirm his enlightenment of life, I sensed nil. He was as much a cadaver as anyone stretched out in a coffin at a funeral home.

"Come with me, Mark! Let me save you!" I shouted against the roar of the wind.

"I would, but you see my boots are made of concrete!"

I looked, and it was true. It wasn't any ordinary concrete mind you. It was the stuff from the WPA era—the kind of cement that was much harder and heavier than what one encounters today.

"But you walked here! Come with me!"

He had developed the beginning of bags under his eyes, and there was a new wrinkle on his forehead. It appeared he was aging at a faster pace than should be the case. Hanging his head low, he replied in a voice nearly inaudible, "I can't. I'm too tired."

"Why did you come here, of all places?" I asked knowing the answer would either lift my spirits, or cut like a knife.

"I'm searching for eternal happiness. Have you seen the Sun Singer?"

Ah! A piece of shared history. Perhaps I was still in his life.

"It's far away from here, Mark, but I can help you get there," I offered. "We have to take the road to Monticello to find it. I know the way."

At last, one corner of his mouth began to turn up, then the other. Soon, I saw what only a true love could describe as a smile.

"You would do this for me?"

"There is nothing I wouldn't do for you, Mark. I'll always be by your side."

"Isn't it too late to begin the journey? It'll be night soon," he said, looking at the darkening sky above.

I had him with this one. "Our love will light the way." Not particularly original, but I was proud of my comeback, nonetheless.

I reached out for him and he took my hands. As promised, the glow of day extended from us to such a degree that surrounding objects could cast shadows. After removing our gloves, I clasped his hands in mine and stood before him. I could barely feel it, but it was growing. No, not that...his soul. He still retained a glimmer of it, and the flame was on the rise. The longer we stood hand-in-hand, the stronger the flame.

"I can hear them!" he shouted.

"Hear who?" I asked.

"Exactly," was his reply.

"I don't understand?" was my naïve response. I even invented this fantasy, yet he beat me to the punch line.

"I hear the Who," he quipped.

It was at that precise moment I knew Mark was saved from certain death. Yet, I still had to get him to Monticello.

"Take one step!" I commanded.

With what seemed to be Herculean effort, he lifted one foot and planted it squarely in front of himself.

"Now take another!" I repeated.

With less effort, he lifted his other foot and took the next step on our journey together. His smile was unmistakable, and tears of joy ran down his face, only to be frozen into tiny icicles.

"This will take forever!" he shouted at me.

"We have forever!" I replied, wanting so desperately for that to be the case.

It was not to be.

"I hear screams!" he shouted, a look of anguish and despair returning once again.

I heard them, too. It was coming from the Who. Looking beyond Mark, I could see the flashing yellow lights of a snowplow, and it was coming directly toward us.

"We have to hurry, Mark! Take another step!"

This time, he was unable to move.

"Try the other foot!" I cried out, not willing to lose him again.

Once more, there was no forward motion.

The cries of the Who became louder, and I knew our situation was grim at best.

"You said you could take me to Monticello! Why are you stopping!"

With a great deal of disappointment, I replied, "All I can do is guide you, Mark. You're the one who must make the journey. The desire must come from within."

"But I don't have the strength to do it on my own, Collette. Who can help me?"

I had to pull away from him and the nearing onslaught of the snowplow. But as I ever so reluctantly retreated from the love of my life, I said to him as I had so many times, "Find the Fuller Brush Man. He can take you the rest of the way."

"But I want you to take me there, Collette!" he screamed as our collective light faded and was replaced by that from the unkind halogens that adorned the top of the blade.

"You have to find the Fuller Brush Man, Mark. Seek him out. Don't stop until you find him."

Just as the snowplow made its final approach toward Mark, I could see a familiar, daunting figure in the driver's seat—that of Esmeralda. But before she would have swept him from his feet, she made a final turn—a turn directly toward me. My time was up. The last I saw of Mark, he was reaching out to me. Yet, unable to move in his concrete boots, his final action was incapable of sparing me death.

SEAN'S TWITCHING IN BED awakened Dixie who had been fast asleep by his side. She felt his skin. He was perspiring heavily and trying to talk. He sounded frantic as he mumbled. Dixie thought she heard him say, "Not the snowplow…not the snowplow…run to Monticello…have to get to Monticello." His voice got increasingly louder to the point at which Dixie was certain the nursing staff would hear him. Rather than waiting for matters to escalate to that level, she gently tried to awaken him from his nightmare.

"Sean…Sean," she said into his ear as she pushed his shoulder.

Bolting upright in bed, Sean began gasping for air. Unsure if his condition was due to the accident or simply an overactive subconscious, Dixie quickly dressed and stepped outside to get a nurse. It wasn't long before several nurses and Dixie stood alongside Sean. Albeit the wee hours of the morning, and even though Sean was on medication for pain, Dixie had never seen such a wild expression on his face as the one he had at that moment. It was a combination of panic, fear, and pain. And it terrified her.

With some supplemental oxygen and a great deal of coaching by the nurses, Sean slowed his breathing to the point where he could once again begin to speak and make sense of his awakened state.

"Mr. Marcum, how are you feeling now?" asked one of the nurses.

Sean replied by holding up one thumb.

"I'm going to take away this oxygen mask. If you feel short of breath again let me know, and I'll give you the oxygen."

Sean held up his other thumb.

A physician who had been summoned by the nurses entered the room. Having come from the emergency room where the on-call doctors work at night, he was a bit winded from the trek that probably involved several flights of stairs.

Seeing his patient was awake and seemingly no longer in distress, the young-looking doctor introduced himself.

"Good morning. I'm Dr. Mollenhauer. How are you doing?"

With the panic attack subsided, Sean's distress was now replaced by pain.

"I hurt like a bitch," Sean replied.

"Why is he hospitalized? the doctor asked the Charge Nurse.

"He was involved in a rollover motor vehicle collision yesterday evening on the Tri-State and was ejected from his vehicle. There was a loss of consciousness. Dr. Hudsen saw him in the ER and diagnosed a mild concussion and a lot of musculo-skeletal strains, bumps and bruises, but nothing significant. He's here overnight for observation. In the morning, he's getting a repeat head CT and another ultrasound of his spleen and liver."

"Sounds like you're a lucky man," the doctor said to Sean. "I can see why you'd be in a lot of pain. Where exactly do you hurt?"

Thinking for a few moments, Sean replied, "Everywhere north of my toenails and south of the hair follicles on my head."

"I need you to narrow that down a bit for me," the doctor requested. "What about here?" he asked, pressing on a large bruise that had formed on the left side of his chest.

Sean jumped and groaned in pain. The doctor mercilessly poked and prodded Sean until he was satisfied he knew from where all the sources of pain emanated. After listening to Sean's chest, he asked him to stand up.

Once he complied with the doctor's request, Sean stood before the crowd totally naked.

"Are you hot?" The doctor asked, noting Sean's lack of any clothing.

"No," Sean replied sheepishly, providing no reason for being undressed.

Dixie tried to avoid eye contact with the nurses and doctor, the extent of her 'care' now clear for all to imagine.

"Walk over to the wall and back for me," the doctor requested.

Doing as asked, Sean walked with a significant limp and a list to one side.

"Does it hurt to walk?"

Obviously more embarrassed now than in pain, Sean replied, "Not too much."

"Okay. Go ahead and get dressed."

Dixie fetched the unused hospital pajamas that had been left for him. After assisting him into them, she eased him back into bed.

"What was going on when the nurses called me?" the doctor asked Sean.

Unwilling to discuss particulars about his dream involving the *Road*, he made up what he felt was a more understandable response. "I was having a nightmare about the accident, and I guess I just freaked out."

Addressing Dixie, Mollenhauer asked, "Were you with him when this began?"

"Yes. He seemed to be sleeping just fine when he suddenly began talking. I tried to wake him, and he suddenly sat straight up and began gasping for air. He was sweating like crazy, and I thought he was having a heart attack."

By now, the nurses had connected Sean to a monitor that was able to measure and display his current vital signs and heart rhythm.

"Everything I see here seems to tie back to the accident experience. You're going to be in a lot of pain—probably worsening over the next few days. I can give you some higher doses of medications, but nothing narcotic until we get the CT in the morning. I can also give you something to help you sleep if you'd like. I'd say the rapid breathing and sweating was due to some residual fear caused by the accident. What would you like me to do for you, Mr. Marcum?"

"I guess I'd like another pain pill. As for something to help me sleep, only if it says single-malt on the label."

After chuckling at Sean's joke, Mollenhauer turned to the nurses and ordered Sean two pills for pain and some food.

"Call me if anything else comes up. By the way, Mr. Marcum, that new ad on television with your wife and daughter cost me the price of a new car. I bought my daughter a new vehicle yesterday afternoon to take with her to college. She's one of Callie's classmates."

"Are you Cecilia's husband?" Dixie asked, believing she made the connection.

"That I am," Mollenhauer replied. "I also want to tell you how impressed I was with Ms. Knudsen. I can't remember her first name."

"April," Sean said.

"Right, April. Very nice. Very professional. Really clenched the deal."

"I'll be certain to pass that along to her," Sean said.

Dixie tried to ignore the praise.

"Is Callie going off to school?"

"Yes," Sean replied. "She's set to leave next week as a matter of fact. However, she's having last minute uncertainties about which college to attend."

"Well, wherever she goes, be sure she goes into journalism, advertising, or marketing. She's exceptional in the public eye, as of course are you, Mrs. Marcum."

"Thank you for the compliment," Dixie acknowledged. In spite of all the advertising she had done for the family business, she had received very few accolades, so she took the flattering remark most graciously.

"I think it's a marvel these days to see a family such as the Darlings and Marcums stick together. The entire community profits from your unity of purpose, and of course this hospital has benefitted as well."

Dixie and Sean were speechless as a result of the doctor's remarks. There was a certain amount of discomfort with how his observations differed from the current reality.

Sensing he had perhaps embarrassed the two, he quickly moved off topic and toward the door. "Anyway, excuse me if I made either of you self-conscious. If there is anything you need, be sure to ask one of the nurses." With that, he and the nurses left the room.

After all the footsteps faded away, Dixie and Sean exchanged glances only briefly before beginning to laugh. Sean was the first to make the obvious remark, "It seems we just can't do it in a hospital without getting caught."

Dixie wasn't certain she should continue to laugh at his observation. The previous incident involving Kim had been the source of so much recent pain. Her focus quickly turned back toward Sean's dream.

"So, were you really dreaming about the accident?"

His laughter slowly subsided, then stopped altogether.

"Gosh, it sucks when you can't even have a nightmare without your wife getting inside of your head."

"I thought that was a sign that we've become essentially one person," Dixie said, taking a different perspective.

"If you want to know, I was dreaming about one of the chapters I read Kim's book."

"And you complain about me getting inside your head..." Dixie said, taking a seat on the bed beside Sean.

Her point was noted by Sean with a shrug of his shoulders.

After a few moments, he asked, "Are you satisfied with our relationship?"

"It's clear that you're not," Dixie replied.

"No, I'm not. For all practical purposes, that's the theme of Kim's book. But I want to know about you. Is our life today what you had always hoped for?"

"What aspects are we speaking about, Sean?"

"I'm talking about the whole ball of wax," he replied, holding his arms out to his side.

She really didn't want to open up her soul like this. Dixie had for the most part always been a dominating, forward-looking, aspiring person. Introspection had never been her forte. However, she thought for a moment about April's words in the parking lot—that April was there should Sean seek her out—and it dawned on her this was one such moment where she needed to be with him and to think with him if she were to keep their marriage intact and April out of the picture.

"I never thought I'd be on the cusp of losing my husband to another woman."

"You're not."

"Well, I feel like I am. Do you want me to share my feelings or not?"

"I'm sorry. You're right. I asked, and I really want to know, so I'll shut up."

"And I'm really worried about you, Sean," she added, stroking his head. "You've got some real issues that now have resulted in your hospitalization."

He acted as though he was waiting for Dixie to add something else to the discussion, but she was quiet, waiting for him to respond.

"So what you're telling me is I'm the source of all your displeasure. Do I have that correct?"

All Dixie did in response to Sean's question was nod.

"I hate to be so blunt, but is there anything you feel *you* should change about *you* that would make you happier?"

Bristling, Dixie replied, "So all of your issues are because of me, is that what you're insinuating?"

"No! I'll be the first to admit I'm obsessed over some things to the point of endangering myself. I'll even go so far as to say I understand why you might think there's something going on between me and April. Those are my problems that are affecting you. I'm trying to work those things out. My question is about you. Are you happy with your circumstances? Face it, Dixie. We'll be empty-nesters starting next week. Financially, we're secure. We could do practically anything we want—anything. What would you do if you took the opportunity to make a change?"

"I can't think like that, Sean," she quickly answered.

"You didn't even try, Dixie," he said.

"Is this why you're attracted to April? Does she play to your fantasies?"

"Damn it, Dixie, give it a rest will you?"

"No, Sean, I won't. Do you know what she told me tonight? She told me she was 'there for you.'"

"She has been," he answered without hesitation. "I can talk to her about all of this shit that's happening. She even referred me to the psychologist I'm seeing....Sterling Berkowitz."

"What has he told you?"

"Well, among other things, that I should be taking my issues to you and not April."

"He sounds like a smart man. I like him already."

"Yeah, well all that advice has done is bring us to where we're arguing at three in the morning and having an otherwise pointless conversation."

"You know, I think I've overstayed my welcome here," Dixie said, completely irritated with Sean by this time. "You're getting yourself worked up into a tizzy, and I still think we need some space between us while *you* work out *your* issues."

"My issues...they're all my issues. Jesus, Dixie, you're such a bitch."

During their long marriage, he had never used such language when referring to her. It was clear to her that at this moment, he no longer cared if his words inflicted pain.

"Goodbye, Sean," was all she said before she picked up her coat and purse, and left.

SEAN STEWED FOR THIRTY minutes or so over how the evening had ended between himself and Dixie. A nurse returned with some food that he was to eat prior to taking the additional medication Mollenhauer had ordered, but his appetite was nonexistent. Dixie's comment that April would be available to him bothered him as much as anything, and he kept mulling over in his mind whether or not he should call her. Hoping that reading some of Kim's book might provide adequate distraction, he removed the soiled cover to the box at which point he found his cell phone and the memory stick containing the image of Kim. Evidently, April had rescued them from the accident scene along with the book. At this point, he succumbed to temptation, picked up his cell phone, and turned on the power. It showed he had a new voice message. He fully expected that Frank had left him yet another callous communication. It was a pleasant surprise when the voice in the message turned out to be April's. Unfortunately, her message did nothing to relieve his angst.

"Sean, I'm not going to the office Saturday. In case you hadn't heard, I've accepted the job working for Frank. There are a lot of reasons, but I don't want to bother you with them. My rationale has nothing to do with you. Anyway, the change is effective immediately. You be sure to take care of yourself. Bye."

From 'she will be there for you' to 'bye' was not a natural progression. Sean was convinced that either Frank or Dixie had persuaded April that in no uncertain terms she had to get out of his life. Angry, deeply hurt, and feeling he had nothing more to lose, Sean got dressed and slipped unnoticed out of the hospital.

Chapter 16

THE CLICK-CLACK OF THE train riding the rails brought back fond memories for Sean. After a short hop on a commuter train into Chicago, he boarded the morning Amtrak heading south. It had been many years since he had taken the train from Chicago's Union Station to Urbana-Champaign. His phone had begun to ring non-stop starting shortly after he fled the hospital. It had been Dixie's number he observed on the caller ID. He was taken aback by how many times she called, and equally surprised that time and time again he refused to answer. To save battery life and avoid the annoyance, he switched the phone off, enabling him to doze when he wasn't gazing out the window of the speeding train.

He looked the worse for wear. The cut on his head was swollen and throbbing, making him quite self-conscious. Despite his otherwise large and accommodating seat, he found it difficult to find a comfortable position. There were grass stains on his pants, and his shirt had blood on it. Fortunately, he was able to cover the latter with his jacket. On top of everything else, he was unshaven. Leaving with only the clothes on his back, his wallet, his phone, and Kim's book, he resembled something of a vagabond.

When the train arrived at Kankakee, the stop was harsh enough to jolt Sean awake. Realizing he needed to let people know he would soon be arriving, he turned his phone back on and dialed his father.

"Yellow." The nasal quality of Barbara's voice always made 'hello' sound like a color.

"Barbara, this is Sean. Is Dad available?"

"Sean, we've been worried sick about you. Dixie called us about six o'clock this morning to tell us you'd left the hospital. Is everything alright?"

"I'm on the train heading toward Urbana. I'll be there in about an hour and a half."

Sean could hear his stepmother repeating everything he was saying, presumably to his father. There were some muffled obscenities in the background.

"Well, here's your father."

Sean wasn't sure he was looking forward to the lecture he was certain to get.

"What's going on?" Raymond asked in a serious tone of voice.

"I'm coming by train to Urbana. I'll get there in about an hour and a half. Are you free this morning or should I meet up with Will first?"

"You didn't answer my question. I want to know what the hell is going on with you."

"Dad, I can explain everything when I get there. I don't want to talk about it over the phone, especially while I'm on the train."

"Well I'll tell you this much. You'd better have some goddamn good answers when you get here."

Sean almost hung up on him, but Raymond was quick to keep Sean engaged.

"Have you called your wife?"

"Nope."

"She's pulling her hair out. They got half the cops in the state looking for you. What the hell kind of a dumb idea did you have when you left the hospital? Dixie said they still had to run some tests on you this morning."

"I just couldn't stay there, Dad."

After a long breath, Raymond continued, "Let me tell you something. I'm an old fart, and I'm done raising kids. Do you know what kind of problems I want to deal with at my stage in life? Here's an example: do I want two or three ice cubes with my glass of scotch? Let me give you another example: should I use a nine iron or a pitching wedge on this approach shot? Hey, how about this one: did the postman put my Social Security check in the neighbor's mailbox? Now that's a good one. But I don't expect to have to worry about my stupid son doing stupid shit when he's fifty-goddamn-three years old! Do you hear me?!"

"Yes, Dad."

"You damn near got killed 'cause you weren't wearing your seatbelt. You knocked yourself out. The doctor wanted to keep you overnight, probably for good reason, then you up and left without telling anyone. And another thing, I think it's pretty chicken-shit when my grandson has to phone me to tell me my son is in the hospital. 'Oh, he's not injured badly', he told me. You're just too damn lazy to call your father!"

"Yes, Dad."

"So I get to stay up half the night wondering if at some point I should have whipped your ass more than I did, or if I whipped it too much and caused brain damage!"

"Dad, you can stop now. I understand you're upset."

"Ah, you don't understand crap."

Sean didn't immediately respond. For a moment, he thought that he heard a strange ringing sound as Raymond spoke. Eventually refocusing on the conversation, Sean asked, "Back to my earlier question, Dad, are you free this morning, or should I meet with Will?"

Not about to lose the first shot with Sean, Raymond replied, "You can call Will and set something up for later on. I'll pick you up. Where are you at now?"

"Kankakee."

"Alright. Guess you'll be here in about an hour or so…that is if you don't jump off the train. Have you eaten anything?"

"No. I'm starving." In truth, though Sean was hungry, he was experiencing a growing sense of nausea that he chalked up to mild motion sickness.

"We'll run out and have us some breakfast."

"I'm not exactly dressed to go out, Dad. What if we pick something up and take it back to the house?"

"You got something you can change into?"

Knowing his response wouldn't be well-accepted, Sean answered, "No. I didn't bring any clothes."

"Jesus H Christ. You're a pain in the ass, did you know that? What are you—homeless?"

"It was a spontaneous decision, Dad."

"That's a piss poor reason to do anything. Last time I made a spontaneous decision, nine months later I ended up with you!"

That response actually brought a grin to Sean's face.

"Dad, is this how our conversation is going to be at breakfast?"

"Nope. It'll be a hell of a lot worse. See you at the station. Oh, and if you haven't called Dixie by the time you get here, I'm putting your ass back on the damn train."

"See you in a bit, Dad."

"I mean it! Call your wife!"

Without another word, Raymond disconnected from his end of the conversation.

Sean nervously fiddled with his phone for a few minutes, debating whether or not to listen to any of the voice messages that had been left for him, and especially pondering if he should give Dixie a call and get it over with. He also was developing a headache, and felt a conversation with Dixie might inadvertently blow up due to how he was feeling more than anything of substance. Procrastinating as long as possible, he decided to phone Will and let him know he was coming. First, he had to listen to the song that was Will's ringtone. After the first verse or two, a young lady with an accent answered the phone.

"Allô?"

The voice was sweet; the accent clearly French. Sean found himself struggling to remember the name of Will's new girlfriend. He finally just had to move on with the conversation after the period of silence dragged on way too long, but she beat him to it.

"Is this Mr. Marcum?"

"Yes," Sean replied, still drawing a blank. "I'm looking for Will."

"This is Giselle," she continued.

Thank God she told me her name, Sean thought.

"I saw the name *Dad* show up on his telephone screen so I knew it was you. Will went out to the bakery to bring home some croissants. He forgot to take his phone with him. I know he wants to talk to you. Madame Suzanne called last night and said you were in an accident. Then this morning a few hours ago, Madame Dixie called and said you had left the hospital and nobody knew where you were. Is everything…wait, I think I hear Will. Yes…here he is."

For the first time since their conversation about the birds and the bees, Sean was nervous about speaking with his son.

"Dad, where are you?"

"I'm coming to Urbana on the train. Your grandfather's going to meet me at the Amtrak station."

"I'll be there, too."

"No. I think I'm in for an ass-chewing. I suggest you stay clear until later on. What are you guys doing this afternoon?"

"I've got a soccer game at three o'clock, but I can get out of it."

"No…no, don't do anything like that. Where's the game going to be played?"

"The same place where you watched me play last time."

"Okay. I can find it."

"Mom said you should be in the hospital. Why did you leave? I mean, when Grandma called last night, it sounded like a pretty bad accident."

"I was fine. I needed to get to Kim's funeral."

"Dad, that's bullshit and you know it. Have you called Mom?"

After a deep sigh, Sean replied, "No."

"Why not?" Will asked emphatically.

"It's a long story."

"Well, it's not that complicated, Dad. Mom's freakin' out and you need to call her."

"Actually, it is complicated, Will. I'll tell you about everything later on."

"What's the deal? Are you guys getting a divorce or something?"

"No, Will. I'm just working through some issues."

"What kind of issues? Callie told me you have a girlfriend," Will said, getting right to the point.

"She what?!"

"Yeah, she overheard Mom tell Aunt Katie that you're humping some lady at work named April. Isn't she one of your assistants?"

"Your mother's mistaken, Will. April's a friend and employee, nothing more." Sean answered in a defensive tone that was loud enough the woman sitting across the aisle glanced at him and shook her head.

"Okay, so if it's no big deal, call Mom."

"Will..."

Cutting his father short, Will demanded, "Dad, do it! I'm not doing it for you."

As Sean spoke with his son, he couldn't help but appreciate that this conversation was a monumental reversal in roles.

"Dad, if you're coming by train, how are you going to get around town when you get here?"

"I'll manage. I think I remember how to navigate the metropolis of Champaign-Urbana."

"Dad, you're turning into a pain in the ass."

That was the second time Sean had been referred to as such in just a few moments.

"I'll have Giselle pick you up when Pops is done spanking you. Just call my phone. One of us will have it."

"Alright, Will. Thanks."

"What are you doing for dinner?"

"I thought we could get together like you suggested the other day."

"Sounds great. A little advance notice would have been nice, but what the heck. We'll go to the store after the game and pick up some things."

"Why don't we just go out and eat?" Sean asked, just as he remembered he had nothing to wear.

"Absolutely not! Giselle and I cook our meals. We're eating here. Where are you going to stay tonight?"

"I'm not sure yet."

"Gee, Dad, you really planned this well, didn't you?" Will pointed out while chuckling.

"Will, mind your manners."

"Well, we have a sofa so if Pops disowns you, you can hunker down here."

"You're enjoying this way too much, son."

"Hey, I figured sooner or later I'd have to take care of you. However, I assumed that would be a few more years down the road. Are you wearing diapers yet?"

"Now, you're being downright disrespectful, Will," Sean said with an extra firm tone in his voice.

"Hey, I'm getting a call from Mom. I'm going to tell her you'll be calling her in the next few minutes. You'd better do it, too. Bye."

"Will!"

It was too late. He had disconnected. Now Sean was committed to calling Dixie, and there was little he could do to get out of it. He dropped his phone into his shirt pocket for just a moment while he thought about what he was going to say to her. In doing so, the phone made a click when it hit something. It was the memory stick containing the image of Kim. With all that had taken place in the previous twenty-four hours, he had nearly forgotten why he was in so much trouble in the first place. As it had so many times in the past, just the thought of Kim gave Sean the strength to take the next step. After all, she'd been the bastion of strength for so many years, having faced an adversary far worse than any of his. It was time to speak with Dixie. The phone barely finished one ring before she answered.

"Sean?" Dixie answered, her voice already breaking.

"It's me," he reluctantly replied. His headache was suddenly worsening.

"Will says you're on a train?"

"I'm on my way to Urbana."

"Why, Sean? Why did you leave like this? Listen to me. The doctor thinks you may have a head injury, and that's why you're acting this way. You could be in critical condition, honey. You need to go to a hospital as soon as you get to town. Have them contact Dr. Hudsen, and give your permission for them to discuss your condition."

"Dixie, I'm perfectly fine," he said as he rubbed his temples. "I just had to get out of town. To be honest with you, I was pissed. Are you the reason April took the job with Frank?"

"Jesus, Sean! I'm worried about your well-being, and all you can think about is that bimbo! I'm not kidding, Sean. I'm going to call Raymond and Will and have them drag you kicking and screaming to the hospital if they have to. Then, when I get there, I'm going to…"

"So it's true then. You're certainly not denying it. You sucked her out of my life, just like you did Kim."

"Sean, that's not the way it was…."

Dixie wasn't able to talk to him any longer she was crying so hard. Sean heard noise on the other end as the phone was taken away from Dixie.

"Sean, it's John. Listen to Dixie. Something's not right with you. When you get to Urbana, just go to the hospital emergency room there and do as Dixie suggested."

"Hey, John! Go fuck yourself!" Sean said. He then disconnected his phone and turned the power off.

The woman across the aisle gave Sean another disapproving look, having drawn her own conclusion about what was going on by eavesdropping on Sean's end of the conversations. As Sean looked uneasily at her, the image of her began to blur slightly and the color of her clothing began to change before his eyes. He quickly closed his eyes, turning his head away from her as he did so.

AS PROMISED, THE TRAIN pulled into the station in Champaign, the city adjacent to Urbana. And as promised, Dixie must have phoned ahead to Raymond and Will. Both were waiting for him on the platform, along with two police officers and two paramedics. It wasn't exactly the same greeting he had received from his grandparents many years before. As Sean stood up, an increasing feeling of vertigo caused him to hold on to the seatbacks. After Sean slowly stepped off the train, Raymond walked up to him. His demeanor was extremely distressed.

"We're going to do this my way, do you understand?"

"Dad…"

"My way, Sean, you got that? Either you can cooperate with these medics and go to the hospital, or I'll tell the cops to put you in handcuffs, and they'll haul you to the hospital."

"Dad, there's no need for this. I'm perfectly…"

"Do you hear me?!" Raymond shouted. He gripped Sean by the shoulders, looked him squarely in the eyes, then said, "I'm not about to lose another member of my family, Sean. You're either hurt or sick. I don't know which, and I don't care. But you're going to the hospital whether you like it or not."

As if to bolster Raymond's position, Will walked up and stood beside his grandfather looking equally concerned.

"So this is my happy homecoming?" Sean asked sarcastically.

"Dad, do as Pops says."

Without so much as a hello, thank you, or anything else for that matter, Sean walked, or more accurately weaved with a limp, to the waiting ambulance, opened the door without asking, and climbed inside with Kim's book tucked safely under his arm.

After handing a note to one of the paramedics, Raymond said, "I wrote down all the information I could pull together about him—name, address, phone number, health problems and so forth. Tell the doctor at the emergency room to phone the number I wrote down for a Dr. Hudsen up in Lake Forest. He can fill in what's been going on in the last twenty-four hours. I guess there's some question that he may have internal injuries or a head injury, and judging from his behavior, if he doesn't have one, he will when I get done with him. So get him the hell out of here. My name and phone number is at the bottom if you need to contact me."

"We'll take good care of him, Mr. Marcum."

"Thanks, fellows. I'll be along after a bit."

"Pops, can I ride to the hospital with you?" Will asked.

Raymond pulled out his wallet and handed Will some cash. "No. I need you to do something. Your father looks like hell. There ought to be a hundred bucks or so there. Go buy him some clothes. Nothing fancy—just some basics to get him through until he gets home. Your mother ought to be here later this afternoon, and she's bringing some of his things."

"I told her I could have driven him home. She didn't have to come all the way down here," Will said.

"I know, Will. But, I think this is one of those *for better or worse* times, and she's really the one who needs to be here for him. In any case, I'm awfully proud of you for stepping up to the plate when the bases are loaded, so to speak. You've turned into quite a responsible man." Raymond sighed before finished with, "I hope your dad turns into one someday here pretty quick."

"I've never seen him like this, Pops. I mean, he's been struggling a lot recently with his job and some garbage about Grandma he just can't let go of. But now, I think that accident really did something to him. He's acting totally weird. Did you see the size of that knot on his head and the way he was walking?"

Raymond nodded before replying, "I don't think I'd use the word 'garbage' when talking about your father's feelings. Your dad and your grandma had a very special relationship. But I figured by now he'd have gotten beyond all of that. Looking more troubled than ever, he said to Will, "Your dad isn't going to want to go home. He wants to go to his friend's funeral. I think her death has kind of pushed him over the edge. You're going to have to help your mom convince him he needs to take it easy. Think you can talk some sense into him?"

"I'll do my best, Pops. By the way, if you don't mind me asking, I know a little about Kim and Dad back a long time ago. What was so special about Kim, anyway?"

After wiping his hands across his face as if to remove all the strain it was exhibiting, Raymond grinned a little and replied, "This is kind of awkward, Will. But your grandma and I really thought them two were going to be married at some point. She made a lot of changes in your Dad—a lot of good changes. Hard tellin' how he might have turned out had she not been in his life during those years. Kimmie was a sweetheart, and your grandma and I all but adopted her as our own. It was tough on all of us when things didn't work out."

"You mean when Mom and Dad began dating," Will concluded. "Did you guys ever feel the same about Mom?"

Raymond wasn't going to go down that path with his grandson, at least not now.

"You're asking a lot of good questions, and you deserve an answer from me. But, if you want an honest, unemotional answer, you'll have to wait until we get your dad back on his feet. Fair enough?"

Will's GQ smile was all the response Raymond needed.

"I hate to bring this up, but if for some reason your folks need to spend the night in town, and they can't get along, who do you want?"

"I can't believe they're acting like this. It's totally stupid. But to answer your question, I don't think I can make a choice like that. You choose, and I'll take whoever is left over."

"Well, I think your mom's under enough stress, so why don't you take her, and we'll take your dad."

"What are you drinking these days?" Will asked, implying his grandfather would need some support from a bottle.

With a chuckle, Raymond answered, "Damn, seems like yesterday you were crapping in your diaper. Now you can buy booze. Tell you what, Will. Surprise me. And be sure to get yourself something to leave at the house for when you and Giselle drop by so I always have something there for the two of you."

Will leaned into his grandfather to give him a hug, shaking his hand at the same time.

RAYMOND ARRIVED AT THE hospital about thirty minutes after Sean left in the ambulance. What had been a relatively small hospital when he moved to Urbana in the late 1940s, had become a behemoth, spanning several city blocks. Raymond had been in many parts of the hospital over the years; some parts he never wanted to see again. Even the emergency room had been moved so it took him another twenty minutes or so to park his car, then to navigate his way to where he hoped Sean would be. Having finally arrived, he walked up to a window marked with a sign saying 'Triage' where a young, attractive nurse was sitting.

"I'm Raymond Marcum. My son, Sean, should have come here about forty-five minutes or so back."

"Hello, Mr. Marcum. You probably don't remember me, but you may know my parents—Glenn and Kristy Hampton?"

"No kidding? You're…uh…" Raymond said, snapping his fingers.

"Tammy," she said, finishing Raymond's line of thought.

"Last I saw you was…golly…a long time ago," he said, reflecting on his past.

"I'll always remember going to the drug store with my mother, and while we waited to get our prescription filled, you'd give me one of those tiny Nestlé Crunch candy bars."

"I must have handed out a million of those damn things to kids over the forty years I had that store. I'm surprised any of your generation has teeth."

"Well it was the best part of being sick, I'll tell you that much."

Raymond was moved by the young nurse's remarks. It felt good to know he'd touched people in such a way.

After typing Sean's name into the computer, Tammy said, "Let me check on Sean for you, and I'll be right back."

"So he made it here?"

"Yes, he's here. I just need to check before I can let visitors back to see him. Give me a few seconds, okay?"

"Fine. I'll be right over here," Raymond said, pointing to some empty seats.

After a few minutes, Tammy opened the door. Raymond could not help but notice the expression on her face had changed to one much more serious.

"Mr. Marcum, Dr. Fletcher will speak with you now."

Raymond was no fool. "What about Sean?"

"The doctor wants to speak with you first. I need you to follow me."

Raymond stood up and walked through the door. But, instead of turning left toward the treatment rooms, Tammy took Raymond gently by the arm to a room marked 'Family Room.' A young doctor with whom Raymond was unfamiliar stood waiting.

"Mr. Marcum, have a seat please. I'm Dr. Fletcher."

"No, I'll stand, thank you. Where's Sean?" Raymond asked anxiously.

"What do you know about his accident yesterday?" the doctor asked.

"Stop beating around the bush, Doc. What's up with Sean?"

"Well, shortly after he got here, he experienced what we call a grand mal seizure. Does he have any history of seizures?"

"No, not that I know of anyway. How is he?"

"Well, we had to sedate him to stop the seizure. Then, to protect his airway, we had to put a tube down his throat to breath for him. That's all routine procedure. I don't want you to worry about that. What concerns me is the underlying cause of the seizure. I just got off the phone with Dr. Hudsen up at Lake Forest, and he said there is reason to believe Sean may have what we call an intracranial hemorrhage as a result of a rather serious traffic accident yesterday. These types of injuries are insidious. Sometimes symptoms show up right away. At other times, they show up weeks after a head injury occurs. That's why Hudsen wanted to do a follow-up CT this morning. Apparently Sean left the hospital last night without being discharged, is that correct?"

"To tell you the truth, you know about as much as I do. So what now?"

"We're doing that CT of his head right now and as many follow-up tests as we can—blood work, ultrasound and CT of his abdomen, some x-rays and such. I'll know more in about fifteen minutes." After pausing to let Raymond absorb the news, the doctor continued, "If he is bleeding inside his head, we may need to do surgery right away. To be honest with you, I've already notified the on-call neurosurgeon and the O-R in anticipation this is the direction things are going."

Raymond took a seat, unable to absorb the sudden change of events.

"Can I get you anything? Do you want us to phone anybody for you?"

"I need to call some people," Raymond replied, his voice cracking. "Can I see him?"

"Not just yet. Let me take care of a few things first. In any event, I'll get you back to him in about twenty minutes. Will that work for you?"

"Whatever you say," Raymond answered reluctantly.

"I'll have someone come back to sit with you so you're not alone."

Raymond nodded as the doctor hastily departed. Raymond reached into his pocket and pulled out his cell phone. He attempted to dial a number several times, but was unable to get through. About the time he was ready to throw his phone, Tammy came into the room.

"Hello again," the young, friendly nurse said. "I switched with one of the other nurses just so I could be with you until your family gets here. What can I do for you?"

"I need to call some people, but I can't get this damn thing to work," Raymond replied, the anguish and frustration of what was happening showing in his eyes.

"Oh, that phone won't work in this room. Use this one," Tammy said, picking up a cordless phone in the room and handing it to Raymond.

Handing his cell phone to Tammy, he asked, "Can you look up a number on that phone for me? Look for the name, Will."

"Sure can," Tammy said enthusiastically.

"I can't figure out how those things work half the time. I had my grandson set it up for me...that's who Will is."

"Here it is. It's local so you won't need to dial the area code and you don't need to dial -9- or anything."

Raymond dialed, and Will was quick to answer.

"Will? Hey, change in plans. I need you to come on to the hospital. Well, your dad's taken a turn and the doctors may want to do an operation here pretty quick. Yeah, you're telling me! No...don't tell her. There's nothing she can do while she's driving. We'll just have to tell her when she gets here. Alright. See you in a bit. Hey, don't dilly-dally. Alright."

"Is he coming?" Tammy asked.

"He'll be here P-D-Q. He's out at the mall. It shouldn't take him long."

"Great. Is there anyone else you want to notify? Is Sean married?"

"Yeah, but his wife's on her way here from the Chicago area. I don't want to call her and tell her this over the phone. She'll drive into a ditch or something. She'll be here later on. I do need to call my wife and let her know what's going on."

"Do you want me to dial that number for you?"

"No. I'm not that old…yet."

Tammy smiled most pleasantly. It was a friendly smile that Raymond most desperately needed at that moment.

"Hey, I brought you something," Tammy said, reaching into her pocket.

After rummaging around for a few seconds, she pulled out a Nestlé Crunch candy bar and presented it to Raymond. She then leaned over and gave him a reassuring hug.

Chapter 17

BY FAR, THE BEST part about Mark—well, other than that part—was his mother. Don't get me wrong. As men go, Mark was a saint. I couldn't have done better if I'd picked him out myself. Wait a minute...I did pick him out myself! Be that as it may, Marian was an incredible woman. I owe my sanity to her. At the risk of breaking my shoulder as I pat myself on the back, I'm quite certain she did equally well by me.

Suffice it to say, what kept us in stitches month after month, year after year, were puzzles. Now, I'm not speaking of the type where you dump a thousand pieces onto a card table, then spend hours turning what inevitably is more than one-half of the pieces face-up. I'm speaking of serious brain-teasers. We literally communicated to Mark and his father subliminally, and we did so when we truly wanted them engaged in the subject. Sure, we could have carried on a conversation with our men much as other women do—you know, where women speak a hundred words and men hear five of them...on an attentive night! That short list of words includes such attention-getters as, beer, sex, dinner, football, and fishing. Instead, we made them think. Rarely did we give them the answer, and never right away. Though Mark and his father often protested our methods, they invariably learned something from each experience...something they would have missed had we simply handed over the goods.

Sadly, there came a point in Mark's life when he no longer had the drive to find the answers to his most pressing problems. Marian and I gave him countless hints and clues, but he never took that information to the next level where he could assimilate it. I used to fault Esmeralda for relentlessly and deliberately distracting him. In the final analysis, however, Mark simply lacked the hunger necessary to find the closure he so desperately needed. I was surprised when Marian's death didn't provide him the catalyst. It's almost as though her death was for naught and that brings us to this chapter in Mark's life. As Mark, himself, now faces his own demise, will his life end without him being able to resolve the ache in his heart? If only he had listened to the Fuller Brush Man when he had the chance...

"MOM, DAD'S WAKING UP!" Callie called out.

After quickly crawling out from under a blanket that had covered her on the hide-a-bed sofa, Dixie made her way over to her husband. She caressed his cheeks with her soft hands before leaning over to give him a warm embrace.

"Can you hear me, honey?" she asked cautiously.

Sean tried to speak, but nothing happened. Instead he nodded a response.

"Callie, go tell the nurse that your dad is waking up."

"Okay," she replied, heading for assistance without any question.

Getting close to him, Dixie asked, "Sean, do you know who I am?"

There was a connection alright. But verbalizing her name was another thing.

"Baby, squeeze my hand if you know who I am."

Dixie was ever so happy to have Sean tightly grip her hand.

As Sean tried to sit up, it appeared he was met with considerable pain in his abdomen. He fought to maintain his equilibrium. He also discovered there were tubes…a tube in his nose, tubes in both arms, and a urinary catheter. Suddenly, the entire situation must have taken on a frightening dimension, causing Sean to panic and begin to struggle.

"Sean, you need to relax," Dixie begged. "Everything's alright, honey. You're at the hospital in Urbana."

Dixie's words provided little reassurance, and Sean's actions now were more visceral than well thought out. He tried sitting up again. This time Dixie had to hold him down so he wouldn't pull out any of his tubes or fall on the side rails of the bed. Fortunately, Callie returned with a nurse just as he was about to overpower her.

"Mr. Marcum, you need to relax," the nurse said.

Sean's response to her was much the same as it was to Dixie's pleading request when she said the same thing. He continued to struggle with both the nurse and Dixie.

"Callie, push that blue button on the wall, would you please," the nurse instructed.

Callie did as requested.

A voice soon called out over a speaker on the wall, "This is the nurses' station."

"I have a Code Blue in 615," the nurse in the room called out.

It wasn't but a few seconds before a second nurse arrived, followed shortly by two other women dressed in scrubs.

"Is Kandahar still on the floor?" the first nurse asked.

"I think he's down in 602," one of the other nurses replied.

"One of you go get him. Now!"

As it turned out, Kandahar was just entering Sean's room. He had heard the call for a Code Blue and assumed he might be needed.

"Mr. Marcum, I'm Dr. Kandahar. You need to lie back in bed before you hurt yourself." He wedged himself in front of Dixie, saying, "Excuse me Mrs. Marcum, but let me in here next to him."

Dixie moved to the foot of the bed where she put her arm around Callie who was now shaking nervously from all the commotion.

Getting face to face with Sean, Kandahar said, "Sean, listen to me right now. If you don't relax and stop fighting, I'll have to give you some medicine to calm you down. I'm your neurologist. You suffered a head injury a while back, and you're just now waking up. I know all of this is confusing, but I want you to relax and listen to what I have to say to you."

Sean continued thrashing about the bed uncontrollably as he tried in vain to get out.

Kandahar looked up at one of the nurses and ordered, "Get me some Ativan." She quickly left the room to do as requested. "Sean, here's the deal. I'm going to give you a little medication to help you relax. I'm not going to put you to sleep. We need you to be interactive, but you have to calm down so I'm going to help you with that."

Sean relaxed some, possibly realizing that if he didn't cooperate, the doctor would take matters into his own hands.

Kandahar continued, "It's not unusual for a person with your type of injury to wake up disoriented and afraid. We need to get you grounded again with your person, time, and whereabouts." Taking Sean's hand and placing it on a bandage that covered the upper left quadrant of his abdomen, the doctor went on to say, "Also, you had surgery on your spleen while you were recovering from your head injury. We had to take part of it out. That surgery site hasn't healed yet obviously, so the more you try to move, the more your belly is going to hurt."

The nurse returned with a syringe and a small vial. She got Kandahar's attention.

"Give him 2 milligrams and we'll see what happens," he requested.

Dixie watched as two nurses and Kandahar held Sean still, while a third with the medication connected the syringe to one of his IV lines and administered the drug.

"Just a little bit of medicine, Sean. It will help you relax while you get settled."

It took a while, but slowly Sean felt the effects of the medicine. He lay back in bed, and everyone was able to cautiously release their grips on his arms and legs.

Kandahar motioned toward Dixie and Callie, saying, "Why don't both of you come back up here now?"

Dixie approached stoically, while Callie still whimpered slightly as she clung to her mother's arm. They got close enough that Sean was able to see both of them.

"Sean, you may have some difficulty speaking because we have a feeding tube in your throat. If you can understand what I'm saying, I want you to nod your head," the doctor instructed.

As Sean slowly nodded, Callie gripped her mother's arm excitedly.

"How long ago did he come around?" Kandahar asked.

"Just a couple of minutes ago," Callie answered. "I went for the nurse right away."

"Have either of you heard him speak?"

"He seems to try, but nothing happens," Dixie answered.

"What exactly do you mean, Mrs. Marcum?" Kandahar pressed.

"Well, he sort of parted his lips when I asked him questions, but he didn't articulate anything."

"I see. I'm not too worried about that just yet. After all, he's been sedated and in a coma for, what, three, going on four days now. Let's get him reoriented, and try to get some things back to normal, and then we can have a better idea of his true mental status. Can I count on the two of you to help him out?" Kandahar asked, looking back and forth at Dixie and Callie.

"Absolutely. In fact, there will be others here in a little while who can also help," Dixie replied.

"Good. I'm going to have the nurses remove the feeding tube. I feel confident he's ready to start eating on his own. I'll order a bland diet for a couple of days to get him used to solid food again. I want you to assist him only to the extent necessary because he needs to try to feed himself as much as possible. I also want you to get him up and start walking him around once he's had something to eat. Take him to the elevators and back once every hour. Be sure when he gets up that you let him sit on the edge of the bed for a minute. He's on medication to lower his blood pressure, and he might faint if you stand him up too quickly. Other than that, try speaking with him. Tell him what's been taking place. Get him to answer questions. If he can't verbalize an answer, get him to answer physically in some manner. Don't make him write just yet. He may need more time for that fine motor skill to come around. Keep an eye out for unusual behavior or anything that looks like a seizure—he might have convulsions or simply develop a blank stare. Let the nurse know immediately if anything like this happens. I need to finish my rounds on this floor, but I will be back in about two hours. I know these are a lot of instructions, so do either of you have any questions?"

Dixie exchanged looks with Callie to gauge her reaction to Kandahar's question before replying, "No. I think we're good. Thanks for everything, Dr. Kandahar."

"These are all good signs," he added. "The fact that he has awakened on his own and has made some associations tells me he is on the road to recovery."

Dixie noticed an immediate change in Sean's facial expression following Kandahar's remark. She reached for his hand, at which point he reached back meeting her half way. Though hoarse and garbled, all in the room clearly heard him say, "Road to Monticello…Find the Fuller Brush Man."

While she was relieved by Sean's burst of excitement and the smile on his face, Dixie had to fight not to show her disappointment in Sean's choice for his first spoken words since lapsing into a coma.

RAYMOND SAT QUIETLY IN a cafeteria chair pouring over a stack of papers. He was reading Kim's book. He had started and stopped reading the book a number of times, finding it often stirred up emotions he had long ago laid to rest, or at least so he'd thought. But each time he stopped reading, he found himself inexplicably drawn back to it. The book, he realized, wasn't just an essay about Sean. It was as much as anything a treatise on everything that surrounded him. It was also exceptionally well written, a quality that Raymond, a prolific reader, couldn't overlook. As he immersed himself into the second half of the book, he was interrupted by a familiar voice.

"Raymond, do you mind if I join you?"

Looking up at his visitor, Raymond gladly welcomed the interruption.

"How ya' doing, Ben?" Raymond asked as he stood up to greet his company. "Take a seat. Can I get you something to eat or maybe something to drink?"

"No. I can't stay too long," he replied, sitting down. "I just met with Sean. He's looking good."

"That he is, the dumbass," Raymond replied as he sat down. "He's talking a lot better now, too."

Ben chuckled at Raymond's hard line regarding his son.

"Did you break the news to him about where Kimmie is buried?" Raymond inquired, getting right to the point.

"No," Ben replied sheepishly.

"Why not? That was part of the deal we made. I'm sure as hell not going to tell him."

"I know, Raymond. I'm just procrastinating."

"Well, you know the first thing he's going to want to do when he gets released is go to the cemetery. He needs to know ahead of time. But first, you need to take Dixie aside and inform her. She's likely to pitch a fit. You need to get that over with before you tell Sean. Was she with him when you left?" Raymond continued.

"No. Will and his girlfriend are with him. Dixie went out with Callie to take care of her situation at the sorority. I guess Callie missed some of the rush activities while she was caring for Sean, and those with 'say' were making noises that they might not let her pledge. After breaking her arm and having to sit out the volleyball season, Dixie wasn't going to sit idly by and let that happen to Callie as well. I suspect she's going to shake things up a bit."

"Waste of damn money, if you ask me. It's just wrong that a sweet, bright, attractive girl like that with a limitless future would have to kiss anyone's butt to get into a sorority. I think you and Sean did right thirty years ago when you ran naked through that place. I hope you relieved yourself behind some heavy piece of furniture."

Ben continued to chuckle at Raymond's frank opinions regarding just about everything.

"How'd he handle your meeting? He was upset to beat hell about not being at Kim's funeral."

"He must have apologized twenty times. I made sure he knew I wasn't offended and I'm really not. It was just one of those unpredictable things. And I let him know you and Barbara attended. He was so worried about getting me the picture of Kim I'd asked him for. A woman who works with him got a copy into my hands the day before the funeral."

"April?"

"You know her?" Ben asked.

"I know *of* her," Raymond replied unhappily. "I hear there may be some hanky-panky going on between her and Sean. You heard anything?"

Shaking his head, Ben answered, "No. In any case, I don't think Sean could be unfaithful ever again. He really regretted what he did to Kim."

"Well, you know what they say—once a sinner, always a sinner."

Again shaking his head, this time more emphatically, Ben countered, "Raymond, trust me on this one. Sean won't stray. Besides, Dixie would have killed the two of them by now if anything had happened between them."

Now it was Raymond's turn to chuckle as he said, "You got that right. She's got the grace of a ballerina and the demeanor of linebacker."

After the yucking settled down, Raymond picked up a few pages of the book and said, "Kimmie's book here...pretty good stuff...pretty tough medicine, too. You know, she was just like a daughter to us. Ever read it?"

Leaning back in the chair with his hands locked behind his head, Ben replied, "She used me as a subject matter expert."

"In other words, a man."

"Exactly. Besides, Sean and I were pretty tight for a lot of years. I had a good idea what was going on between those big ears."

"You'd be a first. I gave up trying to figure him out a long time ago. Until recently, I didn't think I had to worry about him anymore. Has he ever talked to you about this Fuller Brush nonsense? That's all he keeps talking about when he gets me alone."

Resting his elbows on the table, Ben answered, "Did Nadine ever mention anything about it?"

"Hell no," Raymond replied throwing his hands in the air. "Sean's got this hair-brain idea that she was sending him some sort of message when she wrote those words at the end of her journal. Other than that, and the fact that about once a month she bought a few things from ol' man Drake, I never gave this Fuller Brush stuff a second thought."

"Sean says he's had several dreams about Kim since she died. In each dream, she mentions something about how he has to find the Fuller Brush Man."

"Well, I've read more than half of her book, and she hasn't mentioned it so far."

"Did Nadine communicate in riddles?"

"Not until she hooked up with Kimmie. The two of them used to drive me and Sean nuts. They'd never say what was on their mind. They always had some elaborate…oh, what do you call it…all I can think of is brain fart."

"Brain teaser?"

"Yeah, brain teaser. Those two could come up with the wildest things. It was kind of funny at first, but damn, after a few years, I was about to go get fitted for a straight jacket. Do you think there's anything to this notion of Sean's about the Fuller Brush Man?"

"What do you mean…like Drake was Sean's father or something?"

Sitting back in shock at the suggestion, Raymond replied, "Well, first of all, Drake was queer as a four dollar bill. He just happened to be gay before anyone knew about or talked about gay people. Secondly, since you two used to run around the college naked, I assume you've seen that big mole on his butt. Well, I got the same thing. He's all mine."

"Well, I just learned a whole lot more than I'd asked for," Ben quipped. After hesitating a moment, Ben continued, "There is something to it, you know. Kim told me before she died that she was going to give Sean some kind of hint that would solve the mystery of Nadine's words in her journal. She didn't tell me what it was, but she said it would be in this book she wrote for him. She really wanted him to figure it out because she said it would bring closure to his past and set him on a positive course for the future."

"In other words, it's another brain teaser. Well, it's gonna be a while before he figures it out, I guess. Did he tell you he's having a hard time reading 'cause of his headaches?"

"They sound pretty bad. Does the doctor know what's causing them?"

"He said it's a problem with how his brain is assimilating what he's seeing. I guess there's some sort of focus or depth perception problem that makes reading a severe strain. The doc says it ought to straighten out in a few weeks after the rest of the residual blood trapped in that thick skull of Sean's is reabsorbed." Raymond fiddled with some crackers on his plate before continuing, "Back to this April thing. Does Sean know you got the picture you wanted for the funeral?"

"Yeah. I told him it was perfect."

"Does Sean know how the picture got to you?"

"Well, I sort of lied. I told him Dixie got it for me."

"Now that was a stretch. You know as well as I do Dixie was jealous as hell about Kimmie's past with Sean. He'll see right through that. Why didn't you tell him the truth?"

"Because Sean would have told Dixie that it was April who got me the picture, and that's a truth I don't think Dixie could handle at this time given all the strain between them."

Raymond realized Ben must have also felt there was probably more going on between Sean and April than he was letting show. Grinning, he said, "I guess you should have told him it was delivered by the Fuller Brush Man. That would have kept him busy."

Chapter 18

AFTER SEVEN DAYS IN the hospital, Sean was undergoing his final tests and examinations, hoping to get the doctor's approval to be discharged. It had been an emotionally taxing time for Dixie, but she dutifully remained by his side almost constantly save for a few hours here and there with Callie and Will. In spite of the offer to bed down at Raymond and Barbara's home, she respectfully declined—a rebuff that was expected. Dixie never felt completely at ease with Sean's family. There was always a latent need to get out of the shadow cast by Kim when she was alive, let alone now that she was deceased. That feeling was about to take on a whole new dimension.

Dixie had set out clothes for Sean to wear upon leaving the hospital, making clear her confidence that his injury would soon be a thing of the past. As she sat on the hide-a-bed sofa patiently reading a novel, there was a knock on the door to Sean's room.

"Come in," Dixie said.

Ben entered the room. "Is this a good time?"

She had been expecting Ben. After marking her page in the book, Dixie set it down and said, "Sean will be back in about thirty minutes. He just went for *hopefully* his last CT scan. Do you want me to call you when he gets back?"

Closing the door, Ben answered, "Actually, I'd like to speak with you for a few minutes if that's alright."

"Sure. What's up?"

Taking a seat on the bed, he asked, "Are you okay with this trip to the cemetery?"

The conversation was between Dixie and Ben now. There was nobody else in the room to absorb the direct nature of his question.

"Ben, you know how I feel about Kim. There was always tension between us, and now there will never be a chance for either of us to change that. As much as I'm sorry about Kim's death—and I truly am, Ben—I'm sorry her relationship with me never got resolved." Dixie could tell there was more on Ben's mind so she asked, "Is that all you wanted to know?"

"No. There's a detail about Kim's burial that I need to tell you about before we get to the cemetery, and before I tell Sean."

"I can't imagine how her burial could be so mysterious. What is it?"

After pausing to get up enough strength to say it, Ben replied, "Kim's buried next to Nadine."

The silence was deafening. All Dixie could feel was the hair standing up on the back of her neck.

"You're joking, right?" Dixie asked.

"It was one of her last requests. The two plots next to Raymond's and Nadine's were available, so I bought them. Raymond was alright with it."

Incredulous, Dixie asked, "And you never stopped to think about what this would do to Sean…to me for that matter?"

"Well, I looked at it this way, Dixie. It really wasn't up to Sean where my wife was to be buried, and I knew you would disapprove. There was no way for the three of us to have a discussion about it."

Ben's honest and unquestionably accurate assessment of the situation set Dixie on fire.

"Your wife?!" Dixie said. She rose to attention, her face turning red with anger. "I've got news for you…Sean may as well have been married to your wife all these years. It's clear he never stopped thinking about her."

"And who do we have to thank for that?!" Ben yelled back, sinking into the brawl.

"Jesus, Ben! Couldn't you and Kim have just resigned yourselves to the fact that you lost and I won?! Get over it!"

"I lost?! That's crap—I won! I got the prize! Sean's the one who got the turkey!"

"This is complete bullshit, Ben," Dixie answered, the tone of her voice matching Ben's. Sticking her pointed finger into his chest, she continued, "You know Sean will freak out over this. He can't even look at his own mother's grave. Now you plant Kim next to her? What are you trying to do to him?"

"He needs to get past his mother's death."

"And this is supposed to help? He can't handle it, Ben!" Dixie argued while throwing her arms into the air in frustration.

"What do you want me to do, Dix? Dig Kim up?"

"Yes!" she replied with cold-hearted quickness.

"Well that's not going to happen!" Ben yelled at the top of his lungs.

There was a knock on the door and a nurse entered, asking, "People…your voices are carrying up and down the hallway. Is everything alright?"

Neither Dixie nor Ben would answer immediately.

"Mrs. Marcum, I need the two of you to keep your voices down. If there's a problem here, you need to take it outside of the hospital."

"There is a problem," Dixie stated emphatically. "This man needs to be escorted out of the hospital. He's causing a conflict, and Sean doesn't need this kind of stress right now. I don't want him to have any contact with me or Sean until we get out of here. Is that understood?"

"Sir, I need you to leave as Mrs. Marcum requested," the nurse instructed Ben.

Instead of complying with the request, Ben got into Dixie's face and said, "You are the most despicable person I have ever met, Dixie Darling."

"It's Marcum!"

"You're not good enough for that name!"

"Sir, you need to leave now or I'll have to call security," the nurse requested again as she was joined by another.

"That won't be necessary," Ben said as he brushed past the nurses. Stopping just outside the door, he turned and finished with, "Take Sean to the cemetery yourself, Dixie. It's a fitting end since you'll be digging your own grave as you try to explain it all to him. But don't come crawling to me."

DR. KANDAHAR SPENT FIVE minutes speaking way over the vocabulary level of both Dixie and Sean. They were thankful when he finally concluded his remarks in words that both could understand.

"The long and short of it, Sean, is it appears the bleeding inside your head has stopped. While there remains some trace blood in the subdural space, it's not causing you any significant deficits. The symptoms you are experiencing—headaches and visual disturbances and the occasional dizziness—should subside over the next two weeks. During that time, you need to rest as much as possible, do no lifting of objects weighing more than ten pounds, and do not put your head lower than your torso. When you sleep, keep your head elevated slightly above the rest of your body. As a general rule, do not exert yourself in any manner that would elevate your heart rate above one hundred beats per minutes for any length of time. We really want to keep your blood pressure low until all signs of your injury are gone. You cannot have alcoholic beverages until you are cleared. And finally, take all the medications we have prescribed exactly as written. I'll be transferring care to Dr. Cardiff Best in Lake Forest. He knows all about your case. You need to schedule a follow up appointment with him in two weeks, and if you have any worsening of your symptoms or if new symptoms develop, I want you to contact him immediately. Do either of you have any questions?"

Dixie and Sean exchanged looks before he replied, "No. I think you've laid everything out for us. There is one thing. I was seeing a psychologist before all this happened. Like we told you, I'm trying to work out some personal matters. Is it alright if I continue to keep appointments with him?"

"Certainly. I'd, of course, advise you to tread lightly on subjects that might get you too worked up. But if the purpose is to bring comfort to your life, I think this would be a perfect time for you to see this man. What's his name, if I may ask?"

"Sterling Berkowitz."

"Dr. Berkowitz? I know him. He is, among other things, a forensic psychologist. I've testified in several court cases with him. He is a very brilliant man. I've not met anyone as perceptive as he. Watch yourself."

"I know what you mean. I've only seen him once, and he found out more about me after two hours than I could tell anyone in a year."

"You are lucky, Sean. Your injuries could have been much worse. Instead, you've been given a new lease on life. I suggest you take account of your circumstances. Your future lies before you once again."

"Thanks, Doc. I don't know what to say. One thing's for sure. I'm not going to check out of a hospital like I did before."

"Check out? You walked out," Dixie said as she smiled and held Sean's hand.

"You're right, Babe. I really screwed up."

"There's something else I want to say, Sean. Dixie was here with you from the onset of your hospital stay. Her actions demonstrated a commitment of love and caring that always makes me humble when I see it. Take her out and buy her something nice. She earned it."

"You're absolutely right, Doc. I'm very lucky. It's time I started to do a better job of showing it."

"Well then," Kandahar closed, "the nurse will be in shortly with some paperwork you need to sign, your discharge instructions and some prescriptions. After that, you are on your way. Good luck to you Mr. Marcum. Let's not meet this way again, shall we?"

"Nothing personal, Doc, but I don't ever want to see your face again…that is unless you're in the market for a new car."

"You'll cut me a deal?"

"Ask for me personally."

"I might just do that."

DIXIE WAS BETTING ALL her chips that the next half hour would go as planned. Any unanticipated circumstances and all the accolades Dr. Kandahar had doled out earlier would be a thing of the past. When Sean asked the whereabouts of Ben, who was supposed to take him to the cemetery, Dixie told him that Ben needed a break from all the events surrounding Kim's death, and that he was fatigued and too emotionally drained to go back another time. Sean fell for that. To make the rest work, Dixie prayed that there would be at least one more recently dug grave—hopefully one that was marked with anything but a name. Finally, she had to hope that Sean would avoid going to his mother's grave just as he had each time he visited his home town in the past few years. If all of the lies held together, she'd be able to get Sean out of Urbana and back on home soil in Lake Forest where she could deal with the turbulence if—but more likely when—he found out about her deception.

As soon as Dixie crested the hill at the entrance to the cemetery, she scanned the horizon from end to end looking for a suitable grave for her ruse. It wasn't long before she spied one that she felt deserved to be her objective.

"Are you sure you know where it is?" Sean asked.

Making up everything as she drove, Dixie replied, "Ben gave me very clear instructions. He said it was on the other side of the cemetery from your mother's grave. I'm supposed to take the main entrance, then take the first left." After slowly proceeding to the far end of the cemetery, Dixie said, "There. I think that's it. He said it was under a big elm tree."

She pulled her vehicle to a stop and turned off its engine. The two sat quietly, fearing what was about to happen, though for entirely different reasons.

Taking his hand in hers, Dixie asked, "Are you sure you want to do this? Nothing says we have to do this today. We can come back in a week or two if you want."

Looking out the window at the grave, Sean answered, "No. I want to see it. I need to get this behind me. Do you want to come with me or stay here?"

"I want to be with you, honey."

"Alright, let's go."

The two met outside the passenger door and linked arms. Dixie closed her eyes as she prayed that her plan would work. Sean closed his eyes as well. She knew he was unwilling to accept that Kim was now buried, and that he had missed the funeral. In unison, they walked forward about twenty paces over the flat turf, then opened their eyes. They had come to a stop several feet in front of the fresh mound of dirt. There were flower arrangements placed neatly around the grave. One's ribbon said Mother; another's said Wife; yet another's said Sister. Nothing specifically identified this grave from their vantage point. It was here that Sean turned, buried his head in Dixie's shoulder and broke down crying. She felt horrible deceiving Sean this way, but at the same time she was convinced that this was best for not only him, but for the two of them. After a few minutes, Sean took Dixie's hand and led her back to her SUV, never looking back at the grave. Her ploy had worked.

Just before he got into the vehicle, Sean glanced off in the distance to where his mother was buried. Dixie noticed where he was looking and nervously asked, "Is everything alright?"

After a moment, Sean replied, "It looks like someone was buried over near Mom's grave. I think there were some plots left. I hope they didn't get the ones next to her. I'd sort of hoped we might be buried there someday. I guess that's kind of morose…sorry."

Hoping her next question would get them quickly on their way, Dixie asked, "Do you want to go see your mother's grave?"

Sean was quick to respond, "No. I don't feel up to it. I feel like all my blood got sucked out of me. I just want to go home."

Dixie wasn't going to waste any time. She held the door open for him, and he quickly sought refuge. It occurred to her that it had been a long time since she had heard him refer to Lake Forest as 'home.' After getting him settled in, she didn't delay getting out of the cemetery and on the road back to their Chicago suburb.

Chapter 19

FROM SEAN'S POINT OF view, the trip back to Lake Forest seemed to take no time at all. He had fallen asleep within a few minutes of leaving Urbana, and hadn't awakened until Dixie pulled into the garage some three and a half hours later. It wasn't long before Sean realized that he disliked the ten pound rule. It seemed he confronted it with every turn. One never realizes how often one is faced with lifting ten pounds or more until he's not allowed to do it. Every box and bag that needed to be brought in from the Lexus when he and Dixie arrived home was at least that heavy—even Dixie's purse weighed ten pounds. Once she had single-handedly unloaded the vehicle and they were inside, Sean took her in his arms and held her for a long time. If she wondered how he would react to coming home, she had her answer.

"Dix, I'm so sorry about all that I've put you through the last couple of weeks."

As he leaned back to look at her, she responded, "Hey, this is what marriage is all about. I'm sure Ben had to help Kim a million times. What I did for you was just a blip."

"No, it was a lot more than a blip, Dix. You were...spectacular. I just can't come up with a good enough word, but that one will have to do for now."

"Well, thanks. The main thing is that we're home...finally!" Dixie said, rubbing her face.

"It feels so empty," Sean said, looking around and taking note of the silence.

"I know what you mean," Dixie echoed. "When Callie was away on trips, at least we knew she was coming back at some point. Now, the kids are just...gone. It's scary."

"Did you get to spend some quality time with Giselle and Will? When they came to the hospital to see me, we just touched on some frivolous matters in their lives. I think the two of them were sparing me the shock of some momentous announcement."

"I don't know if you can call it quality time. I was there with them, but I was always thinking of you in the back of my mind. Will wanted to tell you something, but as you suspected, he was protecting you. So I have been chartered to do the deed."

"Oh? What's the news?"

"You need to sit down first."

"She's pregnant?"

"No...not yet anyway. Come on. Let's go sit for a while."

Dixie stopped by the bar and poured herself a glass of apricot brandy before joining Sean who had taken a seat on the sofa in front of the fireplace.

"I'm not supposed to drink," Sean said.

"It's for me, lunkhead. But, I might let you have a sip."

"Could I just lick it off of your lips?"

"I suppose that could be arranged."

Dixie took a drink of brandy, then let Sean kiss her. He held the kiss a long time, ending with a slow lick across her lips.

"Now that's the way to drink brandy," he said with a smile. "So what was Will's big news?"

"Well, as you might expect, they're getting married. They haven't picked a date, but it will be next June after they graduate."

"Wow. That relationship moved quickly."

"You're telling me. Anyway, Giselle seems to be perfect. She's smart, she's gorgeous, she's talented, and she has a wonderful personality. She's almost too perfect, but then I wonder if I'm just turning into a mother-in-law prematurely. She's about to take my son away from me, and I just don't want to face that reality."

"You're not losing a son, you're gaining a daughter."

"No," Dixie said, shaking her head. "I'm not there yet."

"How's Will with all of this?"

"Will's so in love. I've never seen him like this. I just don't want her to break his heart. But, at this point they're really, really, really in love."

"Where are they living?"

"He sublet his apartment and moved in with her. She has this condo that's unlike anything you or I ever lived in when we were going to college."

"What about her parents?"

"Loaded…brilliant. He's the CFO for company that owns hotels and resorts throughout Europe, and she's a professional chef. Giselle is their one and only child so they spared nothing giving her what she wanted. All things considered, it appears she has a pretty good head on her shoulders."

"If she could have anything she wanted, why on earth did she end up in Illinois?" Sean asked, puzzled by her choice.

"Do you remember Will's senior class trip went to Provence?"

"Sure do. It cost us a fortune."

"No, Sean. It got Will the love of his life and you a future daughter-in-law. He met Giselle on that trip. She was in Provence with her parents on holiday at the same time. They've been corresponding ever since without us knowing it. Your son is a romantic, just like his father."

"I'll be damned," Sean said with a proud smile on his face. "I am so amazed by him. He has a dream and he chases after it. Not only that, he catches it!" Sean had to pause to wipe tears from his eyes before asking, "Is that it?"

"Well, no. I'm not sure how you'll handle this, but here it goes. Her parents bought a mansion in Monticello."

"My Monticello?"

"Yep. They now own that beautiful old Victorian in the middle of the block on Millionaire's Row. You know—the one with the gables. They're spending the next six to nine months renovating the place, and they hope to open in the summer of next year under the name Château Giselle. It's supposed to be a high end spa, boutique hotel, and gourmet restaurant. Guess who the chef's going to be?"

"Giselle's mother?"

"Guess again."

"Giselle?"

"You're getting closer."

"You're kidding?"

"Nope. You're the father of a soon-to-be gourmet chef."

"Jesus. Your dad's going to crap when he hears this."

"Surprise, surprise, again. Daddy's into the project for three-hundred grand."

"What?" Sean asked, shocked at this added dimension to the news.

"You heard me. Daddy's invested in the château."

"So he knows Will isn't going to be in the auto business?"

"Yep."

"And he knows Will is marrying Giselle?"

"Yep. He told me he has their honeymoon covered. They just need to say where and when."

"And he knows Will is going to be a chef?"

"That's right."

"And he didn't shit an Osterizer?"

"Nope. I had all the same concerns. Will said he called Daddy last week and had a long talk with him. He said they spoke for about three hours. I even called Daddy just to make sure Will wasn't making up all of this. Daddy's alright with the whole concept. He even told me he was impressed with the architectural and business plans. He just wants Will and Giselle to finish college with top grades, and he doesn't want any great-grandkids for at least five years."

"I don't believe what I'm hearing," Sean said, flopping back in the sofa. "The man hates my guts, yet he bends over backward for Will in ways I never would have thought possible."

"He doesn't hate you, Sean. The two of you just aren't on the same page."

"Same page my ass. He's up to something. Did you warn Will?"

"Sean, I truly think Daddy's not going to be any trouble. Anyway, it appears Will can handle himself quite well."

After kicking off his shoes, Sean remarked, "Jesus. My son the chef…married to a French chick…living in a château. What next?"

Touching Sean's hand excitedly, Dixie replied, "Do you want to know about Callie?"

"Is she pregnant?"

"Sean! Cut it out. At least consider the likelihood we raised two smart kids."

"Okay. Sorry. I'll ignore the possibility that either of my children is having sex and let you carry on."

"She pledged Kappa like she wanted, and she met a nice boy from Darien. They met when she and Will were unloading her car the day she drove down for college. He noticed the cast on her arm and offered to help. She introduced him to me the other evening. He's a sophomore and seems to be real nice. He told her he was glad to meet a Kappa driving a conservative car who didn't have to flaunt her capitalist parents' wealth."

"Holy shit! What a line!" Sean laughed. "Give me a hit of that brandy," he said, reaching for the glass.

Dixie took a drink then held the glass up in the air out of Sean's reach. Her puckered lips led Sean's to what they desired.

Following a long kiss, Dixie said, "There's one more thing about Callie's new guy I think you'll be interested in."

"Oh. Here it comes."

"He plays on the rugby team."

"Oh my God…it's payback time. It all sounded good until you said that."

"That's what Daddy said to me thirty years ago."

"You mean my bad relationship with your father was formed when he found out I played rugby?"

"Well, that and a few other things. But rugby probably iced the cake."

"She's on the pill, right?" Sean asked with a blank expression on his face.

"Sean!" Dixie replied, pointing a finger at him.

"When can I meet the guy?"

"Not until you decide you're going to be nice."

"Where's my phone? I need to call her," Sean said, trying to sit up.

"No!" Dixie answered, holding him back on the sofa. "No phone calls. No Callie. No Will. Nothing but me for two weeks."

Resigning himself to be a passive observer, Sean asked, "What's the guy's name?"

"Darryl Mosciewicz."

"Darryl Mosciewicz?" Sean asked, shaking his head.

"The Fourth."

"You're kidding me. Let me guess—he's pre-Med?"

"That would be correct. His family is Polish."

"I can't believe she's dating another Polack."

"And, he's Jewish," Dixie replied with a wry expression.

"Oh, that's so much better."

"Hey, Archie, right about now, somewhere in Darien, there's a Jewish mother in distress saying, 'oy veh,' for the very same reason."

"Right, Edith. What's Frank got to say about that?"

"He's checked them out. His father is a surgeon, and the family is in some good circles."

Sean unexpectedly leaned forward and held his head in his hands as he grimaced.

Alarmed, Dixie asked, "Sean, are you okay?"

"Yeah. Just got a headache all of the sudden."

"And you wonder why Will and Callie didn't want to share their news with you while you were in the hospital. They absolutely love you, Sean. They don't want to contribute in any way to your injuries or delay your recovery. Do we need to go to the hospital?"

"No. Just let me lay down in the bedroom for a few minutes. Maybe I got a bit too excited with all of the updates from the college front."

Sean stood up only to catch himself falling backward. Had the sofa not been there, he would have hit the floor hard.

"Sean, are you sure we don't need to go to the hospital?"

"I'll be fine. Let me lay down right here for a while. If things don't get better, then we can consider going. I've seen enough of the inside of hospitals for a lifetime."

"Why don't you get out of your clothes? Nobody's here but me, and I forbid anyone to come over until at least the day after tomorrow."

Sean slipped out of his shoes and slacks while Dixie got him a pillow and covered him with a blanket. He opened his eyes and gazed back at hers.

"Is this what our life is going to be like from now on?" Sean asked.

"I hope so," Dixie replied as she bent down to kiss him.

Sean made a grunting sound as he remembered something.

"I forgot to thank you for what you did for Ben at Kim's funeral."

Looking puzzled, she took a seat beside him on the sofa and replied, "I don't follow you."

"You know…you got Kim's picture to Ben. That was really important to him, and it was important to me as well. I don't know how you did it, but thanks."

Still confused, Dixie said, "Honey, I didn't see Ben until two days after Kim's funeral. I don't know what you're talking about."

Not willing to accept her answers, Sean pressed on with, "I had this picture of Kim that I'd kept forever. I took it back when we were in high school. She requested that Ben check to see if I still had it so it could be copied, framed and displayed at the funeral. I was able to get that done before all of this nonsense took place. It was in my folio. You didn't see it?"

"Nope," Dixie replied curtly. "Your folio is in a box filled with bits and pieces of personal items John collected from your car at the body shop".

"Wait…I had the picture on memory stick in my shirt pocket when I had my accident. Did you find that?"

"Yes. It's in a bag with the rest of your clothing over on the table."

"And you didn't give it to Ben to use at Kim's funeral?"

"No. Why are we talking about Kim?" she asked, the tone in her tone of voice less kind than it had been a few moments earlier.

"I just wanted to thank you, Dix. I thought you had something to do with getting Ben the picture."

"And I just want to move forward with our lives without obsessing about Kim like you have Nadine for all these years. Is that too much to ask?" She asked, getting up from the sofa.

"It may be, Dix," Sean said, slowly getting up on one arm. "Just because she's dead doesn't mean she's forgotten."

Crossing her arms with disgust, Dixie said, "Great. I don't know how many times you've said those exact words in relation to you mother. Here we go again, only this time, it's Kim you won't let go of."

"Is this what our life's going to be like from now on?" Sean asked, repeating his earlier question, this time with a markedly different bent.

"That's entirely up to you, Sean. You're the one with the problem."

The entire conversation that was taking place seemed eerily familiar—like a replay of the one he had with Dixie a few weeks prior at the hospital in Lake Forest, resulting in his hasty departure…and ultimately an acute worsening of his injuries. He didn't want to relive those experiences. As he looked up at Dixie, he could tell by the expression on her face that she was likely having similar thoughts.

"Sorry, Dix."

"Me, too."

After a pause, Sean made a proposal. "I know this is a lot to ask of you. But I want to finish Kim's book. I think I have maybe forty or fifty pages to go, and I'm really anxious to see how it ends. I don't think I could finish it with these headaches. If you would read them to me, I promise only to mention Kim from now on in the presence of Berkowitz."

Dixie agreed without hesitation. "Certainly, honey. I'll be glad to do that for you."

Chapter 20

FOR THE NEXT THREE weeks, Sean's body recovered bit by bit. The bruises changed color from blue, to purple, then to brown before disappearing altogether. The pain that racked his body slowly abated. With some light stretching and daily massage offered by Dixie, he regained his upright posture and fluid gait. More importantly, Sean's vision returned to normal, and his headaches decreased in both severity and frequency.

Dixie cared for him much as she had while he had been in the hospital. The antiseptic smell was replaced by the fresh air as the two of them walked leisurely among their gardens and the woods that backed up to their property. The winds of late summer turned cooler as autumn pushed in. Time passed without deadlines, without the daily commute, and without having to deal with Frank. It was as therapeutic a setting as there could possibly be. Yet, Sean remained deeply troubled. The end of the book failed to provide him with his long sought-after relief. And his misery was now compounded by Kim's death.

A SOMBER SEAN LABORED to read out loud the ending of Kim's book to Dr. Berkowitz. It ended, as had the movie *The Fuller Brush Man* so many times, without ending Sean's pain.

As it becomes increasingly difficult for me to maintain any train of thought, I worry what will become of Mark. He's yet to complete his journey to Monticello. Alas, I will undoubtedly make my final journey before him. I'm too tired to be frustrated any longer. If I have any emotion regarding Mark's predicament at this point, it's hopefulness. He's a big-hearted person; the kind who should rise above turmoil if for no other reason than the fact that he is surrounded by so many people who can only have kind feelings toward him, lest he be incapable of caring for himself. Sadly, there are a few who would like to see him falter in his mission to find happiness. I carry disdain for these people, but there is nothing more I can do than repeat the warnings I've stated throughout our story.

It must be affirmed, now that I'm soon going to go live with the Who, that goodness will prevail for Mark. I've given him the lessons he must know, and the hints to nudge him through the darkness to the light that lies before him. The only thing that remains is he must...

Sean turned over the last page of Kim's book and placed it in the lid of the box in which it was delivered to him. He was pale as a ghost, and fatigue showed on his face.

Looking up at Dr. Berkowitz, Sean picked up an envelope and said, "And that's how it ended. She said the ending was contained in this envelope, but all it has in it is this blank piece of paper."

"You sound disappointed. I'd say it was something of a masterpiece," Berkowitz said.

Shaking his head, Sean countered, "No. It's not even close. It's torturous. There's no ending. If this was a book intended to guide me to some kind of epiphany, it fell far short of that goal."

As he sat with his legs calmly crossed, Berkowitz tugged at his beard and began making a number of observations.

"Sean, Sean, Sean…there's so much about you that Kim told me in her book. First of all, let me start by saying yours is a first. In all my years of psychotherapy, I've never had a client read to me a full length novel that was in effect a third-person portrayal of said individual. You've heard of the proverbial fly on the wall? Kim was that fly—and I say that most flatteringly."

After setting the box down on the table, Sean rubbed his face and said, "You know, Doc, when Dixie read me the end of the book, I sensed she felt a certain degree of pleasure. She didn't come out and voice it or outwardly show it, but I could feel it. Do you know what I mean? That Kim left me hanging in a lurch brought her immense satisfaction."

"Kim and Dixie were rivals for thirty-some odd years, Sean," Berkowitz answered with his hands clenched into fists. Opening one hand as if to add a visual to his point, he continued, "In my experience, when one of the combatants goes away, no matter the reason, the remaining one experiences at first a period of euphoria, followed by a much longer period of confusion. Think of the U.S. and Soviet Union. As a country, we're still in search of a good replacement for the enemies called Russians. She just hasn't progressed to that point yet. Give her time."

"I won't hold my breath," Sean said, shaking his head.

Uncrossing his legs, Berkowitz leaned forward saying, "Be that as it may, let's get back to Mark and Sean. I let you slide on your assignments. You recall the first time that we met, you were to come up with a response to two questions. I didn't press the matter in part due to all of the recent events in your life—Kim's passing, the accident, changes at home with Callie going off to college and Will's life changes, and the strain between you and Dixie. The book was billed as therapy in and of itself. I thought we should let it play out and see what it had to offer. Believe me when I tell you it offered complete insight into Sean Marcum."

"So what did it tell you, Doc?"

"That! For one thing!" Berkowitz shouted, throwing his hands into the air.

"That?" Sean replied with a puzzled look. "I don't understand."

"It's not a matter of what the book told me, Sean. What did it tell you? You continually place the responsibility for your situation on others."

"You mean I'm a lot like Red Jones."

"The main character in that movie you've told me so much about—The Fuller Brush Man?"

"Right. He always had an excuse for each predicament in his life."

"Well, Sean, let me make it perfectly clear that *you* are the cause of everything you experience—past, present, and future."

After pondering the doctor's statement for a moment, Sean said, "Do you think that's the message my mother was trying to convey?"

"No," Berkowitz quickly replied as he took off his glasses and rubbed his eyes. "In fact, I'm more convinced than ever before that you're chasing a red herring. Let's stay focused on Kim's book for now, shall we?"

Frustrated by the direction that the discussion was taking, Sean replied, "As I said earlier, there was no ending; there was no closure."

"Fine, then. As to one of my questions, what do you think about the character Mark in Kim's book?"

"He's a loser," Sean said bitterly.

"And you've come to this conclusion because…?"

"Because he couldn't find his way."

"And what way was that?"

"You know, I pay you a lot of money to give me answers, not to ask more questions."

Berkowitz persisted, "Did Collette give Mark the answers he sought?"

Giving in to his therapist's perseverance, Sean replied, "In a manner of speaking."

"Bah!" Berkowitz said, brushing off Sean's answer with his hand. "Her guidance was as plain as the nose on your face, Sean."

"Really? Give me one example."

"No…*you* give *me* an example. Think, Sean! Think!"

"Doc!" Sean shouted, standing up angrily. "I could head off in any number of directions in this discussion." Turning back to Berkowitz with a desperate expression, he begged, "Pare it down to one thing, could you?"

Letting out a big sigh with enough drama that Sean knew he was reluctant to give in to his request, Berkowitz answered, "Can we discuss one's inability to complete what one starts?"

Defensively, Sean responded, "Look at all the things I've started and finished!"

"Such as?" Berkowitz asked, shrugging his shoulders.

"A business for one thing!"

"Ho, hum," the doctor said, glancing over to the wall.

"I'm married!"

Putting his finger in his mouth and pulling it out with a pop, Berkowitz said, "At present, unhappily and, though reconciled after a sort, recently separated."

"I have two children!" Sean said angrily.

"A son and daughter, much like the majority of the baby-boom generation."

Struggling to get any positive feedback from Berkowitz, Sean stated, "I've led a normal, happy adult life!"

"Being chased by ghosts, no less. Not to mention the Fuller Brush Man."

"And you think Mark did better than me?"

"No. He's just as big of a loser as you are."

After sitting back down, Sean said, "I never thought I'd hear a psychologist tell a patient that he's a loser. Isn't there something fundamentally wrong about that?"

"Oh, I can say that to you," Berkowitz said gleefully. "I call it a jump-start, and in this setting, it is therapeutic."

"Now you're simply being cruel. This isn't funny, you know."

"With that I can whole-heartedly agree," Berkowitz chuckled. "Your entire life, personified by Mark in Kim's novel, is a Greek tragedy cast in modern times."

Sean simply sat motionless, mentally beaten to a pulp. Berkowitz sat patiently with his legs crossed once more, waiting for him to come around.

Finally, Sean said, "I never completed anything that someone else didn't start for me."

The grin on Berkowitz' face slowly expanded until it pushed both of his ears back. Wringing his hands, he coached Sean along, saying, "Keep going, keep going."

"I really didn't have any focus in life until Kim came along. She led me into or through every facet of our relationship. She was the director of the play that was my life. She was the suitor and the entire reason we met in the first place. She held my hand as she pulled me around the bases of our love life, if you will. She convinced me to go on to college instead of making some otherwise poor choice. She showed me who my mother really was. She showed me, though in hind sight, the importance of having roots and being true to them. She taught me about family."

"And how did she do these things, Sean?"

"I don't know…I guess she usually pointed me in the right direction…"

"And then what?" Berkowitz interrupted.

"I usually figured out what she wanted me to learn."

"No, Sean. You always figured out what she wanted you to learn. That is, until now."

"You've got that right."

Sensing he was getting close, Berkowitz asked, "Tell me, what would you do each time she left a matter open-ended?"

"I'd finish it. It might take a long time, but I'd finish it."

"To her satisfaction?"

"I think so. Yes."

"And now, *The Road to Monticello* is unfinished. What do you think she wants you to do with that?"

Sean's face twisted in any number of expressions as he debated how to respond. Finally settling on a response he was comfortable with, he said, "Finish it?"

Berkowitz' ear-to-ear grin reappeared along with a nodding head and a finger of approval pointing directly at Sean.

"You think she left the book unfinished so that I would complete it? Are you nuts?"

"Think about it, Sean. Who better to write the closing chapters of what ultimately is *your* book, than *you*?"

"I don't know anything about writing."

"Remember what she told you in the letter that accompanied the book? She said, 'Buried deep inside of you is a soul that I once touched. It was a soul with dreams so vivid, and a passion for life that was palpable. I know. I felt it. We nurtured it together.' It's about those dreams, Sean. It's about that passion for life. That's all the book is about. The words will come. They're the easy part. More importantly, it's what you choose to do with your life from here forward."

"I can't do it, Doc," Sean said as he shook his head.

"What did you say a few moments ago? You said, 'I never completed anything that someone else didn't start for me.' This is your moment, Sean. You've been given the challenge by someone you loved and trusted implicitly to determine how your life will turn out; to create your own destiny."

After absorbing what Berkowitz said, Sean asked, "Where do I begin?"

"You begin right here and now!"

"But what direction do I take?"

"That, Sean, is…up…to…you. After all, why do you think the last page of her book is a blank sheet of paper?"

Still not convinced, Sean asked, "You really think that's why her book ended this way?"

"Sean, Kim was brilliant. From the descriptions you've given to me about her, and judging by her writing, everything that Kim, or Collette for that matter, did or said in her life had meaning, purpose, intent, forethought, and premeditation. She was a thoroughly calculating individual. Do I think she purposely ended her book as she did? You're damn right I do."

Doubting Berkowitz' conclusion, Sean asked, "Do you think she ever really wanted me to find the Fuller Brush Man? I mean, she says that to me over and over in my dreams."

"First of all, Sean, they're your dreams, not Kim's or Collette's. The belief that the Fuller Brush Man is the be-all and end-all is your creation. Rather, I feel the Fuller Brush Man is a means to achieve an end. That end is Monticello, which if I may be so bold as to interpret, is a metaphor for your total happiness. I don't know that she intended for you to pack your things and move to Monticello. I fully believe she wanted you to achieve the complete bliss the two of you always envisioned having there. Could you, perhaps, have that same bliss in Lake Forest…with Dixie?"

Sean struggled with the notion that he would have to agree with Berkowitz' analysis.

"That seems like such a reach at this point, Doc."

"Like boots made of concrete?" The doctor replied, relating to a chapter in Kim's book.

"Exactly. And remember, that's where Dixie ran over Kim with a snowplow."

"That was one possible outcome. Recall that was Esmeralda and Collette, not Dixie and Kim. We don't exactly know how that ended, do we? Although, Collette continued as the protagonist in the story, so I would surmise there was some type of intervention—maybe it was Mark. Have you thought about that?"

"Couldn't have been him," Sean said without hesitation. "Mark didn't have the strength to take steps with those concrete boots."

"Did he lack the strength, or the will?"

"He lacked the strength. His will was there."

"And you, Sean? What about your will?"

Sean remained silent for several moments. He was simply exhausted after nearly two hours. At this point, the doctor decided it was time to move off of this subject and on to another.

"Sean, do you recall the second question?"

He did. It was the one question Sean had hoped to never have to answer because the subject was so gut-retching. Knowing he couldn't escape Berkowitz, Sean replied, "You asked me if there was one thing I could tell Kim today, what would it be?"

Berkowitz could tell by Sean's expression and the tears forming in his eyes that this would be difficult, yet he had to push Sean through it.

"And have you given any thought to that question?"

Sean nodded as he replied, "Hours and hours and hours."

"What would you tell her, Sean?"

It was hard for Sean to get the words out. Even as he did so, his voice was breaking.

"When we all knew Kim's cancer was terminal, I had this unrelenting feeling of being so relieved it was Ben who was having to live through her final months, weeks, and days—and not me." Sean took several long breaths, then continued, "Here, she spends much of her adult life, even as she's dying, doing her best to guide me through my fog. Then, when it came time for me to step up and reach out to her, I turned and ran. I not only let her down, but Ben, too. It was the ultimate act of disloyalty." After pausing to pull himself together once more, Sean finished with, "So to answer your question, Dr. Berkowitz, I would tell Kim that I am deeply, deeply sorry for doing nothing for her in the end, and in fact finding comfort in the misery of another by simply failing to face the reality of the situation."

"That's quite a realization, Sean," Berkowitz said, handing Sean a box of tissues. "You identified a weakness, you took responsibility, and you stated your remedy. Unfortunately, as we both know, you will have to find a different outcome. What might that be?"

"I suppose I could…"

"Ah, ah! What did I say?"

"I could finish the book as Kim wished."

Continuing to guide Sean, Berkowitz added, “In a manner…”

“…In a manner that would clarify my destiny and guide me to that end.”

“And you have the…”

“…I have the will to do so.”

Sean wasn’t sure who was more relieved by getting to the point at which they were in the session, he or Berkowitz.

Wrapping up the sitting, the doctor asked, “Is there anyone with whom you feel you should discuss this prior to beginning such an endeavor?”

“I really ought to make sure Ben’s alright with it.”

“I wholeheartedly agree. And who else?”

“Dixie?”

“I would think so. But you know what? I think she will be completely supportive of your venture. Why wouldn’t she be?”

Chapter 21

"GOOD MORNING, MR. MARCUM! How are you feeling?" asked Louisa, one of the receptionists at Sean's Toyota dealership.

"I'm doing pretty well, actually. No lasting damage, anyway. The doctor cleared me only yesterday to get behind the wheel of a car so I figured I would stop in to check on the insurance claim. Marco over at the body shop wants to total my car, but the claims adjuster is balking, so I wanted to take a look for myself. Either way, I'll probably just get rid of it. Do you know where I might find a good car?"

"You've come to the right place," Louisa answered with a smile. "Let me tell you, Mr. Marcum, since you ran that last sequence of ads on television—you know, the back-to-school one—it's been crazy around here. I think I heard some of the guys say they're probably having one of their best months ever. Sales are definitely the thing that's keeping morale up."

Reading between the lines, Sean asked, "So, how is it going with the temporary management?"

"How soon will you be back?" Louisa replied with a sorrowful expression.

"That bad?"

Leaning across the counter to get closer, she confided, "It's horrible. How can you stand being related to that man? He never says anything positive about anybody or anything. It's nothing like when you and April were here."

Sean had almost forgotten that April was no longer at his dealerships on a regular basis. He had been expecting to see her, but now realized that was unlikely to happen unless he went out of his way to find Frank, which was undoubtedly where April would be.

"Have you seen April recently?" Sean asked.

"Last week she dropped in with Mr. Darling for a short while. From what I hear, she spends most of her time at the other group dealerships playing good cop while he plays bad cop." Noting Sean's pensive look, Louisa added, "I really wish she would come back."

Just then, Louisa remembered something. Reaching for a note underneath the blotter on her desk, she handed it to Sean as she said, "I almost forgot…a man came here looking for you last week. He said his name was Sam Ricci. Do you know him?"

With a mixture of enthusiasm and skepticism, Sean replied as he took the note from Louisa, "Absolutely. He's a banking associate I work with on occasion."

"He said he's been trying to get in touch with you, but you apparently aren't returning his calls. He said he urgently needs to talk with you about something."

"I'm not returning anyone's calls. Dixie has my phone hidden someplace as a way to keep me from getting any stressful phone calls during my convalescence. I never realized how dependent I'd become on the darn thing. It's got to be like cigarettes, only at least for a smoker, there's a nicotine patch or gum to curb the urge."

"You know you can check your messages without having your phone with you," Louisa pointed out.

"No, I didn't know that. But, as Callie would say, I'm just a Neanderthal when it comes to stuff like that."

"Did you configure your voice mail so you could check your messages?"

"I don't know. April set it up for me."

"Then you should be capable of checking voice messages remotely. She helped me set mine up. Just dial your number and before it puts you into your voice mail, press the star key and it will ask for your password. Do you know your password?"

Reaching for his wallet, Sean pulled out April's business card that he had tucked behind a credit card. Turning it over to the back side, he showed Louisa, "Look, here it is. I always wondered what the heck this number was for that she jotted down with 'p/w' scribbled under it. Thanks. I'll check my messages later today. And thanks for the heads-up on Sam Ricci. I need to give him a call." With a wink, Sean added, "Uh, keep this between the two of us, okay?"

"That's why I had the note hidden in the first place," Louisa said, winking back. "Mr. Ricci didn't speak very highly of Mr. Darling."

"Huh. That's interesting," Sean remarked, curious as to why Sam wanted to speak with him, especially after Frank had gone out of his way to make the point the day of the accident that he had recruited Ricci onto his side. Looking around before venturing further into the business, Sean asked, "Is *he* here today?"

"No, *he* comes in maybe twice a week. The place pretty much runs itself thanks to how you and April have it set up."

With an accomplished smile, Sean said, "Thanks. That's good to know…I guess. I'm going up to my office for a while. If *he* shows up, give me a warning ring."

"Sure thing, Mr. Marcum."

After briefly mixing with some of the sales staff on duty, Sean walked up the split level to his corner office. It was refreshing to see his home-away-from-home again. Once he had turned on the lights, he could quickly see that Frank had spent little or no time in the office, as all of the work that he had left on the desk prior to his accident was still as it was his last afternoon there. Sean logged into his computer, and pulled up a few recent reports that were automatically generated each day. Louisa was right. Business had been good. The ads April had put together clearly worked even better than anticipated—the proof was in the numbers.

Sean had another clandestine mission. Having scanned the inventory at his dealerships, he found that the red Lexus coupe he had special-ordered was still unsold. He didn't want to buy it for Callie, particularly since her new boyfriend had given her a gold star for her choice to drive a conservative vehicle. No—this time, he was thinking of himself. He just needed to find a way to justify the purchase so that it didn't appear to even the most the casual observer, let alone Frank, as though he was experiencing a mid-life crisis on top of all the other issues facing him.

Deciding to follow through on his newfound insight into how to check his voice messages, Sean dialed the number for his mobile phone, then entered the appropriate keys and code to get his messages. It worked! There was one problem. He had twenty-seven messages. Not interested in hearing them all at the time, he decided to make just three calls—first to April, then to Sam Ricci, and finally Ben.

April had been on speed-dial for so long, he couldn't be sure of her number. It took a few minutes of scribbling combinations of phone numbers on a piece of paper before Sean came up with one he was confident enough to be accurate that it warranted at try. It rang several times before April answered.

"Hello?" She answered.

"April, it's Sean."

"Oh, hello, Don. I'm right in the middle of something. Can I return your call a bit later?"

Sean understood the code, and replied, "Can't talk, huh?"

"That's right, Don. Can I call you back at this number?"

"I'll probably still be here. If there is no answer, call Louisa and she can try to patch me through if I'm somewhere in the building."

"Are you over the flu?"

Again, code. "I'm doing much better. I miss seeing you."

"Me too, Don. I'll get back to you shortly."

"Sounds good. Talk to you then."

Sean hung up, but soon thereafter realized a sensation of warmth that he hadn't experienced in several weeks. Being honest with himself for once, he knew it was the sound of April's voice that had resulted in the rush he was experiencing. He definitely wanted to speak with her some more. Actually, he wanted to see her even more than that.

Next, he dialed Sam Ricci, the number for whom Louisa had jotted down on the piece of paper now before him. A woman answered the phone with a perfectly obvious Chicago accent.

"Good morning. Sam Ricci's office. This is Darla speaking. How may I help you?"

"Darla, this is Sean Marcum. Is Sam available?"

"Mr. Marcum, it's good to hear your voice again. Sam's in with someone at this time, but please hold and let me see if he wants to take your call."

"Fine. I'll be happy to wait."

Sean patiently passed the time listening to WLS-AM radio over the phone while he was on hold. One after another, his employees whom he hadn't yet seen that morning, filed in to shake his hand or gave him a thumbs-up from the doorway. It was the kind of support he especially needed given that during the week leading up to his accident, he was certain their loyalties toward him had been challenged by some of his actions.

"Mr. Marcum, Sam will speak with you now. Let me transfer you."

"Thanks, Darla. You take care."

After a few clicks and rings, Sam answered.

"Sean, how the heck are you?"

"I'm doing much better, thank you very much."

"The family was sort of mum about what had taken place. We didn't exactly know how bad-off you were. Are you back at work?"

"No, not exactly. I'm still under orders from my doctor not to be at work."

"So, that would explain why caller ID says North Shore Toyota?"

"Ah, you caught me," Sean said, laughing at being pinpointed. It occurred to him that he needed to be careful who he phoned as they, too, would know from where he was calling.

"Look, I don't want to beat around the bush. Besides, my other customer is going to be back from the can in a minute or two so let me get to the point. Do you still want to do the deal?"

Sean was shocked, to say the least, by Ricci's question.

"You mean going independent and starting my own Volvo and BMW dealerships? I thought Frank scuttled those plans."

"No, not that I'm aware of," Ricci replied. "What makes you say that?"

"Well, he told me he had spoken with you about some of my…recent problems…and you decided not to lend me the money. In fact, it was that very message that caused me to have my accident."

"Sean, Frank's a lying sack of shit, and that's about as nice as I can put it. He called me to let me know you were going through some setbacks and that basically he wanted to build on the land you've spoken to me about and start up the same dealerships. I told him point blank that he was worse than a thief, made some reference to the possibility that his parents weren't married, and hung up on him. Sean, your plan still stands. I'm ready when you're ready."

Setbacks? Sean thought to himself. That was really a positive way to describe all the problems he had confronted recently. He took several deep breaths, trying to relax after realizing that, once again, Frank had lied, if for no other reason than to delay his progress…probably until he could get his own funding together.

"Sam, I'd say I'm shocked and dismayed by what you just said, but then we're talking about Frank."

"Say no more. So, what's the plan?" Ricci asked.

"Sam, I really want to do it. But quite honestly, Frank took all the wind out of my sails on this one, and I'm caught totally off guard by your generous offer. Let me think on it and get back to you tomorrow. Okay?"

"I'll be in Milwaukee tomorrow on business. Give Darla a call, and she can relay a message to me. If you're in, we jump all over it. If you have cold feet, I'll give you another week to think about it. Hell, I want to see you make the move as much as you do."

"Sam, you're my hero."

"Hey, you pull this off, and I'll build a goddamned statue in your honor."

"Bye, Sam."

"Adios amoeba."

Suddenly, Sean was feeling a high unlike anything he had experienced in recent memory. First, he was anxiously anticipating a call back from April. Now, he was fully engaged in talks, once more, of going independent. His exhilaration was probably not just cause for him to call Ben, but he was next on Sean's mind. He had to speak with him about finishing Kim's book. Perhaps his high spirits were an indication that he was on his way toward Monticello. *Completing the book should be a breeze,* he thought.

Expecting Ben might still be away from his office, he called him at home. Sean was about to hang up when Ben finally answered. He was out of breath.

"Hello?"

"Ben, it's Sean. Can you talk now?"

"Yeah. Let me catch my breath for a few seconds. I was just working out."

"Good. Sounds like you're getting back to life as usual."

"Well, no," Ben disagreed as his breathing slowed. "It will never be life as usual again. But, I'm moving ahead. I can't be stuck in a rut forever. I guess I'm creating a new usual."

"I like that—'creating a new usual.' Mind if I use that in my book?"

"Your book? Are you writing a book?"

"In a manner of speaking. That's why I'm calling you. I finally finished reading Kim's book, and my shrink and I have come to the conclusion that Kim left it open-ended with the intent I should write the ending."

"Really? I figured the ending would have pushed you to the brink of…I don't know… but something dire."

"Nope. I think I know what I'm supposed to do. She wants me to decide where the character, Mark, is headed and take him there. I'm supposed to find a way for him to get to Monticello. And you know what? I think I can do it. I just want to be sure you have no objections to me writing an ending to her book."

"Objections? No. I'm just happy you seem to have put Kim's death in perspective."

"From the sounds of it, the same can be said for you, too, Ben."

"I guess so. Anyway, I need to know…you weren't upset by where she was buried at the cemetery?"

"No. Not at all. It's a beautiful location. Let me ask you, did you buy two plots?"

"Actually, I did. I felt a bit guilty at first, but Raymond told me the ones next to him were open so I figured that would be a place for you and Dixie someday if you wanted to go that route."

"Thanks, but I'd rather be buried next to my mother. It would be a lecture on life in perpetuity if Dad and I were buried side-by-side. For that matter, the last time I checked on the plots next to my mother, those were available. Since we're all facing our mortality sooner and sooner, I guess I'd better hurry up and buy those."

There was a long pause before Ben said, "Sean, you did say you went to the cemetery, correct?"

"Yeah. Dixie took me there the day I left the hospital. She said you were out of sorts and couldn't make it so she accompanied me instead."

"And you saw Kim's grave?"

Puzzled by Ben's questions, Sean replied with a tentative tone to his voice, "Uh, yes. Why?"

"Next to Nadine's grave, right?"

After stopping to comprehend just what Ben was saying, Sean asked, "Kim's not buried in the South end of the cemetery along the row of elm trees?"

With a deep sigh, Ben answered, "No, Sean. Kim's buried next to Nadine. Dixie took you to the wrong gravesite."

Foolishly, Sean gave Dixie the benefit of the doubt, and said, "I guess she was confused. She said you gave her directions."

"Sean, I didn't give her directions at all. I told her Kim was buried next to Nadine, and she had a shit-fit. That's why I didn't take you to the cemetery myself. To be honest, I was about ready to throw Dixie out the window of the hospital. I'm still pissed at her. Dude, I hate to tell you this, but your wife took you for a little joyride. I'll tell you another thing, I hate her even more now than before you called, and I didn't think that was possible. Lying to you about Kim's grave is complete shit, man…complete shit."

Sean couldn't agree more. He, too, was now about ready to spit nails.

"Ben, I'm terribly sorry for what she did. It's taken disrespect to a new level."

"Hey, she learned from the master himself—ol' Frankie boy."

There was a long period when neither of the friends spoke until Ben broke the silence and asked, "So, now that you know where Kim is buried, are you alright with that?"

Sean was feeling so many emotions at that point that he had to be very careful to give a truthful and rational response.

"I guess, the more I think about it, burying Kim next to Mom makes sense. The two were so close. I suppose they'll be close forever this way."

"You're sure?" Ben pressed.

"Yeah, Ben. It was really a good idea. I never would have thought of doing it. Whose idea was it, anyway?"

"Kim's. She asked me a little less than a week before she died. I cleared it with Raymond. Are you mad I didn't ask you?"

"No, you did the right thing. I would have told you, 'no,' and we would have missed an opportunity to create an everlasting relationship between Kim and someone she really loved like a mother. Does it bother you that she still had these attachments to my family?"

"No, not at all. With that in mind, please don't buy the plot next to me. The thought of being buried next to you for eternity is a frightening concept."

"Hey, the feeling's mutual."

"Good. Glad we got that clear."

There was some chuckling as the two made light of a very awkward situation.

It crossed Sean's mind that there was possibly another untruth that needed to be addressed.

"Ben, let me ask you something else while we're trudging through all of the latest scandals."

"Why not? Go for it."

"You told me that Dixie gave you the picture for Kim's funeral. I mentioned it to Dixie and she didn't know what I was talking about. You did get the picture, correct?"

Now having to face his own fabrication, Ben replied, "Yes, I did get the picture. Dixie's right. She had nothing to do with it."

"Then how did you get it?"

After some hesitation, Ben replied, "Your friend April drove all the way down here and personally gave me both the printed picture, which she had beautifully framed, and a digital copy as well."

"She drove to Urbana? Did she by any chance…"

"Yes, Sean, she attended Kim's funeral. I was very pleased to meet her. She told me about how Kim's book had affected you. I'm glad you have somebody to share it with. I'm not at all surprised that person isn't Dixie."

Sean bit his knuckles as he analyzed the markedly different actions by the two women who were closest to him.

When Sean had no response, Ben asked, "Sean, are you still there?"

"You see what I'm up against, don't you, Ben?"

"You mean Dixie versus April?"

"I'm growing very fond of April."

"Bullshit, Sean. You're way past fond, and so is she. But, Kim wanted you to make things work with Dixie. Personally, I think you married a witch. But personal feelings aside, I have to ally with Kim whether I think that's best for you or not." After letting Sean digest his remark for a moment, Ben finished with, "As your dad would say, 'Put that in your pipe and smoke it.'"

Sean rubbed his head as it began to ache once more. He had thought those symptoms were a thing of the past as it had been several days since he had experienced a headache of the magnitude he was feeling.

"Dude, are you there?"

"Yeah, Ben, I'm here. Look, I need to go now. This call has been good, but I'm really stressed now, and I have to go lay down somewhere for a while."

"Are you still having headaches? How's your vision? Sorry I neglected to ask about your recovery."

"They're a lot better. I don't have near the problems I did when I left the hospital. However, I still get killer headaches from time to time. They usually don't last long, but they really kick my ass when I get them. Look, I'll call you again soon. I need to make plans for another trip to Urbana so I can see Kim's grave for real this time."

"Just give me a holler. I want to go over the inscription for the headstone with you. Kim had an idea she said you could relate to, so I'm waiting until we can talk about it before I order the stone."

"Sounds good, Ben. I…I really look forward to it. Hey, I'll catch you later, okay?"

"Sure thing. Bye."

"Bye."

Sean turned around so he was facing away from the bright light coming in through the windows along the side of his office and closed his eyes. He found that when he had these headaches, he could calm himself down by thinking peaceful thoughts about his past with Kim in Monticello. Occasionally, he fantasized about being alone and intimate with April. Usually, after about fifteen minutes, the headache was gone. While he was lost in his zone, he felt a hand softly touch his shoulder. It was an unmistakable touch, and one that he longed for. When he turned around, there she stood—April.

"I expected you to call me," Sean said.

"I was afraid you'd leave, and I'd never get to speak with you let alone see you," April said, leaving no doubt she was as much in pursuit of him as he was of her. "I raced over. Are you disappointed?"

After a calculated delay, Sean replied, "Not in the least."

"You said you felt fine, but don't look too well."

"Well, I just received some shock therapy from Ben, and now I have the headache from hell. It seems Dixie found it in her to deceive me by taking me to some other poor soul's grave instead of Kim's. Ben then proceeded to tell me you attended her funeral. You really wanted to go with me, didn't you?"

"Yes, I did. Since you couldn't be present, I wasn't going to let the funeral take place without somebody close to you in attendance—one who thinks like you and can appreciate Kim, her work, and the relationship the two of you had."

"April, I don't know what to say. You just continue to outdo yourself time and time again." After re-familiarizing himself with April's outward, physical beauty for a moment, Sean asked, "How was it?"

"As funerals go, it was very nice. It was upbeat, though not without a lot of emotions. Kim's boys are really special, and I got to spend some time with Ben. He's really a nice man. I can see the two of you getting into a lot of mischief in your day."

"My day?"

"You know what I mean," April replied, chuckling at her gaffe.

"Did you meet my father?"

"I saw him, but I steered clear. I don't think he knows who I am."

Changing subjects, Sean said, "I made a lot of progress this morning with Berkowitz. There's a lot to tell you, but I need to get out of here before I get sick from this headache."

Sean stood up, but quickly realized he not only had a headache, but he was starting to feel dizzy again. Not wanting to risk another accident, and not caring in the least what Dixie felt about his actions, he asked April, "Would you mind driving me home? I don't think I'm well enough to do it myself."

As April stared passionately at him, she asked, "Yours or mine?"

Seeing the door to April's heart open wide once more, Sean replied without the slightest hesitation, "Yours."

Chapter 22

DIXIE, HER MOTHER, AND Katie were enjoying lunch at the Club, much as they did twice each month. Suzanne had chosen a later time than usual for them to get together—a time when there were fewer diners present. Dixie was certain lunch was soon going to become another unsolicited lecture about life, and she wasn't looking forward to having to deal with her mother in that way. That never mattered to Suzanne.

The conversation began in earnest shortly after the waitress delivered the beverages and salad orders. The matriarch of the Darling clan, in a poorly veiled attempt at showing her concern, asked Dixie, "So, how are matters coming along in Sean's treatment with Dr. Berkowitz?"

Setting her fork on her plate and folding her hands under her chin, Dixie replied, "Gosh, Mom, how long did it take you to bring up Sean's therapy this time? Ten minutes? Five? You're becoming oh-so predictable. Next time we dine, I'll be sure to bring a written and bound report I can hand to the two of you."

"Dixie, what do you expect us to discuss? The weather?" Katie asked. "You knew the conversation would come around to Sean sooner or later."

The sister's-in-law each relished conversations such as these—the kind where Suzanne would put the spotlight on just one of them. But, more often than not, it was Dixie who found herself being scrutinized. After all, she was blood.

With an atypical look of abhorrence for her favorite relative, Dixie said, "Katie, we don't discuss you and John because discussing Play-Doh is just plain boring."

Katie's jaw dropped at the insult, but no words came out.

"Case in point…just a few weeks ago, I pacified your unimaginative, void, little brain with details ad nauseam about the first time Sean and I had sex in college. Mind you, this was at your request. Wasn't that enough? Do you want me to tell you about the blow job I gave him in the hospital after his accident?"

"Dixie!" Suzanne said sternly with a firm, but quiet voice. Her face reddened with embarrassment, she continued, "I won't have this type of discussion in a public setting. In fact, I won't have it at all!"

"Why not, Mom?" Dixie asked. "You picked the venue and the subject. You're the one who wanted to have an open, public discussion about the problems in my husband's life. Just what are the rules for our conversation here today at lunch?"

"Don't you see what Sean's doing to you?" Suzanne said. "Never have you spoken to me or to Katie for that matter in such a callous way. He's turning you against the two of us."

"No, Mom. To that end, I think the two of you are doing a spectacular job without any help whatsoever from him."

"Fine then," Suzanne said. Her body language indicated that the tone of the conversation was anything but fine.

"Good. Now with Sean out of the conversation, let's talk about Callie or Will." Dixie hoped to making a seamless segue onto a new topic as she retrieved her fork and began eating her salad.

"What about that April woman?" Suzanne asked, ignoring Dixie's choice of subject. "I doubt she's out of the picture as far as Sean's concerned, not to mention the fact that I don't like the idea of a floozy like her working in your father's office."

After she finished swallowing her first bite of spinach leaves topped with pine nuts and light vinaigrette, Dixie said, "Well that was Daddy's solution to the problem, Mom. If you don't like what he did, take it up with him. I wanted him to take her pheasant hunting in South Dakota next month and have an accidental shooting. He chose a more socially acceptable option."

"Suzanne's right, you know," Katie added. "Until she's completely out of the picture, she'll be a big problem for you and Sean."

"What do you suggest, Katie?" Dixie posed. "Should I put her up in a condo in Aspen like Daddy did for John's little girlfriend Lori?"

The catfight was on.

"Girls, I think we've had enough of this conversation..." Suzanne strongly suggested.

"Don't dig up old scandals, Dixie," Katie said as her nostrils flared. "There are plenty of scorpions out there if we start turning over rocks. Anyway, that was five years ago. He's done with her."

"Pffftt!" Dixie snorted. "You picked the weapons, Katie. Don't chose one if you can't use it to defend yourself."

Keeping the focus on Sean, Katie said, "You're in denial about April, Dixie. That's your problem."

"You know Katie, maybe I am," Dixie said, once more setting down her fork. "But guess what? Sean's trying to deal with his problems. He's taking time off from work, he's seeing a professional, and I'm going to stand by his side and see him through this thing. Sean says there is no relationship between the two of them, and for now she's for all practical purposes out of the picture, and I'm center stage."

"You deceived him, Dixie. You couldn't even take him to see his ex-girlfriend's grave," Katie pointed out, continuing to rub Dixie's nose in her husband's weakness. "And you say he's dealing with his problems?"

"Recovery is a process. It doesn't happen overnight."

"'Re-covery?' You need to be worried about dis-covery. Sean's going to find out what you did, and you'll both be talking to Berkowitz—in marriage counseling."

"Berkowitz has his methods. I have mine."

"He has a PhD," Katie said.

"And I have a wedding ring, not to mention thirty-one years of blood, sweat, and tears invested in this marriage. You seem to discount the value of that asset way too often."

Dixie pushed her salad plate to the side, no longer having an appetite, and waved for the waitress to come over. Within a few seconds, she was standing at Dixie's side, proudly displaying her white ruffled shirt and black vest. A clean, pressed and folded cloth was draped over her arm.

"Liesl, would you bring me a glass of champagne, please?"

"Certainly Mrs. Marcum. Would you prefer Brut, Extra-dry, Sec, Vintage, or non-Vintage."

"Jesus Christ! Make it house, wet, cold, and bubbling. Just spare me the details." Glaring at Suzanne, she ended her order with, "And be sure to charge it to Mother's account."

"I'll be glad to select for you. You usually drink Vintage Extra-dry. Can I get anyone else something to drink from the bar?"

"Don't you think it's a bit early to start drinking?" Suzanne asked with a disapproving tone in her voice.

Dixie fired back, "Oh, bite me, Mother."

The waitress was uncomfortable with the argument she had stumbled into, and nervously rocked back and forth, waiting for clarification.

"Liesl, champagne please?" Dixie repeated, becoming frustrated with the delay.

"Bring me one, too," Katie requested, deciding alcohol was in order for her as well. "Make it the same as Dixie's, and charge it to Suzanne's account as well."

There was a pause while Dixie, Katie, and the waitress waited for Suzanne to make up her mind. Not wanting to appear aloof, she finally said, "Oh, what the hell. I guess if I'm paying for an afternoon drunk, you may as well bring me one, too."

"Right away, ladies," Liesl said, as she dutifully charged off to retrieve the libations.

After a few moments of silence, Suzanne started in once more with, "So, Dixie, are you going to tell me how Sean's therapy is going, or not?"

Unable to fathom Suzanne's persistence and lack of tact, Dixie replied, "Mother, I thought you invited me out for lunch. Can't we just drop it?"

"Honey, I'm your mother, not your friend. If you want to socialize, go out with one of them. When you're with me, I run the show. I want to know how Sean's doing. This is the point at which you answer my question."

Dixie knew there was no escape from her mother's questioning. If she didn't answer now, Suzanne would simply phone repeatedly until she was satisfied, or invite herself over to Dixie's house. Reluctantly, she answered, "He's seen Berkowitz a total of five times now, including his first visit that took place the day of the accident. Sean says they are pouring over Kim's book looking for clues as to what's bothering him. They were supposed to finish it this morning."

"Don't you think that just perpetuates Sean's issues?" Katie asked.

"I don't know, Katie! It's better than having him sit around the house, moping all day long. When he comes home he seems calm, he shares his thoughts and feelings with me, and he wants to be with me." Becoming visibly emotional, Dixie finished with, "I feel closer to him now than I have in a long time, and it's all because of that damn book."

"Do you think he's getting closer to you because both kids are gone now?"

"No, Mom, I don't. That's way too simple and Sean's way too complex. No...he's doing what I think most men do at some point in their lives—he's taking a look at himself. But instead of staring into the proverbial mirror, he's doing a self-exam through Kim's eyes. By way of her book, she's giving him an objective point of view that he otherwise never would have had."

Before the next question could be asked, Liesl returned with three elegant, long-stemmed glasses filled with bubbling liquid.

"Ladies, your drinks." The waitress laid down three napkins upon which she placed the glasses. After that, she set a small box of tissues on the table close to Dixie.

"Rough day, Mrs. Marcum?"

With a brief chuckle, Dixie replied, "I guess you could say that."

"Would the three of you like me to set a table for you in the Iroquois Room? Nobody's booked that today so you can have it all to yourselves."

It was a generous offer. The Iroquois Room had four tables that each would seat four patrons in a pleasant, intimate setting overlooking the woods that flourished adjacent to the Club.

Suzanne agreed. "Yes, let's do that. Thank you, Liesl."

"Just take your drinks with you, and I'll get everything reset at your new table. I'll bring you fresh everything, all from scratch."

"That's very sweet, Liesl. I'll remember this," Suzanne said with a wink. That was code for, 'You'll get a nice cash gratuity in a parchment envelope at Christmastime.'

It only took a minute to walk down the short hallway to their new dining area. Once there, it didn't take long for the conversation to pick up where it left off.

"What was her motive?" Katie asked Dixie.

"Who's motive?"

"Kim's. Why did she write that book for Sean?"

"You know, I skimmed over most of it, and read the last fifty pages or so completely, but I'd say the intent was purely therapeutic."

"For her?" Suzanne asked

"I suspect that was part of it. But, it truly appears she wanted to help Sean," Dixie replied.

"If you ask me, it was her last attempt to destroy your marriage…hopefully a futile attempt," Katie said.

"Well, I'm not asking you," Dixie answered.

"I'm just saying…" Katie continued.

"What are you saying, Katie? That my marriage can't withstand a few bumps? Some bimbo doesn't have a chance at wrecking it, nor do voices from the grave."

Suzanne and Katie wondered if Dixie truly believed what she was saying. Along with her last two responses, Dixie managed to consume all of her champagne.

"I think there's something you're not telling us, dear," Suzanne said. "I can believe you when you tell me Sean will come to grips with the fact that you didn't really show him that woman's grave. After all, you simply have to give him the excuse you shared with me. He's certain to admit that he doesn't like visiting his mother's gravesite. Then, there were the circumstances of his head injury, and the need to keep him calm after being discharged from the hospital. That is all very convincing. So, before you drown yourself in another glass of champagne, why don't you level with us about what's really troubling you?"

About the time Dixie was ready to speak, Liesl returned with the glasses of water, three freshly-prepared salads, and a second glass of champagne to replace the one that was empty.

As Dixie was about the tip the glass up to her lips, Suzanne stopped her when she raised her finger and said, "Ah!"

Dixie set the glass back down and put her head in her hands as she rested her elbows on the table. Looking down at her salad, she said, "I've done something quite terrible to Sean."

"Is Rick Klugman back in the picture again?" Katie asked. She could tell by the glare she got from both Suzanne and Dixie that her remark was way out of line and unfortunately not out of earshot from Liesl who was still tidying up.

Liesl involuntarily stopped what she was doing at the suggestion Dixie was having a relationship with someone other than Sean—not to mention a very well-known man in business circles who was married, and a member-in-good-standing of the Club. Suzanne looked at her and made a motion as if she was buttoning her lip. Liesl nodded, indicating she was sworn to secrecy. The wait staff of the Club was used to keeping anything remotely sensitive to themselves, or risk losing their jobs, not to mention their year-end cash windfall from the members.

Once Liesl had left the room, Dixie said, "I cannot believe you brought up that prick's name!"

Looking defensively at Suzanne, Katie said, "She started it." Glancing back at Dixie, she added, "What did you say? Don't chose your weapon if you can't use it to defend yourself"

"Katie!" Suzanne said. "That's enough. Never mention his name again. Frank is not aware of that matter, and he had better never find out."

"So what if Frank's in the dark. At least Sean knows. Doesn't he, Dixie?"

Dixie's stare could have burned a hole through Katie at that moment.

"Oh, my. You said you told Sean all about your secret get-together in Wisconsin. I guess he'll need a few dozen more sessions with Berkowitz when you tell him about that."

"If you were important to my life in some way Katie, I'd be upset that I like you less and less by the minute." Turning back toward Suzanne, Dixie returned to her original confession, and said, "I completely changed the end of Kim's book."

"You what?" Suzanne asked.

"Her book ends with her saying something to the effect that she is worried about the character that portrays Sean, and that he may never find Monticello, which is a metaphor for happiness in life. Her last line goes, 'I've given him the lessons he must know, and the hints to nudge him through the darkness to the light that lies before him. The only thing that remains is that he must…', and then she finishes the book by sealing the last page in an envelope. That page read, 'Find the Fuller Brush Man.'"

"You've got to be kidding," Suzanne said.

"No. I was shocked when I read it. Sean's been obsessed for nearly seven years with those last words that his mother wrote in her journal before she passed away. I could see it starting all over again, only much worse. It would be like another broken mirror—seven more years of bad luck for us."

"So, what did you do?" Suzanne asked before sipping her champagne.

"I hid that envelope in our closet and replaced it with another containing just a blank sheet of paper."

"Why on earth did you do that?" Katie asked.

"The blank sheet of paper? Because Sean was about to wake up, and I didn't have time to type up anything. I wouldn't have known what to write that sounded like it came from Kim. Besides, she typed in a font that wasn't typical. I would have had to figure that out as well."

"So, when Sean read the ending, all he saw was a blank sheet of paper? How did he react to that?" Suzanne asked, not knowing what to expect.

"He was really upset," Dixie replied. "He saw the ending as a total sham. He had such high expectations for the book, and was really let down. But, I look at it this way. He would have been far worse off had he seen the actual ending. Not to mention the fact that Kim's ending was, in my opinion, as much of a terrible ending as what I came up with."

"Why do you say that?" Katie asked.

"Because her ending would have sent him back into the same spiral he's been in for years. At least with my ending, it might make him think there's more to it."

Suzanne reached across the table and put her hand on Dixie's as she said, "I can see why you did it, dear. Why are you beating yourself up?"

"When I look back on it, I just see it as another breach of trust. I can't help but feel he's going to find out, and when he does, I worry about the damage I will have done to us."

Katie chuckled as she said, "Just tell him you slept with Rick Klugman. That should take his mind off of it."

It took only an instant for Dixie to take her glass of water and throw the contents into Katie's face. She didn't bother explaining what she was doing or where she was going. She quickly downed the second glass of champagne, grabbed her coat and handbag, and left the others at the lunch table gathering their wits.

A taxi had just dropped off a couple at the Club and was conveniently available for Dixie to take home. Before anyone could stop her, not that they could have done so at that point, she gave the driver her destination and was whisked away.

She didn't bother holding back her tears. In all likelihood, the driver had seen a woman crying before. Nonetheless, from time to time, Dixie would look in the rear view mirror only to see him quickly look away from the mirror and focus on the road before them.

And then it happened. As they waited at a traffic light, she saw Sean with April pass before them in her vehicle.

"Driver, turn right here and follow that silver car that just went by."

"Ma'am, I'm in the middle…"

"Just do it!" Dixie shouted.

The cabby was able to get the attention of the driver in the vehicle to the right of them, who graciously allowed them to turn right at the next opening in traffic.

"Speed up," Dixie said.

“Ma’am, I’m already exceeding the…”

“I’ll give you one-hundred dollars!”

The cabby sped up until there were only two vehicles between them and April’s car. After about ten minutes of clandestine tailing, Dixie saw April and Sean pull into a sub-level garage of an upscale condominium. Dixie recognized the address from greeting cards and invitations she had mailed to it—this was April’s residence.

“This is as far as I can go, Ma’am. I can’t follow them past the gate unless you want me to talk to the guard. Do you want out here?”

Dixie found herself at a loss for words. Only a short while earlier, she was defending her husband against allegations of infidelity. Now, in her mind, she had all the proof she needed…proof that she had been wrong.

“No. I don’t. Please take me to the address on Tarleton Gardens I gave you earlier.”

“Yes, Ma’am.”

Chapter 23

APRIL WAS PAID A handsome salary and she earned a lot in bonuses, but Sean was surprised by the lavishness of the condominium she owned, not to mention the building itself and surrounding grounds. Her residence was on the eighth floor of the ten-story structure. Any residence facing east that was above the seventh had a view of the lake in the distance. Sean knew enough about local real estate to put a price tag on her condo at over a million dollars. He concluded that April either came into some money along the way, or she was outstanding at managing personal finances.

Upon entry, one couldn't help but notice the open floor plan, culminating with wall-to-wall, floor-to-ceiling windows on the eastern exposure so as to take in the view. Her choice in décor was modern—probably Scandinavian. A silver Persian cat that April quickly picked up and cuddled, enthusiastically greeted her shortly after entering.

"Oh, Miss Elinor. How was your day?" She asked with a squeaky voice saved for animals and small children. The cat gave her a "meow" that she took to mean feed me.

"Why don't you lie down for a while in the guest bedroom?" April suggested as she put the cat back on the floor. "I'll feed the kitty, brew some chamomile tea for us, and warm up some soup that I made last night."

Sean was already feeling guilty for having asked April to take him to her home. She, quite the contrary, seemed very much at ease. The degree of comfort with which she spoke and carried on actually made him more uncomfortable.

She was quick to pick up on this, and walked up close to him where she put her arms around his neck and looked into his eyes. "You know as well as I do where this is going. You called me for a reason. Now, we're together and alone. Let me help you relax. This little rendezvous has been a long time coming."

She spoke in vagaries, but her message was so very clear. At this point, she pulled him closer and kissed him softly. Sean offered zero resistance. He was certain there were no pharmaceuticals on the open market, legal or otherwise, that could produce the same effect as her kiss. As his heart rate accelerated, he felt warmth permeate his body. She had effectively cast her spell upon him. When their lips separated, Sean put his hands around her waist, keeping her close as their reciprocal gaze telegraphed a message of mutual desire.

"Just don't take too long. I want to be with you," Sean said.

April took him by the hand down a hallway to a large, well-appointed bedroom where she guided him toward a king-sized bed.

"Make yourself comfortable. My favorite quilt is at the foot of the bed to cover with. I'll be back shortly."

"Nice guest room," Sean said.

"It's not the guest room. It's my room. I've upgraded you."

Before Sean could respond, April took off down the hall toward the kitchen. It was probably her way of testing his resolve. The fact of the matter was that she was right on the money. He did know precisely where this was going. Honestly, he had called her for this very reason, and he was nearly euphoric that they were alone together. April was spot-on. This moment had been a long time coming. He took off his shoes and cardigan, then reclined on the bed, pulling the quilt up over him. It was an extraordinarily comfortable bed, and he melted into it.

April didn't waste time in the kitchen. In the few minutes it took for his eyes to close and remain closed so he could forget about his headache, she returned. For over three decades, Sean had watched only Dixie undress in front of him. It had become such a familiar act that he took it for granted. He couldn't begin to describe the degree of exhilaration he felt watching April go through nearly identical motions. He always knew she had an attractive figure beneath her typically conservative business and casual attire, but as she removed her items of clothing one by one, she slowly unveiled a body that Sean had only seen on the covers of magazines at grocery store check-out lines, generally with the caption, "You Could Have a Figure Like This!" She stopped when she got down to her matching baby-blue panties, bra, and silk camisole. Making a point to put away the clothes she had removed, she ensured he had ample time to study both sides of her. Then, she gracefully slipped on a pair of warm up-pants, tying them at the waist. Finally, she joined him on her bed.

"How's the headache?" She asked.

"Headache? What headache?" he responded, quite honestly, in fact.

After slipping beneath the quilt until their bodies touched, she said, "See, I can sell cars, and heal the sick and infirmed."

"A regular 'Florence Night-in-wheel,'" Sean joked with perfect timing, evoking laughter from his bedmate.

Becoming serious once more, April asked, as she put her head on his chest, "So, why did you call me today?"

Following a moment of reflection, Sean replied, "Well, the little white angel over my right shoulder kept saying, 'Tell April what you learned at Dr. Berkowitz' today. You've solved the mystery of the book.' But then, there was this little dark angel over my left shoulder that kept saying, 'Make up some lame-assed excuse to see April. You're out on your own, and you don't have to work. Dixie's locked up your phone, and she'll never be able to track you down. Maybe, just maybe, you'll end up under a quilt on her bed while she lies naked next to you.'"

"Naked? You're moving way too fast for me, Sean Marcum," April said, unbelievably masking her own motives. "I only wanted to get comfy. You see, I'm done working today. This is how I dress when I want a lazy afternoon at home." April heard the whistling of a tea kettle and excused herself. "I need to get our tea and check on the soup. I'll be right back. Why don't you make yourself comfortable as well?"

"I don't have any warm-up pants," Sean said half-heartedly.

"I'm sure you can come up with some acceptable alternative…" She replied with a sexy smile.

As April once again left the room, Sean watched, taking note of her fabulous physique…and privately comparing it to Dixie's. The only distinction he could come up with was that April's body was taut in all the right places, while Dixie's was soft in all the right places. They were both beautiful, though each in their own unique way.

The die was all but cast as to the afternoon activities, so Sean quickly stripped down to his birthday suit, folded his clothes and set them on a chair. Hearing footsteps returning toward the bedroom, Sean quickly crawled back under the covers, but not before April passed through the doorway and saw the object of her pursuit in the buff.

"Nice ass."

"Isn't that supposed to be the guy's line?" Sean asked, pulling the quilt up to his waist.

April set down the tray with the soup, tea kettle, and cups she was carrying. Swiftly turning around, she wiggled her butt several times. Sean didn't need any more prompts.

"Nice ass," he said.

"There, now we're even," she said, turning back to face him and sporting a mischievous grin. She picked up the tray and took it to a small, round table with two chairs overlooking the balcony near the floor-to-ceiling windows. "I don't know what you're doing over there, Sean," she said, looking back over her shoulder. "I never eat in bed. There's too much chance of getting things…wet."

"You have me at a disadvantage, my dear," Sean responded, noting the disparity in their dress at the moment.

"Would you like me to level the playing field?" April asked as she turned around and pulled loose the drawstring of her pants. Not waiting for Sean to answer, she slowly and sensuously removed what remained of her clothing, setting the items to the side. She was as confident in the nude as she was on the showroom floor, and with good reason.

Sean rolled off the bed and joined her at the window. The two lovers coveted each other's bodies as he approached. The design of the balcony and the orientation of the building provided privacy for the two as they stood before Lake Michigan, embracing flesh to flesh.

"How do you like your tea?" April asked.

Leaning in to kiss her, Sean replied, "With lots and lots of cream."

SEAN AWOKE TO FIND April lying next to him, naked and uncovered, leaning up against several pillows, and deeply entrenched in Kim's book. Even after he turned over onto his side facing her, she remained consumed by her reading.

"I don't think Berkowitz will be happy about this," Sean said, hoping to break her concentration.

"What…me reading the book? He knows you and I have been reading it together."

"You told him?" Sean asked knowing he had been specifically advised not to involve April with the book.

"Of course."

"When?" He asked, wondering how long Berkowitz had this knowledge, and also if it might have influenced any of the discussion in his therapy sessions.

"Sean, I'm reading. Can this wait a minute? I'm almost at the end."

"So you talk about me during your therapy sessions?" He asked, ignoring her request.

April gave up trying to read, put the papers down so as to not mix up what she had read with what remained. "We discuss the problems in my life, Sean. Lately, you've made the cut."

"I'm a problem? What do you talk about?"

"Well, Sean, for one thing, he's been desperately trying to keep me from doing what I just did—making glorious love with you. Do you think I should ask for my money back?"

"He told me the same thing. At least for me, it was a spontaneous act brought about by a random meeting. Yours was premeditated sex. No refund for you."

April punched him affectionately in the ribs as she countered, "You, my friend, are full of crap." After a kiss, she continued, "So, you talk about me during your therapy sessions?" April asked, turning the tables around.

"Touché," Sean replied. Changing subjects, he asked, "What do you think about the book?"

"I wish I'd known Kim," she replied with unqualified certainty. "I would probably know a lot more about myself had she written a book about me."

"Well, she would never have known how good you are at making love," Sean pointed out.

"From what you've told me and from what I've read, she never knew how good you are at making love."

"Touché again."

Though they had just made love, he soon found his mind wandering back to Kim's book. He couldn't blame Kim for what had just taken place. To that end, Ben had earlier made it clear that being unfaithful to Dixie was far from Kim's wishes. But, recalling what Dixie had done at the cemetery gave him reason to bring her into the moment with April.

"Am I wrong to be mad at Dixie for what she did?"

"I would truly be hurt if that was the only reason you are here. Is it?"

Sean recognized a baited question, and his years with Dixie trained him how to respond. "No, it wasn't. I think it was a foregone conclusion we'd be paramours some day. But I'll be honest with you, April. What Dixie did *to* me at the cemetery hastened this outcome.

Of greater significance, however, what you did *for* me by attending the funeral hastened it even further."

"Wow, that was good...really good," April remarked before delivering another kiss. "For the record, have you given any thought to the possibility that Dixie may have felt it was in your best interest not to go to the gravesite? If she was honestly trying to protect you, perhaps you should reconsider your judgment of her."

"Are you taking Dixie's side?"

Without looking at Sean, April answered, "Think for a moment. Even I know you're troubled by the anniversary of your mother's death. Am I correct?"

"Well, I suppose."

"Ah, forbidden word!" She said, looking back at him.

"Yes, doctor."

"So, it's easy to presume you have difficulty visiting her grave. Is that the case?"

Sean now looked away from April, confirming her hypothesis.

"And you were advised to avoid stressors during your convalescence, am I correct?"

"How did you know that?" Sean asked.

"Ben told me," she replied with a shrug of her shoulders.

Reflecting on his thoughts and actions since his phone call with Ben, Sean realized April could be correct. He had never even considered the possibility that Dixie might have been taking steps to protect his health.

April could tell by Sean's body language that he now had regrets. "Did I just torpedo my chances for an encore?"

His response surprised her. April's brutally honest analysis of the situation apparently had no effect on his feelings for her at that moment. In short order, he rolled over on top of her and passions began flying once more.

HAVING CARNAL KNOWLEDGE WITH one's lover the first time *might* be a forgivable offense blamed on the heat of the moment or a lapse in judgment. But a second time…Sean knew it was a conscious choice. As he lay next to her studying her beautiful features, he understood that he would forever be bound to April in an unspeakable way except when alone with her. Not even Dr. Berkowitz would be sympathetic to his decision to take this young, striking, vivacious woman into his life the way he had. For her part, she was so thoroughly satisfied by his second dive into the cookie jar, that she had fallen blissfully asleep soon after their shared climax.

Taking note of the time shown on a clock on her dresser, Sean knew he was well past the point of any believable excuse for his absence from the grid, but he also knew it was time that he returned home to face whatever consequences might befall him. As he dressed, April was roused by the subtle noises he was making in her otherwise silent room.

"You're welcome to stay."

After tucking in his shirt, he lay down on the bed next to her one more time and they embraced. She looped her leg over his as if to keep him next to her, an outcome that was most unlikely. She did manage, however, to nurse one more passionate kiss from him.

Once their lips parted, he said, "I'm sorry I dragged you into my life this way."

It was not exactly the response she was looking for, but one that deserved a reply. "If you look closely, there are no scratches or bruises on either of us. I hate to say that our afternoon was spent having consensual sex—that's way too academic. Let's just call today a new beginning. There's nothing specific to that description." She made certain she had his attention as she finished with, "I want to make it perfectly clear, Sean. You are welcome to stay. You are welcome to come back. Like I've told you before, I'll always be here for you."

It was not exactly the response he was looking for either, but one that, also, deserved a reply. "April, I won't try to put my feelings about you into words right now. They'd be too charged by what's taken place this afternoon. Let me be clear about one thing. I haven't felt about a woman for a long time the way I feel about you right now…right at this very moment. But, if there is to be anything to our relationship after today, I have to return to Dixie and deal with the situation at home."

"What are you going to do?"

"I have no idea. If she's as cunning as I think she is, she knows where I've been today. I wouldn't be a bit surprised to find her parked out front waiting for me with an AK-47."

"Then stay here. You could be right, and I don't want anything to happen to you."

"You realize my days with Darling Motors are over," Sean said.

"So are mine," she echoed. "You see, we have common ground already."

"I think you're making light of a shit storm that's about to unfold."

Rolling onto her back, with a harsh expression unlike anything Sean had seen before on her face, April said, "Let it happen. Bring it on, Sean. All I want right now is you, and I'm willing to weather anything."

Moved by her commitment, he leaned over and kissed her again.

"You can't leave until I read the last five pages of Kim's book. You owe me that much."

Sean responded by pulling up a pillow and planting his head on it.

April reached for the remaining, unread pages, hunkered down next to him, and began reading them out loud. Sean listened intently. Kim's words always sounded different coming from someone else's mouth than when he read them. It was as if Kim's spirit embodied the reader. April read the story enthusiastically, the inflection in her voice adding emphasis to Kim's message. He closed his eyes as he listened to the end all over again. But when she was done, the book's conclusion was unchanged.

April opened the envelope containing the final, blank page. "What's this?"

"It's the ending. Berkowitz and I concluded that it's a sign I'm supposed to write my own ending for her story, taking Mark to Monticello, and thereby me to the happiness I'm seeking."

"That's your great revelation?" April asked. She was clearly underwhelmed by the ending.

"Do you disagree?"

"Well…sort of. I mean, Kim's a deep thinker. A blank sheet? Come on…"

April flopped back onto her pillow and studied the piece of white paper at length.

"What are you looking at?" Sean asked.

"I'm looking for more. There's got to be more."

Suddenly, something occurred to April and she sat up, reached into the lid of the box containing the printed pages of Kim's book, and began holding several of them up to the light coming in from the balcony. She would look at a printed page, then the blank page, then another printed page, and once again, the blank page.

Turning to Sean, she said, "Uh…this blank sheet of paper isn't the ending."

Propping himself up on one elbow, Sean asked, "What do you mean?"

"Look at these pages with the printing." One-by-one she held up several pages to the light. "What do you see?"

"It's a piece of paper with Kim's text on it."

"No! Do you see the watermark? The printed pages all say Strathmore. These pages are a cotton-based paper—very classy. That's consistent with everything else about her book. It came wrapped in fine tissue. Remember when we opened the box for the first time? The tissue had no wrinkles."

"I have very little recollection of that moment, let alone the condition of the tissue paper. How did you happen to notice it?"

"Oh, men! Berkowitz has me looking more and more each day at little details such as this."

"Yeah, but tissue paper wrinkles. Look at it now."

"I know, but prior to your accident when we first opened the box with her manuscript, it was wrinkle free. That took a lot of effort. She was meticulous in her choice of papers. She took painstaking measures to type in a font that's not among your usual, run-of-the-mill choices. There wasn't even a bent corner on a single sheet of paper. Then, she ends the book with a cheap piece of copy stock paper in a low-priced security envelope?" Shaking her head as she held up the envelope and blank page, April concluded, "Call me mistrustful, but this isn't the end of Kim's book."

Sean was astonished by that possibility.

"Who else has read Kim's book?" April asked.

"It's only been you and me, April. I won't even let Berkowitz touch it. The only time it's been out of my hands since I got it was when I had my accident, and from that point until it was returned to me, you had it in your possession."

"What about Will?"

"No."

"Your father?"

"Hell no!"

All of a sudden, Sean remembered Dixie's revelation while in the shower at the hospital—that she had read Kim's book. The prospect was unthinkable, yet all too plausible. Dixie must have taken the last page of Kim's book, and, in doing so, altered its ending.

April came to the same conclusion. "It's Dixie, isn't it?"

Sean nodded.

"She screwed with Kim's book, then she disrespects her by not taking you to her grave? I'm sorry, Sean, but your wife's got some explaining to do."

"You're telling me," Sean agreed.

"Let me take you home. I want to see the expression on her face when you confront her."

"Am I still welcome here tonight?"

"Tonight, and the rest of your life."

Chapter 24

DIXIE HAD REHEARSED OVER and over again what she was going to say to Sean if and when he came home. She was already furious with Katie for raising the issue of her own sordid, previous improprieties, and angry with her mother for setting up a lunch date that turned into such a fiasco. Katie had called Dixie at home repeatedly until she finally took the phone off the hook, while Suzanne, as anticipated, had invited herself over, only to have her daughter tell her to leave and not return until she was asked. By now, Dixie's gun was loaded for bear.

What she wasn't prepared for was to have April brazenly drive Sean up to the back doorstep of her home. The enraged expression on Sean's face, and the pace with which he approached the kitchen door, indicated to her he was livid. She wondered if perhaps he had discovered her shell game at the cemetery. Add to this his bold, if not outrageous, inclusion of April into their pending confrontation at this explosive moment, and the situation truly scared her. Not knowing how bad the altercation might become, Dixie dialed 911 from her cell phone and urgently requested the police to come to her house. Seconds later, Sean burst through the door.

"You lied to me! How long did you think it would take before I figured out that you purposely took me to the wrong gravesite?!"

Ignoring Sean's question entirely, Dixie fired back as she looked at April standing a few feet behind him in the doorway, "What's she doing here?!"

"Answer my question!"

"Listen to you, Sean! You excoriate me for something I did to the memory of your deceased ex-girlfriend, yet you don't see the problem with bringing this tramp into our lives?!"

As they shouted at one another, they circled about the kitchen, progressively stepping closer until they were face-to-face. April stood in the doorway, excitedly watching as if she had ringside seats at a Las Vegas heavyweight boxing match.

"Tell me! I have to know!" Sean continued. "What was your motive?! I mean, was it simply that you're a mean-spirited person?! Did Frank tell you to fuck with me just to see if I'd jump off the deep end?!"

"You're already off the deep end, Sean!" Dixie replied, pushing him away. "You passed that point months ago! But am I mean-spirited?! No! I made the mistake of following my mother's advice—that somehow it was up to me to make things work between us and to never let you slip through my fingers! That's why I've coped with all of your obsessions for God knows how long! That's why I've stood by your side since your accident! That's why I spent sleepless nights on a sofa in your hospital room wondering if my husband was ever going to be himself again! That's why I read that stupid book to you day and night until I wanted to puke! That's why I gave all of me to you…until now!"

"You didn't give me all of you! You forgot about the truth! It's all been a farce," he said, throwing his hands up in the air. "Everything you've done for me has been pretense so you could continue to manipulate me into becoming some gutless puppet for the Darling family to pound into the ground, day after day, year after year, simply for their amusement! Well I have news for you! Sean Marcum is emancipated as of today! You can tell your daddy that this is his red-letter day! I'm out of here! He can have you back!"

Determined to keep the focus on Sean's extramarital relationship, Dixie said, "I followed you to her place this afternoon, Sean." Running her fingers through her hair, she continued, "You know, I even defended you today against the assertion by Mother and Katie that you were sleeping with that woman. They were so right, and I was so wrong. All this time you said you were looking for happiness, trying to find yourself, searching for your future. Who would have thought that all she had to do was spread her legs and all your problems would be solved in less than five minutes. You should have had her do it seven years ago when all this nonsense began. It would have saved us all a hell of a lot of grief and a lot of wasted energy."

By now, both parties had launched all of their sorties. But, Sean decided to bring up one more matter, "What did you do with the real last page to Kim's book?"

Her answer mixed with heart-wrenching sobs, Dixie said, "You mean the ending that I kept from you because I feared it would be too much for you? The ending I sheltered you from out of some misguided devotion for a husband who developed separation anxiety as an adult? The ending I couldn't possibly let you see, because I couldn't stand to watch all of your love go lost to a dead woman instead of me? I'll get it for you, Sean. But do me this final favor—wait until you're back at her place before you read it," she said, pointing at April. "I don't want to see what it does to you. I guess there's still a part of me that for some foolish reason cares for you. I can't bear to watch you self-destruct over Kim's choice of ending."

DIXIE LEFT THE ROOM and returned quickly with the envelope. It was as April had suggested—a personalized parchment envelope with Kim's raised initials. Clearly, it had to be the authentic climax for which he was searching. Neglecting to heed Dixie's warning, Sean quickly opened the envelope to find it contained a single sheet of paper with a Strathmore watermark. It was unquestionably the ending that had just weeks ago been crafted by Kim.

He eagerly read it out loud, hoping the words would not only free him of his burden, but demonstrate to both Dixie and April that his quest had been worthwhile.

"...Find the Fuller Brush Man."

Struck by those words, he repeated the ending in a monotone voice.

"…Find the Fuller Brush Man."

It was clear to both women that the pinnacle he'd expected had been anticlimactic at best.

There was a long pause as Sean grappled with the finish he so longed to hear. Recalling verbatim the final words of the last printed page, he pieced together the entire last sentence of Kim's book. "The only thing that remains is he must…Find the Fuller Brush Man." In their entirety, Kim's last words fell short.

Dropping his arms to his side in frustration, Sean turned to April and said, "This means I'm back to square one again." As his emotions turned to anguish and despair, he yelled, "I mean, what the hell did she think I've been doing for the last seven fucking years?! With his voice breaking, he added, "Jesus, this is some kind of curse or something. What did I ever do to anyone to deserve this?"

Neither April nor Dixie gave an immediate answer to his question. Up to now, April had remained at the doorway. But seeing Sean in such distress, she went to his side to offer comfort, saying, "Sean, let's go now. We can talk about this when we get back to my place."

"Honey, you'll be talking about this for years…trust me," Dixie said, taking a seat at the kitchen table and sporting a most unlikable grin as she relished the all too predictable outcome.

"No. I can't go with you," Sean answered, staring at the floor. "Not just yet. This stops here. This stops now." Looking into April's eyes, he continued, "I'm tired of all this Fuller Brush crap, April. I think Kim was just trying to get back at me for dumping her, and torturing me in this way has been her objective all along. No more. This…this has to stop."

"But Sean, your mother said essentially the same thing," April pointed out. "She wouldn't do that to you as well. There has to be more to it than what you think. Let's go talk."

"In a bit," Sean replied as he turned around, breaking free of April's hold. Pushing past Dixie, he said, "I have to take care of some things first."

SEAN WENT INTO HIS office and locked the door behind him. April followed him, but he refused her request to be let in. The silence was deafening until April got the courage to ask Dixie, "What's in this room?"

With a shrug of indifference, Dixie replied, "It's his office. There's a computer, all of his work files, everything you never wanted to know about the Fuller Brush Company—that, by the way, you will be packing and moving to your place—and, oh, yes, a 9mm Glock."

Moments later, there was cursing and screaming along with sounds of objects being thrown and broken. It went on and on. Shortly after the commotion began, the police arrived. Two officers entered through the open kitchen door. They could tell *where* the problem was, the question was *what* the problem was.

"I'm Lt. Baker," the more senior of the two said. "This is Officer Metz," he continued, gesturing to his partner. "Which of you called for assistance?"

Dixie nonchalantly waved her hand.

"What's the problem, ma'am?"

"It seems my husband has lost his mind."

"You're Ms. Darling, correct?" the Lieutenant asked, recognizing Dixie's very public face, but missing on the name.

"Soon, I hope. For now, I'm Mrs. Marcum...Dixie Marcum."

"And your husband's name is?"

"Sean Marcum."

Turning toward April, the Lieutenant asked, "And your name, ma'am?"

Before she could answer, Dixie replied, "That's my husband's whore."

It didn't take long for the two policemen to figure out the situation was some type of domestic disturbance, if not worse.

"I'm April Knudsen," she politely answered for herself.

Looking at Dixie, the Lieutenant asked, "Ma'am, I need to know right now who lives here."

Calmly, Dixie replied, "I do."

"And Mr. Marcum?"

"He's no longer welcome here," Dixie replied. As condescendingly as possible, she continued, "I suspect he's going to have to move in with his sweet little concubine."

"Is Ms. Knudsen welcome here, ma'am?" the Lieutenant asked, remaining unemotional.

Bitterly, Dixie replied, "Not in any way, shape or form. Can you shoot her in the heart? It would do mine wonders to see her hauled off in a body bag."

Ignoring Dixie's absurd request, the Lieutenant motioned for his partner to remove April from the house.

"Ms. Knudsen, come with me," Metz requested, taking her by the arm and hustling her to the patrol car.

Once April was outside, Baker pressed for answers. "Now, get to the point. What's going on with your husband?"

Still not taking the situation as seriously as she should, Dixie replied, "He's mad at the Fuller Brush Man?"

"The what?" Baker asked.

"You know. Those guys who used to go door to door selling brushes, cleaning supplies, and what-not."

Being middle-aged himself, Baker said, "You mean *those* Fuller Brush guys?"

Dixie nodded.

"I don't get it, and I don't care. Why is he in that room?"

"I'm not completely sure, but I think he may be about to kill himself."

Baker's expression indicated he found Dixie's composure, if her assertion was correct, more than a little unsettling.

"Are there any weapons in the room?"

Dixie nodded, but offered little more.

Frustrated by Dixie's unwillingness to be completely forthcoming, Baker railed, "Ma'am, I don't know what's going on between the three of you, but if, as you say, your husband has barricaded himself into his office and he has a weapon, you need to cooperate fully with me or I'll remove you from the house as well and take matters into my own hands. Do you follow me?"

Beginning to get a sense of the grave nature of the problem at hand, Dixie felt more and more a degree of alarm. As she thought about what she was saying, and knowing how upset Sean was about the entire matter, she realized there was a chance—a very good chance—that her husband just might commit suicide. She wasn't ready for that.

"He has a 9mm Glock that he keeps in his desk drawer."

"Do you think he might use it on us?" Baker asked.

Dixie shook her head.

"Do you think he might use it on himself?

Tears began to well up in Dixie's eyes as, this time, she nodded.

With good timing, two back-up officers joined Baker and his partner.

Addressing one of them, Baker said, "Take Mrs. Marcum to your car and stay with her. I want you and Metz to take both units and stage up at Westminster Road." Pointing at the other officer, he continued, "Tatum, you stay with me."

OVER THE NEXT THIRTY minutes, Sean would not reply to any of Baker's attempts to make contact with him. Dixie suggested to the officer tasked with her safety that Dr. Berkowitz be contacted. That idea was passed along to those in charge of the situation, and the incident commander was able to locate the psychologist and request his assistance.

Additional police officers, as well as a group of men dressed in black uniforms and heavily armed, assembled at the dwelling. A helicopter circled above the site eerily illuminating the house and grounds, and marking it as ground zero for all the nosy neighbors who were gathering across the street. From a distance, Dixie watched in horror as people she thought of as friends, congregated in a party-like atmosphere, passing around drinks and snacks to one another as they watched the goings-on with poorly-concealed amusement.

And then matters got worse—Frank arrived. He was in his element now: a pseudo-combat situation, armed men, a chain of command, and air support. Dixie watched through the rear-seat window of the patrol car as her father took in several deep breaths, fully appreciating the unfolding drama. Frantically, she pounded on the window of the locked door to the cruiser. Perhaps it was the persistent thump-thump of the helicopter overhead, or maybe it was the squawking of voices on the many radios. Regardless, Frank was unable to hear Dixie as she tried in vain to get his attention.

All of a sudden, Frank did the unfathomable—he approached the police cruiser holding April, spoke with the officer and shook his hand, then helped April out of the car after the officer opened the door. Dixie watched in disbelief as the two struck up a brief conversation as if they were the best of friends. True, April worked for him, but he must have known that for her to be associated in any manner with the situation, she likely was directly involved. For that matter, she was probably the cause of the entire calamity. Dixie had made her ill-feelings about April perfectly clear to her father on multiple occasions, and she was perplexed that there could be any civility between the two.

The exchange lasted only a short while, but long enough for Dixie to stew in her own juice until it appeared April became self-conscious of the fact that the silhouette inside the vehicle behind the one she had been in was that of Dixie. Once April made Frank aware of Dixie's whereabouts, he abruptly ended his discussion and came to Dixie's aid.

After making small talk with the officer standing-by with Dixie, Frank asked that his daughter be let out of the car. Dixie leaped past her father, raced toward April and knocked her to the ground before Frank and two cops were able to restrain her. Officer Metz helped April to her feet. Other than a torn coat and some missing buttons, she was otherwise unscathed.

Dixie managed to break free from those holding her, spun around and took a swing at the first person she saw—it was her father. His Marine reflexes still sharp, the septuagenarian stopped her punch by catching her fist in his enormous hand. Frank coldly said to his daughter, "You don't want to do that."

After a few moments, Dixie fell into her father's arms. As he comforted her, she said, "Daddy, I told you to get rid of April, but all you did was move her to another location. Now she's taken Sean from me." What Dixie couldn't see as they held each other was the accomplished smile on Frank's face.

"Is he the cause of all this commotion?" Trying to take the situation seriously for Dixie's sake, he continued, "It was inevitable, Dixie. Sean's got lots of issues. It's time you cut your losses and leave him. Let her have him."

As the two walked away from where April stood, she said, "He's upset with me that I didn't take him to see his ex-girlfriend's grave, and that I screwed with the ending of her book."

"Sounds like Sean," Frank said sarcastically. "He knows how to pick his battles."

"Stop maligning him!" Dixie shouted.

"He's a philandering psycho. Stop defending him! What are you going to do? Follow him to her place every afternoon like you did today?"

It suddenly occurred to Dixie that her father seemed much too aware of what had taken place leading up to tonight's row. "How did you know Sean was at April's apartment today?"

Frank hesitated, caught perhaps in his own trap. Fortunately, Berkowitz arrived on scene at that moment. "I need to have a few words with Sean's shrink," Frank said uncomfortably as he stepped toward Berkowitz' car.

Dixie grabbed her father by the arm, spun him around, and looked him in the eyes. "If anyone is going to speak with Dr. Berkowitz, it will be me. When this mess is over, you owe me a damn good answer to my question, Daddy. I have a really bad feeling about you and April right now."

Chapter 25

FIRST, BERKOWITZ HAD TO meet with the incident commander on scene. Though Sean had not yet committed a crime, from the perspective of the police, they had a fifty-three year old male holed up in a house of which he was both owner and resident. He was unable or unwilling to communicate with police inside the residence, and he was potentially armed and posed a threat to himself. There were protocols to follow, and the police were ready for any worst-case scenario.

To Dr. Berkowitz, he was simply dealing with Sean.

Following his briefing from the police, Berkowitz met with Dixie. She explained to him all of the events of the day of which she was aware, leading up to the confrontation in the kitchen. In particular, she highlighted her misrepresentation of the facts at the cemetery, her alteration of Kim's book, and also Sean's involvement with April and his anger when they arrived. The doctor found the revelations about the cemetery and the book startling. That of Sean's romantic tryst with April, not so much.

"This is all very, very disturbing, Dixie," Berkowitz began. "You see, Sean and I came to a markedly different conclusion based upon the blank piece of paper we found at the end of Kim's book.

While we determined Kim wanted Sean to start from scratch—to write his own ending to the story—the actual ending, with the reference to the Fuller Brush Man, totally changes things."

"What do you think Kim meant?" Dixie asked.

"I have no earthly idea at this point, but this new ending has to be explored with Sean. That her ending more or less matches the last written words of his mother is not a mere coincidence. No, it's a huge clue…a huge clue. But, it'll require Sean to reconcile the pieces to this puzzle."

"And what about his affair with April?"

With clinical indifference, Berkowitz replied, "I expect you see it as a terrible violation of the vows he made to you many years ago. I see it as Sean acting out. Please, by no means think that I condone what he may have done with April. I've warned him to stay clear of her from the beginning of our work together. But, what's done is done. We have to pick up the pieces from here and move forward. What I need to know is do you still want to be a part of Sean's life?"

Upset at being put on the spot to answer a question she never thought she would have to respond to, Dixie replied, "I can't give you an answer right now."

Forcing the issue, Berkowitz stated, "Not good enough. When *I* go in to bargain with Sean, I need to know what *we* have to offer."

"And I'm telling you I don't know where I stand with regards to Sean!"

With some hesitation, Berkowitz laid it all on the line. "You do realize I have to be completely honest with him. If he asks about the state of his relationship with you—and he will—I have to tell him everything is up in the air."

"The condition of our relationship is somehow my fault?! He's the one having sex with another woman!"

"That may be the case…"

"No! That *is* the case!"

"…but what you did wasn't right either, and we know Sean's rationality was already in a fragile condition."

"What I did and what he did aren't the same thing—not even close."

"What both of you did was to commit a serious breach of trust. I'm not going to debate relative degrees with you, Dixie."

The incident commander broke up the conversation by tapping Berkowitz on the shoulder. "Doctor, we need to get you up to the house now. Wrap things up here."

"Fine. It'll be just a minute," he replied.

Dixie paced back and forth, literally not knowing what to do. It was then that she received a call from an angel. Callie was phoning.

"Just a moment, Dr. Berkowitz. Let me take this call." Walking up the road, away from all the action, Dixie answered as calmly as possible, "Hi, Baby."

"Hi, Mom. I can't talk too long 'cause Darryl's taking me out tonight. But I wanted to let you know that Kappa had a planning meeting today, and we're throwing a giant party, and like, having all kinds of events this year for Homecoming Weekend, and I signed up both of you guys to be speakers."

"Really? That's…interesting, Callie. What are we to speak about?"

"You have to give a speech about how Kappa made you what you are today, and like, Dad has to give a speech on being married to a Kappa all these years. Guess what, like, almost everyone I meet from the northern suburbs knows us from our TV ads, and of all the parents of the new pledges, you guys have been married the longest. That is like, so cool."

"Well…I'll have to check with your father…."

"What's to check? Darryl's parents are coming down for the weekend. I talked it over with Will, and like, we're all having dinner Friday night cooked by Giselle and him over at her place. You and Dad will be at the sorority Saturday morning, and Grandpa's cooking bratwursts at his place for lunch. I told him they had to be, like, Kosher or something. The football game starts at three o'clock."

"It seems as though you covered all the bases. I just need to make sure we have nothing else going on, sweetie."

"Mom?! Is everything okay? You're, like, acting weird. Kappas don't turn down requests from other Kappas. Besides, it's Homecoming, and like, it's the first time both Will and I are at college together."

"I'm not turning you down, Callie. Just let me check with your father. I'm certain…he'll be able to make the trip by then."

"Why wouldn't he be able to travel? Is he still having headaches?"

"No…well, occasionally. He's doing better…"

"Mom, what aren't you telling me? Is there something else going on?"

"No, honey. I'm just tired. It's been a long day, and I got sick from lunch with Grandma and Aunt Katie."

"You're sure there's nothing you need to tell me?"

"Positive. Look, I need to run. I have to help your father with something."

"Is he still reading that stupid, idiotic book?"

Dixie was shocked by Callie's candor. It was both awkward and painful that Callie took such an irreverent view of Kim's book—probably a reflection of the same feelings she had felt about it.

"It's not 'stupid' Callie. It's very important to your father. I'll call you in the morning, okay?"

"'Night, Mom."

"Don't stay out too late…"

There was no reply. Callie had already disconnected. Dixie just had her first taste of delivering motherly advice to her college-aged daughter over long distance.

Callie's phone call had another overpowering effect. It underscored the two most important things in life she had in common with Sean—Callie and Will. Of all their successes and failures, the children had been true blessings. That was enough to encourage Dixie to throw her support to her husband one more time.

Returning to Berkowitz, she said, "Tell him I'm still with him, but you need to go before I change my mind."

Through his thick beard, Dixie thought she saw a grin on Berkowitz' face. Soon after, he was whisked toward the house to meet with Sean. As Dixie watched him walk away, there was a tap on her shoulder. It was Katie. She was a welcome sight.

DESPITE HIS PROTESTS, THE police outfitted Dr. Berkowitz with an armored vest. Then, they ushered him to a chair near the door to Sean's study. A thick, bullet-proof, clear Lexan plate, held upright and in position by heavy-duty supports, protected him from any possible threat of gunfire originating from Sean's direction.

Sean hadn't spoken a word since he locked himself in his study. The police had repeatedly called the house phone that also rang at Sean's desk. But he never answered it, and ultimately must have unplugged it. Lieutenant Baker informed Berkowitz that he had heard movement and unrecognizable mumbling coming from the office, so they knew Sean was still alive.

After getting as comfortable as possible in the chair, Berkowitz began with nothing more than an introduction. "Sean, it's Berk."

There was what appeared to be the sound of someone nervously tapping a pen or pencil on a desk, but no verbal response.

"Sean, I know you're in there. I'm here to listen to what's on your mind."

"What's this going to cost me?" Sean answered.

"Oh, outcalls like this run about two-hundred fifty an hour, three-hundred if I'm in a bad mood. But we can stretch out a payment plan for you. You're credit's good with me."

Berkowitz had what could only be described as an unorthodox way of mixing humor into any serious discussion.

"Really? Not after Dixie takes me to the cleaners," Sean said.

"To that end, I have some good news. I was just outside speaking with Dixie, and she wants to work things out with you."

After a short pause, Sean replied, "Where is she now?"

"She's still out there. The police have her at a safe distance from the house because, to be quite honest Sean, nobody knows what you plan to do. Is there a weapon in the room?"

After another pause, Sean replied, "Actually there is. I'd forgotten about that."

Berkowitz and Baker heard a drawer open and Sean pull back the slide action of an automatic handgun. Berkowitz wondered if he had made a mistake mentioning the gun in the first place. Now it was too late. The doctor continued his conversation while Baker relayed to the others over the radio that there was now a verified weapon involved.

"Doc, I screwed up big time," Sean continued. "I was wrong to bet my future and my entire existence on Kim's book. Did you know that all this time, she wanted nothing more than to screw me over?"

Berkowitz couldn't help but notice Sean placed more significance on Kim's book than he did the events that had taken place between him and April. But he was going to let Sean lead the conversation in a direction he felt most comfortable.

"Are you speaking of the real ending you discovered tonight?"

"Yes I'm speaking of the real ending I discovered tonight," Sean said, parroting Berkowitz.

"Sean, it would require Kim to have had an unimaginable penchant for vengeance if, as you suggest, she went to all of this trouble just to hurt you. Not one time have you ever indicated to me that Kim had a mean bone in her body. Not once, in that masterful work Kim wrote, did her spirit, portrayed by Collette, do anything that would directly inflict pain upon you. My God, she's the savior of the Who! I think we should give her true intentions a more thorough examination."

"Doc, Doc, Doc, Doc, Doc…," Sean countered. "I simply can't wade through this bullshit any longer. If there's a message in Kim's book, it's lost in the translation."

"We can take a break," Berkowitz said, sympathizing with Sean's plight. "We've come to terms with a great number of matters during our sessions, Sean. Maybe I've been too aggressive with you. I'm not suggesting that we necessarily jump back into Kim's book right away. Let's let things gel for a while. That'll give you time to get your new county tax sticker. I noticed this morning that it's still expired."

Sean chuckled as he said, "You know something Doc? You're one sick son-of-a-bitch."

"Hey, I minored in sick son-of-a-bitch during my undergrad years at college. You're the beneficiary of all my hard work."

There was a long silence as Berkowitz waited for Sean to say something. He eventually asked, "Sean, are you still with me?"

"What am I going to say to April?"

Somewhat surprised that Sean was willing to discuss the matter, Berkowitz answered, "Well, Sean, that all depends to whom you wish to have allegiance in the years ahead—April or Dixie."

"My allegiance is with April. Dixie burned her bridges."

"Sean, I wasn't speaking about now. I'm speaking about the future. It's easy to get caught up in your present circumstances."

Avoiding answering Berkowitz' question, Sean replied, "Where's April?"

"I believe I saw her outside as well."

"Is she with Dixie?"

"Not hardly."

"April's been spectacular through this whole mess, Doc. She knows what I'm going through. For Christ's sake, she went to Kim's funeral on my behalf."

"Sean, we've been over this several times already. Dixie and April have hugely different stakes and interests in their relationship with you. I'd be cautious of betting that April is completely altruistic with her actions. As for Dixie, that relationship has been tested by time."

"I don't see how you can be so judgmental about April?" Sean argued.

"No, Sean. At issue here is how you can *not* be judgmental about April. You're smitten. She says jump, and you're already three feet off the ground. To put it another way, you're thinking with those two lumps between your legs instead of the bigger lump on top of your shoulders."

"It's not about sex, Doc."

"Oh, Sean. Pul-ease! What did you do with her this afternoon? Review sales figures? Did you chart out an investment plan for your future? Did you discuss the outlook for your careers? Did you discuss her family? Yours? Did you climb Mount Crumpet to visit the Who? Or did you just mount April?"

There was another long delay as Sean absorbed what Berkowitz said. Eventually, he replied, "You're being cruel now, Doc."

"Sean, I'm simply trying to move this process along. I'm not handing out cherry-flavored cough syrup today. You're getting Paregoric. What do you think was the central message in Kim's book?"

Bitterly, Sean replied, "You screwed me over, now it's my turn to slowly suck the life out of you."

"Really, Sean? Tell me, what did you do to your mother that she felt screwed over and needed to ruin your life as well? Their written messages to you are all but identical."

"Kim used those words in a different context."

"You have no idea of the context under which they wrote those words. You think you know, and you project that into your own reality. But realistically, Sean, you don't understand the context any more than the very meaning of the words themselves. Why have we been belaboring the point for the last several weeks?"

Sean gave no answer.

"So what's it going to be, Sean? I'm sitting out here wearing a ridiculous bullet-proof vest talking to you through a door and a monolith of plastic. I'd much rather speak with you face-to-face, get you cooled off, and back to your wife. What do you say?"

The relative calm of the conversation was instantly turned into calamity by the sound of a single gunshot.

As Berkowitz looked at Lieutenant Baker, he said, "Oh, my. That can't be good."

FROM THE SAFE LOCATIONS where police had taken Dixie and April, all they heard was a POP. Under normal circumstances, the sound would have been dismissed as nothing more than a random noise. This time, there was no doubt in the minds of anyone what had just taken place—a gun had been fired. It echoed eerily between the homes so that it sounded as though there were multiple shots from several locations. The sound was quickly followed by indecipherable chatter on the police radios. Looking toward the open door of the house, Dixie saw Officer Tatum usher Dr. Berkowitz out of the house—his hands held up to his face in what appeared to be an expression of disbelief.

Dixie was frozen in place, unable to believe what was happening. As if to prevent her sister-in-law from witnessing any more of the morbid events that were unfolding, Katie stepped into Dixie's line of view, put her arms around her, and pulled her toward the rear seat of the police car. The two crawled inside where the gravity of the situation began to sink in. Out of all the talk on the radio, both ladies clearly heard the most horrible words, "Scene is secure, repeat, scene is secure."

It was over. That's when Dixie lost all of her composure.

Katie tried to remain calm so as to comfort her closest friend, but it was all but impossible. Katie's eyes would tear up, she would wipe them and look at the scene, only to have her eyes tear up again. She watched with obscene curiosity as Berkowitz and several officers disappeared inside the house. But after a brief wait of less than ten minutes, two officers emerged, followed by Dr. Berkowitz, then Sean and Lieutenant Baker. Katie gasped and tugged at Dixie's arm.

"Dixie! He's alive! Look, he's alive!"

Although he appeared sheepish and completely submissive to the police and Berkowitz, he looked otherwise uninjured. Once more, Dixie found herself on the wrong side of a locked door. After pounding on the window, the officer outside opened the door and she ran as quickly as she could to Sean. Surrounded by the officers and Dr. Berkowitz, Sean and Dixie embraced as the others looked on guardedly. Words were hard to come by for both of them, but there was plenty of communication between the two in the form of touch.

Finally, Berkowitz broke the silence.

"Dixie, I'm admitting Sean to an inpatient care facility in Wisconsin with which I am associated. It's clear to me at this point that Sean needs some time to work through matters in a monitored, safe environment. His treatment will be under my supervision, but the therapists he'll be working with are employed by that facility."

Looking into Sean's eyes, Dixie asked, "Is this what you want?"

Before he could answer, Lieutenant Baker stepped into the conversation, saying, "Mrs. Marcum, your husband doesn't have a choice given the circumstances. We, along with Dr. Berkowitz, believe Sean presents a threat to himself and perhaps others. His options were to either submit to a voluntary committal under the care of Dr. Berkowitz, or we would have to execute an emergency detention and take him to a hospital that deals with patients who have psychiatric problems. He chose the first option. He's also being charged with unlawful discharge of a firearm which is a Class C misdemeanor here in Lake Forest. He's not under arrest, but when he's done with his stay at the clinic, he'll have to go before a Magistrate here in Lake County, pay a fine, and possibly face a probated sentence of some kind."

"What's the name of this facility? Where exactly in Wisconsin is it located?" Dixie asked with mounting agitation.

"I'm afraid I can't disclose that information, Dixie," Dr. Berkowitz answered. "It's confidential so that family members respect the patient's privacy. This rule is not unique to Sean's situation. This is the case for all patients of this facility."

"How will I know if he's alright?" Dixie asked warily. "I don't like this arrangement. I don't like it one bit!"

"He'll be able to correspond with you through me once a week. If the therapists at the facility feel he's progressed to a point where it's appropriate, he'll be allowed to call you. I know this is hard for you, but right now this treatment is entirely focused around Sean's needs."

After another long embrace, Sean said, "I'm sorry, Dixie. I'm sorry I caused all of this trouble. I'm sorry about everything."

Dixie realized he had been speaking in a monotone. Despite the enormity of what had taken place, Sean was virtually devoid of all emotion. It was obvious to Dixie that Sean had reached the bottom of his own personal abyss. She had no choice but to let him go. Besides, she could only agree with Berkowitz' assessment that Sean had unquestionably become a threat to his own well-being. She was just thankful that she had this chance to hold him again, and to look forward to rebuilding their lives together. Following a long kiss, she reluctantly allowed the police to lead him away. Katie joined her once more and the two proceeded back to the house.

THOSE FORMING THE CIRCLE weren't the only ones watching the reunion, so were April and Frank. As the group walked past Frank, he mumbled loud enough for Sean to hear, "I thought I was finally rid of you." Sean stopped as Frank callously continued, "You're so incompetent you can't even blow your own brains out."

April shook her head, unwilling to acknowledge the cruelty of what Frank had said. It appeared for a moment that Sean was about to do the same. He took two steps away from Frank in the direction the police had been escorting him when he suddenly bolted from the group, turned, and tackled Frank. Before the police could restrain him, he'd dealt Frank no less than four solid blows to his face.

As police helped Frank to his feet, he shouted, "I want that crazy son-of-a-bitch charged with assault! Do you hear me?! I want his ass in jail!"

Sean was hurriedly placed into a police car along with Dr. Berkowitz and taken away as Frank continued to bark out orders to unsympathetic ears. Finding himself anything but the center of attention, Frank brushed his clothes off, walked back to his car, and left.

April now found herself alone, surrounded by police and a dwindling crowd of unfamiliar spectators. She was certain that she wasn't the only person at the scene to notice Sean never spoke with her—never even making eye contact with her—as he walked from the house to the police car. Having just over an hour earlier audaciously driven up to Sean's back door, she now surreptitiously got into her car and left.

Chapter 26

DIXIE RECOGNIZED THE OVERSIZED policeman standing in her kitchen wearing a black uniform, as the one who earlier had been outside and in charge of the situation. He was in the company of another man wearing a sport coat with a badge hanging over its pocket. The latter, an investigator, was taking photographs of Sean's study which had been pretty much turned upside-down during his outburst of anger. The gun that presumably had been fired was sitting on Sean's desk in a plastic bag. A thick wire safety device ran through its barrel, locking the gun in an open and harmless condition. The room still smelled like burned gun powder.

"Did he shoot at anyone?" Dixie asked.

"No ma'am," the Incident Commander replied.

"Did he shoot at himself?" she asked, trying to figure out what had taken place.

The investigator picked up a shattered picture frame from the floor then handed it to Dixie. The 5 by 7 photograph that barely remained contained within the bent metal frame, had a hole through the middle of it. Yet, there was enough of the photograph remaining for Dixie to recognize the subject. It had been the cherished picture of Kim that Sean kept in his desk drawer.

"Who's that?" Katie asked.

"Sean's old flame—the one who wrote the book that started this entire mess."

"Maybe he needs some anger management while he's in Wisconsin," Katie chortled. The look on Dixie's face made it clear she wasn't impressed by her attempt at humor.

"You know something?" Dixie began. "It may be over…it may finally be over. I mean, this woman has been numero uno in his life of late…probably for longer than I want to know. Judging by this picture, I don't think he holds her in the same regard anymore. Add to that the destruction in this room, and Kim may accompany the Fuller Brush Man as a distant nightmare." Walking around the office, kicking through the objects that had been strewn about, she added, "I don't think I've ever appreciated a trashed room so much."

"The picture's pretty much destroyed. What about her book? I think it needs to go away, too," Katie said.

"You're right. You're absolutely right." After looking about Sean's office for a few seconds, Dixie remembered that he had taken the book with him to his appointment with Dr. Berkowitz earlier in the day. "Crap! It's probably in his car, and I suspect that's still parked outside Berkowitz' office. I saw Sean in April's car when I was coming home from lunch, and she drove him here tonight."

"He was with April while you were at lunch with us?" Katie asked.

"Do *not* go there with me right now, Katie Darling!" Dixie said, glaring at her. "I swear I'm about to slap the person closest to me, and you're less than an arm's length away!"

"Okay, okay. I'll drop it. I promise," Katie said, holding her arms up in a defensive position.

"We need to go get Sean's car anyway. We can get the book, come back home, open a bottle of champagne, start a fire in the fireplace, and celebrate as we burn each page."

"Now that's what I call anger management," Katie said approvingly. "You go girl. But I think I should stay here overnight just to make sure you don't burn the house down. Let's go get Sean's car, and on the way home I'll stop at home and get a few things."

Dixie realized it was not only a good idea for her to have some companionship, it was also an opportunity for the two of them to work through some of the problems that had surfaced recently in their relationship. There was no one else in Dixie's circle of friends she trusted so dearly, nor one who had so much in common with her as Katie.

"Do you need us here for anything?" Dixie asked the policeman.

"No, ma'am," the Commander replied. "We're just wrapping up a few things, and we'll get out of your hair. I'm glad things ended the way they did. For a while, I thought the outcome would be a lot worse."

Dixie nodded before asking, "Are you taking the gun with you?"

"No, ma'am. It's registered to your husband. He committed no felony, therefore I have no legal reason to take the gun away."

"If I insist, will you take it?"

"I can do a temporary confiscation if you would like. That normally requires some paperwork, but you know what, I'll just take it with me tonight, and you can come by the station sometime tomorrow and fill out the form."

"Wonderful. I want it out of here—and take all the bullets, too."

"Certainly, ma'am."

KATIE AND DIXIE MADE haste to Berkowitz office. Not finding Sean's car there, they drove to Sean's dealership where they found his car still parked. Unfortunately, Dixie didn't find what she had set out for.

"Shit! It's not here!" Dixie said.

"Maybe he left it in Berkowitz' place or even here at his office." Katie suggested.

"No. No way. That book was attached to him like an arm. I'll bet he took it with him to that bitch's place. I'll bet she has it," Dixie said, pulling on her hair.

"What are you going to do?"

"Do we know anybody who lives at The Terrace?" Dixie asked. "You know…it's that high-rise condo place over near the lake."

"Is that where she lives?"

"Yep," Dixie replied, thoroughly disgusted.

"Where does she get the money for that? John and I have checked into buying one of those condos, and they cost a fortune."

"Who knows?"

"Do you know the Wilson's…Chuck and Leah Anne?"

"Yeah. Do they live there?"

"I'm pretty sure they do. JJ went to a birthday party there about six months ago. There was talk of Chuck getting transferred, but I still see Leah Anne at the store occasionally. It's possible they've moved, but I'd bet they're still there. What are you planning, Dixie?"

"I'm going on a scavenger hunt. I'm looking for a book titled, 'The Road to Monticello.'"

"You're asking for trouble by going there. You know that, don't you?"

"There won't be any trouble." Crossing her arms and sporting a diabolical expression, Dixie added, "All she has to do is hand over the book, and I'll let her live."

Putting her hands on her hips, Katie said, "Let me go with you."

"No. This is between just me and her," Dixie said, unconsciously rolling up her sleeves as she spoke. "Why don't you take Sean's car and pick up the things you want for tonight. Meet me at home in about thirty minutes."

"Dixie…"

"It'll be fine. I promise I won't get into any trouble."

There was no way Katie was going to change Dixie's mind, so she said, "Call me as soon as you leave. If I don't hear from you within an hour, I'm coming to get you."

"You'll hear from me. See you in a while."

DIXIE HAD TO RESTRAIN herself several times from driving too fast while she was making the short drive to April's condominium. With a little luck, she thought maybe she could sweet-talk the security guard into letting her into the building. She hoped she wouldn't have to unnecessarily disturb the Wilson's, but at least she had a back-up plan to get inside the building. Pulling up to the main gate, she was met by a kind-looking, middle-aged, black man in uniform.

"Good evening, ma'am. How may I help you?"

"Hello. I'm Dixie Marcum. I'm here to see Leah Anne Wilson."

"I'll ring her right away, ma'am."

His response wasn't what Dixie had hoped for. But as the guard picked up the telephone to dial, he continued to study Dixie. Finally, a big smile came across his face.

"Say, aren't you the lady who does those TV ads for cars?" he asked as he put the phone receiver back on its cradle.

Trying to hide her anticipation that perhaps her TV personality had become a skeleton key, she replied, "That's right. 'You'll always get a Darling deal at Darling Motors.'"

"I thought I recognized you," the guard said as he pointed at Dixie with delight. "I bought a car there last year…a Toyota. Actually, it was a truck…one of them small trucks."

"Great! That's my husband's dealership."

"Yeah. Now I know. Gosh, you're practically a movie star, Ms. Marcum. You probably know Ms. Knudsen? She lives here, too."

Hoping she wouldn't choke on her words, she answered, "April? She's a sweetheart, isn't she?"

"Just a doll of a lady," the guard agreed. "She helped me get a good price on my old truck that I traded in—really nailed the deal for me. You just missed her. She came zipping by here about twenty minutes ago."

"I know. She was just over at my place."

"Gosh, ma'am. This is the high point of my evening, and it's only just begun. Say, would you mind signing this piece of paper? The wife collects autographs. She'll get a kick out of knowing I met you today."

Dixie took the clipboard holding the blank sheet of paper. "Who should I make this out to?"

"Oh, uh…just say, 'Happy Birthday Wilmeena.' That's spelled, W-I-L-M-E-E-N-A. It's her birthday today."

"I gathered that," Dixie said. After a few seconds of writing, Dixie handed the clipboard back to the guard. "What's your name?"

"Cletus Jackson, ma'am."

"Well it's sure been a treat to meet you, too, Mr. Jackson."

"Thank you, ma'am. The pleasure's been all mine, I'm sure."

"Can you go ahead and ring Leah Anne for me?" Dixie asked, putting the finale on her ruse.

Jackson made a 'pffftt' noise, then pressed a button and the large, black iron gate began to swing open.

"You go on up. She and Mr. Wilson live in 504, but I suspect you know that ma'am. She doesn't like me to delay her friends any longer than necessary. You can park over to the right in one of the spaces marked for visitors. As soon as I see you're at the door, I'll buzz you in."

"Thank you, Mr. Jackson. I'll be sure to tell the Wilson's how gracious you were."

"Ma'am, you were wonderful to me. Thank you, and have a splendid evening."

Dixie didn't linger any more. She quickly followed the guard's instructions and parked her car. Once she was at the door, there was a buzzing sound at the lock, and she was able to walk right in. She made sure she waved at the guard. It was the least she could do for having duped him.

The mailboxes offered no clues as to April's condominium number, but she was fairly certain it was 808, the same number as Frank and Suzanne's street address. When she had addressed Christmas cards in the past, she made that association so her number would be easy to remember.

Once outside April's door, she hesitated for just a moment. She really didn't want a confrontation. The events of the day had already proved to be exhausting. She hoped she could simply get the book and leave. After taking a deep breath, she pushed the door chime, and shortly after, heard footsteps approaching the door. There was a pause as, most likely, the person on the other side peered through the security window in the door. In short order, the door opened.

April stood there, not in the least bit apologetic nor conciliatory.

"I came for the book," Dixie said brusquely.

April put her finger on a red button of a security alarm control panel just inside the door. "In about five seconds, I'm pressing the panic button. That's how much of a head start I'm giving you."

Dixie thought to herself, *so much for not making a scene.* "Oh, cut the bullshit, April. Just give me the damn book and I'll leave."

Seeing an opportunity to inflict pain, April replied, "Why don't you get it yourself. It's on the bed where Sean and I were reading it earlier today."

"Hum. 'Reading it,' Dixie said, unwilling to give April the pleasure of believing she had been hurt. "I've never heard it stated quite that way. I always called it fucking."

Before April could reconsider her offer, Dixie walked past her and made her way down the hallway that she presumed led to the bedrooms. As she looked around, Dixie said, "Nice. Very nice indeed. You should be proud of yourself, April. You really fucked your way to the top...literally. I mean, the eighth floor. My God."

"I earned every bit of the money I needed to purchase this condo, Dixie, and none of my money has come from your Sean. In fact, you may find it interesting that I have no desire to take Sean from you. My desire lies in something much more sacred to you than your husband. By no means do I want to demean poor Sean. He did turn what would have been an otherwise dull afternoon into a fabulous soirée. He's really quite good in the sack. It's such a shame that being in your presence makes him want to put a bullet in his head."

Finding the box containing Kim's book on April's bed, she picked it up and said, "Delude yourself all you want, slut. Sean's mine, and always will be. He's gone to an inpatient rehab facility for a while to exorcise you from his body and soul. Once that evil is gone, I'll be here for him. As for your other fantasies, I can understand why you would covet what I have since you have nothing of any value in your empty life except this brothel you operate. But rest assured, whatever else of mine you think you want, you won't get either. You obviously don't know who you're dealing with. So be on notice, I plan to put an end to you. Suffice it to say, when the Darling's make a pledge of exile, that individual is history. Pack your shit. Armageddon is coming."

Unaffected by Dixie's threats, April answered, "I'll leave if and only if I want, when I want. You don't intimidate me in the least,

Dixie. For one thing, Sean and I became one today in that we consummated more than our relationship. We sealed a friendship by understanding Kim's book together. I wasn't the one who tricked him into believing a bogus ending to the book, completely changing the book's meaning and intent. You're guilty as charged. Kim's purpose is now quite clear to me. I know exactly why she ended the book the way she did, and I intend to be Sean's guiding light. If you had anything resembling intelligence—not to mention true devotion to your husband—you'd have understood Kim's conclusion as I have. You speak of delusion? Don't be righteous. I feel sorry for you, Dixie."

Dixie understood one thing. She absolutely loathed April Knudsen. April could match her verbal assault word for word, yet she wasn't going to give April the satisfaction of getting physical again as she had several weeks prior at the hospital parking lot, or in front of her house just a short time ago. No. She had to find a way to take her out of the picture…completely.

Chapter 27

DIXIE ARRIVED BACK AT her house to find Katie in pajamas, and snuggled under a blanket. While she sat on the sofa with her feet propped up on the coffee table in front of the fireplace, she unabashedly sipped champagne. She held up her nearly empty glass to Dixie and smiled widely.

"Why don't you make yourself at home?" Dixie asked sarcastically.

"I knew you would approve. I just love gas fireplaces. They light up so quickly. I brought a bottle of champagne with me because I knew one wouldn't be enough."

"Four wouldn't be enough!"

"Went that bad, huh?"

"Royal, fucking bitch!" Dixie said, tossing the book on the coffee table.

"Are you speaking about me, or April?" Katie asked.

Cocking her head to one side, Dixie replied, "Did you check the study to see if the cops took Sean's gun?"

"Dixie..."

"What happened to, 'I'll come after you if I don't hear from you in one hour'?"

"I had the utmost confidence in your self-control," Katie replied, pulling the blanket up high around her neck.

"Ah!! I wanted to strangle her!" Dixie said, throwing her arms into the air. Scanning around the room, she asked, "Did you pull out a glass for me?"

"I got it out of the cabinet, but left it on the bar. I was afraid you might be throwing things when you got home, and I know how you love your Lalique," Katie said as she took one final sip.

Dixie took Katie's empty glass and walked over to the bar. She set the glass on the counter, pulled the open bottle of champagne out of the wine cooler, and took two gulps from it before returning to the sofa.

"Screw etiquette," Dixie said, wiping her mouth with the sleeve of her sweater.

As she raised her eyebrows, Katie said, "My, we have an attitude tonight, don't we?"

"Watch this!" Dixie replied. After setting down the champagne bottle on the coffee table, she removed her shoes and threw them into the far corner of the living room, slipped out of her slacks and threw them the opposite direction, then yanked her sweater over her head and tossed it onto the grand piano. Sitting on the sofa next to Katie, she said, "Give me some of that blanket."

"I will, if you first hand me the bottle."

Dixie complied with Katie's request, then got under the blanket with her sister-in-law.

"I have never hated a person more than I hate April Knudsen. It's bad enough that she's screwing my husband, but then she has to rub my nose in it."

"I don't blame you," Katie said, lending a sympathetic ear. "But remember, you went to her place. She didn't seek out you."

"Whose side are you on?"

"Yours, of course. But somebody has to be your conscience."

After letting out a deep breath, Dixie asked, "How did you come to grips with Lori after John's affair?"

Katie first took two long gulps of champagne before she replied, "A lot like this. Don't you remember? In fact, it was almost exactly like this. Right here on this sofa. Except, we were drinking tequila."

"You know, I haven't had tequila since that night," Dixie said with a grimace.

"Really? Me neither."

Once the giggling had died down, Dixie said, "You know, the thing that bugs me the most about my conversation with April tonight is that she claims to understand the meaning behind Kim's ending to her frickin' book."

"No. You're kidding."

"Nope. She says I lack both the intelligence and devotion to Sean needed to figure out the significance of what she wrote."

"Ignore what she said. You're smart, and God knows how devoted you are to Sean."

"Right," Dixie said, burying her face into Katie's shoulder. "And look at the situation I'm in."

After taking a drink from the bottle, Katie said, "Would you like to read it again with me tonight?"

Holding her wrists out to Katie, Dixie replied, "Quick, get me a razor blade."

"Seriously, I'd be happy to read it to you. You just have to lay there and drink. Face it, Sean is too connected with the author, and lacks a woman's intuition. He'll probably never understand what his old girlfriend was trying to say to him. As for you, you're anything but objective, and that taints your interpretation."

"Can't I simply burn the book, kill April, and commit Sean to an institution for the remainder of his life?"

"You mean, take the easy way out? No."

"Bitch. Hand me the bottle."

Katie gave the bottle to Dixie before continuing, "You know, it's probably a good thing that Sean's out of the picture for a while. The two of you need some time to heal your wounds. He's in a place where April can't be a part of the equation, and the book is here."

"Did I tell you that she ended her book the same way as Nadine ended her journal?"

"No, you didn't. That can't be some weird twist of fate, Dixie. There has to be a reason for that. Now, even *I* want to know what the meaning is behind the book."

Dixie took a drink of champagne. "I wonder who he's thinking about right now—me, Kim, or April?"

"It could be his mother that he's thinking about."

"Oh, God," Dixie said before taking another gulp. "Why would he be thinking of Nadine, pray tell?"

"There's an association between Sean, his mother, and Kim, and I'll bet it's buried somewhere in that book. For that matter, she's probably the root of the message Kim's been trying to deliver."

"So you're not going to let me burn it, are you?"

"Do as you want, Dixie, but I think you're missing an opportunity."

"Well, I'll tell you one thing. I've never thought of reading this book as an opportunity. It's more like an encumbrance."

"I'll take that as a 'yes.' Can you hand me the book?"

Begrudgingly, Dixie sat up, pulled the lid off the box, removed the three-inch stack of paper, and handed it to Katie.

"Wow! Strathmore. Nice paper. She was obviously trying to make an impression."

Giving Katie a queer look, Dixie begged, "Can we skip the platitudes?"

"Actually, no. This is the kind of detail that becomes an integral part of the message. There is more to this book than words. It's a cacophony of subliminal, significant details." Proud of her choice of words, Katie added, "Listen to that! And after a glass and a half of champagne!"

"Jesus! This is going to be a long night." Getting up from the sofa, Dixie said, "Let me get into my PJs and pop open another bottle. I'll be right back."

DIXIE HADN'T YET RETURNED from changing clothes when the house phone rang. After several unanswered rings, Katie took the call much as she would on any other occasion.

"Marcum residence," she answered.

"Dixie?" inquired the unrecognizable woman's voice on the other end.

"No. This is her sister-in-law Katie. Dixie's unable to come to the phone just this second. Can I help you?"

"This is her sister-in-law from the other side, Kelly…Sean's sister."

"Right," Katie replied, now able to make the connection. "We met a few years ago when he and Dixie hosted Christmas at their place."

"I remember it well," Kelly chimed. "That was the time Callie drove Sean's car through garage door."

"That's the one. Poor thing, she'd only had her license for two weeks." Following a short exchange commiserating the events before and after that small family crisis, Katie asked, "So, Dixie mentioned you've been in Europe. Was it a vacation or work?"

"A little of both, actually. I had a conference in Copenhagen for a week, then Chuck met me in Spain, and we took a 13-day cruise on the Mediterranean. We just got back this afternoon."

"I'm jealous. John never takes me anywhere."

"It was wonderful and very relaxing, which is probably contrary to how I can say things must be at Sean's home these days."

Following a deep breath, Katie said, "As you suspect, it's a mess right now. How much do you know about the last three weeks?"

"Well, that's what I want to find out. Dad told me quite a bit when I spoke to him earlier tonight, but I got the feeling I was just getting the press release. I'm looking for the exclusive."

"I hope you have some time. Tell you what, Dixie just walked into the room. How about I hand you over to her?"

"Sounds good. It was nice speaking with you again," Kelly said quite sincerely.

"You, too."

Dixie approached Katie, unaware she had answered the phone. Covering the speaker of the telephone receiver with her hand, Katie said, "Dix, Kelly's on the phone."

Dixie's arms went limp at her sides as she hung her head. The civil conversation that was taking place between Katie and Sean's sister was not likely to continue. While Dixie and Kelly got along amicably for the most part, Sean's sister had over the years taken on more and more of a mother-in-law role. It had gotten to the point where Dixie could only take small doses of Kelly at any given time because it took so much energy to justify her place in Sean's life—something that Dixie found increasingly none of Kelly's business. To Kelly, Sean being her brother trumped him being

Dixie's husband. Under the circumstances, this was likely to be a difficult conversation at best.

"Open this and pour me a glass," Dixie demanded of Katie as she exchanged the bottle of champagne for the telephone receiver. Putting the phone to her ear, Dixie fought to be on her best behavior. "Kelly, welcome home. It's good to hear your voice."

"What's going on with my brother?" she responded quite tersely.

Right... Dixie thought. *Let's just jump in with both feet.*

"Let's see, Kelly. Since you've been gone, he's suffered...we'll call them a series of physical and psychological traumas. I assume you know his old girlfriend, Kim, passed away."

"That I do," Kelly replied. "Are you going to blame his problems on her?"

That remark lit Dixie's fire. "You know what, Kelly? I'm sorry for you that it is I, and not Kim, who became your sister-in-law. But after thirty years, don't you think it's about time you got over it?"

"Kim was very special to a lot of members of the family, not just Sean. Show some respect, particularly now that she's dead."

"Respect? What about me, Kelly? When will I ever meet your criteria to be Sean's wife? Huh?"

"I didn't call to fight with you, Dixie."

"You could have fooled me!" She replied before taking a swallow of champagne.

"So, are you going to finish telling me what's happening with Sean?"

No longer attempting to make nice, Dixie replied, "Short version...he's had a complete melt down. It's the twentieth anniversary of your mother's death, Kim died, he was nearly killed in a car accident, he fled the hospital against medical advice, only to lapse into a coma and later have his spleen surgically removed. He missed Kim's funeral, but not to worry because she sent him a six-hundred page fantasy chronicling his life through some fictional characters, not to mention the voice of Theodore Seuss, and she ends it with the same words that concluded Nadine's journal...something about the Fuller Brush Man. Finally, he completely lost his mind, had sex with his new lover—whom you need to meet to see if she meets your definition of sister-in-law—and then had a standoff with police, that ended in gunfire. At this moment, he's being taken by his shrink to an unnamed house for the insane somewhere in Wisconsin where I hope he spends the rest of his life!"

"Don't take that tone with me, Dixie Darling!"

"It's Marcum!"

Katie took the phone away from Dixie, presuming the conversation had deteriorated into nothing more than a screaming war of words. Before she could hang up on Kelly, Dixie grabbed it back from her.

"Listen to me and listen good, Kelly. I've had it with people testing the sanctity of my marriage to Sean. He's my husband, and I am a Marcum. Nobody, including you, will get in the way of that. Do you understand?"

After a long pause, Kelly replied, "I'm glad to hear those words come from you. And I apologize for coming across a bit overprotective of my little brother."

"Kelly, he's fifty-three. He doesn't need you to fight for him anymore. That's my job."

Apparently convinced Dixie was still supportive of Sean, Kelly asked, "Were you exaggerating about the gun and Sean being institutionalized?"

The conversation appeared to be taking on a new tone. Giving Kelly the benefit of the doubt, Dixie answered, "No, unfortunately. He locked himself in his office tonight for about an hour and a half. Police were here, and finally Sean's psychologist talked him out, but not before he put a bullet through a picture of Kim that he'd kept since they dated."

"That's a bit over the top," Kelly replied, seriously understating the magnitude of what Sean had done.

"Ya' think?"

"Was he hurt?"

"Physically, no. But emotionally, Sean's hit bottom. I've never seen him this low, nor so troubled. He's simply given up, and the police and his psychologist were convinced he was a threat to himself giving him no choice but to accept a voluntary commitment to some inpatient facility. And no, I don't want him to spend the rest of his life there. I miss him terribly."

"And you don't know the name of this place?"

"No. Dr. Berkowitz, his therapist, says that's confidential. We can communicate to Sean via him only."

"Well, when I tell Dad about this, I'm sure the good doctor will regret being said conduit. He's not Mr. Patience when it comes to Sean and me. He's the only person more protective of Sean than I am."

"…and me," Dixie added.

"This is true. So, who's the wench?"

"A woman he works with. She's divorced, about ten years younger than me, and has the body of a college girl. Worse yet, she's e-v-i-l. There's something cunning and underhanded about her I have yet to discover. But at this point, Sean can't see past her breasts or her pouting lips."

"How long has this been going on?"

"In truth, I think they finally had sex for the first time just today. Beyond that, there's been an emotional attachment for some time. I don't know how long."

"So, there's still hope for you guys, right?"

"I don't know, Kelly. I want to say yes, but then I get to thinking about what happened, and I want to kill both of them. Is there hope? Yes, there's hope. Can I promise we'll get past this? No. In all honesty, everything's up in the air. Until he gets out of the clinic, we can't begin to solve our problems."

"I guess I don't blame you for being hurt. Does Dad know about her?"

"I'm not sure. Raymond and I aren't exactly confidants. Do you know what I mean?"

"Tell you what. I do know how to talk with Dad. Let me bring him up to date on things. He'll want to speak to you, but I'll tell him to wait until tomorrow. Okay?"

"How about the day after tomorrow?" Dixie suggested.

"Sure. But promise me you'll call if anything else comes up."

"Absolutely. Was there anything else, Kelly? Because I have a splitting headache, and I've got to go lay down before I fall down."

"Actually, Dixie, there is one more thing I need to tell you about."

"Can it wait?"

"I don't think it should. It might be relevant to Kim's book."

"Tell you what, Katie and I were just about to make it a night of reading Kim's book again, looking for anything that could help bring some closure to what's bothering Sean. Could you tell her? Seriously, I have to lie down."

"That should work. I just need to give this message to someone."

"Fine, here she is," Dixie said, handing the phone to Katie.

"Hi, Kelly. It's me again," Katie said.

"So, what do you know about Sean's old girlfriend, Kim?"

"Just bits and pieces. I know they were close, and I know how they parted company."

"Did you know that she and my mother frequently communicated to Sean and our father through riddles?"

"So I've heard. And they weren't necessarily easy to solve from what little Dixie has told me."

"That's probably an understatement. In any event, I was going through my mail today, and I found a short note from Kim postmarked two days before she died."

"Really? What's it say?"

"Well, her handwriting was very difficult to read. But, I believe she wrote these words: 'Dear Kelly, By now you know I have passed on. I sent to Sean a book that holds the key to his future happiness with Dixie. He was never good at riddles. You, on the other hand, had the same talent as Nadine for solving them. You may need to intervene if Sean is unable to himself solve the enigma within my book. While Sean probably thinks the book is totally about him, it is actually written as much for Dixie. Tell her the following, as it will put an end to that which perplexes her. *Evil speaks through the one whose coif doth change.* She'll know what I mean. I'll see you at the Whobilation. Regards, Kim.'"

"Not another riddle for Sean? Why couldn't she communicate in plain English?"

"She always explained to the rest of us that it wasn't the answer to life's questions that was of great consequence. It was the journey. As the message pointed out, this challenge is for Dixie, not Sean. Let her work with it for a while."

"If you say so. I'll break it to her and see what she thinks. You may be getting a call to help us."

"I'll give it some thought, too. But to be honest, I'm at a loss at this point. Maybe there is a reference to this evil-doer in the book. In any case, you have a good evening."

"Bye, Kelly."

Sitting back down next to Dixie, Katie gleefully said, "You'll be glad to know you aren't the mouth of evil."

Even though she had a pillow pulled over her head, Dixie heard Katie's remark and was able to say, "What on God's green earth are you talking about?"

"Evil speaks through the one whose coif doth change."

Pulling the pillow off her face just enough so that one eye peered past it, Dixie again asked, "I repeat, what on God's green earth are you talking about?"

"It turns out Kim sent Kelly a final letter. It was actually more of a note, but in short she said her book is as much for you as it is for Sean. The book, she said, holds the key to Sean's future happiness with you. But there is this ominous warning—evil speaks through the one whose coif doth change."

"What's that mean?" Dixie asked, pulling the pillow back over her eyes.

"It sounds like she's warning us about someone who changes her hair all the time, and you've always been a brunette with more or less shoulder length hair."

Quickly pulling the pillow off her face, Dixie exclaimed, "Oh, my God." She ran into Sean's ramshackle office and began looking for a large picture album on his bookshelf. Finding the one she was looking for, Dixie returned to where Katie sat waiting, and opened the book to the last page. It contained a picture of Sean with his employees at their annual award banquet that had taken place during that spring. Pointing to April in the photo, Dixie said, "Look, she's got shoulder-length blond hair."

"Okay, so what?" Katie acknowledged.

Turning to the prior page, Dixie said, "Last year…it's blond, but cut short and perm'd."

"Oh my…" Katie said, understanding where Dixie was going with her thoughts.

Turning each page to the previous year, April changed her hair no less than once each year. Finally, Dixie reached the picture from ten years ago—the year that April started working for Sean. Her hair was red. Recalling her mother's revelation immediately after Sean's accident, "A certain redhead and I had a confrontation she'll never forget", Dixie turned pale.

"Dixie, what's wrong?"

"I'm almost afraid to say. It's too awful even to think of." Turning to look at Katie, Dixie asked, "Isn't there a way you look up the names of property owners on the web site of the city tax assessor?"

"Yeah. I've done that a time or two. Why?"

Quickly going to the computer in Callie's room, Dixie searched the internet for the City of Lake Forest, and soon found the link to the database for which she was looking. After typing in the address 1000 The Terrace, Dixie was faced with a list of fifty names. But it was the one next to 808 that interested her the most. As Katie looked on, Dixie scrolled down to that number. The name Permes Delfisi was listed.

With a puzzled look, Katie said, "Is that Greek or Italian?"

"I'm not sure," Dixie replied as she continued to study the name. "I have a feeling it's neither." Then, a terrifying possibility crossed her mind. Grabbing a piece of paper, she jotted the name down and began rearranging the letters. Once she was satisfied she had found the correct order of the letters for both names, she held the paper up for Katie to see.

"Semper Fidelis?" Katie read out loud. "Are you sure?"

"Believe me. Growing up at home, those words were drilled into my subconscious. They adorned pillows, beer mugs, coozies, stationary, and various objets d'art throughout the house."

"It sounds like something Frank would say. What's the meaning of this?"

Looking up at Katie, Dixie replied, "It means we have a conspiracy on our hands. It also means Sean never stood a chance."

Chapter 28

DIXIE DROVE TO HER parents' house early the next morning, and let herself in as she typically did. She found her mother sitting at the table in the kitchen addressing some invitations.

"You look tired, honey. Pour yourself a cup of coffee and take a seat."

Dixie said nothing and had no desire for coffee, though she could have used it. Her stomach was upset enough from the overnight revelation. She had dark circles beneath her eyes from exhaustion, and she lacked her usual make-up. The look on her face was enough to convince Suzanne that their conversation was going to be anything but cordial.

Again taking note of Dixie's appearance, Suzanne asked, "What's wrong, dear? Katie told me she was going to keep you company last night. Did you girls stay up too late?"

After taking her seat, Dixie finally said, "We did stay up late, Mom. In fact, we were up all night." Skipping the pretense, Dixie continued, "We were talking about the person who owns a condominium at The Terrace—the one that is presently occupied by a once-upon-a-time red-haired woman. What do you know about those arrangements?"

There was a short hesitation to Suzanne's response, and Dixie thought she detected her mother squirm ever so slightly.

"I'm not certain I understand your question, Dixie." Before Dixie could respond, Suzanne stood up and went to the sink where she took up the spontaneous chore of washing the few cups and plates leftover from breakfast.

"Where's Daddy?" Dixie asked.

"He left for work an hour ago. He told me he was going to be in meetings all day so don't bother trying to get in touch with him."

Dixie had already checked her father's schedule with his secretary, and his day was open.

"Mother!" Dixie shouted, pounding the table with her fist.

Completely flustered, Suzanne dropped a plate in the sink breaking it. She then commenced to fiddling with her hair as she avoided eye contact with Dixie.

"I am your one and only daughter! Turn around and quit lying to me!" Demanding both attention and answers, Dixie stood up from the table, grabbed her mother by the shoulders, and pulled her so the two stood face-to-face. "Is April Knudsen the woman Daddy had an affair with?"

Suzanne made incomprehensible sounds as she avoided answering Dixie's question.

"Damn it!! Answer my question!!" Dixie screamed, jerking her mother by the shoulders at the same time.

Tears beginning to stream from her eyes, Suzanne nodded.

Realizing how much the truth must have hurt her mother, Dixie hugged her tightly while they sobbed in unison.

After a minute or two, Dixie pleaded, "Why, Mom? Why is she still in the picture?"

Suzanne took a seat at the table and wiped the tears from her eyes with a napkin she had taken from a stack in a large ceramic bowl. Dixie poured both of them coffee before joining her.

"She is a vile and malevolent creature," Suzanne started to say between sniffles. "Not too long before John had his relationship with Lori, April came to work for the company. About two years later, she and your father were at an auto show together, and she seduced him. Well, Frank may be a lot of things, but a good liar he's not. I can't remember exactly what it was that caught my attention about his behavior, but I asked him point blank if he had a girlfriend, and he most unconvincingly answered, 'no.' A few days later I asked him again, only this time he came clean. I told him she had to go, but she threatened to expose him publicly. Somehow, she got wind that we had set Lori up in Aspen with a condo and a stipend to keep her quiet. Knowing what we did for Lori, she demanded a similar compensation. However, she didn't want cash. The developer of The Terrace and Frank have a friendship that goes back a long way, so he got a deal on the condo where she lives. She liked working for the company and refused to leave, so we moved her to Sean's business instead of having to pay her anything per se and prayed for the best."

"Did it ever occur to you that she might do the same thing again?" Dixie asked.

"Oh, dear God, yes. I've worried about her ever since I found out about her and Frank. Underneath that beautiful exterior and wonderful personality is a malicious, immoral, and evil human being. In all honesty, I trusted Sean implicitly. I figured she'd be in bed with Frank Junior, John, or Stephen in no time if we'd put her to work for one of them. But you and Sean, you always seemed so close, and until recently, he was so grounded. He just never struck me to be the kind of man to stray."

"Did it ever occur to you she might strike up a romance again with Daddy?" Dixie asked, knowing the subject was painful.

"I suspect since we are having this conversation, you've discovered that reality. Your father is a powerful and demanding man, Dixie. I know I told you that I've kept him in check all these years, but in truth that's not the case. He says he still loves me, and in his own way, he shows that he does. That's enough for me. I'm seventy-five years old, honey. Starting over is not an option I want to pursue. Living alone isn't one either." Reaching out to touch Dixie's hand, she asked, "Can you forgive me, honey?"

Dixie shook her head in disbelief as she replied, "Mom, I may someday forgive you. But today isn't that day. As for Daddy, I've lost all respect for him. So much of the misery in this family could have been prevented if he'd only dealt with April a long time ago." Wiping the tears from her cheeks, she continued, "My God, Sean almost took his own life last night, Mother! Now he's stuck in a loony bin at least in part because she repeated with Sean what she did to Daddy. Poor Sean was so vulnerable. All she had to do was hand him a parachute, and he grabbed for it. He never realized it was the pack with the anvil in it."

"I hate to point this out, Dixie, but nobody held a gun to Sean's head and told him to be unfaithful."

"Are you sure, Mom? What's Daddy's role been in all that's taken place in Sean's life recently?"

"What are you trying to imply?" Suzanne replied resentfully.

Pointing a finger at her mother, Dixie said, "I think Daddy knew April was the perfect weapon to use against Sean. He only needed to wait until the right time to unleash her."

Suzanne responded by slapping her daughter across the face as she yelled, "Don't ever make such an accusation like that against your father! He only wants the best for this family and his children! There's no crime in that!"

Reeling from the blow, Dixie said, "Right, Mom. Semper Fi...always faithful." As she got up and headed toward the door, she added, "Perhaps it's not his motives that lack good judgment. It's his methods I question."

"Where are you going?!"

"I'm going to pay our wicked little friend a visit. Then, I'm off to find Daddy."

"Honey, just leave matters as they are! You don't want to stir this mess up any more than it already is. It'll get ugly real fast."

"Mom, it passed ugly a long, long time ago!" Dixie shouted, slamming the door behind her as she left.

DIXIE TOOK SOME TIME to calm down following her visit with her mother. After waiting in line at a Starbucks drive-through for a mocha latte, she sat in her parked SUV, made four phone calls, put on some make-up, and brushed her hair. In all, it was maybe forty-five minutes before she reached April's residence. It was with good fortune that Dixie found her favorite security guard, Cletus Jackson, on duty again as she pulled up to the gate.

"Don't you ever go home?" Dixie asked in a friendly tone.

"Good morning, Mrs. Marcum. Yes, I went home late last night. But the day man called in sick. Only being here a year, I'm the one with the lowest seniority. So here I am again. Are you here to see the Wilsons again?"

"No. Actually, I'm here to see April Knudsen," Dixie replied, successfully concealing all of her anger.

"You, too? Mr. Darling came by here a little while ago saying he had a meeting with her as well. Are the three of you working on a commercial or something?"

Trying to hide her gut reaction, Dixie asked, "Frank Darling?"

"That's right. I expect you know him. He's the big boss over all the Darling dealerships, am I correct?"

"Uh, yes," Dixie answered, not willing to reveal her relationship to the person being discussed. "How well do you know him?"

"Mr. Darling? He comes here all the time to see Ms. Knudsen. She's his niece. He owns the place where she's staying, but he's letting her stay there while her husband's deployed overseas. He's in the Navy. Didn't you know that?"

"Of course," Dixie answered, thinking quickly. "She talks about Scott all the time. It has to be a real hardship, having your husband gone for so long."

"You got that right. I was in the Air Force for twenty-seven years. I had a couple of hitches in places I didn't want to take Wilmeena and the kids, so I was away from home for long periods. It's tough on a family. But Miss April will get through it. She strikes me as a very devoted wife." Leaning forward and speaking in a softer voice, he added, "She never has any callers, if you know what I mean."

"I couldn't agree with you more, Mr. Jackson," Dixie said, hoping she wouldn't say what was really on her mind. "After God made April, he threw away the mold."

"That's right…he threw away the mold," the guard echoed with a chuckle. "Say, you want me to let them know you're here, or do you just want to go on up?"

"She's in 808. I know the way. They're probably in the middle something, and I don't want to bother them." In fact, her intention was quite the opposite. Dixie hoped to catch them in a compromising position.

"Well, you go and park right where you did last night, and I'll buzz you in again."

"Thank you, Mr. Jackson. You're so sweet. By the way, we're expecting a few others. Let me write down their names for you. If you would, just let them up, too."

After examining the quickly-written list of names, the guard said, "Absolutely, Mrs. Marcum. I'll be sure to let them up. You have a good day, ma'am."

"You, too, Mr. Jackson."

In the few minutes it took Dixie to park, walk to the elevator, and take it to the eighth floor, she had contemplated what she was going to do, what she was going to say, and even if she could go through with it. Her spirit at this moment was driven by a peculiar mix not only of intense anger, but also deep sorrow about what she had discovered—even more so, what she was likely to learn. She quickly found her resolve and herself at the point of no return, when her knock on April's door was quickly answered.

Standing only in her stilettos, panties, stockings clipped to a sexy garter, and an open, button-down shirt, April said with a smug smile, "I expected you to return sooner or later. You have the book. Did you leave something else behind?" Looking up and down at Dixie, April continued, "Tsk Tsk. It's easy at times like these to understand why a man as vibrant as Sean would run from a woman like you to a woman like me."

Dixie pressed the -2- button on her cell phone—the speed dial for her father. In seconds, she heard a phone playing the Marines' Hymn—his ring tone—coming from the direction of the bedroom where she had collected Kim's book the evening before.

"Hi, baby. How are you today?" he answered, unaware Dixie was at the door.

"I need to meet with you, Daddy," she replied cagily.

"I'm tied up at the office right now. Can we make it later?"

Dixie made her way past April to the hall leading to the bedrooms. There, she spotted Frank standing most unflatteringly in his boxers and undershirt. His mouth fell open as they both disconnected the call at the same time.

"Get dressed!" Dixie demanded. "Meeting time is now!" She turned and walked into April's living room where she coolly took a seat in a plush chair.

April approached Dixie, continuing to smile as she reveled over the pain present in the heart of Frank's daughter, for which she assumed responsibility. When she was close enough for her liking, she leaned forward, putting her hands on the arms of the chair. With her shirt gaping open and her goods on display, she said, "As I told you last night, my desire lies with something more sacred to you than Sean. And do you want to know something else? I have the Darlings by their collective balls. Don't think for second I haven't thought this through."

Frank hurriedly stepped into the living room, still tucking his shirt tails into his pants. Before he had finished, he said, "Dixie, let's go. You and I need to talk."

"Sit down, Frank!" Dixie insisted. Pointing to the chair across from her, she said, "The talking is going to take place right here."

Knowing when he had met his match, Frank did as instructed. April moved behind him where she calmly stood with her hands on his shoulders.

With total confidence and control of the situation, Dixie explained, "In just a few minutes, Daddy, there will be four more visitors knocking at the door: Marvin Rabinowitz, Sam Ricci, Lieutenant Don Baker from the Lake Forest Police Department, and Devon Brookshire from the Tribune."

"Dixie, you don't…"

"Shut up, Frank!" Dixie shouted at her father. After regaining her composure, she continued to explain herself. "When they arrive, you will explain to them, as I already have, that Little Miss Silk Stockings here has been extorting the Darling family."

"Dixie, you're opening up a can of…"

"For the last time, Frank, shut up!"

Seemingly unaffected by what Dixie was saying, April said, "This ought to be entertaining. The Trib will have a field day with this one."

"That they will," Dixie said, not disputing April's remark. "And here's the exclusive I've promised Brookshire. First of all, let me preface this by reminding you that Darling Motors is one of the largest advertisers in the Tribune. That will have a lot of influence in the approach he takes."

April's smile began to slowly fade as Dixie continued.

"As I was saying, Daddy, you're going to tell the entire story about you and April to Marvin. If Lieutenant Baker feels there is just cause, and based upon my conversation with him not a half-hour ago, I'm quite certain he will, April will likely be taken into custody and charged with felony extortion. Once she is on her way to jail, you and Marvin will draft a memo of dissolution, severing the assets in Darling Motors you own. I understand, and fully expect, it will take weeks for auditors to accurately assess what is yours. But when that's done, they will place a dollar value on all of those assets, and you will place that amount in escrow at Sam Ricci's bank. I expect you to get no more than one-fifth of the net worth of the company, so be very careful how you slice the pie or this will end up in court. When that's done, you're stepping down as President of Darling Motors. You're overdue for retirement, and you need to take Mom on a long, therapeutic vacation far away from here."

Bristling, Frank asked, "And just who in the hell is going to take my place...Sean?" Frank was convinced that was the hand Dixie was playing.

"No. Marvin and the governing board will see to it that I take over Darling Motors. You have Sean pegged correctly, Daddy. He doesn't want to run a conglomerate. He just wants to be left alone to do his job. That and sell BMWs and Volvos. Besides, the Boys will never take Sean seriously, and they also lack respect for one another. They *will* listen to me, and the Board respects me."

"You are naïve if you think for one second that you have all the bases covered, Dixie," Frank advised his daughter.

"True. There is one tainted detail remaining, and I expect you to see to it as well. You're going to have Lieutenant Baker investigate what's been taking place in Aspen with Lori. If what's occurring there is also extortion, it'll be come-to-Jesus-time for her as well. Oh, and before I forget, by the end of the day tomorrow, this place had better be listed 'For Sale.'"

April's smile was now completely gone. As she left her place behind Frank and slowly approached the Darling with the biggest balls, she warned Dixie, "The Tribune is going to roast your family, Dixie, and you along with them. I don't care what the Darling advertising budget is. No journalist worth his salt will be able to resist a family scandal the magnitude of this one."

As seriously as she could possibly be, Dixie replied, "Brookshire may choose to do so, April. I can't control what's written. But I know this much. My father and our family have done far more for this community than you ever will, and when all is said and done, people in this community remember that first and foremost. When the community needs help, they call Frank Darling. If some underfunded project requires money, Frank gets the appeal. When there is a charitable cause that desires leadership, Daddy carries the torch. When local governments want to bounce ideas off of up to now one of the region's most reputable men, Frank's their choice. On the other hand, if some unfortunate, misguided, wayward man needs a quick fuck, you get the call. May I remind you of what I said last night...Armageddon's coming. Pack what little is yours, and get the hell out."

Just as April lunged at Dixie, the first two of the visitors arrived—Lieutenant Baker and Devon Brookshire. All Frank could do was look on in horror while April clawed at and pulled Dixie's hair. While Baker wrested April from her physical attack on Dixie, Brookshire snapped several photographs. Moments later, Marvin Rabinowitz and Sam Ricci walked into the room together. As the company's attorney watched the beginnings of a corporate debacle unfolding, Sam Ricci was clearly relishing the moment. To make matters worse, April took a swing at Lieutenant Baker. That was all it took for him to forcefully subdue her and place her in handcuffs as she screamed.

"The Darlings are all crooks! They're all a bunch of liars!" April shouted as she struggled, kicking her shoes off in the direction of Dixie, narrowly missing her both times. After she managed to spit at Dixie, she continued, "Your father promised me this place and a job. There was no blackmail. It was just payment for the years of pleasure I brought to this giant of a man in the twilight of his life. As for Sean, he may never have the pleasure of having me again. But I'll always be on his mind."

Dixie stood, faced April, and defiantly said, "Check back with me on that, say in about…twenty years."

Ms. Marcum, you can file assault charges against Ms. Knudsen if you want," Baker said.

"Will that get her out of my sight immediately?" Dixie asked.

"That can be arranged. My partner is standing-by downstairs."

"Then file away," Dixie replied, pounding the final nail into April's coffin.

As he pulled April's arm, Baker said, "Let's go, Ms. Knudsen."

Before Baker could get her away from Dixie, April managed to lean back into Baker and get off one last kick, catching Dixie in the nose with her heel and knocking her to the ground. Wasting no more time, Baker rustled April out of the room.

Frank pulled out a handkerchief and gave it to Dixie who was dazed and bleeding slightly from her nose. With tears running down his cheeks, he tried to pull her up to hold her, only to have her push him away.

As she cried, Dixie said, "I want the truth, Daddy. Did you conspire with April to jeopardize my marriage with Sean?"

"It's not like it seems, honey," he replied, defending himself. "Let me explain how things really are."

"How things are?! How things are?! What about Semper Fi, Daddy?! Where is 'always faithful'?!"

"Baby, Sean was never good enough for you. I tried to accept him. I tried for thirty years. But he's a loser, Dixie. My responsibility is to my God, my country, my company, and my family. Sean never made the cut."

Looking into her father's eyes one last time, Dixie made clear, "Well, *my* responsibility is to *my* family, and those I love, Daddy." Tearfully, she concluded, "As for that, you don't make the cut."

Once she had struggled to get to her feet, Dixie left without saying another word.

Chapter 29

DESPITE TWO WEEKS OF pleading with Dr. Berkowitz, Dixie was not allowed to contact her husband. He explained repeatedly that Sean was having a mixed response to both the counseling, as well as the medications doctors at the clinic had prescribed for him. Even with aggressive therapy, Sean was slipping deeper and deeper into depression, and was nearing the point of becoming completely non-communicative as he withdrew from those trying to help. It mattered not, any of the revelations regarding Frank and April that Dixie told Berkowitz. All he would say was that Sean was in an extremely fragile condition, and they were still working toward turning the corner in his decline and achieving a breakthrough.

This left Dixie faced with the unenviable task of trying on her own to come up with a solution to the mystery that plagued Sean's mind—how to find the Fuller Brush Man. If there was anyone who could help, it was Ben. She had telephoned him several times and each time he hadn't answered the phone or returned her call. Dixie left beseeching voice messages, but to no avail. Finally, at Raymond's request, Ben half-heartedly agreed to a meeting with

Dixie. This was to be a meeting of old adversaries searching for a common thread.

CONVENIENTLY, BEN HAD TO attend to business in the Chicago area. When he had finished with that, he paid a visit to his old friend's home in Lake Forest that was occupied by the one woman he detested more than anyone. His reluctant knock on the door was answered by a nervous and equally hesitant Dixie.

"Hello, Ben. Thanks for coming by."

Without entering, Ben said, "You realize I am only here because of Sean."

"Me, too." As the face-off continued at the door, Dixie asked, "Won't you come in and have a seat…please?"

Ben went as far as the first chair he came to in the living room. There he took a seat, waiting for Dixie to make the first move. She took a seat on the sofa, farther into the living room and not between Ben and the door, giving him the impression he was free to leave at any time. It was all posturing up to this point.

"Sean's in a clinic where he can…"

"I know. Raymond told me everything."

"Everything?"

"His obsession with the Fuller Brush Man; his torment over the anniversary of his mother's death; the grieving over Kim; his inability to understand her book; his decline into depression; and his affair with another woman. Please tell me there's nothing else."

"Well, there's also Frank."

"Oh, yes. How could I possibly have overlooked your father?"

There was a long period of silence until Ben asked, "What can we do for Sean, Dixie? He's really in a pickle."

With a long breath, Dixie said, "There have been changes, and I think there are more to come. First, let me tell you that Frank is out of the company. When Sean returns to work, he won't have Daddy impeding him in any way."

"Who's he going to work for? He only gets along with John."

"He'll work for me. I'm the new President of Darling Motors as of a week ago."

"Your father quit? Retired?"

"He failed to discharge his duty. I had him removed," Dixie said with a cold-hearted expression.

"My God. Nothing is sacred to you people," Ben said, unable to fathom Dixie's action against her father.

Dixie explained, "He paid the woman Sean slept with to seduce him. She's been Frank's mistress for years. What Sean did was unconscionable, but it is forgivable. As for my father, that's another story."

"Frank sent his mistress to screw Sean? As I said, nothing is sacred to you people."

"Stop saying that!" Dixie shouted. "One thing is sacred to me, and that's my marriage. I won't let anything destroy that. If that means I have to be subordinate to Sean's memory of Kim, that's an easy choice for me to make. But I want him in my life for all time, and I'm missing out on precious days while he's gone. I have to get him back, and I need your help bringing him home."

Ben began to choke up as he thought about all that Dixie had said to him.

"Did I say something wrong?"

Shaking his head, Ben replied, "Those words you spoke—those very words. I find you now to be in the situation I've been in for years—that I had to be subordinate to Kim's memories of Sean. But I wanted nothing more than to live with her for all time…time that's been stolen from me."

Moving to the chair closest to Ben, Dixie took a seat and said, "I'm sorry, Ben. There's nothing I can do to replace Kim, or the years together you'll never have. But at the risk of sounding totally selfish, I still have time to be with Sean. Will you help me?"

Digressing, Ben divulged, "Kim lived her life with Sean through her book. Have you read it?"

"At least ten times."

"She was as obsessed about creating a happy life for him—even if it was fictional—as he is with finding the Fuller Brush Man. In her book, she cast you as the arch-villain Esmeralda. In reality, she lived her life vicariously through you. She envied you. She even spied on you."

"Spied on me?"

"It was rather heartbreaking. She called it research. Regardless, she would travel to Lake Forest at least once a year, change her appearance in some way, don a wig, and go car shopping at Sean's dealerships. She would also follow you as you went about your day. She has volumes of notes that she took. They're all packed in boxes. I don't feel good that I have them, and you should have the option of taking them or destroying them."

Sitting back in her chair, Dixie said, "I'm shocked. I don't know what to say." Looking uneasily at Ben, she asked, "This is an awkward question, but I have to ask it anyway. Was Kim ever diagnosed with any psychological problems?"

Leaning forward, Ben replied, "She was in and out of therapy. In recent years, as I watched her become more and more preoccupied with her book, and Sean more and more possessed by what was troubling him, I truly thought I was witnessing a race to see who went completely bonkers first. For the most part, she was extraordinarily bright and intuitive, and very passionate about her cause. She threw herself into writing that book in hopes it would one day guide Sean and you to a level of happiness we experienced until the moment she died. But, as the cancer began to wear her down, she started to take on another personality. On the outside she was Kim. But on the inside she was increasingly becoming Collette. That aside, she respected you, Dixie. She grew to like you. She watched you care for Sean and your family. She watched you live the life with him that you took from her. But in the end, there was no longer any resentment. Was she healed of the pain you and Sean inflicted upon her? I believe so. Was she content? Absolutely."

Dixie walked over to Ben and put her arms around him. "You and I aren't as dissimilar as I once thought. It must have been grueling to have Sean embedded in your lives to that extent. I know I always felt Kim's presence."

"But for me it was worth every second, Dixie. I wouldn't trade any part of our life together for anything. If it had been a man other than Sean, I might have felt differently. But I knew Sean was never going to be a physical threat to my marriage. Despite all of your ups and downs, the two of you really love and care for each other. And Kim and I were able to talk about the two of you very openly."

Kneeling before him, Dixie continued, "It would be wrong to let all of Kim's hard work go to waste. You must know what Kim meant when she said, 'Find the Fuller Brush Man'."

Rubbing his hands over his head nervously, Ben replied, "I do have a theory, and you're not going to like it."

"What's that?"

"Kim was envious of the unending attention Sean paid to his mother. She told me once that he would think of his mother incessantly, because she had ended her journal with what he felt were words of great importance. The ending to Kim's book might be Kim's way to keep Sean thinking about her forever."

Shaking her head in disbelief, Dixie said, "No. I can't believe that either of them would torment him like that. Doing so would be practically malicious, and we're speaking of two people who loved him."

"Well, that's all I can come up with," Ben concluded, shaking his head.

"Try, Ben! Try!"

"I said that's all!"

Shaking her head, Dixie said, "I'm sorry. This whole thing is simply so frustrating."

It was with good fortune that the house phone rang. Dixie excused herself to take the call. Forcefully lifting the receiver off of its cradle, Dixie answered most unreceptively, "Yes?"

"Dixie, this is Dr. Berkowitz. How are you doing?"

"I'm fine. Is everything alright with Sean?" She asked, fearing the worst.

"Yes. Is everything fine with you?"

"Why do you ask?"

"I sense from the tension in your voice that you're under a lot of stress."

Leaning against a door frame with her fist against her forehead, she said, "I've been going over and over this Fuller Brush bullshit with Sean's friend, Ben. It gets on my nerves."

"Were you just speaking with Ben by phone?" Berkowitz asked anxiously.

"No. He's visiting me at our home in Lake Forest. He was up here on business and paid me the courtesy of stopping by to discuss Sean's situation."

Excitedly, Berkowitz inquired, "Dixie, ask him if he can go to Wisconsin tomorrow."

"To see Sean?" Dixie asked, beginning to anxiously pace the floor.

"Yes. I want him to meet with Sean at the clinic."

"What about me?" Dixie asked suspiciously.

Not mincing his words, Berkowitz replied, "Unfortunately, it appears Sean still views you as part of his problem. He opened up today and became quite upset about not being able to see Kim's grave. He was so disturbed, the staff had to sedate him. He won't be up to any more conversation today, but tomorrow I'd like him to speak with Ben."

"Why? Did anybody inform him that I've already accepted blame for that? I told you to tell him. Have you?"

"That's irrelevant, Dixie. The fact remains he hasn't seen her grave."

"Ben can't take him to see Kim's grave. What's Ben going to do? Draw him a picture?"

"In a manner of speaking," Berkowitz replied. "You see, during Sean's outburst, he mentioned that Ben had invited him to Urbana to review an inscription that was going to be on Kim's headstone. I think it's imperative that Sean get some closure on Kim's death in order for us to make progress in his treatment, and I feel speaking with Ben about this detail is just what he needs."

"No. Absolutely not. If anybody is going to see Sean, it will be me. I can bring the inscription to Sean just as easily as Ben can."

"Dixie, I think Sean's turned that corner we've been waiting for. I promise you, in time Sean will be back in your arms. However, this is not the appropriate time for that to take place. This is for Ben and Sean to deal with. I understand how difficult this is for you. I commend you for being so passionate about his release. But please, trust me."

Grudgingly, Dixie agreed. "I'll speak to Ben and call you back."

"Thank you, Dixie. You're doing the best thing for Sean. I'll wait for your call."

Returning to where she had left Ben sitting alone, Dixie said, "That was Sean's doctor. Sean's beginning to engage with the therapists again. Berkowitz says Sean mentioned something about meeting with you to go over an inscription for Kim's headstone. Is there any truth to this?"

"Yeah. I mentioned it to him the same day he wigged out. Of course, that was right after I told him you deliberately took him to the wrong gravesite."

"Look, Ben, I can't undo my mistake. It was horrible, selfish, unkind, egregious…"

"Try just plain shitty!" Ben interrupted.

"What do you want me to say, Ben? What do you want me to do? I've fallen on my sword. I'd love to apologize to Sean, but they won't let me near him."

"There's probably a good reason for that."

"Oh, piss off!" Dixie said angrily as she turned to leave. Once it dawned on her that she was in her own home, she turned, and with a confused grin said, "I'm sorry, Ben."

After thinking about what he had said, Ben reached out for Dixie. "I'm sorry, too. That wasn't a fair thing for me to say. You must be pulling your hair out over all this."

Beginning to whimper, she acknowledged, "I don't know how much longer I can hold out for him, Ben. Berkowitz says Sean still views me as a source of his problems, and I'm helpless to do anything that might change his mind."

Ben stood up and took Dixie in his arms.

"Ben, can you go see Sean in Wisconsin tomorrow? Berkowitz thinks talking to Sean about the inscription will be very constructive, not to mention very timely."

"I suppose I can rearrange my plans. Where's he at?"

"I have no idea. The doctor may not even tell me, preferring to speak with you directly. In any case, I told him I would ask you and get back to him. So, you are willing to do this?"

"If it will get Sean home quicker, I'll do anything."

Dixie was fortunate to get Ben to visit Sean. But at the same time, she had a burning curiosity about the inscription Ben was going to share with her husband. "Would it be too much to ask you to share Kim's inscription with me? I promise I won't say anything. I just need to know. Please?"

Ben pulled a folded piece of paper from his pocket and handed it to Dixie. No sooner had she read those brief words than she fell back crying in Ben's arms.

Chapter 30

IT WAS AN EXCEPTIONALLY gloomy, early-October day at the clinic near Chippewa Falls where Berkowitz had placed Sean. Despite a stone exterior, there was a presence about the facility that was a very accommodating. Once inside, in so many ways it didn't resemble a clinic—bright, cheerful, well-decorated, with comfortable furniture and ample glass so one could look out onto pleasantly manicured lawns and sculpted gardens. Yet, doors opened and closed securely only for those with a card key.

Berkowitz gave Ben a short list of topics that he could discuss with Sean, and a long list of what he could not. Beyond that, Ben was given no script. Though it took him over five hours to drive from Lake Forest, Ben still arrived in time to enjoy a late lunch with Sean. It was the first time in years the two long-time friends had dined together. Unfortunately, under the parameters Ben operated, the conversation was spotty, and it was hard to dig deeply into any subject. Nonetheless, it was clear to Ben that Sean was profoundly embittered. Having been sheltered from all that had taken place since the night of his flap, Sean still believed April was his salvation and saw Dixie as a hateful woman, jealous of Kim, and willing to manipulate any situation so that it suited her needs at his expense.

After lunch, the two stepped out onto the patio where both took a seat on a rock wall overlooking a one-acre lake. The trees at the other side of the lake reflected their new autumn colors in the glassy water. The setting was very similar to Allerton Park.

"It's pretty out here. Too bad it's a nut house," Sean said, half-jokingly.

"Don't get used to the place," Ben replied. "Dixie wants you back."

Having had several weeks for the entire subject of his marriage to percolate, Sean was quick to respond, "I don't plan to go back to her, Ben. It's time for me to start over…completely over."

"Do you want my opinion?" Ben asked.

"No. Keep it to yourself," Sean replied.

Ignoring Sean's request, Ben said, "You're being too hasty, Sean. Finish working things out here. I think you'll come away with a fresh outlook, rather than a desire to start over."

Sean stood and irately said, "You don't get it, do you Ben? Do you know what happened that night back at the house?" Looking out onto the lake, Sean's face took on an expression of disgust as he continued, "I had that gun in my mouth with the hammer pulled back. You don't know what it's like to chase something as long as I have. Then, as soon as you think there may be hope, someone points you down another endless road. And the worst part about it was that it was Kim who paved the way. She threw me in front of the fucking snowplow, Ben. That's when I realized I hated Kim more than I hated myself. Mercifully, I put a bullet through her picture. Symbolically, I put a long overdue end to my relationship with her."

Berkowitz had warned Ben that Sean might share some bitter feelings about Kim, and that he would have to simply let him have his say without objecting. But he couldn't let these remarks go without comment.

"Do you know what was so perfect about my marriage to Kim?'

"No, and I don't want to hear it."

"Tough shit. Stand there and listen. The best part about our marriage was that we told each other years and years ago that we'd stick it out."

"Every couple reads the same stupid vows, Ben. For better, for worse; For richer, for poorer; In sickness and in health; blah, blah, blah. It's all horseshit."

"No, it's not! Hey, I'll be the last person to defend a lot of what Dixie has done. But I've come to realize she's done it all out of the immeasurable love she has for you."

"You're on crack."

"Living with you can't be a walk in the park either! You let this Fuller Brush bullshit run your life since your mom died! Talk about obsessing over the ultimate in mundane!"

"Obviously you've never had a person affect you the way my mother affected me."

"Oh, yes I did. I was married to her."

"My mother was trying to tell me something."

"Big deal! Is it worth throwing away your marriage while you search for whatever it is you're looking for?"

Sean stopped to think. Everyone was telling him essentially the same thing. He didn't want to hear any more.

"What was it like?" Sean asked.

"What?"

"When she died."

Carnal knowledge wasn't as intimate as Kim's death had been. But Ben reluctantly shared those days.

"Sean, your ex-girlfriend, my wife, and the mother of my boys weighed sixty-seven pounds the day before she died. The last month, I carried her wherever she wanted to go. She could no longer walk. Her pain was unbearable. Two weeks prior, she began shitting on herself. A week prior, she stopped eating food. Her cheeks were sunken and she had dark circles under her eyes. But you would have recognized her. Her eyes were as blue as always. And she never lost her ability to smile or laugh. We fought her cancer together. It was hard. You talk about suicide. Ending her pain along with mine crossed my mind more than once. She had to begin her next journey when she was ready. Let me tell you something else—I loved her more the day she died than I did the day I married her."

Sean said nothing.

Ben struggled with his thoughts. He was angry that Sean had developed such ill regard for Kim. At the same time, it was almost liberating that Sean no longer coveted his late wife. And then there was the reaffirmation of their friendship—one that had seen them through the best and worst times of their lives. Ben knew it was time to take care of the matter for which Berkowitz had sent him. It was time to confront the matter of the inscription.

"I promised you we'd take a look at the inscription for her headstone. Are you ready for that?"

Sean nodded.

BEN PULLED OUT A folded piece of paper and handed it to Sean as he explained, "They're very simple words, yet they carried a great deal of meaning for Kim. Actually, according to her, they're not at all original. She wanted me to make it perfectly clear to you who should get credit for them. It was something your mother said to her many years ago."

"My mother?"

"That's right."

Sean unfolded the note and read the inscription that Kim had written.

Make It Work; Make It Last; Guarantee It No Matter What...

Sean was stunned by those words. He abruptly took a seat in a wooden patio chair at a table directly behind Ben. His mind began to spin as years of patient investigation and analysis spontaneously compressed into this single moment. It was as if every door that had mercilessly slammed closed at the end of each fruitless chapter of his journey since the beginning of his quest, suddenly sprang open.

As Ben looked out over the lake, he continued with his explanation. "Kim told me she once asked your mother, 'What was the key to a long and fruitful marriage?' She loved your parents, and she cherished every word Nadine spoke. Her answer to Kim's question is what you now hold in your hand." With tears in his eyes and his voice breaking, Ben added, "Kim said it guided her through the difficult, final years of our marriage, and in retrospect, even though I never saw these words until a month ago, I find that they are so true…so very true. I was following this advice before I had even heard it."

Expecting Sean to give some kind of feedback, Ben turned around to find his friend holding the note in front of his face, trembling as he silently read the words over and over again.

"Dude, are you alright?"

The sun broke through the clouds almost mystically illuminating Sean's face. He started to smile and tears slowly ran down his cheeks.

"Sean, I didn't mean to upset you. Can I get you any…"

"It's the Fuller Brush Man," Sean said in a low voice.

"What's that Sean?"

"It's the Fuller Brush Man. It's the Fuller Brush Man, Ben! It's the Fuller Brush Man!!"

Sean stood up, grabbed Ben, and began to cry uncontrollably. One of the therapists, who had been surreptitiously observing the meeting from inside the building, came to Sean's aid.

When she finally, carefully separated the two, what she saw on Sean's face was an expression both of elation and enormous relief.

"I'm not sure I follow you, Sean."

Though his voice was cracking, Sean found the strength to elaborate. "It's the answer to the riddle, Ben. Listen to me. In 1906, Alfred C. Fuller formed the beginnings of The Fuller Brush Company. He was the original Fuller Brush Man. 'Make It Work; Make It Last; Guarantee It No Matter What' was the company's mantra. For that matter, it still is today. My mother apparently usurped that phrase. She put it in the context of how to secure a long-lasting marriage. It's perfect, Ben. That was the message my mother tried to convey to me in her journal. That was the message Kim tried to convey with the end of her book. They were guiding me in my marriage. They must have known Dixie and I were in trouble. 'Make It Work; Make It Last; Guarantee It No Matter What.' I've seen these very words a hundred times. They're right there on the Fuller Brush website. The answer was right before me, staring me in the face for years. But I never got it, not until you handed me this piece of paper. Kim must have watched me struggling to solve the riddle. She guided me to the solution, Ben. To think that it's Kim's epitaph that's giving me a new beginning. It's as if she died, so I could live. That's so...so ironic...so poetic...so much like Kim. We solved it, Ben. We found the Fuller Brush Man." Emotionally exhausted by the revelation, Sean took a seat in the chair once again.

Ben was nearly as shocked and overwhelmed as Sean by the discovery. Clearly, the breakthrough had a profound effect on him just as it did on Sean. But he didn't want to steal the moment from Sean. He walked up to his friend, put a hand on his shoulder, and asked, "So, Sean, what are you going to do with this revelation? You've been given a sign. You'd better not piss it away."

Sean looked up at the therapist, who had been intently listening as she jotted down notes about what had transpired. "I need to call my wife. Please. I need to call Dixie. Dear God, hopefully I'm not too late. I'm not exactly sure what I'm supposed to do, but I know one thing for certain. I can't give up on the two of us. Call Dr. Berkowitz and tell him I have to talk to her right away."

Homecoming

ONE MONTH LATER…

Dinner with Giselle and Will went spectacularly. Taking into account the culinary wishes of the Mosciewicz family, the two prepared a wonderful vegetable medley, cod cakes, and for the main course, a fish bouillabaisse. Dessert was a simple raspberry tart served with an apéritif. The meal was exquisite, and the presentation divine. Darryl's parents complimented the two time and time again for dinner, and also for their hospitality. It was clear to Sean and Dixie that Giselle and Will were going to be very successful in their future endeavor, Château Giselle.

The next day, the dégustation gastronomique was Raymond's famous Brats. Again, considering the kosher diet of his Jewish guests, Raymond went out of his way—literally—to find a suitable meat. He made 'shopping' for his meal the perfect excuse for a three-day hunting excursion near the region surrounding the common borders of Iowa, Missouri, and Illinois where he bagged his limit of pheasant in each state, using them as the base for his wurst. He jokingly called his trip a terrible hardship, but the joy in his face as he talked about the trip gave away his true feelings. Once the delicate meat was ground with his secret recipe for filler and spiced to taste, the six-inch sausages were a backyard party masterpiece.

Schedules at large events are seldom perfect. Such was the case with the arranged times in which Dixie and Sean were to fulfill their obligation to Callie by giving speeches at one of the myriad of Kappa Kappa Gamma homecoming events. With some of the activities running long, the planners had scheduled time conveniently after the Marcum family feast, rather than first thing that morning. From a practical perspective, it was two hours prior to the start of the football game, and all the parents were gathered at the sorority in preparation for that big affair.

Dixie wasn't certain how she would be received given the recent publicity about the Darling family business. Devon Brookshire hadn't been entirely kind in his Tribune exposé. But the article was more a chronicle of a company implosion, than a sordid sex scandal. Dixie's choice of Brookshire was a calculated decision. She knew of his reputation as a sleuth, and he pursued the backgrounds of both women who had their hands in the Darling's pockets—April Knudsen and Lori Scott. It was Brookshire who discovered April had truly been married…but, a long time ago, and not to a sailor named Scott. Scott had been her maiden name. It was no coincidence that she and Lori shared the same last name—they were sisters. Both were conniving, shrewd, and ruthless gold diggers in search of wealth and comfort that others would have to pay for. That they targeted the same family played on the sympathy of nearly all who knew the Darlings. And it was as Dixie expected. Their friends, associates, and the community rallied around the good Darling name, recognizing the family's abundance of virtue and were willing to overlook the turpitude.

Dixie spoke in general terms about the lessons she learned as a Kappa while in college, and how she had been guided in many of the Kappa ways by both her grandmother and mother. But she took the humble road rather than toot her horn, realizing she and her family could become, once again, a target for opportunists. After ten minutes of giving her sorority much of the credit for her success, she decided to let her gritty rise to glory speak for itself. For Dixie to take the podium under such circumstances in front of nearly one hundred parents earned her a standing ovation, along with Callie who stood beside her, her arm around her mother's waist.

Brookshire's article didn't specifically say Sean had a relationship with April, but it didn't take a rocket scientist to figure it out. Nor was his bout with depression and obsessive-compulsive disorder a well-kept secret. That Callie's parents could stand before a crowd and openly discuss the ups and downs they had experienced only made them more human. The trials and tribulations Sean and Dixie had lived through separately and together were experiences known to many of the other parents.

As Sean took the podium, he was met with a hug and kiss from Callie. When he looked in her eyes as she stepped away, he knew she wasn't thinking, *look at me*. She was thinking, *look at him…this is my dad.* Once Callie had taken a seat next to Dixie in the front row, Sean found it hard to take his eyes off of them. Only a month earlier, he never would have envisioned being a keynote speaker with his girls still supporting him. It was the happiest moment of his life.

"Callie told me I was to give a talk about what it's like to be married to a Kappa for thirty-one years. As I look around this room, I see a lot of men with salt-and-pepper hair, others have full heads of grey hair, and still others are balding. I see all of you gents sitting next to a fine-looking woman. I'm quite certain each of you knows what it's like to be married to a woman who was transformed by this institution—that is, assuming your lady-friend beside you is in fact your wife."

There was a round of laughter before Sean continued, "It would be pointless to string out some mind-numbing speech. But there are words that come to mind when I think of my wife, Dixie, and I feel they best express what it's like to still be wearing this matching wedding band we had put on lay-away, many, many years ago…against her father's wishes, I should add."

When the chuckles died down, Sean went on to say, "Words like devoted, tenacious, protective, nurturing, patient, charming, and loving come quickly to mind." There were nods of agreement in the audience. "But from the era that gave you a woman taught within these very walls, how to *properly* hold and smoke a cigarette, comes yet another set of qualities. With that in mind, words such as hard-charging, zealous, creative, demanding, forceful, awe-inspiring, and even brutal come to mind."

Again there were chuckles.

"On one hand she can be a Vermont Teddy Bear. But when necessary, she can be a grizzly."

Dixie gave Sean a crooked smile as she gleefully took in his remarks, while others in the audience laughed.

"She's the whole package." With added emphasis, Sean continued after searching for the right words, "But I don't think I realized that until recently. For that oversight, I beg my wife's forgiveness."

Dixie blew him a kiss.

Now looking more serious and introspective, Sean said, "I spent a lot of years thinking the grass in the next field would be greener, when what I should have been doing was feeling the lush softness and comfort of the grass upon which I stood. At the risk of making my little plot of terra firma resemble a well-used rugby pitch, I plan to occupy my place just to the right of Dixie until one or both of us ends up planted under some patch of earth…hopefully a long time down the road."

Nobody in the room said a word, but nearly every couple took the pause in Sean's speech as their cue to embrace each other warmly as husband and wife.

"For those of you with doubts about your marriage—and it happens to all of us at some point—let me leave you, both husbands and wives, with these words of wisdom from the Fuller Brush Man: 'Make It Work; Make It Last; Guarantee It No Matter What'."

Spontaneously, the parents and sisters gave Sean a standing ovation.

When the applause had died down, Sean digressed. Sporting a mischievous smile, he went on to say, "Ending on a lighter note, I think it would be entertaining for me to share with you how Dixie and I first met."

Dixie's eyes got wide as the audience encouraged Sean to continue with what was expected to be a humorous, perhaps lurid, anecdote.

"Do all of you have memories of panty raids?"

Dixie hid her face in her hand and shook her head as everyone in earshot nodded and chuckled.

"What about streaking?!" Sean shouted enthusiastically.

Mortified by the professed actions of her mother and father years earlier, Callie said, "Daddy!"

Several of the men in the audience, along with one woman, yelled out, affirming their knowledge of, if not their participation in, such activities. They obviously related well to those antics of which Sean was speaking.

"Well, put those two together, and that's how Dixie and I first met."

There were howls from the crowd. Though her face was red as a beet, Dixie thoroughly enjoyed the yarn. She even stood to take a bow, acknowledging herself as a willing accomplice.

"I suggest anyone wishing to use the women's shower on the third floor stay out of there for at least the next twenty minutes because when I'm done speaking, I'm taking Dixie up to where it all began for some passionate necking. Thanks for giving me your time, and may we always remember Chief Illiniwek! See you at the game."

Sean took only a few steps away from the podium when Dixie walked up to embrace him.

Callie walked up to them and said under her breath, "Guys, cut it out. You're, like, embarrassing the heck out of me."

Not heeding Callie's plea, Sean threw Dixie over his shoulder and raced up the stairs like the college youth he once was. Nobody followed.

Epilogue

IT WAS A HOT July 4th when Dixie and Sean returned to Monticello for the Grand Opening of Château Giselle. The holiday fell on a Thursday giving many first-time guests, including Sean and Dixie, the chance to stay through the long weekend. From all appearances, the *Grand Venue*, as it was dubbed, went flawlessly for the newlyweds Will and Giselle. Also staying at the château were Giselle's parents, and one other important couple, Frank and Suzanne, who had just returned from their own vacation in Provence.

A great deal had transpired during the months since Homecoming aside from the new family enterprise in Monticello. Callie found that her boyfriend, Darryl, had too little time for her as his studies intensified. Her participation in an improvisational acting guild provided her ample distraction from that fizzling relationship, and piqued her interest in the performing arts. All Sean and Dixie had to do was make a casual suggestion that she pursue an acting career, and she quickly applied to the Bristol Old Vic Theatre School in London. Following a spectacular audition in New York, Callie was off to train overseas for her new vocation.

Sean continued to meet regularly with Dr. Berkowitz until he finally put to rest all his troubles surrounding the deaths of his mother and Kim that had fueled his obsessive and self-destructive behaviors. Dixie agreed with Sean that with her at the helm of Darling Motors, it would not be a healthy situation for him to work within the framework of the family business. The Group gave Sean what he had hoped for—the ability to go independent. Dixie assumed Sean's role of General Manager at the Lexus and Toyota dealerships in addition to her Group responsibilities. Sean started his BMW and Volvo businesses right next door as he had previously planned. It was an arrangement that favorably rewarded Dixie and Sean both personally and financially. He replaced his Toyota with a modest 3-series BMW. It occupied a space on the driveway at night. Inside the garage was Sean's yellow 1968 Mustang Fastback.

It had been nine months since either Dixie or Sean had spoken to the elder Darlings. Will, ever so wise for his years, insisted upon a reunion, and arranged for it to take place at the newly-restored boutique guest lodge. Surprisingly, Dixie was less enthusiastic about the meeting than Sean.

After the two had settled into their room, she and Sean started down the staircase on their way to visit some local antique stores. It was then that they encountered Frank and Suzanne checking in with the réceptionniste.

Confident after the better part of a year out from under Frank's domination, Sean proceeded without hesitation to where his in-laws stood. Suzanne, looking much happier and refreshed than he remembered, was quick to give Sean a hug and a kiss on his cheek. Sean then turned to Frank. The two men stared at each other for a few moments before Frank extended his hand. It was a highly-charged and symbolic gesture. As Sean took his hand and as they shook, the two exchanged a smile. It was going to be a good weekend.

Dixie stood on the third step from the bottom, still apprehensive about the meeting. Slowly, Frank walked over to her and stood at the bottom of the stairs. Following a deep breath, Dixie took the last three steps, and as Sean and Suzanne looked on, descended contently into her father's open arms. It was the first time Sean ever saw his father-in-law cry. One couldn't have hoped for a better reunion. It was going to be a spectacular weekend.

FOLLOWING THE AFTERNOON PARADE, Ben, Sean, and Dixie left to make their pilgrimage to the cemetery. Sean still had never seen Kim's grave, but Dr. Berkowitz, and more importantly, Dixie, felt the time was right for him to confront that which he so feared. The engraved headstone had recently been set in place. Thick grass now covering the plot made for a seamless carpet, spanning both Nadine's grave and Kim's. As the roots of the grass became intertwined, so did the lives ever-after of the mother and erstwhile daughter-in-law.

Ben, Dixie, and Sean stood quietly in front of the two graves. Sean accepted that having Kim buried next to his mother made the experience that much easier. Clearly, he surmised, there would never be any loneliness. If fact, they were probably working on a puzzle together.

Ben and Sean placed flowers on the graves, embraced one another, shed a few tears, shared a few memories, then turned to walk slowly back to their cars.

Dixie stayed behind. She felt the closure to so many events in her life nearly overwhelming. She wanted so badly at that moment to share her deepest gratitude with Nadine and Kim. They had liberated Sean from the bondage that had for so long imprisoned him, and, in doing so, had given her husband back to her. What's more, their marriage was stronger than ever. Delicately crouching before both graves, she whispered, "Thank you." Never had so few words been packed with so much meaning.

"Dix? Are you coming?" Sean called.

After wiping the tears from her eyes, she joined her husband, hand-in-hand as they set out to make it work, make it last, and guarantee it no matter what.

THAT EVENING, INSTEAD OF going to see the fireworks, Sean and Dixie ventured away from Château Giselle to the far end of Allerton Park. There, Dixie sat ever so contently on the hood of Sean's yellow Fastback, with the statue of the Sun Singer behind her. Her silhouette was framed by the peach and orange hues from the clouds of a fabulous central Illinois sunset. Sean snapped a picture that he would cherish for all time. He had finally found everything he had been searching for at the end of The Road to Monticello.

~~ The End ~~

Author's Note

My mother died of pancreatic cancer on March 12, 1987. She kept a journal. In it, her last written words really were *Fuller Brush Man.* As far as I am concerned, I know what she was talking about.

I was fortunate to have had a relationship with a truly wonderful woman during high school and my first years of college. She died of breast cancer on June 30, 2010. Though we parted ways many years ago, I can't help but think of how she, along with my mother, perhaps unknowingly, helped shape me to be the decent man, father, and husband that I am today. She married a better man than me, and raised a lovely family. Their life together will be a lesson of love in and of itself for all time.

I will never be able to thank these two women enough. And I can never again embrace them. But as a tribute to them, I hope all who read this book come to understand, as I have, the beauty of a long-term relationship.

… Doug Carlyle